THE INVENTOR IS ALWAYS PROMETHEUS

"There is no great invention, from fire to flying, that has not been hailed as an insult to some god."
—J.B.S. Haldane

Many people see themselves through the weary eyes of pessimism—they see humankind as a race of failed angels, inherently flawed, destined for eternal frustration. No one accuses pessimists of enthusiasm or youthful vision.

Optimists see a species evolving toward immortality. Certainly there are shortcomings, pitfalls, drawbacks to every advance the human race makes. But optimists look to the future with confidence that we can use our brains, our hands and our hearts to constantly improve the world.

Anti-science, anti-technology Luddites are pessimists.

And optimists are . . . the

PROMETHEANS

Look for all these TOR books by Ben Bova

BEN BOVA

PROMETHEANS

A TOM DOHERTY ASSOCIATES BOOK

PROMETHEANS

Copyright © 1986 by Ben Bova

First printing: September 1986

A TOR Book

Published by Tom Doherty Associates, Inc.
49 West 24 Street
New York, N.Y. 10010

Cover art by Ron Walotsky

ISBN: 0-812-53219-8
CAN. ED.: 0-812-53220-1

Printed in the United States

0 9 8 7 6 5 4 3 2 1

To Ray Bradbury,
a Promethean if ever there was one.

ACKNOWLEDGMENTS

Contents

Introduction

There are two kinds of people in the world: Luddites and Prometheans. This book is about Prometheans.

But first let me tell you what a Luddite is, and then what a Promethean is, so that you can decide for yourself which type of person you are.

History has not been kind to Ned Ludd, the unwitting founder of the Luddite movement of the early nineteenth century. Webster's *New World Dictionary* describes Ludd as feeble-minded. The *Encyclopaedia Britannica* says he was probably mythical.

The Luddites were very real, however. They were English craftsmen who tried to stop the young Industrial Revolution by destroying the textile mills that were taking away their jobs. Starting in 1811, the Luddites rioted, wrecked factories, and even killed at least one employer who had ordered his guards to shoot at a band of rioting workmen. After five years of such violence, the British government took harsh steps to suppress the Luddites, hanging dozens and transporting others to prison colonies in far-off Australia. That broke the back of the movement, but did not put an end to the underlying causes that had created the movement. Slowly, painfully, over many generations, the original Luddite violence evolved into more peaceful political and legal activities. The labor movement grew out of the ashes of the Luddites' terror. Marxism arose in reaction to capitalist exploitation of workers. The Labour Party in Britain, and socialist governments elsewhere in the world, are the descendants of that early resistance against machinery.

Today the progeny of those angry craftsmen live in greater comfort and wealth than their embattled forebears could have dreamed in their wildest fantasies. Not because employers and factory owners suddenly turned beneficent. Not because the labor movement and socialist governments have eliminated human greed and selfishness. But because the machines—the machines that the Luddites feared and tried to destroy—have generated enough wealth to give common laborers houses of their own, plentiful food, excellent medical care, education for their children, personally owned automobiles, television sets, refrigerators, stereos, all the accouterments of modern life which we take so much for granted that we almost disdain them, but which would have seemed miracles beyond imagination to the original Luddites.

We still have the Luddite mentality with us today: people who distrust or even fear the machines that we use to create wealth for ourselves. The modern Luddites are most conspicuous in their resistance to high technology such as computers and automated machinery, nuclear reactors, high-voltage power lines, airports, fertilizers and food additives. To today's Luddites, any program involving high technology is under immediate and intense suspicion. In their view, technology is either dangerous or evil or both, and must be stopped. Their automatic response is negative; their most often used word is *no*.

Opposing the Luddite point of view stands a group of people who fear neither technology nor the future. Instead, they rush forward to try to build tomorrow. They are the Prometheans, named so after the demigod of Greek legend who gave humankind the gift of fire.

Every human culture throughout history has created a Prometheus myth, a legend that goes back to the very beginnings of human consciousness. In this legend, the first humans are poor, weak, starving, freezing creatures, little better than the animals of the forest. A godling—Prometheus to the Greeks, Loki to the Norse, Coyote to the Plains Indians of America—takes pity on the miserable humans and brings down from the heavens the gift of fire. The other gods are furious, because they fear that with fire the humans will exceed the gods themselves in power. So they punish the gift-giver, eternally.

And, sure enough, with fire the human race does indeed become the master of the world.

The myth is fantastic in detail, yet absolutely correct in spirit. Fire was indeed a gift from the sky. Undoubtedly a bolt of lightning set a tree or bush afire, and an especially curious or courageous member of our ancestors overcame the very natural fear of the flames to reach out for the bright warm energy. No telling how many times our ancestors got nothing for their troubles except burned fingers and yowls of pain. But eventually they learned to handle fire safely, to use it. And with fire, technology became the main force in human development.

Technology is our way of dealing with the world, our path for survival. We do not grow wings like the eagle, or claws like the bear, or fleet-running legs like the deer. We make tools. We build planes, we make clothing, we manufacture automobiles. The English biologist J.B.S. Haldane said, "The chemical or physical inventor is always a Prometheus. There is no great invention, from fire to flying, that has not been hailed as an insult to some god."

In a broader context, we might say that the basic difference between the Luddites and thePtometheans is the difference between an optimist and a pessimist. Is the glass half full of water or half empty?

Many human beings see themselves, and the entire human race, through the weary eyes of ancient pessimism. They see humankind as a race of failed angels, inherently flawed, destined for eternal frustration. Thus we get the myth of Sisyphus, whose punishment in Hades was to eternally struggle to roll a huge stone up a hill, only to have it always roll back down again as soon as he got it to the summit. It sounds very intellectual to be a pessimist, to adopt a world-weary attitude; at the very least, no one can accuse you of enthusiasm or youthful vigor.

The optimists tend to see the human race as a species evolving toward immortality. We are perfectible creatures, they believe. Optimists can be accused of naiveté, but they can also point to recent history and show that human thought has improved the human condition immensely within the few short centuries in which science has come into play. Certainly there are shortcomings, pitfalls, drawbacks, to every advance the human race makes. But the optimists look to the future with the confidence that humankind can use its brains, its hands and its heart to constantly improve the world.

Incidentally, it is this difference between the pessimists and optimists that causes a fundamental resistance among the pessimists to science fiction. Especially among those who specialize in the literature of the past, the optimistic literature of a brighter tomorrow is anathema. They simply cannot fathom it; they are blind to what science fiction says. Even *within* the science fiction field, its practitioners often fall prey to this ancient schism, regarding darkly pessimistic stories as somehow more "literary" than brightly optimistic ones.

There is a bit of the pessimistic Luddite in each of us, and each of us is something of an optimistic Promethean. This book, though, deals exclusively with Prometheans, men and women who do not fear technology but rather embrace it and use it to build the future.

About half of this book is fiction, short stories of the relatively near future. The other half is nonfiction, speculative essays and articles that relate to the fictional pieces in a general way. Fact and fiction both deal with Prometheans, real and imagined, the kind of people who call down the lightning from the sky—and then use it to make a better world.

—Ben Bova
West Hartford, Connecticut

Sam Gunn

The basic idea for this story occurred to me back in the years when I was an editor. For the better part of a decade I tried to get one writer after another to write a story for *Analog* or, later, *Omni* around this idea. All I ever got for my troubles was a series of blank stares and muttered promises to "give it a shot."

When I finally stopped being an editor and began to write short fiction again, I tackled the idea myself. *Sam Gunn* is the result. Sam is a true Promethean—inventive and irreverent, feisty and tough, good-hearted and crafty. Ed Ferman, editor and publisher of *The Magazine of Fantasy and Science Fiction* not only bought the story, he published it in his magazine's 34th anniversary issue, which pleased me no end.

By the time I was finished with the story, it occurred to me that Sam is too good a character to drop. There will be more tales about Sam Gunn, and maybe even a novel about him. But that's for the future. Here's what Sam looked like when I first set my inner eye on him.

The spring-wheeled truck rolled to a silent stop on the Sea of Clouds. The fine dust kicked up by its six wheels floated lazily back to the mare's soil. The hatch to the truck cab swung upward, and a space-suited figure climbed slowly down to the lunar surface, clumped a dozen ponderously careful steps, then turned back toward the truck.

"Yeah, this is the spot. The transponder's beeping away, all right."

Two more figures clambered down from the cab, bulbous and awkward-looking in the bulky space suits. One of them turned a full three hundred sixty degrees, scanning the scene through the gold-tinted visor of the suit's bubble helmet. There was nothing to be seen except the monotonous gray plain, pockmarked by craters like an ancient, savage battlefield that had been petrified into solid stone long eons ago.

"Christ, you can't even see the ringwall from here!"

"That's what he wanted—to be out in the open, without a sign of civilization in sight. He picked this spot himself, you know."

"Helluva place to want to be buried."

"That's what he specified in his will. Come on, let's get to work. I want to get back to Selene City before the sun sets."

It was a local joke: the three space-suited workers had more than two hundred hours before sunset.

Grunting even in the general lunar gravity, they slid the coffin from the back of the truck and placed it gently on the roiled, dusty ground. Then they winched the four-meter-high crate from the truck and put it down softly next to the coffin. While one of them scoured out a coffin-sized hole in the ground with the blue-white flame of a plasma torch, the other two uncrated the big package.

"Ready for the coffin," said the worker with the torch.

The leader of the trio inspected the grave. The hot plasma had polished the stony ground. The two workers heard him muttering over their helmet earphones as he used a hand laser to check the grave's dimensions. Satisfied, he helped them drag the gold-filagreed coffin to the hole and slide it in.

"A lot of work to do for a dead man."

"He wasn't just any ordinary man."

"It's still a lot of work. Why in hell couldn't he be recycled like everybody else?"

"Sam Gunn," said the leader, "never did things like everybody else. Not in his whole cussed long life. Why should he be like the rest of us in death?"

They chattered back and forth through their suit radios as they uncrated the big package. Once they had removed all the plastic and the bigger-than-life statue stood sparkling in the sunlight, they stepped back and gaped at it.

"It's glass!"

"Christ, I never saw anything so damned big."

"Must have cost a fortune to get it here. Two fortunes!"

"He had it done at Island One, I hear. Brought the sculptor up from Earthside and paid him enough to keep him at L-4 for two whole years. God knows how many times he tried to cast a statue this big and failed."

"I didn't know you could make a glass statue so big."

"In zero gee you can. It's hollow. If we were in air, I could ping it with my finger and you'd hear it ring."

"Crystal."

"That's right."

One of the workers, the young man, laughed softly.

"What's so funny?" the leader asked.

"Who else but Sam Gunn would have the gall to erect a crystal statue to himself and then have it put out in the middle of this godforsaken emptiness, where nobody's ever going to see it. It's a monument to himself, for himself. What ego! What monumental ego."

The leader chuckled, too. "Yeah. Sam had an ego, all right. But he was a smart little guy, too."

"You knew him?" the young woman asked.

"Sure. Knew him well enough to tell you that he didn't pick this spot for his tomb just for the sake of his ego. He was smarter than that."

"What was he like?"

"When did you know him?"

"Come on, we've still got work to do. He wants the statue positioned exactly as he stated in his will, with its back toward Selene and the face looking up toward Earth."

"Yeah, okay, but when did you know him, huh?"

"Oh golly, years ago. Decades ago. When the two of us were just young pups. The first time either of us came here, back in—Lord, it's thirty years ago. More."

"Tell us about it. Was he really the hero that the history tapes say he was? Did he really do all the things they say?" asked the young woman.

"He was a phony!" the young man snapped. "Everybody

knows that. A helluva showman, sure, but he never did half
the stuff he took credit for. Nobody could have, not in one
lifetime.''

"He lived a pretty intense life," said the leader. "If it
hadn't been for a faulty suit valve he'd still be running his
show from here to Titan."

"A showman. That's what he was. No hero."

"What was he like?" the young woman repeated.

So, while the two youngsters struggled with the huge,
fragile crystal statue, the older man sat himself on the lip of
the truck's cab hatch and told them what he knew about the
first time Sam Gunn came to the Moon.

The skipper used the time-honored cliché. He said, "Houston, we have a problem here."

There were eight of us, the whole crew of Artemis IV,
huddled together in the command module. After six weeks of
living on the Moon, the module smelled like a pair of un-
washed gym socks. With a woman President, the space agency
figured it would be smart to name the second round of lunar
explorations after a female: Artemis was Apollo's sister. Get
it?

But it had just happened that the computer who picked the
crew selections for Artemis IV picked all men. Six weeks
without even the sight of a woman, and now our blessed-be-
to-god return module refused to light up. We were stranded.
No way to get back home.

As usual, capcom in Houston was the soul of tranquility.
"Ah, A-IV, we read you and copy that the return module is
no-go. The analysis team is checking the telemetry. We will
get back to you soonest."

It didn't help that capcom, that shift, was Sandi Hemmings, the woman we all lusted after. Among the eight of us,
we must have spent enough energy dreaming about cornering
Sandi in zero gravity to propel each of us right back to
Houston. Unfortunately, dreams have a very low specific
impulse, and we were still stuck on the Moon, a quarter-
million miles from the nearest woman.

Sandi played her capcom duties strictly by the book, especially since all our transmissions were taped for later review.

She kept the traditional Houston poker face, but managed to say, "Don't worry, boys. We'll figure it out and get you home."

Praise God for small favors.

We had spent hours checking and rechecking the cursed return module. It was engineer's hell: everything checked but nothing worked. The thing just sat there like a lump of dead metal. No electrical power. None. Zero. The control board just stared at us as cold and glassy-eyed as a banker listening to your request for an unsecured loan. We had pounded it. We had kicked it. In our desperation we had even gone through the instruction manual, page by page, line by line. Zip. Zilch. The bird was dead.

When Houston got back to us, six hours after the skipper's call, it was the stony, unsmiling image of the mission coordinator who glowered at us as if we had deliberately screwed up the return module. He told us:

"We have identified the problem, Artemis IV. The return module's main electrical power supply has malfunctioned."

That was like telling Othello that he was a Moor.

"We're checking out bypasses and other possible fixes," Old Stone Face went on. "Sit tight, we'll get back to you."

The skipper gave him a patient sigh. "Yes, sir."

"We're not going anywhere," said a whispered voice. Sam Gunn's, I was certain.

The problem, we finally discovered, was caused by a micrometeoroid, no less. A little grain of sand that just happened to roam through the solar system for four and a half billion years and then decided to crash-dive itself right into the main fuel cell of our return module's power supply. It was so tiny that it didn't do any visible damage to the fuel cell; just hurt it enough to let it discharge electrically for most of the six weeks we had been on the Moon. And the other two fuel cells, sensing the discharge through the module's idiot computer, tried to recharge their partner for six weeks. The result: all three of them were dead and gone by the time we needed them.

It was Sam who discovered the pinhole in the fuel cell, the eighteenth time we checked out the power supply. I can remember his exact words, once he realized what had happened:

"Shit!"

Sam was a feisty little guy who would have been too short for astronaut duty if the agency hadn't lowered the height requirements so that women could join the corps. He was a good man, a whiz with a computer and a born tinkerer who liked to rebuild old automobiles and then race them on the abandoned freeways whenever he could scrounge up enough old-fashioned petrol to run them. The Terror of Clear Lake, we used to call him. The Texas Highway Patrol had other names for him. So did the agency administrators; they cussed near threw him out of the astronaut corps at least half a dozen times.

But we all loved Sam, back in those days, as we went through training and then blasted off for our first mission to the Moon. He was funny, he kept us laughing. And he did the things and said the things that none of us had the guts to do or say.

The skipper loved Sam a little less than the rest of us, especially after six weeks of living in each other's dirty laundry. Sam had a way of *almost* defying any order he received; he reacted very poorly to authority figures. Our skipper, Lord love him, was as stiff-backed an old-school authority figure as any of them. He was basically a good Joe, and I'm cursed if I can remember his real name. But his big problem was that he had memorized the rule book and tried never to deviate from it.

Well, anyway, there we were, stranded on the lunar surface after six weeks of hard work. Our task had been to make a semi-permanent underground base out of the prefabricated modules that had been, as the agency quaintly phrased it, "landed remotely on the lunar regolith in a series of carefully-coordinated unmanned logistics missions." In other words, they had dropped nine different module packages over a fifty-square-kilometer area of Mare Nubium and we had to find them all, drag them to the site that Houston had picked for Base Gamma, set them up properly, scoop up enough of the top layers of soil to cover each module and the connecting tunnels to a depth of 0.3048 meter (that's one foot, in English), and then link in the electric power reactor and all the wiring, plumbing, heating and air circulation units. Which we had done, adroitly and efficiently, and now that our labors were finished and we were ready to leave—no go. Too bad we couldn't have covered the return module with 0.3048 meter of lunar soil; that would have protected the fuel cells from that sharpshooting micrometeoroid.

The skipper decided it would be bad procedure to let us mope around and brood.

"I want each of you to run a thorough inventory of all your personal supplies: the special foods you've brought with you, your spare clothing, entertainment kits, the works."

"That'll take four minutes," Sam muttered, loud enough for us all to hear him. The eight of us were crammed into the command module, eight guys squeezed into a space built for three, at most. It was barely high enough to stand in, and the metal walls and ceiling always felt cold to the touch. Sam was pressed in with the guys behind me; I was practically touching noses with the skipper. The guys in back giggled at his wisecrack. The skipper scowled.

"Goddammit, Gunn, can't you behave seriously for even a minute? We've got a real problem here."

"Yessir," Sam replied. If he hadn't been squeezed in so tightly, I'm sure he would have saluted. "I'm merely attempting to keep morale high, sir."

The skipper made an unhappy snorting noise, and then told us that we would spend the rest of the shift checking out *all* the supplies that were left: not just our personal stuff, but the mission's supplies of food, the nuclear reactor, the water recirculation system, equipment of all sorts, air . . .

We knew it was busywork, but we had nothing else to do. So we wormed our way out of the command module and crawled through the tunnels toward the other modules that we had laid out and then covered with bulldozed soil. It was a neat little buried base we had set up, for later explorers to use. I got a sort of claustrophobic feeling, just then, that this buried base might turn into a mass grave for eight astronauts.

I was dutifully heading back for barracks module A, where four of us had our bunks and personal gear, to check out my supplies as the skipper had ordered. Sam snaked up beside me. Those tunnels, back in those days, were prefabricated Earthside to be laid out once we got to the construction site. I think they were designed by midgets. You couldn't stand up in them; they were too low. You had to really crawl along on hands and knees if you were my size. Sam was able to shuffle through them with bent knees, knuckle-walking like a miniature gorilla. He loved the tunnels.

"Hey, wait up," he hissed to me.

I stopped.

"Whattaya think will get us first, the air giving out or we starve to death?"

He was grinning cheerfully. I said, "I think we're going to poison our air with methane. We'll fart ourselves to death in another couple of days."

Sam's grin widened. "C'mon . . . I'm setting up a pool on the computer. I hadn't thought of air pollution. You wanna make a bet on that?" He started to King-Kong down the shaft to the right, toward the computer and life-support module. If I had had the space, I would have shrugged. Anyway, I followed him there.

Three of the other guys were in the computer module, huddled around the display screen like Boy Scouts around a campfire.

"Why aren't you checking out the base's supplies, like the skipper said?" I asked them.

"We are, Straight Arrow," replied Mickey Lee, our refugee from Chinatown. He tapped the computer screen. "Why go sorting through all that junk when the computer has it already listed in alphabetical order for us?"

That wasn't what the skipper wanted, and we all knew it, but Mickey was right. Why bother with busywork? We wrote down lists that would keep the skipper happy. By hand. If we had let the computer print out the lists, Skip would have gotten wise to us right away.

While we scribbled away, copying what was on the screen, we talked over our basic situation.

"Why the hell can't we use the nuke to recharge the fuel cells?" Julio Marx asked. He was our token Puerto Rican Jew, a tribute to the agency's Equal Opportunity policy. Julio was also a crackerjack structural engineer who had saved my life the day I had started to unfasten my helmet in the barracks module just when one of those blessed prefab tunnels had cracked its airlock seal. But that's another story.

Sam gave Julio a sorrowful stare. "The two systems are incompatible, Jules." Then, with a grin, Sam launched into the phoniest Latin accent you ever heard. "The nuclear theeng, man, it got too many volts for the fuel cells. Like, you plug the nukie to the fuel cells, man, you make a beeg boom and we all go to dat big San Juan in thee sky. You better steek to plucking chickens, man, an' leave the electreecity alone."

Julio, who towered a good inch and a half over Sam, grinned back at him and answered, "Okay, Shorty, I dig."

"Shorty! Shorty!" Sam's face went red. "All right, that's it. The hell with the betting pool. I'm gonna let you guys all die of boredom. Serve you right."

We made a big fuss and soothed his feathers and cajoled him into setting up the pool. With a great show of hurt feelings and reluctant but utterly selfless nobility, Sam pushed Mickey Lee out of the chair in front of the computer terminal and began playing the keyboard like a virtuoso pianist. Within a few minutes the screen was displaying a list of possible ways for us to die, with Sam's swiftly calculated odds next to each entry. At the touch of a button, the screen displayed a graph, showing how the odds for each mode of dying changed as time went on.

Suffocation, for example, started off as less than a one percent possibility. But within a month the chances began to rise fairly steeply. "The air scrubbers need replacement filters," Sam explained, "and we'll be out of them inside of two more weeks."

"They'll have us out of here in two weeks, for Christ's sake," Julio said.

"Or drop fresh supplies for us," said Ron Avery, the taciturn pilot whom we called Cowboy because of his lean, lanky build and his slow Western drawl.

"Those are the odds," Sam snapped. "The computer does not lie. Pick your poison and place your bets."

I put fifty bucks down on Air Contamination, not telling the other guys about my earlier conversation with Sam. Julio took Starvation, Mickey settled on Dehydration (Lack of Water), and Ron picked Murder—which made me shudder.

"What about you, Sam?" I asked.

"I'll wait 'til the other guys have a chance," he said.

"You gonna let the skipper in on this?" Julio asked.

Sam shook his head. "If I tell him . . ."

"I'll tell him," Ron volunteered, with a grim smile. "I'll even let him have Murder, if he wants it. I can always switch to Suicide."

"Droll fellow," said Sam.

Well, you probably read about the mission in your history tapes. Houston was supporting three separate operations on the Moon at the same time, and they were stretched to the limit down there. Old Stone Face promised us a rescue flight in a week. But they had a problem with the booster when they tried to rush things on the pad too much, and the blessed launch had to be pushed back a week, and then another week. They sent an unmanned supply craft to us, but the descent stage got gummed up, so our fresh food, air filters, water supply and other stuff just orbited over us about fifty miles up.

Sam calculated the odds of all these foul-ups and came to the conclusion that Houston was working overtime to kill us. "Must be some sort of an experiment," he told me. "Maybe they need some martyrs to make people more aware of the space program."

We learned afterward that Houston was in deep trouble because of us. The White House was firing people left and right, Congressional committees were gearing up to investigate the fiasco, and the CIA was checking out somebody's crackbrained idea that the Russians were behind all our troubles.

Meanwhile, we were stranded on the Mare Nubium with nothing much to do but let our beards grow and hope for sinus troubles that would cut off our ability to sense odors.

Old Stone Face was magnificent, in his unflinching way. He was on the line to us every day, despite the fact that his superiors in Houston and Washington were either being fired directly by the President himself or roasted over the simmering coals of media criticism. There must have been a zillion reporters at Mission Control by the second week of our marooning; we could *feel* the hubbub and tension whenever we talked with Stony.

"The countdown for your rescue flight is proceeding on an accelerated schedule," he told us. It would never occur to him to say *We're hurrying as fast as we can*. "Liftoff is now scheduled for 0700 hours on the twenty-fifth."

None of us needed to look at a calendar to know that the twenty-fifth was seventeen days away. Sam's betting pool was looking more serious every hour. Even the skipper had finally taken a plunge: Suffocation.

If it weren't for Sandi Hemmings we might have all gone crazy. She took over as capcom during the night shift, when most of the reporters and the agency brass were asleep. She gave us courage and the desire to pull through, partly just by smiling at us and looking female enough to make us *want* to survive, but mainly by giving us the straight info with no nonsense.

"They're in deep trouble over at Canaveral," she would tell us. "They've had to go to triple shifts and call up boosters that they didn't think they would need until next year. Some senator in Washington is yelling that we ought to ask the Russians or the Japanese to help out."

"As if either of them had upper stages that could make it to the Moon and back," one of our guys muttered.

"Well," Sandi said, with her brightest smile, "you'll all be heroes when you finally get back here. The girls will be standing in line to admire you."

"You won't have to stand in line, Sandi," Ron Avery answered, in a rare burst of words. "You'll always be first with us."

The others crowded into the command module added their heartfelt agreement.

Sandi laughed, undaunted by the prospect of the eight of us grabbing for her. "I hope you shave first," she said.

A night or two later she spent hours reading to us the suggestions made by the Houston medical team on how to stretch out our dwindling supplies of food, water and air. They boiled down to one basic rule: lie down and don't exert yourselves. Great advice, especially when you're beginning to really worry that you're not going to make it through this mess. Just what we needed to do, lie back in our bunks and do nothing but think.

I caught a gleam in Sam's eye, though, as Sandi waded through the medics' report. The skipper asked her to send the report through our computer printer. She did, and he spent the next day reading and digesting it. Sam spent that day—well, I couldn't figure out where he'd gotten to. I just didn't see him all day long, and Base Gamma really wasn't big enough to hide in, even for somebody as small as Sam.

After going through the medics' recommendations, the skipper ordered us to take tranquilizers. We had a scanty supply of downers in the base pharmaceutical stores, and Skip divided them equally among us. At the rate of three a day, they would last four days, with four pills left over. About as useful as a cigaret lighter in hell, but the skipper played it by the book and ordered us to start gobbling tranquilizers.

"They will ease our anxieties and help us to remain as quiet as possible while we wait for the rescue mission," he told us.

He didn't bother to add that the rescue mission, according to Sandi's unofficial word, was still twelve days off. We would be out of food in three more days, and the recycled water was starting to taste as if it hadn't been recycled, if you know what I mean. The air was getting foul, too, but that was probably just our imaginations.

Sam appeared blithely unconcerned, even happy. He whistled cheerfully as Skip rationed out the tranquilizers, then scuttled off down the tunnel that led toward our barracks module. By the time I got to my bunk, Sam was nowhere in sight. His whistling was gone. So was his pressure suit.

He had gone out on the surface? For what? To increase his radiation dose? To get away from the rest of us? That was probably it. Underneath his wise-guy shell, Sam was probably as worried and tense as any of us, and he just didn't want us to know it. He needed some solitude, and what better place to get it than the airless rocky expanse of Mare Nubium?

That's what I thought, so I didn't go out after him.

The same thing happened the next "morning" (by which I mean the time immediately after our sleep shift), and the next. The skipper would gather us together in the command module, we would each take our ceremonial tranquilizer pill and a sip of increasingly bad water, and then we would crawl back to our bunks and try to do nothing that would use up body energy or air. I found myself resenting it whenever I had to go to the toilet; I kept imagining my urine flowing straight into our water tank without reprocessing. I guess I was beginning to go crazy.

But Sam was as happy as could be: chipper, joking, laughing it up. He would disappear each morning for several hours, and then show up again with a lopsided grin on his face, telling jokes and making us all feel a little better.

Until Julio suddenly sat up in his bunk, the second or third morning after we had run out of tranquilizers, and shouted:

"Booze!"

Sam had been sitting on the edge of Julio's bunk, telling an outrageous story of what he planned to do with Sandi once we got back to Houston.

"Booze!" Julio repeated. "I smell booze! I'm cracking up. I'm losing my marbles."

For once in his life, Sam looked apologetic, almost ashamed.

"No you're not," he said to Julio, in as quiet a voice as I've ever heard Sam speak. "I was going to tell you about it tomorrow—the stuff is almost ready for human consumption."

You never saw three grown men so suddenly attentive.

With a self-deprecating little grin, Sam explained, "I've been tinkering with the propellants and other junk out in the return module. They're not doing us any good, just sitting out there. So I made a small still. Seems to be working okay. I tasted a couple sips today. It'll take the enamel off your teeth, but it's not all that bad. By tomorrow. . . ."

He never got any further. We did a Keystone Kops routine, rushing for our space suits, jamming ourselves through the airlock and running out to the inert, idle, cussedly useless return module.

Sam was not kidding us. He had jury-rigged an honest-to-backwoods still inside the return module, fueling it with propellants from the module's tanks. The basic alcohol also came from the propellant, with water from the fuel cells, and a few other ingredients that Sam had scrounged from miscellaneous supplies.

We lost no time pressurizing the module, lifting our helmet

visors, and sampling his concoction. It was *terrible*. We loved it.

By the time we had staggered back to our barracks module, laughing and belching, we had made up our minds to let the other three guys in barracks B share in Sam's juice. But the skipper was a problem. Once he found out about it, he'd have Sam up on charges and drummed out of the agency, even before the rescue mission reached us. Old Stone Face would vote to leave Sam behind, I knew, if he found out about it.

"Have no fear," Sam told us, with a giggle. "I will, myself, reveal my activities to our noble skipper."

And before we could stop him, he had tottered off toward the command module, whistling in a horribly sour off-key way.

An hour went by. Then two. We could hear Skip's voice yelling from the command module, although we couldn't make out the words. None of us had the guts to go down the tunnel and try to help Sam. After a while the tumult and the shouting died. Mickey Lee gave me a questioning glance. Silence; ominous silence.

"You think Skip's killed him?" he asked.

"More likely," said Julio, "that Sam's talked the skipper to death."

Timidly, we slunk down the tunnel to the command module. The other three guys were there with Sam and the skipper; they were all quaffing Sam's rocket juice and grinning at each other.

We were shocked, but we joined right in. Six days later, when the guys from Base Alpha landed their return module crammed with food and fresh water for us, we invited them to join the party. A week after that, when the rescue mission from Canaveral finally showed up, we had been under the influence for so long that we told them to go away.

I had never realized before then what a lawyer Sam was. He had convinced the skipper to read the medics' report carefully, especially the part where they recommended using tranquilizers to keep us calm and minimize our energy consumption. Sam had then gotten the skipper to punch up the medical definition of alcohol's effects on the body, out of Houston's medical files. Sure enough, if you squinted the right way, you could claim that alcohol was a sort of tranquilizer. That was enough justification for the skipper, and we just about pickled ourselves until we got rescued.

The crystal statue glittered under the harsh rays of the unfiltered sun. The work leader, still sitting on the lip of the truck's hatch, said:

"It looks beautiful. You guys did a good job. Is the epoxy set?"

"Needs another few minutes," said the young man, tapping the toe of his boot against the base that they had poured on the lunar plain.

"What happened when you got back to Houston?" the young woman asked. "Didn't they get angry at you for being drunk?"

"Sure," said the leader. "But what could they do? Sam's booze pulled us through, and we could show that we were merely following the recommendations of the medics. Old Stone Face hushed it all up and we became heroes, just like Sandi told us we would be—for about a week."

"And Sam?"

"He left the astronaut corps for a while and started his own business. The rest you know about from the history books. Hero, showman, scoundrel, patriot. It's all true. He was all those things."

"Did he and Sandi ever, uh . . . get together?" the young man asked.

"She was too smart to let him corner her. She used one of the other guys to protect her; married him, finally. Cowboy, I think it was. They eloped and spent their honeymoon in orbit. Zero gee and all that. Sam pretended to be very upset about it, but by that time he was surrounded by women, all of them taller than he was."

The three of them walked slowly around the gleaming statue.

"Look at the rainbows it makes where the sun hits it," said the young woman. "It's marvelous."

"But if he was so smart," said the young man, "why'd he pick this spot 'way out here for his grave? It's miles from Selene City. You can't even see the statue from the city."

"Silly. This is the place where Base Gamma was," said the young woman. "Isn't that right?"

"No," the leader said. "Gamma was all the way over on the other side of Nubium. It's still there. Abandoned, but still there. Even the blasted return module is still sitting there, as dumb as ever."

"Then why put the statue here?"

The leader chuckled. "Sam was a pretty shrewd guy. He set up, in his will, a tourist agency that will guide people to the important sites on the Moon. They start at Selene City and go along the surface in those big cruisers that're being built back at the city. Sam's tomb is going to be a major tourist attraction, and he wanted it far enough out in the mare so that people wouldn't be able to see it from Selene; they have to buy tickets and take the bus."

Both the young people laughed tolerantly.

"I guess he was pretty smart, at that," the young man confessed.

"And he had a long memory, too," said the leader. "He left this tourist agency to me and the other guys from Artemis IV, in his will. We own it. I figure it'll keep me comfortable for the rest of my life."

"Why did he do that?"

The leader shrugged inside his cumbersome suit. "Why did he build that still? Sam always did what he darned well felt like doing. No matter what you think of him, he always remembered his friends."

The three of them gave the crystal statue a final admiring glance, then clumped back to the truck and started the hour-long drive to Selene City.

Private Enterprise Goes Into Orbit

While Sam Gunn can set himself up in the distillery business, albeit briefly, on the Moon, other entrepreneurs are going into the space business right here on Earth. For more than two decades, space was the almost exclusive preserve of government agencies; no private enterprise allowed. But that is changing, and rapidly. This article was published in Continental Airlines' magazines, largely because the editor recognized that Continental's business travelers would be interested in the opportunities of moving industry into space.

A new industrial revolution is beginning, a hundred miles from where you are right now—straight up. Private companies, large and small, are taking the first experimental steps that will lead to factories in space that manufacture ultrapure medicines, new metal alloys, electronics components and materials that cannot possibly be made on the surface of the Earth.

Before the end of this decade, for example, we may have an entire new line of medicines that are more powerful, yet safer to use, than anything on Earth today. These new pharmaceutical products will be manufactured in orbit.

It is called the EOS Program: EOS standing for Electrophoresis Operations in Space.

"*Eos* is also the name of the Greek goddess of dawn," says David W. Richman, "and we like to think that this program is the dawn of a new era."

Richman is the EOS deputy program manager at McDonnell Douglas Astronautics Company, in St. Louis, Missouri. In partnership with the Ortho Pharmaceutical Division of Johnson & Johnson (the Band-Aid company), and with the help of NASA, McDonnell Douglas has already completed two flight tests of experimental EOS hardware, aboard the sixth and seventh space shuttle flights in April and June 1983.

Under the zero-gravity conditions in orbit, the EOS automated minilab equipment used the phenomenon of electrophoresis to separate complex protein molecules from one another, the first step toward developing new and better pharmaceuticals to treat disease. The EOS hardware separated some seven hundred times more proteins than would have been possible in the same time on Earth, where gravity hampers the process. And the separated materials were more than four times purer than they would have been if they had been produced on Earth.

Ortho Pharmaceuticals, of Raritan, N.J., is revealing very little about exactly which proteins are being studied in space, and what the medical applications of zero-gravity drugs will eventually be. The pharmaceutical industry is so competitive that Ortho, a subsidiary of Johnson & Johnson, is keeping its purposes veiled in deep secrecy.

But McDonnell Douglas's Richman points out that many human diseases are caused by lack of specific proteins, such as hormones and enzymes. If a zero-gravity pharmaceutical laboratory in orbit can produce such vitally-needed proteins in greater abundance and purity than it is possible to obtain on Earth, the pharmaceutical industry may go literally "out of this world" to treat protein-deficiency diseases.

A McDonnell Douglas engineer, Charles D. Walker, joined five other astronauts on the twelfth space shuttle mission in early 1984. He was the first payload specialist to fly in the shuttle for a purely commercial project.

Pharmaceuticals, though, are not the only products that can be manufactured in space. Several companies are studying the possibilities of zero-gravity manufacturing of metals, crystals and materials for electronics equipment. Other companies are getting into the business of launching rockets. They expect to make profits from boosting satellites into orbit within the next few years.

Since the first Sputnik went up, in 1957, space operations have been the work of national governments: the Soviet Union, the United States, a group of Western European nations now called the European Space Agency (ESA), China, Japan and India have all launched their own satellites. But now, here in America, private enterprise is going into orbit, with the help of NASA.

The space agency is working with more than half a dozen private firms, providing technical expertise and facilities that range from a "drop tube" at NASA's Marshall Space Flight Center, near Huntsville, Alabama, to flights aboard the space shuttle.

"We're acting as a sort of marriage broker," says Bob Marshall, Director of Program Development at Marshall Space Flight Center, where the space manufacturing program is based.

Starting in the mid-1970s, Marshall and his NASA colleagues began to identify areas in space research that might be turned into commercial products someday. They contacted more than 400 private firms and began showing them how space operations could benefit them.

"We tried to go in at the highest level in each company," Marshall explained, "and talk to the president or the vice president for research or marketing."

NASA set up regional meetings where space engineers discussed these new ideas with area industrial firms. Then NASA helped the interested companies to "marry" with an experienced aerospace firm. Once that was done, NASA stepped out of the picture—except to provide the technical facilities that each project required.

"We've never turned away a company that showed interest," Marshall says. Some firms have dropped out of the program after an initial investigation. "But I expect most of them will return, sooner or later," states Marshall confidently.

Why try to manufacture things in space? At first the idea sounds strange, even wild. Do these people actually believe that someday there will be factories in orbit?

Yes. The environment of space is new, and can be dangerous. But it is far from useless. The space environment offers four advantages that are extremely valuable for many industrial operations: free energy, controllable temperature extremes, very high vacuum and controllable gravity.

Energy is abundant in space. The Sun shines constantly, and solar energy can be used either directly as heat, or converted into electricity by the same kind of solarvoltaic cells that have powered satellites since the first Vanguard went into orbit in 1958.

The Sun's heat can be used for a wide range of industrial processes. With simple mirrors it is possible to focus sunlight and attain temperatures of many thousands of degrees. Smelting, metalworking, chemical processing, boiling and heating can be done in an orbital factory with direct or concentrated sunlight.

A space factory can easily attain very low temperatures as well, simply by shielding an area from sunlight. A well-shadowed region could be cooled down close to absolute zero. Because vacuum is an excellent thermal insulator (the secret of the Thermos bottle), a space factory could be smelting metals in one place and, only a few yards away, could simultaneously be freezing nitrogen or hydrogen into liquids.

Temperatures can be manipulated up and down the scale, over thousands of degrees, merely by manipulating the amount of sunlight or shade—without burning an ounce of any fuel, without building heaters or refrigerators, without separating the hot work from the cold work by more than a few yards.

Free solar energy means freedom from the heavy and continuous fuel bills of Earthside factories, plus freedom from the pollution that inevitaby accompanies power plants on Earth.

It costs a lot of time and money to make nothing—a vacuum—on Earth. Many industrial processes require vacuum chambers at some stage of their operation; a considerable part of the cost of electronics components, pharmaceuticals, metals and other industrial products stems from the need to pump air out of a chamber and produce nothingness.

Just a hundred or so miles overhead is a better vacuum *for free* than any that can be bought on Earth, regardless of price. The combination of this excellent vacuum with the zero gravity* of orbit yields the possibility of "containerless" processing, which can lead to the routine manufacture of ultrapure materials.

On Earth, when you want to mix liquids you must put them into a container, whether you are mixing a salad dressing or a white-hot molten steel alloy. No matter how well you stir the ingredients, the heavier ones tend to sink toward the bottom of the bowl. And there are always microscopic bits of the container mixed in, too. This contamination does not matter much for most processes, but in areas such as pharmaceuticals, purity is supremely important.

In space everything changes for the better. There are no heavier ingredients in orbit; everything is weightless. There is no "bottom" under weightless conditions. So you do not need a bowl. The materials to be mixed can hang in vacuum, containerless, unsullied by impurities. Space factory technicians could melt down a slab of iron, without fear of drips. The molten metal would simply hang there weightlessly and slowly take on a spherical shape, because of internal tension forces.

These four advantages of the space environment are already attracting industrialists and researchers. Even though it costs thousands of dollars to place a pound of material in orbit, space manufacturing offers the promise of highly profitable new products. This means new industries and new jobs—most of them on Earth.

Would you believe that one of the world's leading manufacturers of farm equipment is working with NASA? The John Deere Company, of Moline, Illinois, has used NASA airplanes to simulate zero gravity in a study of new ways to produce cast iron. About 25 percent of the material this $5-billion-per-year company produces is cast iron. Deere ranks among the largest iron foundry operators in the U.S.

Larry L. Fosbinder, a Deere senior engineer, points out that one of the key factors determining the properties of cast iron is the way graphite particles mix within the iron. One

---

*Purists point out that the condition found in orbit is not exactly *zero* gravity, since the mass of the spacecraft itself exerts a minuscule gravitational force. It is called, therefore, *microgravity* by the experts . . . and zero gravity by everyone else.

way to study how gravity affects the mixture is to eliminate gravity while various samples of mixtures are prepared. Deere has flown experiments aboard NASA F-104 and KC-135 aircraft. The planes achieve weightless conditions for a few seconds to a few minutes by flying a parabolic arc; zero gravity comes when the plane soars through the top of the arc.

James Graham, a senior research associate at Deere, points out that the company has also utilized many other NASA technologies, including new adhesives and computer programs. NASA and the American Foundry Society are also investigating the use of ultrasonic technology to probe the inner details of the composition of various cast iron alloys.

Small companies are working with NASA in space manufacturing, too.

Microgravity Research Associates (MRA), of Coral Gables, Florida, will conduct a series of experiments aboard the space shuttle aimed at developing electronic crystal materials in space. Crystals can be grown larger and purer under zero-gravity conditions than they can be on Earth. Richard L. Randolph, president of MRA, says that the company's experiments aboard the shuttle will be aimed at growing crystals of gallium arsenide, a material that he believes will replace the commonplace silicon chip for many future electronics applications.

"Space-produced gallium arsenide will be making considerable inroads in new applications in electronics and electro-optics," says Mr. Randolph. "The space-produced materials will have superior crystal properties and with that will have superior electronic performance and reliability. [Electronic] equipment that demands the very best performance and reliability will demand space-produced materials."

Seven shuttle flights are planned, in a program that will move from proof-of-concept to demonstration of a full-scale commercial production facility in orbit. Randolph expects to have "meaningful quantities of space-produced crystals" available for evaluation by commercial customers before the end of the 1980s.

Union Carbide Corporation, at Oak Ridge, Tennessee, is studying containerless solidification of metallic "glasses," materials that may someday be used to construct extremely efficient electrical power equipment.

Two companies in Cleveland, TRW and Eaton Corporation, are also working with NASA on various aspects of developing metal alloys under conditions of weightlessness. The DuPont Corporation, Wilmington, Delaware, is engaged in a study of how zero gravity would affect the formation of metals to be used as catalysts—such as the platinum catalytic converters installed to control pollution emissions from automobile engines.

NASA's Marshall Space Flight Center works with the individual private companies in these pioneering efforts. Studies often begin with simple experiments in drop tubes, where a fleeting few seconds of zero gravity are attained while the test object is falling along the length of the tube. The next step is usually to fly experiments aboard the jet aircraft, which can provide up to three minutes of weightlessness as they soar through their parabolic arcs.

Only after these relatively inexpensive tests have proved successful is the experiment packaged for a flight on the space shuttle, where it may be in orbit for anywhere from a few days to two weeks.

Private enterprise is also moving into the business of launching payloads into space.

Since the mid-1960s, the communications satellite industry has blossomed into a multi-billion-dollar global business. Communications companies such as AT&T, RCA, Western Union, Comsat Corporation and many others regularly pay NASA to launch satellites for them. Even at $50 million or more per launch, the satellites are far cheaper than stringing relay stations across a continent or laying cable across an ocean.

So profitable are these communications satellites that the biggest sale ever made by the famous auction house of Sotheby Park Bernet was in 1981, for seven-year leases on seven channels in a new communications satellite. The leases were auctioned for a total of $90.1 million—in a single afternoon.

There are other customers for launch vehicles, as well. The petroleum industry, for example, spends billions of dollars per year exploring remote areas of the world for possible new oil deposits. Satellites are a vital part of such explorations.

When NASA began the space shuttle program in the early 1970s, the agency planned to phase out all its older-type expendable rocket boosters once the shuttle went into operation. NASA's reasoning was that expendable boosters, which can be used only once, would give way to the shuttle, which is reusable, more efficient, and therefore should bring down the costs of launching payloads into orbit.

But private industry sees it differently. While the shuttle is the best vehicle in the world for large and very sophisticated payloads, there are many kinds of satellites that can be placed in orbit with "old-fashioned" throwaway boosters. In fact, NASA's chief competition for commercial customers is the European Space Agency's *Ariane* booster, which is an expendable, one-time rocket rather like the Deltas, Titans and Atlases that were the standbys of the American space program before the shuttle flew.

So while NASA is placing all its payloads in the shuttle, private entrepreneurs are developing their plans for launching satellites aboard expendable boosters—for profit. President Reagan announced his support for this move in May 1983, stating that "the government fully endorses and will facilitate the commercialization of expendable launch vehicles."

The first company to get into the space-launching business was Space Services, Inc., of Houston. Operating from a base they established on Matagorda Island, off the Gulf coast of Texas, SSI successfully launched their Conestoga I rocket on a suborbital test in September 1982. An earlier launch attempt, the company's first, ended abruptly when the rocket blew up on the launch stand.

David Hannah Jr., president of SSI, expects the company's first orbital launch to take place in 1987. "We're getting our funding in order and designing our launching system," Hannah says. He expects to purchase solid-fuel rocket engines from manufacturers such as United Technologies Corporation or Thiokol and to be able to boost satellites of 900 pounds into 500-mile-high orbits.

Hannah sees a market for at least five orbital launches per year, each of which should cost about $10 million. Most of the satellites will carry Earth-sensing equipment for geological exploration of remote areas. Many of the oil companies based in Houston could become customers of SSI.

Space Projects Company, of Princeton, New Jersey, has an even grander vision. The company has proposed to the government that it will raise a billion dollars for the construction of a fifth space shuttle (NASA has been allowed to build only four, to date). This fifth shuttle would be devoted entirely to commercial flights.

Dr. Klaus Heiss founded the firm, which was originally called Space Transportation Company, in conjunction with William Sword, a Princeton financier. Heiss was the econometrician who did the original economic studies, ten years ago, for NASA on the "market" for the space shuttle's launching services. The studies convinced him that there is a vast commercial market for the shuttle.

Space Transportation also intended to develop a business line in expendable rocket boosters, and started a program with Martin Marietta Corporation, which builds the Titan booster at its Denver, Colorado, plant. But in May 1983, Space Transportation sold off this part of its business to Federal Express Corporation. The new company was called Fedex Spacetran.

Someday, when you have a satellite payload that "absolutely, positively, has to get there," you will be able to call Federal Express.

The original Space Transportation Company changed its name to Space Projects, and Dr. Heiss left, while Sword remained as chairman of the company.

It was an amicable parting, Dr. Heiss says. "We had a difference of opinion. They took a short-range view, while I want to look at the longer range."

Dr. Heiss believes it will be another two to three years before a commercial space shuttle program can become a reality. But once it does, he foresees "six to eight commercial shuttle flights per year, and a total U.S. market for commercial launch services of one to two billion dollars per year," with a total world market reaching almost three billion dollars per year.

His main intention now is to "broaden the base of investor

support," for the plan to build a commercial space shuttle, most likely through a combination of Space Projects and other investors—including the general public. "Broad public participation [will be] appropriate" in the commercialization of space, Dr. Heiss believes.

Space Projects, meanwhile, is proceeding with its original proposal to NASA. James Scott Hill, general counsel for the company, says that the proposal to build a fifth shuttle orbiter "is important for the country, and for science, and for space exploration. We would like to see it come to fruition."

While the government has not yet decided on Space Projects' proposal, Hill says, "We're most optimistic. The concept is sound. Private enterprise should be in space. It should not be an exclusively governmental program."

The advent of private launching services, and the success of the shuttle, raises new problems for NASA. Should the agency operate its four-shuttle fleet as a sort of semi-commercial transportation line into space? Or should NASA relinquish control of the shuttle, once all four vehicles have been satisfactorily tested, and allow another government agency or a private firm to operate the shuttle? NASA, after all, is at its best developing new technology and exploring the universe. It was not set up to be a transportation company.

As private enterprise moves into the business of launching payloads into space, as well as developing industrial operations in orbit, what role should NASA play?

Dr. Jerry Grey, publisher of *Aeronautics and Astronautics* magazine and author of the book *Beachheads in Space*, says, "I believe commercial operation of the shuttle is on the way. The shuttle, or its derivatives, will eventually become a private operation." Citing the greater flexibility that private operators would have over a government agency, Dr. Grey believes, "My view is that NASA feels the shuttle isn't ready yet to be turned over to private enterprise," but in "two or three years" it will be. Pointing out that the shuttle program is still in a testing, experimental phase, he adds, "It doesn't make sense for NASA to operate the shuttle once it becomes an operational system. And I think NASA agrees with that."

President Reagan also wants to turn over to private operators the Landsat satellites, which monitor the Earth for natural resources, and the weather observations satellites now under the control of National Oceanic and Atmospheric Administration (NOAA).

While this proposal has been attacked by some members of the Congress and by many scientists, it seems inevitable that private companies will take over more and more functions in space that are now operated by government agencies.

Back in 1979, *Fortune* magazine writer Gene Bylinsky said, ''In the wide and starry band of near-earth space . . . [there is] the possibility of an industrial bonanza. . . . No corporation affected by changes in technology can afford to ignore the new era of innovation that is about to begin.''

Today, that era *has* begun. For many American companies, large and small, new and old, business is definitely looking up.

Vision

We can talk about the practical benefits of going into space, the fortunes to be made in zero-gravity manufacturing, the benefits of new medicines and materials produced in orbit. But there is the human aspect to consider, also. Don Arnold is a Promethean of a slightly different stripe, a reluctant leader who pioneers into a new domain almost in spite of himself. Philosophers have long argued over whether human history is molded by the daring actions of extraordinary men and women, or whether history responds to implacable, inevitable natural forces which individual human actions can do little to bend or shape. *Vision* might help you to decide which side of that argument you are on; then again, it might just add a little weight to both sides of the argument.

Vision, by the way, was originally published in *Analog* magazine's 50th anniversary issue, and marked my return to that venerable magazine's pages as a writer. My first sale to *Analog* was in May 1962, a short story titled *The Next Logical Step* (see *Escape Plus Ten,* published by Tor Books in 1983). When John W. Campbell, Jr. died in 1971 and I was tapped to become *Analog's* editor, I decided not to write for the science fiction magazines as long as I was an editor of one of them; it would have been too much of a conflict of interest, I felt. Although I continued to write science fiction novels, I also withdrew them from consideration for the Hugo and Nebula awards, for the same reason. Once I left *Analog,* however, I was pleased to submit stories and articles to the science fiction magazines once again, and was very happy when Stanley Schmidt picked it for *Analog's* 50th anniversary.

"But if you live in orbit, you can live forever!"

Don Arnold said it in sheer frustration and immediately regretted opening his mouth.

Picture the situation. Don was sitting under the glaring lights of a TV studio, in a deep fake-leather couch that looked comfortable but wasn't. His genial talk-show host had ignored him totally since introducing him as "one of NASA's key scientists." (Don was a NASA engineer, and pretty far from the top.)

On one side of Don sat a UFOlogist, a balding, owlishly-bespectacled man with a facial tic and a bulging briefcase clutched in his lap, full of Important Documents.

On Don's other side sat a self-proclaimed Mystic of indeterminate age, a benign smile on his face, his head shaved and a tiny gem in his left earlobe.

They had done all the talking since the show had started, nearly an hour earlier.

"The government has all sorts of data about UFOs," the UFOlogist was saying, hugging his battered briefcase. "NASA has *tons* of information about how the saucers are built and where they're coming from, but they won't release any of this to the people."

Before Don could reply, the Mystic raised both his hands, palms outward. The cameras zoomed in on him.

"All of the universe is a single entity, and all of time is the same," he said in a voice like a snake charmer's reed flute. "Governments, institutions, all forms of society are merely illusions. The human mind is capable of anything, merely by thinking transcendentally. The soul is immortal—"

That's when Don burst out, "But if you live in orbit, you can live forever!"

It surprised them all, especially Don. The Mystic blinked, his mouth still silently shaped for his next pronouncement. The UFOlogist seemed to curl around his briefcase even tighter. The studio audience out there beyond the blinding glare of the overhead lights surged forward in their chairs and uttered a collective murmur of wonderment.

Even the talk show's host seemed stunned for just a moment. He was the best-dressed man on the set, in a deep blue cashmere sports jacket and precisely-creased pearl gray slacks. He was the only man on camera in makeup. His hairpiece gave him a youthful-yet-reliable look.

The host swallowed visibly as Don wished he could call back the words he had just blurted.

"They live forever?" the host asked, so honestly intrigued that he forgot to smile.

How in hell can I backtrack out of this? Don asked himself desperately.

Then the Mystic started to raise his hands again, his cue to the cameras that he wanted their attention on him.

"Our studies have shown that it's possible," Don said, leaning forward slightly to stare right into the host's baby-blue eyes.

"How long have people lived in orbit, anyway?" the host asked.

"The record is held by two Russian cosmonauts, aboard their space station. They were up there for almost nine months. Our Skylab team was up for 83 days, back in '73-'74."

Don could sense the UFOlogist fidgeting beside him, but the host asked, "And they did experiments up there that showed you could live longer if you stayed in space?"

"Lots of experiments have been done," Don answered before anyone else could upstage him, "both in orbit and on the ground."

"On . . . immortality."

"We tend to call it life extension," he said truthfully. "But it's quite clear that in orbit, where you can live under conditions of very low gravity, your heart doesn't have to work so hard, your internal organs are under much less stress . . ."

"But don't your muscles atrophy? Isn't there calcium loss from the bones?"

"No," Don said flatly. All three cameras were aimed squarely at him. Normally he was a shy man, but nearly an hour of listening to the other two making a shambles of organized thought had made him sore enough to be bold.

"It doesn't?"

"It takes a lot of hard work to move around in low gravity," Don answered. "With a normal work routine, plus a few minutes of planned exercise each day, there's no big muscle-tone loss. In fact, you'd probably be in better condition if you lived in a space station than you are here on Earth."

"Fascinating!" said the host.

"As for calcium loss, that levels off eventually. It's no real problem."

"And then you just go on living," the host said, "forever?"

"For a long, long time," Don hedged. "In a space station, of course, your air is pure, your water's pure, the environment is very carefully controlled. There are no carcinogens lousing up the ecology. And you have all the benefits of low gravity."

"I never knew that! Why hasn't NASA told us about this?"

As Don fished around in his mind for a reply, the host turned on his smile and fixed his gaze on camera one.

"Well, it always seems that we run out of time just when things are *really* interesting." Glancing back along his guests on the couch, he said, "Dr. Arnold, that was fascinating. I hope you can come back and talk with us again, real soon."

Before Don could answer, the host said farewell to the two other guests, mispronouncing both their names.

Don sat up in bed, his back propped by pillows, the sheet pulled up to his navel. It was hot in the upstairs bedroom now that they had to keep the air-conditioner off, but he stayed covered because of the twins. They were nine now, and starting to ask pointed questions.

Judy was putting them into their bunk beds for the night, but they had a habit of wandering around before they finally fell asleep. And Judy, good mother that she was, didn't have the heart to lock the master bedroom door. Besides, on a sultry night like this, the only way to catch a breath of breeze was to keep all the doors and windows open.

Don played a game as he sat up watching television, the remote-control wand in his sweating hand. He found the situation comedies, police shows, doctor shows, even the science fiction shows, on TV so boring that he couldn't bear to watch them for their own sake.

But they were tolerable—almost—if he watched to see how much space-inspired technology he could identify in each show. The remote monitors in the surgeon's intensive-care unit. The sophisticated sensors used by the coroner's hot-tempered pathologist. The pressure-sensitive switch on the terrorists' bomb planted in the cargo bay of the threatened 747.

Judy finally came in and began undressing. The bedroom lights were out, but there was plenty of light coming from the TV screen.

"Better close the door, hon," Don told her as she wriggled her skirt down past her hips. "The twins . . ."

"They're both knocked out," she said. "They spent all day in the Cramers' pool."

"Still . . ." He clicked off the TV sound and listened for the patter of nine-year-old feet.

His wife's body still turned him on. Judy was short, a petite dark-haired beauty with flashing deep-brown eyes and a figure that Don thought of as voluptuous. She stripped off her panties and crawled into the bed beside Don.

Grinning at him, she said, "You worry too much."

"Yeah, maybe I do."

"I thought you were terrific on the show this afternoon. I got so mad when those other two clowns kept hogging the camera!"

"Maybe I should have let them hog it for the whole show," he said.

"No you shouldn't! I sat here for nearly an hour waiting for you to open your mouth."

"Maybe I should've kept it closed."

"You were terrific," she said, snuggling closer to him.

"I was lying," he answered. "Or, at least, stretching the truth until it damn near snapped."

"You looked so handsome on television."

"I just hope nobody at Headquarters saw the show."

"It's a local talk show," Judy said. "Nobody watches it but housewives."

"Yeah . . ."

He started to feel better, especially with Judy cuddling next to him, until almost the very end of the eleven o'clock news. Then they showed a film clip of him staring earnestly into the camera—*I thought I was looking at the host*, Don thought—and explaining how people who live in orbit will live forever.

Don saw his whole career passing in front of his eyes.

He made sure to get to his office bright and early the next morning, taking a bus that arrived on Independence Avenue before the morning traffic buildup. Don was at his desk, jacket neatly hung behind the door and shirt sleeves rolled up, going over the cost figures for yet another study of possible future options for the Office of Space Transportation Systems, when his phone buzzed.

"Uncle Sam wants *you*," rasped Jack Hardesty's voice in the phone receiver.

He saw the show! was Don's first panicked thought.

"You there, Mr. Personality?" Hardesty demanded.

"Yeah, Jack, I'm here."

"Meet me in Klugie's office in five minutes." The phone clicked dead.

Don broke into a sweat.

Otto von Kluge was as American as the Brooklyn Bridge, but many and various were the jokes around NASA Headquarters about his name, his heritage and his abilities. He was an indifferent engineer, a terrible public speaker, and a barely adequate administrator. But he was one of the few people in the office who had a knack for handling other people—from engineers to congressmen, from White House Whiz Kids to crusty old accountants from the Office of Budget and Management.

Despite the low setting of the building's air-conditioning, von Kluge wore his suit jacket and even a little bow tie under his ample chin. Don always thought of him as a smiling, pudgy used-car salesman. But once in a great while he came across as a smiling, pudgy Junker land baron.

Hardesty—bone-thin, lantern-jawed, permanently harried—was already perched on the front half-inch of a chair at one side of von Kluge's broad desk, puffing intensely on a cigaret. Don entered the carpeted office hesitantly, feeling a little like the prisoner on his way to the guillotine.

Von Kluge grinned at him and waved a hand in the general direction of the only other available chair.

"Come on in, Don. Sit down. Relax."

Just like the dentist says, Don thought.

"The TV station is sending me a tape of your show," von Kluge said, with no further preliminaries.

"Oh," Don said, feeling his guts sink. "That."

Laughing, von Kluge said, "Sounds to me like you're bucking for a job in the PR department."

"Uh, no, I'm not . . . I mean . . ."

"Sounds to *me*"—Hardesty ground his cigaret butt into von Kluge's immaculate stainless steel ashtray—"like you're bucking for a job selling brushes door-to-door!"

"Now don't get your blood pressure up, Jack," von Kluge said easily. "Most of the crimes of this world come out of overreacting to an innocent little mistake."

An overwhelming sense of gratitude flooded through Don. "I really didn't mean to do it," he said. "It's just—"

"I know, I know. Your first time on television. The thrill of show business. The excitement. Takes your breath away, doesn't it?"

Don nodded. Hardesty glowered at him.

"Let's just see the tapes and find out what you really said," von Kluge went on. "I'll bet you don't remember yourself, do you, Don?"

"No . . ."

Shrugging, von Kluge said, "It's probably no big deal. We'll just play it cool until it all blows over."

His office door opened slightly and Ms. Tucker, a black secretary of such sweetness and lithe form that she could make bigots vote pro-bussing, said softly:

"Phone for you, Dr. von Kluge."

"I can't be disturbed now, Alma."

"It's Senator Buford," she said, in an awed whisper.

Von Kluge's eyes widened. "Excuse me," he said to Don and Hardesty as he picked up the phone.

He smiled broadly and said, "Senator Buford, sir! Good morning! How are you—"

And that was all he said for the next twenty-two minutes. Von Kluge nodded, grunted, closed his eyes, gazed at the ceiling, stared at Don. As he listened.

Finally he put the phone down, slowly, wearily, like a very tired man at last letting go of an enormous weight. His ear was red.

Looking sadly at Don, von Kluge said, "Well, son, the Senator wants you to appear at his Appropriations Committee hearing. Tomorrow morning."

Don had expected the hearing chamber to be packed with newsmen, cameras, lights, crowds, people grabbing at him for interviews or comments.

Instead, the ornate old chamber was practically empty, except for the few senators who had shown up for their committee's session and their unctuous aides. Even the senators themselves seemed bored and fidgety as a series of experts from various parts of NASA and the Office of Management and Budget gave conflicting testimony on how much money should be appropriated for the space program.

But flinty old Senator Buford, the committee's chairman, sat unflinchingly through it all. His crafty gray eyes drilled holes through every witness; even when he said nothing, he made the witnesses squirm in their seats.

Don was the last scheduled witness before the lunch break, and he kept hoping that they would run out of time before they called on him. Hardesty and von Kluge had drilled him all night in every aspect of the space agency's programs and budget requests. Don's head hadn't felt so burstingly full of facts since his senior year in college, when he had crammed for three days to get past a Shakespeare final exam.

By the time Don sat himself cautiously in the witness chair, only four senators were left at the long baize-covered table facing him. It was a few minutes past noon, but Senator Buford showed no inclination to recess the hearing.

"Mistah Arnold," Buford drawled, "have you prepared a statement for this committee?"

"Yes, sir, I have." Don leaned forward to speak into the microphone on the table before him, even though there was no need to amplify his voice in the nearly-empty, quiet room.

"In view of the hour"—Buford turned *hour* into a two-syllable word—"we will dispense with your reading your statement and have it inserted into th' record as 'tis. With youh permission, of course."

Don felt sweat beading on his forehead and upper lip. "Certainly, sir." His statement was merely the regular public relations pamphlet the agency put out, extolling its current operations and promising wonders for the future.

Senator Buford smiled coldly. Don thought of a rattlesnake coiled to strike.

"Now what's this I heah," the Senator said, " 'bout livin' in space prolongin' youh life?"

Don coughed. "Well, sir, if you're referring to . . . ah, to the remarks I made on television . . ."

"I am, suh."

"Yes, well, you see . . . I had to oversimplify some very complex matters, because . . . you realize . . . the TV audience isn't prepared . . . I mean, there aren't very many scientists watching daytime television talk shows . . ."

Buford's eyes bored into Don. "Ah'm not a scientist either, Mr. Arnold. I'm jest a simple ol' country lawyer tryin' to understand what in the world you're talkin' about."

And in a flash of revelation, Don saw that Senator Buford was well into his seventies. His skin was creased and dry and dead-gray. The little hair left on his head was wispy and white. Liver spots covered his frail, trembling hands. Only his eyes and his voice had any spark or strength to them.

A phrase from the old Army Air Corps song of Don's childhood skipped through his memory: *We live in fame or go down in flames.*

Taking a deep breath and sitting up straighter in the witness chair, Don said, "Well, sir: there are two ways to look at any piece of information—optimistically or pessimistically. What I'm about to tell you is the optimistic view. I want you to understand that clearly, sir. I will be interpreting the information we have on hand in its most optimistic light."

"You go right ahead and do that," said Senator Buford.

*　　*　　*

They lunched in the Senate dining room: dry sherry, mock turtle soup, softshell crabs. Just the two of them at a small table, Don and Senator Buford.

"I finally got me a NASA scientist who can talk sense!" Buford was saying as he cut through one of the little crabs.

Don's head was still reeling. "You know, Senator, that there will be lots of experts inside NASA and outside who'll make some pretty strong arguments against me."

Buford fixed him with a baleful eye. "Mebbe so. But they won't get away with any arguments 'gainst *me*, boy."

"I can't guarantee anything, you realize," Don hedged. "I could be completely wrong."

"Ah know. But like you said, if we don't *try*, we'll never know for sure."

This has got to be a dream, Don told himself. *I'm home in bed and I'll have to get up soon and go testify before Buford's committee.*

"Now lessee what we got heah," Buford said as the liveried black waiter cleared their dishes from the table. "You need the permanent space station—with a major medical facility in it."

"Yessir. And the all-reusable shuttle."

Buford looked at Don sharply. "What's wrong with th' space shuttle we got? Cost enough, didn't it?"

"Yessir, it did. But it takes off like a rocket. Passengers pull three or four gees at launch. Too much for . . . er, for . . ."

"For old geezers like me!" Buford laughed, a sound halfway between a wheeze and a cackle.

Don made his lips smile, then said, "An advanced shuttle would take off like an airplane, nice and smooth. Anybody could ride in it."

"Uh-huh. How long'll it take to get it flyin'?"

Don thought a moment, considered the state of his soul, and decided, *What the hell, go for broke.*

"Money buys time, Senator," he said craftily. "Money buys time."

Senator Buford nodded and muttered, mostly to himself, "I finally got a NASA scientist who tells me the truth."

"Sir, I want you to realize the *whole* truth about what I've been telling you—"

But Buford wasn't listening. "Senator Petty will be our major obstacle. Scrawny little Yankee—thinks he's God's chosen apostle to watch out over the federal budget. He'll give us trouble."

The name of Senator Petty was known to make scientists weep. NASA administrators raced to the bathroom at the sound of it.

Buford waggled a lean, liver-spotted hand in Don's general direction. "But don't you worry none 'bout Petty. Ah'll take care o' him! You just concentrate on gettin' NASA to bring me a detailed program for that space station—with th' medical center in it."

"And the advanced shuttle," Don added, in a near whisper.

"Yeh, of course. The advanced shuttle, too. Cain't ride up there to your geriatrics ward in th' sky on a broomstick, now can I?"

"The twins were twelve years old today."

Don looked up from the report he was writing. It had been nearly midnight by the time he'd gotten home, and now it was well past one.

"I forgot all about their birthday," he confessed.

Judy was standing in the doorway of his study, wrapped in a fuzzy pink housecoat. There were lines in her face that Don hadn't noticed before. Her voice was sharper than he'd remembered.

"They could both be in jail for all you think about them!" she snapped. "Or me, for that matter."

"Look, honey, I've got responsibilities . . ."

"Sure! The big-shot executive. All day long he's running NASA and all night long he's out at parties."

"Meetings," Don said defensively. "It's tough to deal with congressmen and senators in their offices—"

"Meetings with disco bands and champagne and lots of half-naked secretaries prancing around!"

"Judy, for God's sake, I'm juggling a million and one details! The space station, the flyback shuttle booster, and now Senator Buford's in the hospital . . ."

"I hope he drops dead and Petty cuts your balls off!" Judy looked shocked that the words could have come from her mouth. She turned and fled from the room.

Don gave out a long, agonized sigh and leaned back in his desk chair. For a moment he wanted to toss the report he was writing into the wastebasket and go up to bed with his wife.

But he knew he had to face Senator Petty the next morning, and he had to be armed for the encounter. He went back to his writing.

"I think you're pulling the biggest boondoggle this nation's ever seen since the Apollo project," said Senator Petty, smiling.

Don was sitting tensely in a big leather chair in front of the Senator's massive oak desk. On Don's left, in an equally sumptuous chair, sat Reed McCormack, NASA's chief administrator, the space agency's boss and a childhood chum of the President.

McCormack looked like a studious, middle-aged banker who kept in trim playing tennis and sailing racing yachts. Which was almost entirely true. He was not studious. He had learned early in life that you can usually buy expertise—for a song. His special talent was making people trust him.

Senator Petty didn't trust anyone.

From the neck up the Senator looked like a movie idol: brilliant white straight teeth (capped); tanned, taut handsome face (lifted, twice); thick, curly, reddish-brown hair (implanted and dyed). Below the neck, however, his body betrayed him. Despite excruciating hours of jogging and handball, his stomach bulged and his chest was sunken.

"A boondoggle?" McCormack asked easily. "Your colleagues in the Senate don't seem to think so."

Petty's smile turned acid. "Funny thing about my fellow senators. The older they are, the more money they want to appropriate for your gold-plated space station. Why do you think that is?"

"Age brings wisdom," said McCormack.

"Does it?" Petty turned his mud-brown eyes on Don. "Or

is it that you keep telling them they can live forever, once they're up in your orbital old-age home?''

"I've never said that," Don snapped. His nerves were frayed, he realized, as much by Senator Buford's hospitalization as by Judy's growing unhappiness.

"Oh, you've been very careful about what you've said, and to whom, and with what qualifications," Petty replied. "But they all get the same impression: Live in space and you live forever. NASA can give you immortality—if you vote the funds for it.''

"That is *not* our policy," McCormack said firmly.

"The hell it isn't," Petty snapped. "But old Bufe's terminal, they tell me. You won't have him to steer your outrageous funding requests through the Senate. You'll have to deal with me.''

Don knew it was true, and saw the future slipping away from his grasp.

"That's why we're here," McCormack said. "To deal."

Petty nodded curtly.

"If you try to halt construction of the space station, your colleagues will outvote you overwhelmingly," said McCormack.

"Same thing applies to the new shuttle," Don added.

Petty leaned back in his chair and steepled his fingers. "I know that. But I can slow you down. OMB isn't very happy with your cost overruns, you know. And I can always start an investigation into this so-called science of life extension. I can pick a panel of experts that will blow your immortality story out of the water.''

For the first time, McCormack looked uneasy.

"There's no immortality 'story,' '' Don said testily. "We've simply reported the conclusions of various studies and experiments. We've been absolutely truthful.''

"And you've allowed the senators to believe that if they life in orbit they can all become Methuselahs." Petty laughed. "Well, a couple of biologists from Harvard and Berkeley can shoot you down inside a week—with the proper press coverage. And I can see to it that they get the coverage.''

Don gripped the arms of his chair and tried to hold onto his

temper. "Senator Buford is dying and you're already trying
to tear down everything he worked to achieve."

Petty grinned mischievously. "You bet I am."

"What do you want from us?" McCormack asked.

The Senator's grin faded slowly.

"I said we're here to deal with you," McCormack added,
speaking softly. "The President is very anxious to keep this
program going. Its effect on the national economy has been
very beneficial, you realize."

"So you say."

"What do you want?" McCormack repeated.

"The ground-based medical center that's going to be built
as part of your life-extension program . . ."

"In your state?"

"Yes."

McCormack nodded. "I see no reason why that can't be
done. It would be rather close to the Mayo Clinic, then,
wouldn't it?"

"And one other thing," Petty said.

"What is it?"

He pointed at Don. "I want this man—Senator Buford's
dear friend—to personally head up the space station operation."

Don felt his incipient ulcer stab him as McCormack's face
clouded over.

"Mr. Arnold is program manager for the space station
program already," McCormack said, "and also serves as
liaison to the advanced shuttle program office."

"I know that," Petty snapped. "But I want him *up there*,
in the space station, with the first permanent crew."

Don stared at the Senator. "Why . . . ?"

Petty gave him a smirk. "You think living up in space is
such a hot idea, let's see *you* try it!"

Senator Buford's intensive-care bed looked more like a
spacecraft command module than a hospital room. Electronics surrounded the bed, monitoring the dying old man. Oscil-
loscope traces wriggled fitfully; lights blinked in rhythm to
his sinking heartrate; tubes of nutrients and fresh blood fed
into his arteries.

Don had to lean close to the old man's toothless sunken mouth to hear his wheeze:

" 'Preciate your comin' to see me . . . got no family left, y'know."

Don nodded and said nothing.

"Looks like I cain't hold out much longer," the Senator whispered. "How's the space station comin' along?"

"We've got Petty behind it," Don answered. "For a price."

Buford smiled wanly. "Good. Good. You'll get th' whole Senate behind you. They're all gettin' older. They'll all want to go . . . up there."

"I'm only sorry that we're not ready to take you."

Cackling thinly, Buford said, "But I'm goin'! Ah made all the arrangements. They're gonna freeze me soon's I'm clinically dead. And then I'm gonna be sent up to your space station. I'll stay froze until the science fellas figure out how to cure this cancer I got. Then they'll thaw me out and I'll live in orbit. I'll outlive all o' you!" He laughed again.

"I hope you do," Don said softly. "You deserve to."

"Only trouble is, once I'm froze I won't need that advanced shuttle to boost me into orbit. Coulda saved th' taxpayers all that money if I'd known. I can ride the regular ol' shuttle, once I'm dipped in that liquid nitrogen stuff."

He was still cackling to himself as Don tiptoed out of his room.

"I'm coming home, honey! For once, I'll be home in time for the twins' birthday."

Don was floating easily in his "office": a semicircular desk welded into a bulkhead in the zero-gee section of the space station. There was no need for chairs; a few looped straps sufficed to keep one from drifting too far from one's work.

Don took a good look at his wife's face as it appeared in the telephone screen of his desk. Her mouth was a thin, tight line. There were crow's feet at the corners of her eyes. Her hair was totally gray.

"What happened to your hair?" he asked. "It wasn't like that the last time we talked, was it?"

"I've been dyeing it for years and *you* never noticed," Judy said, her voice harsh, strained. "The style is gray this year . . . now I dye it so it's all gray."

"That's the style?" Don glanced at his own reflection in the darkened window above his desk. His hair was still dark and thick.

"How would you know anything about fashion?" Judy snapped, "—living up in that tin can in the sky."

"But I'm coming home early this year," Don said. "Things are going well enough so I can get away a whole month earlier than I thought. I'll be there in time for the twins' birthday."

"Don't bother," Judy said.

"What? But the kids . . ."

"The kids are nineteen and they don't want their Mommy and Daddy embarrassing them, *especially* on their birthday. They want to be with their friends, out on the farm they've set up."

"Farm?"

"In Utah. They've joined the Church of the Latter Day Saints."

"Mormons? Our kids?"

"Yes."

Don felt confused, almost scared. "I've got to talk with them. They're too young to—"

But Judy was shaking her gray head. "They won't be here to talk with. And neither will I."

He felt it like a body blow as he hung there weightlessly, defenselessly, staring into the screen.

"I'm getting a divorce, Don," Judy said. "You're not a husband to me. Not two months out of every twelve. That's no marriage."

"But I *asked* you to come up here with me!"

"I've been living with Jack Hardesty the past six months," she said, almost tonelessly, it was so matter-of-fact. "He's asked me to marry him. That's what I'm going to do."

"Jack Hardesty? Jack?"

"You can live up there and float around forever," Judy said. "I'm going to get what happiness I can while I'm still young enough to enjoy it."

"Judy, you don't understand—"

But he was talking to a blank screen.

Don had to return to Earth for the official opening ceremonies of Space Station Alpha. It was a tremendous international media event, with special ceremonies in Washington, Cape Canaveral, Houston and the new life-extension medical center in Senator Petty's home state.

It was at the medical center ceremonies that Petty pulled Don aside and walked him briskly, urgently, into an immaculate, new, unused men's room.

Leaning on the rim of a sparkling stainless steel sink, Petty gave Don a nervous little half-smile.

"Well, you got what you wanted," the Senator said. "How do you feel about it?"

Don shrugged. "Kind of numb, I guess. After all these years, it's hard to realize that the job is done."

"Cost a whale of a lot of the taxpayers' money," Petty said.

Gesturing at the lavish toilet facility, Don riposted, "You didn't pinch any pennies here, I notice."

Petty laughed, almost like a little boy caught doing something naughty. "Home-state contractors. You know how it is."

"Sure."

"I guess you'll want to start living here on the ground full-time again," Petty said.

Don glared at him. "Oh? Am I allowed to? Is our deal completed?"

With an apologetic spread of his hands, Senator Petty said, "Look, I admit that it was a spiteful thing for me to do. . . ."

"It wrecked my marriage. My kids are total strangers to me now. I don't even have any friends down here anymore."

"I'm . . . sorry."

"Stuff it."

"Listen . . ." The Senator licked his thin lips. "I . . . I've been thinking . . . maybe I won't run for re-election next time around. Maybe . . . maybe I'll come up and see what it's like living up there for a while."

Don stared at him for a long, hard moment. And saw that

there was a single light-brown spot about the size of a dime on the back of one of the Senator's hands.

"You want to live in the space station?"

Petty tried to make a nonchalant shrug. "I've . . . been thinking about it."

"Afraid of old age?" Don asked coldly. "Or is it something more specific?"

Petty's face went gray. "Heart," he said. "The doctors tell me I'll be in real trouble in another few years. Thanks to the technology you guys have developed, they can spot it coming that far in advance now."

Don wanted to laugh. Instead, he said, "If that's the case, you'd better spend your last year or two in the Senate pushing through enough funding to enlarge the living quarters in the space station."

Petty nodded. Grimly.

"And you should introduce a resolution," Don added, "to give the station an official name: the Senator Robert E. Buford Space Center."

"Now that's too much!"

Don grinned at him. "Tell it to your doctors."

There was no reason for him to stay on Earth. Too many memories. Too few friends. He felt better in orbit. Even in the living sections of the Buford Space Center, where the spin-induced gee forces were close to Earth-normal gravity, Don felt more alive and happier. His friends were there, and so was his work.

Don had been wrong to think that his job was finished once the space station was officially opened. In reality, his work had merely begun.

A year after the station was officially opened, von Kluge came aboard as a retiree. His secretary, Alma Tucker, still lithe and wonderful despite the added years, came up to work for Don. They were married, a year later. Among the witnesses was Senator Petty, the latest permanent arrival.

The Buford Space Center grew and grew and grew. Its official name was forgotten after a few decades. It was known everywhere as Sky City.

Sky City became the commercial hub of the thriving space

industries that reached out across the solar system. Sky City's biomedical labs became system-famous as they took the lead in producing cures for the various genetic diseases known collectively as cancer.

Ex-Senator Petty organized the first zero-gee Olympics, and participated personally in the Sky City–Tranquility Base yacht race.

Von Kluge, restless with retirement, became an industrial magnate and acquired huge holdings in the asteroid belt: a Junker land baron at last.

Alma Tucker Arnold became a mother—and a prominent low-gravity ballerina.

Don stayed in administration and eventually became the first mayor of Sky City. The election was held on his ninety-ninth birthday, and he celebrated it by leading a bicycle race all around the city's perimeter.

The next morning, his first official act as mayor was to order the thawing of Senator Buford. The two of them spent their declining centuries in fast friendship.

I don't believe in omens from the gods, but when a meteorite fell into a suburban house in a town near my Connecticut home, and conservative old *Yankee* magazine asked me to write a piece about the event, I took it as a signal that it was time to tell the average New Englander about mining the asteroids. After all, these are the descendants of those intrepid whalers and clipper ship crews who have been described as "iron men in wooden ships." Their children, some of whom are in their teens today, will have the opportunity to set sail for the dark depths of interplanetary space, spend two or three years "before the mast" in a mining vessel that will travel out to the asteroids and come back with enough precious ores to make every crew member rich. They'll be Prometheans for sure!

———————

Contrary to folk wisdom, lightning often strikes more than once in the same place. But Wethersfield, Connecticut, is only the second community in all of recorded history to be hit on two separate occasions by meteorites.

It was nearly 9:20 p.m. on Monday, November 8, 1982, when a six-pound chunk of rock dropped out of the skies and through the roof of the Donahue home in Wethersfield. Wanda and Robert Donahue were watching *M*A*S*H* on television when the meteorite smashed through their roof at some 500 miles per hour, tore through the second- and first-floor ceilings, and into their living room. It bounced through

51

the doorway into the dining room, where it hit a chair and finally rolled under the dinner table, leaving a trail of shattered plaster, splintered wood and a badly dented piece of oak flooring behind it.

The Donahues were in the family room, less than twenty feet from the living room, when the falling star struck. Mrs. Donahue told reporters that it sounded like an explosion. Neither she nor her husband were hurt, though the living room seemed to be filled with smoke, which they later learned was only plaster dust. They called the police, who arrived in moments along with the volunteer fire brigade. Only then did the Donahues discover their celestial visitor resting under their dining-room table.

Eleven years earlier, on April 8, 1971, another meteorite had crashed into the Wethersfield home of Mr. and Mrs. Paul J. Cassarino, a scant mile from the Donahue residence. The only other community in the world known to be have been hit twice by meteorites is Honolulu, and the two falls there were a century apart.

The Cassarinos' insurance did not cover being struck by a meteorite, but the Donahues' home insurance policy did cover being struck by objects from the sky. Robert Donahue says his career in the life insurance business had nothing to do with getting that clause into their homeowner's policy.

"Wethersfield 1982," as astronomers immediately dubbed the stone, came a long way to reach New England. While meteorites found by scientists recently in Antarctica appear to have originated on the Moon and even on the distant planet Mars, Wethersfield 1982 probably came from the still-farther Asteroid Belt, a zone of the solar system more than 100 million miles from Earth's orbit where thousands of millions of small chunks of rock and metal float through space.

The word asteroid means "little star," because that is how they appear in astronomers' telescopes: tiny points of faint light. The first asteroid was discovered on the night of January 1, 1801, by Father Giuseppe Piazzi, a monk who was then director of a small astronomical observatory at Palermo, Sicily. Since then, thousands have been observed, and calculations show that there must be myriads more, too small and distant to be easily seen from Earth.

They really should be called "planetoids," because they are actually not stars, but minor planets—pieces of rock and metal that might have once been parts of a larger planet that broke up, or the building blocks for a planet that somehow never came together.

The largest of the asteroids is the one Fr. Piazzi discovered, Ceres. It is some 450 miles in diameter. Compared to the Earth's nearly 8000-mile diameter or even the Moon's 2000-odd-mile width, Ceres is indeed a minor planet. Yet most of the asteroids are much, much smaller—the size of a mountain, or a football field, or a boulder.

While the Asteroid Belt lies beyond the orbit of Mars, many asteroids swing in orbits that loop close to the Earth. Some of them are caught by the Earth's powerful gravity and pulled to our planet. Every twenty-four hours, some 20,000 tons worth of asteroids strike our world. Most of them are no larger than a grain of sand, but still, if it were not for the protective blanket of our atmosphere, the Earth would look as battered and dead as the Moon.

Almost all of the asteroids that fall toward Earth are burned up completely when they enter the atmosphere. In the vacuum of space these bodies can travel at tremendous speeds with no harm to themselves. But once they enter our atmosphere, traveling at Mach 20 or faster, friction with the air heats them to the point where they glow. Most of them are burned up completely long before they reach the surface.

Wethersfield 1982, for example, must have weighed several hundred pounds when it hit the top of the atmosphere. By the time it rolled under the Donahues' dining-room table, it had been boiled down to slightly less than six pounds. The meteorite weighed precisely 2704 grams, in the metric measurement that astronomers use. That is 5.9488 pounds, to be precise. Another 50 grams (1.63 ounces) of stone chips were found, which had broken off the main body of the meteorite as it banged around the Donahue house. Wethersfield 1982 is 12 centimeters wide (4.72 inches). Its outer crust is a thin smooth layer of charred stone, visible proof of its fiery trip through the atmosphere.

For centuries, learned men refused to believe that meteorites came from beyond the Earth. Thomas Jefferson, who was widely respected as a naturalist as well as a revolutionary philosopher and politician, was among the skeptics. When told that two Yale professors had reported that a meteorite had fallen in Weston, Connecticut, President Jefferson is said to have remarked, "It is easier to believe that two Yankee professors would lie than that stones would fall from heaven." Jefferson the Virginian had his doubts about Yankees, apparently.

However, when a shower of meteorites pelted the French village of L'Aigle in 1803, the *Académie Française* investigated thoroughly and found that stones really do fall from heaven. Today we know that more than 75 million of them hit the Earth every day, although only a few hundred each year survive their blazing passage through the air to reach the surface.

What we call a "shooting star" or a "falling star," astronomers call a meteor. The word "meteor" comes from a Greek root that means "something high up in the air, lofty." Originally, "meteor" was used in English to denote almost anything that happened overhead; hence our word for the study of the weather is *meteorology*, which has nothing to do with falling stars and meteorites.

When an asteroid begins its long slide down Earth's gravity well, astronomers begin to term it a meteoroid. It is still the same object, a chunk of rock or metal that was born billions of years ago and has been floating in space ever since. But now it is heading for a rendezvous with our planet, drawn by the invisible force of gravity toward its destiny.

As the meteoroid ploughs through the upper fringes of our atmosphere, more than fifty miles above Earth's surface, friction from the air heats it until it glows. We see a "shooting star." It is this streak of light in the sky that astronomers call a meteor. If the meteoroid survives its incandescent passage through the air and reaches the ground, it is then known as a meteorite.

So one and the same body can at different stages be called an:

Asteroid, when it is in space;

Meteoroid, when it is falling toward Earth;

Meteor, when it becomes a blazing light in the sky; and

Meteorite, when what's left of it reaches the ground.

Wethersfield 1982 was seen as a brilliant falling star by observers as far away as Albany, New York. Anyone can see meteors on any clear night of the year, with a little patience. On the average, some five to ten meteors will streak across the sky each hour. The best time to watch for them is between midnight and dawn, for reasons of orbital mechanics that need not be explained here, but which can be found in any good astronomy text.

Nothing can compare with the sudden thrill of seeing a falling star. One moment it's there, the next it has winked out, probably completely burned up high in the atmosphere. Usually the meteor streaks through the sky in total silence, giving the impression that it's in a hurry to get to wherever it's going. Most such meteors are caused by meteoroids that are no bigger than a grain of sand.

But larger meteors can be absolutely startling, lighting up the sky for a few brief moments and rumbling like an express train. The noise is a sonic boom caused by the meteoroid's multi-Mach flight through the air. The head of such a meteor, called the fireball, or bolide, is tear-shaped and followed by a long, scintillating trail that sometimes shows spectacular colors. The fireball of Wethersfield 1982 was reported by at least one observer to have broken into two brilliant, flaming pieces. The second meteorite has not yet been found. Presumably, it fell into the woods nearby.

Often a large meteoroid will explode as it gets close to the Earth, blown apart by the heating it experiences as it drives down into the lowest, thickest layers of our atmosphere. Then its fragments pelt a wide area, like celestial shrapnel. Many areas of Earth have been hit by dozens or even hundreds of meteorites from a single such fall.

Some meteorites are truly huge. The largest one ever found, called Hoba West, is estimated to weigh 60 tons. It landed in South West Africa eons ago. The largest meteorite on public display is the 34-ton Ahnighito, which was discovered in Greenland by polar explorer Robert Peary in 1894 and transported (painfully) to the American Museum of Natural History in New York City, where it still rests.

Every schoolchild in America has seen a photograph of the

Meteor Crater in Arizona. Some 20,000 years ago a meteoroid that weighed at least 50,000 tons blasted out this mile-wide hole in the ground. Known variously as the Winslow Crater, the Barringer Crater, and even as Canyon Diablo, this 650-foot-deep scar in the ground is one of the most prominent reminders that our planet has been bombarded by meteoroids in the past and is still under bombardment today.

In 1908 a heavenly object streaked across the skies of Europe, heading eastward, and exploded close to the ground in Tunguska, Siberia. The sound of the explosion was heard a thousand miles away. A nearby witness was deafened by it. A herd of 1500 reindeer was incinerated and trees were knocked flat for an area of several miles around the impact site. Seismographs located thousands of miles from Siberia recorded the tremors caused by the event. When scientists finally got to the remote area where the object hit, they found more than a hundred craters, some of them a hundred feet across. But no fragments of meteorite!

Most astronomers believe the Tunguska meteoroid was actually a small comet that exploded in midair, close to the frozen Siberian ground. Comets are believed to be little more than frozen gases and ices, with perhaps a smattering of stones imbedded in the slush. If such an object exploded at a low altitude, very little solid material would be found afterward.

But other scientists (and laymen) have speculated that the Tunguska fireball was something much more exotic. An alien spacecraft, perhaps, damaged and desperately seeking a safe landing on planet Earth; its nuclear engines exploded just before it could reach the ground. Or, even weirder, a microscopic black hole that bored right through the solid mass of our planet and popped out again in the middle of the Atlantic Ocean and headed back into space.

Whatever caused the Tunguska fireball, if it had arrived in Earth's vicinity just a few minutes later than it did, it could have hit somewhere in Europe with the devastating force of a nuclear explosion. If a similar object should strike a civilized part of the world today, it might easily be mistaken for a nuclear attack and trigger World War III.

Considering how many meteorites hit the ground each year, it is something of a wonder that they have not caused more damage than they have. In 1948 a shower of stones peppered Norton County, Kansas. More than a hundred of them were located afterward, the largest one weighing a ton.

The only person known to be injured by a meteorite was a woman in Alabama who was struck a glancing blow while in bed, in 1954. She was bruised, but appeared more worried about the hole in her roof than her own injury.

There are certain times of the year when meteor showers occur, sprinkling hundreds or even thousands of meteors across the night sky withing a few hours. On rare occasions, the sky can be filled with flaming meteors. In a 1966 shower, a thousand meteors per minute were seen!

The meteors that fall in such showers are believed to be the remnants of comets, rather than refugees from the Asteroid Belt. Comets do not live forever. Each time they travel around the Sun they lose more of their substance, gases and ices evaporating away into the long, beautiful cometary tail. Eventually, all these volatile materials are boiled off, leaving nothing but a huge collection of stones rambling through space along the comet's old orbit like a crowd of marathon runners doggedly following their interminable track.

Some of these orbits intersect the orbit of the Earth, and when they do, some of those stones fall into our atmosphere to blaze briefly and then dissipate into harmless dust.

There are more than a dozen annual meteor showers, returning each year with like celestial clockwork. The most prominent of them are the Perseids, which occur over several nights around August 12, and the Leonids, which come around November 16. The names of the showers refer to the area of the sky that the meteors seem to stream out of: the constellation Perseus, in the case of the Perseids, and Leo for the Leonids.

The meteors appear in all parts of the sky. But if you track their trails backward, they all seem to intersect in one area. This was the first clue that such meteor showers were being caused by a single cluster of objects traveling through space.

Meteor showers are the spawn of comets. Individual meteoroids were once asteroids. And asteroids may be the miner's bonanza of the twenty-first century. For these minor bodies of the solar system contain all the raw materials, the metals and

minerals, that civilization needs for a new age of space-born
industries that can enrich all the people of Earth.

Among the thousands of millions of asteroids in space
there are at least thirty or forty that are more than a hundred
miles across, say, the size of Massachusetts minus Cape Cod.
There are thousands that are more than ten miles across, and
millions that are a mile or so wide. The rule of thumb is that
for every asteroid of a given size, there are ten more that are
one-third smaller.

From the evidence of meteorites, astronomers conclude
that some asteroids are basically metallic in composition,
mostly iron and nickel alloyed naturally into high-grade steel.
Most asteroids, though, are rocky, as is Wethersfield 1982,
which is composed of stony *chondrules*, or spheres.

A single rocky asteroid of the type astronomers call a
carbonaceous chondrite, no larger than the length of a football field, could contain some $15 million in gold—as an
impurity. The real value of such an asteroid would be in the
organic chemicals it contained. A 100-yard-wide asteroid of the
nickel-iron variety contains nearly four million tons of high-
grade nickel steel, worth more than a billion dollars in today's steel industry. One asteroid. There are uncounted myriads
of them.

For eons, asteroids have pelted the Earth, giving us the
evidence that these resources exist in space. Soon now, as
history counts time, human miners and prospectors will head
outward to the Asteroid Belt, armed with electronic gear and
lasers, riding nuclear-powered rockets. They will be followed
by huge factory ships, sailing the silent sea of vacuum for
years at a time, scooping in thousands of millions of tons of
rock and metals, and processing them into finished products
during the long voyage home.

Like the whalers of New Bedford and the iron men who
crewed the wooden ships of old, the men and women who
journey out to the asteroids will be prepared to spend several
years "before the mast." And like the whalers and sailors of
those earlier centuries, they will share in the profits of their
voyages and return to Earth richer than any corsair who ever
waylaid a treasure galleon.

Zero Gee ━━━━━━━━━━━

If you've read the novels *Kinsman* and *Millennium* you have met Chet Kinsman. In this short story, Chet is still a cocky youth who believes that nothing in the world can really hurt him, and that flying—especially into the euphoria of zero gravity—is the biggest kick in life. He learns better. As we all do, sooner or later. Kinsman is a Promethean, and later in his life takes on the burden of Prometheus himself, in a way. At the stage of his life depicted in *Zero Gee*, however, he is just beginning to learn that the Second Law of Thermodynamics applies to everything in the universe, even personal relationships: You always have to pay more than you receive in return. Only in the rare instances of deeply human love do individuals willingly and gladly pay this price; only in those precious relationships does the Second Law yield to the synergy of true love.

━━━━━━━━

Joe Tenny looked like a middle linebacker for the Pittsburgh Steelers. Sitting in the cool shadows of the Astro Motel's bar, swarthy, barrel-built, scowling face clamped on a smoldering cigar, he would never be taken for that rarest of all birds, a good engineer who is also a good military officer.

"Afternoon, Major."

Tenny turned on his stool to see old Cy Calder, the dean of the press-service reporters covering the base.

"Hi. Whatcha drinking?"

"I'm working," Calder answered with dignity. But he settled his once-lanky frame onto the next stool.

"Double scotch," Tenny called to the bartender. "And refill mine."

"An officer and a gentleman," murmured Calder. His voice was gravelly, matching his face.

As the bartender slid the drinks to them, Tenny said, "You wanna know who got the assignment."

"I told you I'm working."

Tenny grinned. "Keep your mouth shut 'til tomorrow? Murdock'll make the official announcement then, at his press conference."

"If you can save me the tedium of listening to the good colonel for two hours to get a single name out of him, I'll buy the next round, shine your shoes for a month, and arrange to lose an occasional poker pot to you."

"The hell you will!"

Calder shrugged. Tenny took a long pull on his drink. Calder did likewise.

"Okay. You'll find out anyway. But keep it quiet until Murdock's announcement. It's going to be Kinsman."

Calder put his glass down on the bar carefully. "Chester A. Kinsman, the pride of the Air Force? That's hard to believe."

"Murdock picked him."

"I know this mission is strictly for publicity," Calder said, "but Kinsman? In orbit for three days with *Photo Day* magazine's prettiest female? Does Murdock want publicity or a paternity suit?"

"Come on, Chet's not that bad. . . ."

"Oh no? From the stories I hear about your few weeks up at the NASA Ames Center, Kinsman cut a swath from Berkeley to North Beach."

Tenny countered, "He's young and good-looking. And the girls haven't had many single astronauts to play with. NASA's gang is a bunch of old farts compared to my kids. But Chet's the best of the bunch, no fooling."

Calder looked unconvinced.

"Listen. When we were training at Edwards, know what

Kinsman did? Built a biplane, an honest-to-God replica of a Spad fighter. From the ground up. He's a solid citizen.''

"Yes, and then he played Red Baron for six weeks. Didn't he get into trouble for buzzing an airliner?''

Tenny's reply was cut off by a burst of talk and laughter. Half a dozen lean, lithe young men in Air Force blues— captains, all of them—trotted down the carpeted stairs that led into the bar.

"There they are,'' said Tenny. "You can ask Chet about it yourself.''

Kinsman looked no different from the other Air Force astronauts. Slightly under six feet tall, thin with the leanness of youth, dark hair cut in the short, flat military style, blue-gray eyes, long bony face. He was grinning broadly at the moment, as he and the other five astronauts grabbed chairs in one corner of the bar and called their orders to the lone bartender.

Calder took his drink and headed for their table, followed by Major Tenny.

"Hold it,'' one of the captains called out. "Here comes the press.''

"Tight security.''

"Why, boys,'' Calder tried to make his rasping voice sound hurt, "don't you trust me?''

Tenny pushed a chair toward the newsman and took another one for himself. Straddling it, he told the captain, "It's okay. I spilled it to him.''

"How much he pay you, boss?''

"That's between him and me.''

As the bartender brought a tray of drinks, Calder said, "Let the Fourth Estate pay for this round, gentlemen. I want to pump some information out of you.''

"That might take a lot of rounds.''

To Kinsman, Calder said, "Congratulations, my boy. Colonel Murdock must think very highly of you.''

Kinsman burst out laughing. "Murdock? You should've seen his face when he told me it was going to be me.''

"Looked like he was sucking on lemons.''

Tenny explained. "The choice for this flight was made mostly by computer. Murdock wanted to be absolutely fair, so he put everybody's performance ratings into the computer and out came Kinsman's name. If he hadn't made so much noise about being impartial, he could've reshuffled the cards and tried again. But I was right there when the machine finished its run, so he couldn't back out of it.''

Calder grinned. ''All right then, the computer thinks highly of you, Chet. I suppose that's still something of an honor.''

''More like a privilege. I've been watching that *Photo Day* chick all through her training. She's ripe.''

''She'll look even better up in orbit.''

''Once she takes off the pressure suit . . . et cetera.''

''Hey, y'know, nobody's ever done it in orbit.''

''Yeah . . . free fall, zero gravity.''

Kinsman looked thoughtful. ''Adds a new dimension to the problem, doesn't it?''

''Three-dimensional.'' Tenny took the cigar butt from his mouth and laughed.

Calder got up slowly from his chair and silenced the others. Looking down fondly on Kinsman, he said:

''My boy—back in 1915, in London, I became a charter member of the Mile High Club. At an altitude of exactly 5,280 feet, while circling St. Paul's, I successfully penetrated an Army nurse in an open cockpit . . . despite fogged goggles, cramped working quarters and a severe case of windburn.

''Since then, there's been damned little to look forward to. The skin-divers claimed a new frontier, but in fact they are retrogressing. Any silly-ass dolphin can do it in the water.

''But you've got something new going for you: weightlessness. Floating around in free fall, chasing tail in three dimensions. It beggars the imagination!

''Kinsman, I pass the torch to you. To the founder of the Zero Gee Club!''

As one man, they rose and solemnly toasted Captain Kinsman.

As they sat down again, Major Tenny burst the balloon. ''You guys haven't given Murdock credit for much brains. You don't think he's gonna let Chet go up with that broad all alone, do you?''

Kinsman's face fell, but the others lit up.

''It'll be a three-man mission!''

"Two men and the chick."

Tenny warned, "Now don't start drooling. Murdock wants a chaperon, not an assistant rapist."

It was Kinsman who got it first. Slouching back in his chair, chin sinking to his chest, he muttered, "Sonofabitch . . . he's sending Jill along."

A collective groan.

"Murdock made up his mind an hour ago," Tenny said. "He was stuck with you, Chet, so he hit on the chaperon idea. He's also giving you some real chores to do, to keep you busy. Like mating the power pod."

"Jill Meyers," said one of the captains disgustedly.

"She's qualified, and she's been taking the *Photo Day* girl through her training. I'll bet she knows more about the mission than any of you guys do."

"She would."

"In fact," Tenny added maliciously, "I think she's the senior captain among you satellite-jockeys."

Kinsman had only one comment: "Shit."

The bone-rattling roar and vibration of liftoff suddenly died away. Sitting in his contour seat, scanning the banks of dials and gauges a few centimeters before his eyes, Kinsman could feel the pressure and tension slacken. Not back to normal. To zero. He was no longer plastered up against his seat, but touching it only lightly, almost floating in it, restrained only by his harness.

It was the fourth time he had felt weightlessness. It still made smile inside the cumbersome helmet.

Without thinking about it, he touched a control stud on the chair's armrest. A maneuvering jet fired briefly, and the ponderous, lovely bulk of planet Earth slid into view through the port in front of Kinsman. It curved huge and serene, blue, mostly, but tightly wrapped in the purest, dazzling white of clouds, beautiful, peaceful, shining.

Kinsman could have watched it forever, but he heard sounds of motion in his earphones. The two girls were sitting behind him, side by side. The spacecraft cabin made a submarine look roomy: the three seats were shoehorned in among racks of instruments and equipment.

Jill Meyers, who came to the astronaut program from the Aerospace Medical Division, was officially second pilot and biomedical officer. *And chaperon*, Kinsman knew. The photographer, Linda Symmes, was simply a passenger.

Kinsman's earphones crackled with a disembodied link from Earth. "AF-9, this is ground control. We have you confirmed in orbit. Trajectory nominal. All systems go."

"Check," Kinsman said into his helmet mike.

The voice, already starting to fade, switched to ordinary conversational speech. "Looks like you're right on the money, Chet. We'll get the orbital parameters out of the computer and have 'em for you by the time you pass Ascension. You probably won't need much maneuvering to make rendezvous with the lab."

"Good. Everything here on the board looks green."

"Okay. Ground control out." Faintly. "And hey . . . good luck, Founding Father."

Kinsman grinned at that. He slid his faceplate up, loosened his harness and turned in his seat. "Okay, girls, you can take off your helmets if you want to."

Jill Meyers snapped her faceplate open and started unlocking the helmet's neck seal.

"I'll go first," she said, "and then I can help Linda with hers."

"Sure you won't need any help?" Kinsman offered.

Jill pulled her helmet off. "I've had more time in orbit than you. And shouldn't you be paying attention to the instruments?"

So this is how it's going to be, Kinsman thought.

Jill's face was round and plain and bright as a new penny. Snub nose, wide mouth, short hair of undistinguished brown. Kinsman knew that under the pressure suit was a figure that could most charitably be described as ordinary.

Linda Symmes was entirely another matter. She had lifted her faceplate and was staring out at him with wide, blue eyes that combined feminine curiosity with a hint of helplessness. She was tall, nearly Kinsman's own height, with thick honey-colored hair and a body that he had already memorized down to the last curve.

In her sweet, high voice she said, "I think I'm going to be sick."

"Oh for . . ."

Jill reached into the compartment between their two seats. "I'll take care of this. You stick to the controls." And she whipped open a white plastic bag and stuck it over Linda's face.

Shuddering at the thought of what could happen in zero gravity, Kinsman turned back to the control panel. He pulled his faceplate shut and turned up the air blower in his suit, trying to cut off the obscene sound of Linda's struggles.

"For Chrissake," he yelled, "unplug her radio! You want me chucking all over, too?"

"AF-9, this is Ascension."

Trying to blank his mind to what was going on behind him, Kinsman thumbed the switch on his communications panel. "Go ahead, Ascension."

For the next hour Kinsman thanked the gods that he had plenty of work to do. He matched the orbit of their three-man spacecraft to that of the Air Force orbiting laboratory, which had been up for more than a year now, and intermittently occupied by two- or three-man crews.

The lab was a fat, cylindrical shape, silhouetted against the brilliant white of the cloud-decked Earth. As he pulled the spacecraft close, Kinsman could see the antennas and airlock and other odd pieces of gear that had accumulated on it. *Looking more like a junkheap every trip.* Riding behind it, unconnected in any way, was the massive cone of the new power pod.

Kinsman circled the lab once, using judicious squeezes of his maneuvering jets. He touched a command-signal switch, and the lab's rendezvous-radar-beacon came to life, announced by a light on his control panel.

"All systems green," he said to ground control. "Everything looks okay."

"Roger, Niner. You are cleared for docking."

This was a bit more delicate. *Be helpful if Jill could read off the computer . . .*

"Distance, eighty-eight meters," Jill's voice pronounced firmly in his earphones. "Approach angle—"

Kinsman instinctively turned, but his helmet cut off any possible sight of her. "Hey, how's your patient?"

"Empty. I gave her a sedative. She's out."

"Okay," Kinsman said. "Let's get docked."

He inched the spacecraft into the docking-collar on one end of the lab, locked on and saw the panel lights confirm that the docking was secure.

"Better get Sleeping Beauty zippered up," he told Jill as he touched the buttons that extended the flexible access-tunnel from the hatch over their heads to the main hatch of the lab. The lights on the panel turned from amber to green when the tunnel locked its fittings around the lab's hatch.

Jill said, "I'm supposed to check the tunnel."

"Stay put. I'll do it." Sealing his faceplate shut, Kinsman unbuckled and rose effortlessly out of the seat to bump his helmet lightly against the overhead hatch.

"You two both buttoned tight?"

"Yes."

"Keep an eye on the air gauge." He cracked the hatch open a few millimeters.

"Pressure's okay. No red lights."

Nodding, Kinsman pushed the hatch open all the way. He pulled himself easily up and into the shoulder-wide tunnel, propelling himself down its curving length by a few flicks of his fingers against the ribbed walls.

Light and easy, he reminded himself. *No big motions, no sudden moves*.

When he reached the laboratory hatch he slowly rotated, like a swimmer doing a lazy rollover, and inspected every inch of the tunnel seal in the light of his helmet lamp. Satisfied that it was locked in place, he opened the lab hatch and pushed himself inside. Carefully, he touched his slightly adhesive boots to the plastic flooring and stood upright. His arms tended to float out, but they touched the equipment racks on either side of the narrow central passageway. Kinsman turned on the lab's interior lights, checked the air supply, pressure and temperature gauges, then shuffled back to the hatch and pushed himself through the tunnel again.

He reentered the spacecraft upside-down and had to contort

himself in slow motion around the pilot's seat to regain a "normal" attitude.

"Lab's okay," he said finally. "Now how the hell do we get her through the tunnel?"

Jill had already unbuckled the harness over Linda's shoulders. "You pull, I'll push. She ought to bend around the corners all right."

And she did.

The laboratory was about the size and shape of the interior of a small transport plane. On one side, nearly its entire length was taken up by instrument racks, control equipment and the computer, humming almost inaudibly behind light plastic panels. Across the narrow separating aisle were the crew stations: control desk, two observation ports, biology and astrophysics benches. At the far end, behind a discreet curtain, was the head and a single hammock.

Kinsman sat at the control desk, in his fatigues now, one leg hooked around the webbed chair's single supporting column to keep him from floating off. He was running through a formal check of all the lab's life systems: air, water, heat, electrical power. All green lights on the main panel. Communications gear. Green. The radar screen to his left showed a single large blip close by—the power pod.

He looked up as Jill came through the curtain from the bunkroom. She was still in her pressure suit, with only the helmet removed.

"How is she?"

Looking tired, Jill answered, "Okay. Still sleeping. I think she'll be all right when she wakes up."

"She'd better be. I'm not going to have a wilting flower around here. I'll abort the mission."

"Give her a chance, Chet. She just lost her cookies when free-fall hit her. All the training in the world can't prepare you for those first few minutes."

Kinsman recalled his first orbital flight. *It doesn't shut off. You're falling. Like skiing, or skydiving. Only better.*

Jill shuffled toward him, keeping a firm grip on the chairs in front of the work benches and the handholds set into the equipment racks.

Kinsman got up and pushed toward her. "Here, let me help you out of the suit."

"I can do it myself."

"Shut up."

After several minutes, Jill was free of the bulky suit and sitting in one of the webbed chairs in her coverall-fatigues. Ducking slightly because of the curving overhead, Kinsman glided into the galley. It was about half the width of a phone booth, and not as deep nor as tall.

"Coffee, tea or milk?"

Jill grinned at him. "Orange juice."

He reached for a concentrate bag. "You're a hard girl to satisfy."

"No I'm not. I'm easy to get along with. Just one of the fellas."

Feeling slightly puzzled, Kinsman handed her the orange juice container.

For the next couple of hours they checked out the lab's equipment in detail. Kinsman was reassembling a high-resolution camera after cleaning it, parts hanging in midair all around him as he sat intently working, while Jill was nursing a straggly-looking philodendron that had been smuggled aboard and was inching from the biology bench toward the ceiling light panels. Linda pushed back the curtain from the sleeping area and stepped, uncertainly, into the main compartment.

Jill noticed her first. "Hi, how're you feeling?"

Kinsman looked up. She was in tight-fitting coveralls. He bounced out of his web-chair toward her, scattering camera parts in every direction.

"Are you all right?" he asked.

Smiling sheepishly, "I think so. I'm rather embarrassed . . ." Her voice was high and soft.

"Oh, that's all right," Kinsman said eagerly. "It happens to practically everybody. I got sick myself my first time in orbit."

"That," said Jill as she dodged a slowly-tumbling lens that ricocheted gently off the ceiling, "is a little white lie, meant to make you feel at home."

Kinsman forced himself not to frown. *Why'd Jill want to cross me?*

Jill said, "Chet, you'd better pick up those camera pieces before they get so scattered you won't be able to find them all."

He wanted to snap an answer, thought better of it, and replied simply, "Right."

As he finished the job on the camera, he took a good look at Linda. The color was back in her face. She looked steady, clear-eyed, not frightened or upset. *Maybe she'll be okay after all.* Jill made her a cup of tea, which she sipped from the lid's plastic spout.

Kinsman went to the control desk and scanned the mission schedule sheet.

"Hey, Jill, it's past your bedtime."

"I'm not really very sleepy," she said.

"Maybe. But you've had a busy day, little girl. And tomorrow will be busier. Now you get your four hours, and then I'll get mine. Got to be fresh for the mating."

"Mating?" Linda asked from her seat at the far end of the aisle, a good five strides from Kinsman. Then she remembered, "Oh . . . you mean linking the pod to the laboratory."

Suppressing a half-dozen possible jokes, Kinsman nodded. "Extra-vehicular activity."

Jill reluctantly drifted off her web-chair. "Okay, I'll sack in. I am tired, but I never seem to get really sleepy up here."

Wonder how much Murdock's told her? She's sure acting like a chaperon.

Jill shuffled into the sleeping area and pulled the curtain firmly shut. After a few moments of silence, Kinsman turned to Linda.

"Alone at last."

She smiled back.

"Uh, you just happen to be sitting where I've got to install this camera." He nudged the finished hardware so that it floated gently toward her.

She got up slowly, carefully, and stood behind the chair, holding its back with both hands as if she were afraid of falling. Kinsman slid into the web-chair and stopped the camera's slow-motion flight with one hand. Working on the fixture in the bulkhead that it fit into, he asked:

"You really feel okay?"

"Yes, honestly."

"Think you'll be up to EVA tomorrow?"

"I hope so . . . I want to go outside with you."

I'd rather be inside with you. Kinsman grinned as he worked.

An hour later they were sitting side by side in front of one of the observation ports, looking out at the curving bulk of Earth, the blue and white splendor of the cloud-spangled Pacific. Kinsman had just reported to the Hawaii ground station. The mission flight plan was floating on a clipboard between the two of them. He was trying to study it, comparing the time when Jill would be sleeping with the long stretches between ground stations, when there would be no possibility of being interrupted.

"Is that land?" Linda asked, pointing to a thick band of clouds wrapping the horizon.

Looking up from the clipboard, Kinsman said, "South American coast. Chile."

"There's another tracking station there."

"NASA station. Not part of our network. We only use Air Force stations."

"Why is that?"

He felt his face frowning. "Murdock's playing soldier. This is supposed to be a strictly military operation. Not that we do anything warlike. But we run as though there weren't any civilian stations around to help us. The usual hup-two-three crap."

She laughed. "You don't agree with the colonel?"

"There's only one thing he's done lately that I'm in complete agreement with."

"What's that?"

"Bringing you up here."

The smile stayed on her face but her eyes moved away from him. "Now you sound like a soldier."

"Not an officer and a gentleman?"

She looked straight at him again. "Let's change the subject."

Kinsman shrugged. "Sure. Okay. You're here to get a story. Murdock wants to get the Air Force as much publicity as NASA gets. And the Pentagon wants to show the world that we don't have any weapons on board. We're military, all right, but *nice* military.''

"And you?" Linda asked, serious now. "What do you want? How does an Air Force captain get into the space cadets?"

"The same way everything happens—you're in a certain place at a certain time. They told me I was going to be an astronaut. It was all part of the job . . . until my first orbital flight. Now it's a way of life.''

"Really? Why is that?"

Grinning, he answered, "Wait'll we go outside. You'll find out.''

Jill came back into the main cabin precisely on schedule, and it was Kinsman's turn to sleep. He seldom had difficulty sleeping on Earth, never in orbit. But he wondered about Linda's reaction to being outside while he strapped on the pressure-cuffs to his arms and legs. The medics insisted on them, claimed they exercised the cardiovascular system while you slept.

Damned stupid nuisance, Kinsman grumbled to himself. *Some ground-based MD's idea of how to make a name for himself.*

Finally he zippered himself into the gossamer cocoon-like hammock and shut his eyes. He could feel the cuffs pumping gently. His last conscious thought was a nagging worry that Linda would be terrified of EVA.

When he awoke, and Linda took her turn in the hammock, he talked it over with Jill.

"I think she'll be all right, Chet. Don't hold that first few minutes against her.''

"I don't know. There's only two kinds of people up here: you either love it or you're scared sh—witless. And you can't fake it. If she goes ape outside. . . .''

"She won't," Jill said firmly. "And anyway, you'll be there to help her. I've told her that she won't be going outside until you're finished with the mating job. She wanted to get pictures of you actually at work, but she'll settle for a few posed shots.''

Kinsman nodded. But the worry persisted. *I wonder if Calder's Army nurse was scared of flying?*

He was pulling on his boots, wedging his free foot against an equipment rack to keep from floating off, when Linda returned from her sleep.

"Ready for a walk around the block?" he asked her.

She smiled and nodded without the slightest hesitation. "I'm looking forward to it. Can I get a few shots of you while you zipper up your suit?"

Maybe she'll be okay.

At last he was sealed into the pressure suit. Linda and Jill stood back as Kinsman shuffled to the airlock-hatch. It was set into the floor at the end of the cabin where the spacecraft was docked. With Jill helping him, he eased down into the airlock and shut the hatch. The airlock chamber itself was coffin-sized. Kinsman had to half-bend to move around in it. He checked out his suit, then pumped the air out of the chamber. Then he was ready to open the outer hatch.

It was beneath his feet, but as it slid open to reveal the stars, Kinsman's weightless orientation flip-flopped, like an optical illusion, and he suddenly felt that he was standing on his head and looking up.

"Going out now," he said into the helmet's mike.

"Okay," Jill's voice responded.

Carefully, he eased himself through the open hatch, holding onto its edge with one gloved hand once he was fully outside, the way a swimmer holds the rail for a moment when he first slides into the deep water. Outside. Swinging his body around slowly, he took in the immense beauty of Earth, dazzlingly bright even through his tinted visor. Beyond its curving limb was the darkness of infinity, with the beckoning stars watching him in unblinking solemnity.

Alone now. His own tight, self-contained universe, independent of everything and everybody. He could cut the life-giving umbilical line that linked him with the laboratory and float off by himself, forever. And be dead in two minutes. *Ay, there's the rub.*

Instead, he unhooked the tiny gas gun from his waist and, trailing the umbilical, squirted himself over toward the power pod. It was riding smoothly behind the lab, a squat truncated cone, shorter, but fatter, than the lab itself, one edge brilliantly lit by the sun; the rest of it bathed in the softer light reflected from the dayside of Earth below.

Kinsman's job was to inspect the power pod, check its equipment, and then mate it to the electrical system of the laboratory. There was no need to physically connect the two bodies, except to link a pair of power lines between them. Everything necessary for the task—tools, power lines, check-out instruments—had been built into the pod, waiting for a man to use them.

It would have been simple work on Earth. In zero gee, it was complicated. The slightest motion of any part of your body started you drifting. You had to fight against all the built-in mannerisms of a lifetime; had to work constantly to keep in place. It was easy to get exhausted in zero gee.

Kinsman accepted all this with hardly a conscious thought. He worked slowly, methodically, using as little motion as possible, letting himself drift slightly until a more-or-less natural body motion counteracted and pulled him back in the opposite direction. *Ride the waves, slow and easy.* There was a rhythm to his work, the natural dreamlike rhythm of weightlessness.

His earphones were silent; he said nothing. All he heard was the purring of the suit's air blowers and his own steady breathing. All he saw was his work.

Finally he jetted back to the laboratory, towing the pair of thick cables. He found the connectors waiting for them on the side wall of the lab and inserted the cable plugs. *I pronounce you lab and power source.* He inspected the checkout lights alongside the connectors. All green. *May you produce many kilowatts.*

Swinging from handhold to handhold along the length of the lab, he made his way back toward the airlock.

"Okay, it's finished. How's Linda doing?"

Jill answered, "She's all set."

"Send her out."

She came out slowly, uncertain wavering feet sliding out first from the bulbous airlock. It reminded Kinsman of a film he had seen of a whale giving birth.

"Welcome to the real world," he said when her head cleared the airlock-hatch.

She turned to answer him and he heard her gasp and he knew that now he liked her.

"It's . . . it's . . ."

"Staggering," Kinsman suggested. "And look at you—no hands."

She was floating freely, pressure suit laden with camera gear, umbilical flexing easily behind her. Kinsman couldn't see her face through the tinted visor, but he could hear the awe in her voice, even in her breathing.

"I've never seen anything so absolutely overwhelming . . ."

And then, suddenly, she was all business, reaching for a camera, snapping away at the Earth and stars and distant Moon, rapidfire. She moved too fast and started to tumble. Kinsman jetted over and steadied her, holding her by the shoulders.

"Hey, take it easy. They're not going away. You've got lots of time."

"I want to get some shots of you, and the lab. Can you get over by the pod and go through some of the motions of your work on it?"

Kinsman posed for her, answered her questions, rescued a camera when she fumbled it out of her hands and couldn't reach it as it drifted away from her.

"Judging distances gets a little wacky out here," he said, handing the camera back to her.

Jill called them twice and ordered them back inside. "Chet, you're already fifteen minutes over the limit!"

"There's plenty slop in the schedule; we can stay out a while longer."

"You're going to get her exhausted."

"I really feel fine," Linda said, her voice lyrical.

"How much more film do you have?" Kinsman asked her. She peered at the camera. "Six more shots."

"Okay, we'll be in when the film runs out, Jill."

"You're going to be in darkness in another five minutes!"

Turning to Linda, who was floating upside-down with the cloud-laced Earth behind her, he said, "Save your film for the sunset, then shoot like hell when it comes."

"The sunset? What'll I focus on?"

"You'll know when it happens. Just watch."

It came fast, but Linda was equal to it. As the lab swung in its orbit toward the Earth's night-shadow, the sun dropped to the horizon and shot off a spectacular few moments of the purest reds and oranges and finally a heart-catching blue. Kinsman watched in silence, hearing Linda's breath going faster and faster as she worked the camera.

Then they were in darkness. Kinsman flicked on his helmet lamp. Linda was just hanging there, camera still in hand.

"It's . . . impossible to describe." Her voice sounded empty, drained. "If I hadn't seen it . . . if I didn't get it on film, I don't think I'd be able to convince myself that I wasn't dreaming."

Jill's voice rasped in his earphones. "Chet, get inside! This is against every safety reg, being outside in the dark."

He looked over toward the lab. Lights were visible along its length and the ports were lighted from within. Otherwise, he could barely make it out, even though it was only a few meters away.

"Okay, okay. Turn on the airlock-light so we can see the hatch."

Linda was still bubbling about the view outside, long after they had pulled off their pressure-suits and eaten sandwiches and cookies.

"Have you ever been out there?" she asked Jill.

Perched on the biology bench's edge, near the mice colony, Jill nodded curtly. "Twice."

"Isn't it spectacular? I hope the pictures come out; some of the settings on the camera . . ."

"They'll be all right," Jill said. "And if they're not, we've got a backlog of photos you can use."

"Oh, but they wouldn't have the shots of Chet working on the power pod."

Jill shrugged. "Aren't you going to take more photos in here? If you want to get some pictures of real space veterans, you ought to snap the mice here. They've been up for months now, living fine and raising families. And they don't make such a fuss about it, either."

"Well, some of us do exciting things," Kinsman said, "and some of us tend mice."

Jill glowered at him.

Glancing at his wristwatch, Kinsman said, "Girls, it's my sack time. I've had a trying day: mechanic, tourist guide, and cover boy for *Photo Day*. Work, work, work."

He glided past Linda with a smile, kept it for Jill as he went by her. She was still glaring.

When he woke up again and went back into the main cabin, Jill was talking pleasantly with Linda as the two of them stood over the microscope and specimen-rack of the biology bench.

Linda saw him first. "Oh, hi. Jill's been showing me the spores she's studying. And I photographed the mice. Maybe they'll go on the cover instead of you."

Kinsman grinned. "She been poisoning your mind against me." But to himself he wondered, *What the hell has Jill been telling her about me?*

Jill drifted over to the control desk, picked up the clipboard with the mission log on it and tossed it lightly toward Kinsman.

"Ground control says the power pod checks out all green," she said. "You did a good job."

"Thanks." He caught the clipboard. "Who's turn in the sack is it?"

"Mine," Jill answered.

"Okay. Anything special cooking?"

"No. Everything's on schedule. Next data transmission comes up in twelve minutes. Kodiak station."

Kinsman nodded. "Sleep tight."

Once Jill had shut the curtain to the bunkroom, Kinsman carried the mission log to the control desk and sat down. Linda stayed at the biology bench, about three paces away.

He checked the instrument board with a quick glance, then turned to Linda. "Well, now do you know what I meant about this being a way of life?"

"I think so. It's so different . . ."

"It's the real thing. Complete freedom. Brave new world. After ten minutes of EVA, everything else is just toothpaste."

"It was certainly exciting."

"More than that. It's living. Being on the ground is a drag, even flying a plane is dull now. This is where the fun is . . . out here in orbit and on the Moon. It's as close to heaven as anybody's gotten."

"You're really serious?"

"Damned right. I've even been thinking of asking Murdock for a transfer to NASA duty. Air Force missions don't include the Moon, and I'd like to walk around on the new world, see the sights."

She smiled at him. "I'm afraid I'm not that enthusiastic."

"Well, think about it for a minute. Up here, you're free. Really free, for the first time in your life. All the laws and rules and prejudices they've been dumping on you all your life . . . they're all *down there*. Up here it's a new start. You can be yourself and do your own thing . . . and nobody can tell you different."

"As long as somebody provides you with air and food and water and . . ."

"That's the physical end of it, sure. We're living in a microcosm, courtesy of the aerospace industry and AFSC. But there're no strings on us. The brass can't make us follow their rules. We're writing the rule books ourselves. . . . For the first time since 1776, we're writing new rules."

Linda looked thoughtful now. Kinsman couldn't tell if she was genuinely impressed by his line, or if she knew what he was trying to lead up to. He turned back to the control desk and studied the mission flight plan again.

He had carefully considered all the possible opportunities, and narrowed them down to two. *Both of them tomorrow, over the Indian Ocean. Forty to fifty minutes between ground stations, and Jill's asleep both times.*

"AF-9, this is Kodiak."

He reached for the radio switch. "AF-9 here, Kodiak. Go ahead."

"We are receiving your automatic data transmission loud and clear."

"Roger, Kodiak. Everything normal here; mission profile unchanged."

"Okay, Niner. We have nothing new for you. Oh wait . . . Chet, Lew Regneson is here and he says he's betting on you to uphold the Air Force's honor. Keep 'em flying."

Keeping his face as straight as possible, Kinsman answered, "Roger, Kodiak. Mission profile unchanged."

"Good luck!"

Linda's thoughtful expression had deepened. "What was that all about?"

He looked straight into those cool blue eyes and answered, "Damned if I know. Regneson's one of the astronaut team; been assigned to Kodiak for the past six weeks. He must be going ice-happy. Thought it'd be best just to humor him."

"Oh. I see." But she looked unconvinced.

"Have you checked any of your pictures in the film processor?"

Shaking her head, Linda said, "No, I don't want to risk them on your automatic equipment. I'll process them myself when we get back."

"Damned good equipment," said Kinsman.

"I'm fussy."

He shrugged and let it go.

"Chet?"

"What?"

"That power pod . . . what's it for? Colonel Murdock got awfully coy when I asked him."

"Nobody's supposed to know until the announcement's made in Washington . . . probably when we get back. I can't tell you officially," he grinned, "but generally reliable sources believe that it's going to power a radar set that'll be orbited next month. The radar will be part of our ABM warning system."

"Antiballistic missile?"

With a nod, Kinsman explained, "From orbit you can spot missile launches farther away, give the States a longer warning time."

"So your brave new world is involved in war, too."

"Sort of." Kinsman frowned. "Radars won't kill anybody, of course. They might save lives."

"But this *is* a military satellite."

"Unarmed. Two things this brave new world doesn't have yet: death and love."

"Men have died . . ."

"Not in orbit. On reentry. In ground or air accidents. No one's died up here. And no one's made love, either."

Despite herself, it seemed to Kinsman, she smiled. "Have there been any chances for it?"

"Well, the Russians have had women cosmonauts. Jill's been the first American girl in orbit. You're the second."

She thought it over for a moment. "This isn't exactly the bridal suite of the Waldorf . . . in fact, I've seen better motel rooms along the Jersey Turnpike."

"Pioneers have to rough it."

"I'm a photographer, Chet, not a pioneer."

Kinsman hunched his shoulders and spread his hands helplessly, a motion that made him bob slightly on the chair. "Strike three, I'm out."

"Better luck next time."

"Thanks." He returned his attention to the mission flight plan. *Next time will be in exactly sixteen hours, chickie.*

When Jill came out of the sack it was Linda's turn to sleep. Kinsman stayed at the control desk, sucking on a container of lukewarm coffee. All the panel lights were green. Jill was taking a blood specimen from one of the white mice.

"How're they doing?"

Without looking up, she answered, "Fine. They've adapted to weightlessness beautifully. Calcium level's evened off, muscle tone is good . . ."

"Then there's hope for us two-legged types?"

Jill returned the mouse to the colony entrance and snapped the lid shut. It scampered through to rejoin its clan in the transparent plastic maze of tunnels.

"I can't see any physical reason why humans can't live in orbit indefinitely," she answered.

Kinsman caught a slight but definite stress on the word *physical.* "You think there might be emotional problems over the long run?"

"Chet, I can see emotional problems on a three-day mission." Jill forced the blood specimen into a stoppered test tube.

"What do you mean?"

"Come on," she said, her face a mixture of disappointment and distaste. "It's obvious what you're trying to do. Your tail's been wagging like a puppy's whenever she's in sight."

"You haven't been sleeping much, have you?"

"I haven't been eavesdropping, if that's what you mean.

I've simply been watching you watching her. And some of the messages from the ground . . . is the whole Air Force in on this? How much money's being bet?''

"I'm not involved in any betting. I'm just—"

"You're just taking a risk on fouling up this mission and maybe killing the three of us, just to prove you're Tarzan and she's Jane.''

"Goddammit, Jill, now you sound like Murdock.''

The sour look on her face deepened. "Okay. You're a big boy. If you want to play Tarzan while you're on duty, that's your business. I won't get in your way. I'll take a sleeping pill and stay in the sack.''

"You will?''

"That's right. You can have your blonde Barbie doll, and good luck to you. But I'll tell you this—she's a phony. I've talked to her long enough to dig that. You're trying to use her, but she's using us, too. She was pumping me about the power pod while you were sleeping. She's here for her own reasons, Chet, and if she plays along with you it won't be for the romance and adventure of it all.''

My God Almighty, Jill's jealous!

It was tense and quiet when Linda returned from the bunkroom. The three of them worked separately: Jill fussing over the algae colony on the shelf above the biology bench; Kinsman methodically taking film from the observation cameras for return to Earth and reloading them; Linda efficiently clicking away at both of them.

Ground control called up to ask how things were going. Both Jill and Linda threw sharp glances at Kinsman. He replied merely:

"Following mission profile. All systems green.''

They shared a meal of pastes and squeeze-tubes together, still mostly in silence, and then it was Kinsman's turn in the sack. But not before he checked the mission flight plan. *Jill goes in next, and we'll have four hours alone, including a stretch over the Indian Ocean.*

Once Jill retired, Kinsman immediately called Linda over to the control desk under the pretext of showing her the radar image of a Russian satellite.

''We're coming close now.'' They hunched side by side at

the desk to peer at the orange-glowing radar screen, close enough for Kinsman to scent a hint of very feminine perfume. "Only a thousand kilometers away."

"Why don't you blink our lights at them?"

"It's unmanned."

"Oh."

"It *is* a little like World War I up here," Kinsman realized, straightening up. "Just being here is more important than which nation you're from."

"Do the Russians feel that way, too?"

Kinsman nodded. "I think so."

She stood in front of him, so close that they were almost touching.

"You know," Kinsman said, "when I first saw you on the base, I thought you were a photographer's model . . . not the photographer."

Gliding slightly away from him, she answered, "I started out as a model. . . ." Her voice trailed off.

"Don't stop. What were you going to say?"

Something about her had changed, Kinsman realized. She was still coolly friendly, but alert now, wary, and . . . sad?

Shrugging, she said, "Modeling is a dead end. I finally figured out that there's more of a future on the other side of the camera."

"You had too much brains for modeling."

"Don't flatter me."

"Why on earth should I flatter you?"

"We're not on Earth."

"Touché."

She drifted over toward the galley. Kinsman followed her.

"How long have you been on the other side of the camera?" he asked.

Turning back toward him, "I'm supposed to be getting your life story, not vice versa."

"Okay . . . ask me some questions."

"How many people know you're supposed to lay me up here?"

Kinsman felt his face smiling, an automatic delaying action. *What the hell*, he thought. Aloud, he replied, "I don't know. It started as a little joke among a few of the guys . . . apparently the word has spread."

"And how much money do you stand to win or lose?" She wasn't smiling.

"Money?" Kinsman was genuinely surprised. "Money doesn't enter into it."

"Oh no?"

"No, not with me," he insisted.

The tenseness in her body seemed to relax a little. "Then why . . . I mean . . . what's it all about?"

Kinsman brought his smile back and pulled himself down into the nearest chair. "Why not? You're damned pretty, neither one of us has any strings, nobody's tried it in zero gee before. . . . Why the hell not?"

"But why should I?"

"That's the big question. That's what makes an adventure out of it."

She looked at him thoughtfully, leaning her tall frame against the galley paneling. "Just like that. An adventure. There's nothing more to it than that?"

"Depends," Kinsman answered. "Hard to tell ahead of time."

"You live in a very simple world, Chet."

"I try to. Don't you?"

She shook her head. "No, my world's very complex."

"But it includes sex."

Now she smiled, but there was no pleasure in it. "Does it?"

"You mean never?" Kinsman's voice sounded incredulous, even to himself.

She didn't answer.

"Never at all? I can't believe that. . . ."

"No," she said, "not never at all. But never for . . . for an adventure. For job security, yes. For getting the good assignments; for teaching me how to use a camera, in the first place. But never for fun . . . at least, not for a long, long time has it been for fun."

Kinsman looked into those ice-blue eyes and saw that they were completely dry and aimed straight back at him. His insides felt odd. He put a hand out toward her, but she didn't move a muscle.

"That's . . . that's a damned lonely way to live," he said.

"Yes, it is." Her voice was a steel knifeblade, without a trace of self-pity in it.

"But . . . how'd it happen? Why . . . ?"

She leaned her head back against the galley paneling, her eyes looking away, into the past. "I had a baby. He didn't want it. I had to give it up for adoption—either that or have it aborted. The kid should be five years old now. . . . I don't know where she is." She straightened up, looked back at Kinsman. "But I found out that sex is either for making babies or making careers; not for fun."

Kinsman sat there, feeling like he had just taken a low blow. The only sound in the cabin was the faint hum of electrical machinery, the whisper of the air fans.

Linda broke into a grin. "I wish you could see your face: Tarzan, the Ape-Man, trying to figure out a nuclear reactor."

"The only trouble with zero gee," he mumbled, "is that you can't hang yourself."

Jill sensed something was wrong, it seemed to Kinsman. From the moment she came out of the sack, she sniffed around, giving quizzical looks. Finally, when Linda retired for her final rest period before their return, Jill asked him:

"How're you two getting along?"

"Okay."

"Really?"

"Really. We're going to open a Playboy Club in here. Want to be a bunny?"

Her nose wrinkled. "You've got enough of those."

For more than an hour they worked their separate tasks in silence. Kinsman was concentrating on recalibrating the radar mapper when Jill handed him a container of hot coffee.

He turned in the chair. She was standing beside him, not much taller than his own seated height.

"Thanks."

Her face was very serious. "Something's bothering you, Chet. What did she do to you?"

"Nothing."

"Really?"

"For Chrissake, don't start that again! Nothing, absolutely nothing happened. Maybe that's what's bothering me."

Shaking her head, "No, you're worried about something, and it's not about yourself."

"Don't be so damned dramatic, Jill."

She put a hand on his shoulder. "Chet . . . I know this is all a game to you, but people can get hurt at this kind of game, and . . . well . . . nothing in life is ever as good as you expect it will be."

Looking up at her intent brown eyes, Kinsman felt his irritation vanish. "Okay, kid. Thanks for the philosophy. I'm a big boy, though, and I know what it's all about. . . ."

"You just think you do."

Shrugging, "Okay, I think I do. Maybe nothing is as good as it ought to be, but a man's innocent until proven guilty, and everything new is as good as gold until you find some tarnish on it. That's *my* philosophy for the day!"

"All right, slugger," Jill smiled, ruefully. "Be the ape-man. Fight it out for yourself. I just don't want to see her hurt you."

"I won't get hurt."

Jill said, "You hope. Okay, if there's anything I can do. . . ."

"Yeah, there is something."

"What?"

"When you sack in again, make sure Linda sees you take a sleeping pill. Will you do that?"

Jill's face went expressionless. "Sure," she answered flatly. "Anything for a fellow officer."

She made a great show, several hours later, of taking a sleeping pill so that she could rest well on her final nap before reentry. It seemed to Kinsman that Jill deliberately layed it on too thickly.

"Do you always take sleeping pills on the final time around?" Linda asked, after Jill had gone into the bunkroom.

"Got to be fully alert and rested for the return flight," Kinsman replied. "Reentry's the trickiest part of the operation."

"Oh. I see."

"Nothing to worry about, though," Kinsman added.

He went to the control desk and busied himself with the tasks that the mission profile called for. Linda sat lightly in the next chair, within arm's reach. Kinsman chatted briefly with Kodiak station, on schedule, and made an entry in the log.

Three more ground stations and then we're over the Indian Ocean, with world enough and time.

But he didn't look up from the control panel; he tested each system aboard the lab, fingers flicking over control buttons, eyes focused on the red, amber and green lights that told him how the laboratory's mechanical and electrical machinery was functioning.

"Chet?"

"Yes."

"Are you . . . sore at me?"

Still not looking at her, "No, I'm busy. Why should I be sore at you?"

"Well, not sore maybe, but . . ."

"Puzzled?"

"Puzzled, hurt, something like that."

He punched an entry on the computer's keyboard at his side, then turned to face her. "Linda, I haven't really had time to figure out what I feel. You're a complicated girl; maybe too complicated for me. Life's got enough twists in it."

Her mouth drooped a little.

"On the other hand," he added, "we WASPS ought to stick together. Not many of us left."

That brought a faint smile. "I'm not a WASP. My real name's Szymanski. . . . I changed it when I started modeling."

"Oh. Another complication."

She was about to reply when the radio speaker crackled, "AF-9, this is Cheyenne. Cheyenne to AF-9."

Kinsman leaned over and thumbed the transmitter switch. "AF-9 to Cheyenne. You're coming through faint but clear."

"Roger, Nine. We're receiving your telemetry. All systems look green from here."

"Manual check of systems also green," Kinsman said. "Mission profile okay, no deviations. Tasks about ninety percent complete."

"Roger. Ground control suggests you begin checking out your spacecraft on the next orbit. You are scheduled for reentry in ten hours."

"Right. Will do."

"Okay, Chet. Everything looks good from here. Anything else to report, ol' Founding Father?"

"Mind your own business." He turned the transmitter off. Linda was smiling at him.

"What's so funny?"

"You are. You're getting very touchy about this whole business."

"It's going to stay touchy for a long time to come. Those guys'll hound me for years about this."

"You could always tell lies."

"About you? No, I don't think I could do that. If the girl was anonymous, that's one thing. But they all know you, know where you work . . ."

"You're a gallant officer. I suppose that kind of rumor would get back to New York."

Kinsman grinned. "You could even make the front page of the *National Enquirer*."

She laughed at that. "I'll bet they'd pull out some of my old bikini pictures."

"Careful now," Kinsman put up a warning hand. "Don't stir up my imagination any more than it already is. I'm having a hard enough time being gallant right now."

They remained apart, silent, Kinsman sitting at the control desk, Linda drifting back toward the galley, nearly touching the curtain that screened off the sleeping area.

The ground control center called in and Kinsman gave a terse report. When he looked up at Linda again, she was sitting in front of the observation port across the aisle from the galley. Looking back at Kinsman, her face was troubled now, her eyes . . . he wasn't sure what was in her eyes. They looked different: no longer ice-cool, no longer calculating; they looked aware, concerned, almost frightened.

Still Kinsman stayed silent. He checked and double-checked the control board, making absolutely certain that every valve and transistor aboard the lab was working perfectly. Glancing at his watch: *Five more minutes before Ascension calls*. He checked the lighted board again.

Ascension called in exactly on schedule. Feeling his innards tightening, Kinsman gave his standard report in a deliberately calm and mechanical way. Ascension signed off.

With a long last look at the controls, Kinsman pushed himself out of the seat and drifted, hands faintly touching the grips along the aisle, toward Linda.

"You've been awfully quiet," he said, standing over her.

"I've been thinking about what you said a while ago." What was it in her eyes? Anticipation? Fear? "It . . . it has been a damned lonely life, Chet."

He took her arm and lifted her gently from the chair and kissed her.

"But . . ."

"It's all right," he whispered. "No one will bother us. No one will know."

She shook her head. "It's not that easy, Chet. It's not that simple."

"Why not? We're here together . . . what's so complicated?"

"But—doesn't anything bother you? You're floating around in a dream. You're surrounded by war machines; you're living every minute with danger. If a pump fails or a meteor hits. . . ."

"You think it's any safer down there?"

"But life *is* complex, Chet. And love . . . well, there's more to it than just having fun."

"Sure there is. But it's meant to be enjoyed, too. What's wrong with taking an opportunity when you have it? What's so damned complicated or important? We're above the cares and worries of Earth. Maybe it's only for a few hours, but it's here and now, it's us. They can't touch us, they can't force us to do anything or stop us from doing what we want to. We're on our own. Understand? Completely on our own."

She nodded, her eyes still wide with the look of a frightened animal. But her hands slid around him, and together they drifted back toward the control desk. Wordlessly, Kinsman turned off all the overhead lights, so that all they saw was the glow of the control board and the flickering of the computer as it murmured to itself.

They were in their own world now, their private cosmos, floating freely and softly in the darkness. Touching, drifting, coupling, searching the new seas and continents, they explored their world.

Jill stayed in the hammock until Linda entered the bunkroom, quietly, to see if she had awakened yet. Kinsman sat at the control desk feeling . . . not tired, but strangely numb.

The rest of the flight was strictly routine. Jill and Kinsman did their jobs, spoke to each other when they had to. Linda took a brief nap, then returned to snap a few last pictures. Finally, they crawled back into the spacecraft, disengaged from the laboratory, and started the long curving flight back to Earth.

Kinsman took a last look at the majestic beauty of the planet, serene and incompatible among the stars, before touching the button that slid the heat-shield over his viewport. Then they felt the surge of rocket thrust, dipped into the atmosphere, knew that air heated beyond endurance surrounded them in a fiery grip and made their tiny craft into a flaming, falling star. Pressed into his seat by the acceleration, Kinsman let the automatic controls bring them through reentry, through the heat and buffeting turbulence, down to an altitude where their finned craft could fly like a rocketplane.

He took control and steered the craft back toward Patrick Air Force Base, back to the world of men, of weather, of cities, of hierarchies and official regulations. He did this alone, silently; he didn't need Jill's help or anyone else's. He flew the craft from inside his buttoned-tight pressure suit, frowning at the panel displays through his helmet's faceplate.

Automatically, he checked with ground control and received permission to slide the heat-shield back. The viewport showed him a stretch of darkening clouds spreading from the sea across the beach and well inland. His earphones were alive with other men's voices now: wind conditions, altitude checks, speed estimates. He knew, but could not see, that two jet planes were trailing along behind him, cameras focused on the returning spacecraft. *To provide evidence if I crash.*

They dipped into the clouds and a wave of gray mist

hurtled up and covered the viewport. Kinsman's eyes flicked to the radar screen slightly off to his right. The craft shuddered briefly, then they broke below the clouds and he could see the long, black gouge of the runway looming before him. He pulled back slightly on the controls, hands and feet working instinctively, flashed over some scrubby vegetation, and flared the craft onto the runway. The landing skids touched once, bounced them up momentarily, then touched again with a grinding shriek. They skidded for more than a mile before stopping.

He leaned back in the seat and felt his body oozing sweat.

"Good landing," Jill said.

"Thanks." He turned off all the craft's systems, hands moving automatically in response to long training. Then he slid his faceplate up, reached overhead and popped the hatch open.

"End of the line," he said tiredly. "Everybody out."

He clambered up through the hatch, feeling his own weight with a sullen resentment, then helped Linda and finally Jill out of the spacecraft. They hopped down onto the blacktop runway. Two vans, an ambulance and two fire trucks were rolling toward them from their parking stations at the end of the runway, a half-mile ahead.

Kinsman slowly took off his helmet. The Florida heat and humidity annoyed him now. Jill walked a few paces away from him, toward the approaching trucks.

He stepped toward Linda. Her helmet was off, and she was carrying a bag full of film.

"I've been thinking," he said to her. "That business about having a lonely life. . . . You know, you're not the only one. And it doesn't have to be that way. I can get to New York whenever . . ."

"Now who's taking things seriously?" Her face looked calm again, cool, despite the glaring heat.

"But I mean—"

"Listen, Chet. We had our kicks. Now you can tell your friends about it, and I can tell mine. We'll both get a lot of mileage out of it. It'll help our careers."

"I never intended to . . . I didn't . . ."

But she was already turning away from him, walking

toward the men who were running up to meet them from the trucks. One of them, a civilian, had a camera in his hands. He dropped to one knee and took a picture of Linda holding the film out and smiling broadly.

Kinsman stood there with his mouth open.

Jill came back to him. "Well? Did you get what you were after?"

"No," he said slowly. "I guess I didn't."

She started to put her hand out to him. "We never do, do we?"

Living and Loving in Zero Gravity ▃▃▃

This is obviously a companion piece to *Zero Gee*, even though they were written more than fifteen years apart. When I left the world of magazine editing to become a full-time writer, I set myself the challenge of selling pieces to all the major magazines that might conceivably publish either fact or fiction about science, high technology and the future. I tried a few ideas with the articles editor of *Playboy* with no success. It was my agent, bless her, who shrewdly suggested that I ask if *Playboy* would be interested in a piece about the physiology of weightlessness. Of course, I didn't quite phrase my query to the magazine in exactly those terms . . .

———————————

Nearly fifteen years ago I wrote a short story about a man and a woman making love in the weightlessness of an orbiting space station. It was science fiction then; it will be history long before another fifteen years have passed.

If you like waterbeds, you're going to love orbital space. The floating sensation of weightlessness has made every astronaut who's gone into space euphoric. Even those who suffered at first from disorientation and nausea quickly became acclimatized to zero gravity and enjoyed it tremendously. The American astronauts who spent months in Skylab back in 1973–74 learned to fly through their commodious space station, weightlessly gliding through a world that had neither "up" nor "down."

Sooner than most people realize, tourists are going to begin riding into orbit. NASA is already selecting ordinary citizens to ride on the space shuttle. Private entrepreneurs are getting into the business of launching rockets. Inevitably, today's Jet Set will become tomorrow's Rocket Set, heading into orbit for zero-gravity fun and games.

We take gravity quite for granted, the one "gee" force that we experience here on Earth. It shapes our bodies, our lives, even the way we think and play. We leave the comfortable floating dark world of the womb and start fighting gravity from the instant of birth. Our bones, our muscles, our blood circulation systems must all work against gravity every moment of our lives. Gravity pulls us down, bends our spines and gives us backaches, makes our faces and breasts sag, hurts us when we fall.

But in zero gravity the body undergoes some marvelous changes. You become wasp-waisted. Your legs thin down. Your face becomes somewhat puffier for the first few days. Skylab astronaut William Pogue thought his face had taken on an oriental cast, with higher cheekbones and narrower eyes than he had on Earth. All this happens because the body's internal fluids are no longer being pulled downward by gravity. Even the placement of the internal organs shifts a little in zero gee. After a few days of weightlessness, the facial puffiness goes away as the body begins to adjust its fluid production to meet the conditions of zero gee.

Dieting is easier in space. You tend to eat less because you are doing less physical work under zero-gee conditions, and the body demands less fuel.

And you tend to grow a couple of inches taller when in orbit because the spine unbends and lengthens. All our lives our spines have been pressed into an ess-shape by the downward-pulling force of gravity. In zero gee, the spine unbends and you gain an inch or two in height. Unfortunately for all the unhappy short people of the world, that added height is taken away once you return to Earth and its one-gee environment. If you want to stay two inches taller, you must stay in orbit.

In 1961, when Yuri Gagarin became the first man to fly in orbit, medical doctors feared that the human mind and body could not stand up to the conditions of space flight: the enormous stresses of a high-gee "blastoff," then zero gravity and all its attendant physical and psychological changes, and finally the strain of returning to Earth and a one-gee environment again. In particular, the medics worried about three major problems of space flight.

First, zero gravity affects the delicate balancing mechanisms in the inner ear. Ever since the first lungfish crawled out of the sea, land-dwelling creatures have developed internal systems for telling them which end is up. For two-legged critters such as we are, who move around the surface of our world by teetering our weight on one foot while we swing the other forward, the balancing devices built into our inner ears are crucially important. When they go awry, we fall on our faces; we can't walk straight and in some cases we can't even stand up at all.

The inner ear's mechanisms are very sensitive to gravity; it's their job to be. It is their message to the brain that gives us that sick-in-the-stomach feeling we have when we are falling.

In orbit, we are "falling" all the time. Weightlessness has often been called "free fall" by scientists and astronauts. In effect, a satellite is falling as it hurtles around the Earth, but its forward speed is so huge—18,000 miles per hour for a low orbit—that the curve of its fall is wider than the size of the Earth. So the satellite, and everyone in it, continues to fall endlessly as long as it is in orbit.

The inner ear's balancing system does not like this. It is built to warn you when you are falling, to get your attention by making you feel queasy and panicky. NASA medics knew that this would happen when astronauts went into orbit. They trained the astronauts aboard planes that flew special maneuvers which produced a few precious seconds of zero-gee conditions. Such training flights are still called "whoopee missions." Still, most of the astronauts (and cosmonauts) who have gone into orbit have felt queasy, sensitive, and even downright sick for the first few hours or days of their missions.

"Space sickness" is somewhat like sea sickness. You get over it after a while. Training and knowledge of what to expect can help. So can medication, such as Dramamine. Space tourists won't get the kind of intensive training that the astronauts receive, but they will have a full panoply of pharmaceutical products, from improved anti-vertigo drugs to tranquilizers, to help them ward off the physical and psychological impact of "space sickness."

The two other problems that worried space medics were the loss of muscle tone and the loss of bone calcium that come from long exposure to weightlessness. After twenty-two years of space flight, we know that these fears were not groundless, but they were exaggerated. The experiences of our Skylab astronauts and the many Russian cosmonauts show that living in space for months at a time has positive medical benefits.

The Russians are far ahead of us in long-term experience with weightlessness; they have had cosmonauts aboard their Salyut space stations for more than six months at a time. Their current record is 237 days in orbit, and they will probably shatter their own record before very long.

What the medics have learned from these man-years of orbital experience is that the human body adapts to the disappearance of gravity quite nicely. Muscle tone can deteriorate, but exercise can make up for that. The Skylab astronauts had an exercycle in their space station and often pedaled around the world in 80-some minutes. Such exercise keeps up the muscle tone not only of the legs, but of the heart as well, which is equally important. In zero gee, the heart's workload is reduced because the blood it is pumping through the circulatory system is weightless. So it is important to maintain the heart muscle's tone—in anticipation of returning to Earth and its one-gravity environment.

Calcium loss caused more worry among the medics than anything else. The longer an astronaut remained in orbit, it appeared, the less calcium the body produced. This could make the bones so weak that the astronauts could not stand up on Earth once they returned. But the Russians, thanks to their longer-term missions, learned that calcium production levels off after about four months of weightlessness. And the calcium production in the body never gets low enough to cause a serious medical problem. What is happening is *adaptation*: the wonderfully plastic nature of our bodies allows us to adapt to the zero-gravity environment. The bones are not experiencing the kinds of stresses they feel on Earth, so they do not need to be as rigid. Therefore, calcium levels are automatically decreased by the body's internal feedback controls. Once one returns to Earth, calcium levels go back to normal within a few days.

The body adapts to zero gravity. Even the queasiness of "space sickness" disappears after a while. The problems that worried the medics years ago were mainly problems of how the astronauts would fare when they returned to Earth. As long as a person stays in orbit, his or her body will adapt to weightlessness automatically. Almost all our internal bodily functions operate independently of gravity—a heritage of those primeval ages when our ancient ancestors lived in the sea, floating in a sort of zero-gee world underwater.

In orbit, we return to a weightless existence. As our Skylab and shuttle astronauts have shown, living in zero gee can be fun. You can float effortlessly from one end of the cabin to another, maneuvering with nothing more than fingertip touches against the bulkheads. There are no backaches in zero gee. No post-nasal drips.

Of course, adjusting to life on Earth again after a month or more in orbit presented the Skylab astronauts with a few mental problems, as well as physical ones. Most of them complained of feeling dull, heavy and uncomfortable for days or even weeks after coming back from zero gee. They also had to keep reminding themselves that if they released an object from their hands it would crash to the floor instead of floating obediently in midair, waiting to be picked up again.

Although the first astronauts and cosmonauts were highly-trained jet jockeys from the ranks of military fliers and test pilots, already the space shuttle is carrying non-pilot "payload specialists" into orbit, and scientists who work in the spacelab that the shuttle carries into orbit. NASA is developing plans to build a permanent station in orbit, which the space agency unromantically calls the Space Operations Center (SOC).

The entrepreneurs who today are launching rockets for profit will someday build space stations of their own in orbit, space habitats where ordinary people can live and work for months or even years at a time. Space habitats where tourists can go for zero-gee vacations.

Imagine your very own two-week vacation in orbit. It could happen before the end of this century. The *Love Boat* of 1999 might have wings on it.

At today's prices it would cost more than $100,000 to fly into orbit aboard the space shuttle. But just as engineering improvements made commercial air travel feasible in the 1930s, improvements in shuttle-type craft can bring down the ticket price of a ride into orbit to something like the price of a round-the-world cruise aboard a luxury liner, by the late 1990s. Expensive, yes; but not impossible, especially for the vacation of a lifetime.

The space shuttle of the 1990s will not take off like a rocket. It will look like two airplanes, one riding piggyback on the other, rather like today's shuttle orbiter riding atop its Boeing 747 carrier when it returns to Cape Canaveral after having landed at Edwards AFB in California.

Today's shuttle subjects its crew to three or four gees during the few minutes' liftoff. The all-reusable piggyback shuttle of the 1990s will take off like a commercial airliner. The passengers will sit back and sip their champagne as the orbiter separates from the lifter beneath it, up about 100,000 feet, and accelerates smoothly toward the space station, some two hundreds miles higher.

Once the orbiter's rocket engines shut down, the passengers get their first feel of zero-gee. Under the watchful eyes of the stewards and stewardesses, you can unfasten your safety belt and float out of your seat. You feel as if you are falling, but several weeks of group sessions with the spaceline's psychologist (all part of your fare) have at least prepared you mentally for the stomach-in-your-throat sensation.

Thanks to the experience of the Skylab astronauts, the interior of the space liner's cabin is decorated with strong designs of bright colors, which give you a clear sense of up and down. Even though your inner ear is sending out distress signals, your eyes tell you that the floor is beneath you, the ceiling is overhead, and you are perfectly safe. Still, when the stewardess floats by and offers you an anti-vertigo pill, you take it and slosh it down with champagne.

The cabin attendants are wearing one-piece coverall uniforms of powder blue. The stewardesses are required to wear "comfort bras" of the type designed for NASA's women astronauts. The spaceline company wants no excessive jiggling during the flight. Most of the passengers are wearing equally utilitarian coverall outfits, on the advice of the company, although the clothing locked away in the passengers' luggage is bound to be quite a bit different.

Perhaps it is a coincidence, but the passengers on this flight are divided exactly equally: ten men and ten women. Most of them are your own age, give or take a year. Does the company match tourists by age and sex? Certainly.

By the time the orbiter docks at the space station, all the passengers are feeling fine, although a couple of them have bumped their heads against the softly-padded ceiling of the cabin. It's fun to tow your luggage and float through the cabin's airlock into the reception area of the orbital hotel. Here too, the interior design stresses visual cues that identify which way is up. The hotel lobby looks rather ordinary and Earthlike, with a carpeted floor and a registration desk staffed by smiling young men and women who have their shoes firmly locked into the metal gridwork behind the desk, so that they don't go floating disconcertingly off toward the ceiling.

Other areas of the hotel take full advantage of zero gravity, and have furniture built into the walls and ceiling as well as the floor. What difference does it make, as long as you are weightless?

The bellhop could be a robot, but the hotel management is careful to use human beings—psychology students, mostly—who can spot the symptoms of physical or psychological distress as they guide the tourist through the circular tubes that are the corridors of this hotel. The bellhop chatters pleasantly about "the little things" that make a big difference in weightlessness. You have to be careful about shaving, eating and housecleaning in orbit because whiskers, crumbs and litter do not drop to the floor; they float in the air currents and sooner or later end up sticking to the filter screens over the air vents.

The bellhop tells the story of the Skylab astronauts, who found that small drops of liquid and crumbs from their meals would float around the interior of their space station until they stuck on the wall or the open-grid ceiling just above their dining table. The ceiling became quite dirty, because even though the astronauts could see it, they could not get their hands into the area to clean it. Near the end of the mission it looked like the bottom of a birdcage, and the astronauts took pains not to look at it—especially while they were eating.

Every astronaut who has been in orbit has experienced the heady euphoria that comes with weightlessness. It is as if the body suddenly realizes it is free of a burden it had taken totally for granted, and every nerve begins to tingle with the excitement of this new freedom. Once you realize that you are not going to become nauseated, that weightlessness actually feels wonderful, this excitement begins to grip you. It is a new experience, unlike anything on Earth.

The orbital hotel offers a modest variety of activities for its guests. There are observation bubbles on the outer shell of the hotel, where you can use a small telescope to observe the construction crews at work on other satellites, thousands of miles away, or inspect the surface of the Moon, or gaze out at the stars which stare steadily back at you, without the twinkling effect caused by the Earth's turbulent layers of air.

There is zero-gravity volleyball, with a net that looks like a circular trampoline floating in the middle of a big, heavily-padded gymnasium. There is zero-gee ping-pong, with no net at all, and no table, either. The object is to keep the ball from hitting a wall surface. You quickly get out of the habit of saying "ceiling" or "floor." All six surfaces of any cube-shaped enclosure are called "walls."

Of course, many of the hotel's rooms are not cube-shaped at all. Your bedroom is built like the interior of a padded egg, with no furniture in sight. There is no need for a bed; a simple zip-up webbed bag will hold you in if you're afraid of drifting around the room in your sleep. The closets are built into the walls behind the padding.

Everyone's favorite activity is Earth-watching, and you have chosen to do it from outside the metal shell of the hotel. Along with half a dozen other members of your flight, you are going EVA. Three hotel staffers help you to wriggle into your space suits, which come in small, medium, and large sizes and in garish day-glo colors. You strike up a conversation with your fellow tourists, especially the pretty redhead next to you. But once the hotel staffers lower the space helmets over your heads and seal them to the suits' collars, all you can see of each other is a bulbous helmet with a mirrored visor, riding atop a bulky, cumbersome suit that would weigh at least ninety pounds on Earth. Here, of course, it weighs exactly as much as you do—nothing.

Suit radios, oxygen, heaters, air-circulation fans—and all the joints and seals of the awkward suits—are minutely checked by the hotel people. Then at last they walk you into the big airlock, attach your safety cords and open the outer hatch.

It's like jumping off the highest diving board you can imagine, or stepping out of an airplane. You put out one booted foot and then the other, and you're walking on nothing. Space-walking. You can hear your heart pounding in your ears, but in an instant you forget all about it.

Because you see the Earth. An immense, beautiful, gleaming curve of deepest, richest blue, the jewel of creation, wrapped in dazzling clouds of pure white. The oceans are shot through with colors ranging from aqua and absolute green to surprising browns and reds formed by algal growths that trace out long swirling patterns of ocean currents for hundreds of miles. The land is brown, mostly, wrinkled where mountain chains fold. They look pitifully small from up here. You can see snow on some of the peaks. Your guides tell you where to look, and you see that Dakota's Black Hills really are black.

The panorama of Earth glides before your eyes, land and sea and clouds, and it is so lovely, so endlessly fascinating, that you are shocked when the guides tell you that two hours have gone by and it's time to get back inside.

All of you are surprised, as you struggle out of the space suits, to find that you are thoroughly soaked with perspiration. The space suits that protected you from freezing or broiling in the vacuum outside have also prevented your body's normal moisture from evaporating off your skin. The sweat will not drip off you, of course; it puddles up on your skin like beads of water on a newly-waxed automobile.

You "swim" your way back toward your rooms for a

quick shower before dinner. As you glide along the tubelike corridors you make a date for dinner with the redhead. She's from Minnesota, and the farthest above the ground she's been before this has been at the top of the IDS Tower in downtown Minneapolis.

Bathing in zero gee is different from the way it is done on Earth. When you wet a washcloth the water sticks to the fabric like a puddle of jelly. Touch the washcloth to your body and the water sticks to your skin. Spread it around carefully until you are completely wet, then lather in the soap. Don't worry about dripping water; it will not fall, even if you shake it loose from your body. You use a vacuum cleaner attachment to get the soapy water off your skin, then reverse it into a hot air blower to dry yourself.

Fashions in zero gee are quickly evolving away from the strictly utilitarian, such as the coveralls everyone wore on the shuttle. After all, if you've spent enough money to get to this orbital hotel, you're not going to be satisfied with a unisex jumpsuit. Men seem to be going in for uniforms with long vertical design elements that emphasize their newfound height and zero-gee induced slimness. Women prefer wispy, billowing fashions, although most of them want to show off their new wasp-waisted hourglass figures and longer-looking legs. Freed from the need for bras and other gravitationally-required restraints, both women's and men's zero-gee styles are more exotic than anything possible on Earth—where there is always the danger of something falling off.

Hair fashions are also different, for both sexes, because long hair has the tendency to float out wildly from its roots. Zero-gee Afros were popular at first, but short hair styles now are the mark of men and women who have been to space. Of course, snug hair coverings can be made very decorative, too, and there are plenty of those visible as you enter the dining room with your date.

Ever-mindful of their guests' comfort, the hotel has kept its dining room as Earthlike as possible, with a definite floor and no furniture on any other surface. The waiters glide along effortlessly, though, and no one ever drops a tray of food in zero gee. The chairs all have seatbelts, so that you don't inadvertently drift away in the middle of the meal. Burping and other sudden expulsions of gas are not only impolite in zero gee, they can start you moving if you're not strapped down.

Soft candlelight is unlikely, because a candle flame will quickly extinguish itself in zero gravity. Under weightless conditions, the hot carbon dioxide given off by the flame remains right there around the flame itself; hot air is not lighter than cold air in zero gee, and the candle soon dies in its own pollution. But the tables are lit by flickering electric candles, and the mood of the dining room is quite nicely romantic.

Dinner features orbital delicacies such as frog's legs and roasted rabbit: animals that offer a high percentage of meat to bone, and don't need large amounts of feed to fatten them. Hydroponic vegetables, grown in the hotel's own zero-gee garden, are a mainstay of the menu. The *pièce de résistance* is the hotel's special dessert: Sundae *à la* Skylab. One of the Skylab astronauts mistakenly put a serving of ice cream into the food warmer; it melted, of course. But being weightless, it melted into a large, sublimely thin, hollow ball. He carefully refroze the ball, then filled it with strawberries: the first ice cream sundae in orbit.

After dinner and an exhilarating round of zero-gee disco, you bring your date back to your room, that intimate dimly-lit ovoid chamber where the wall surfaces are warmly padded so that you can float effortlessly. Sex in zero gee is mind-boggling. Floating weightlessly in your own cozy, private universe, where every slightest touch produces a gentle movement, is the ultimate in sensuousness.

Like almost all other inner functions, the human body is perfectly well adapted to accommodate weightless sex. If anything, the absence of gravity should give a boost to a man's ability to have and maintain an erection, since the blood that engorges the penis's tissue is weightless and can be pumped that much more easily by the heart.

Free of the need to support yourself on a surface of any kind, sexual play can involve the entire body, both arms and legs simultaneously. No cramped limbs from having to support your weight or your partner's. The actual physical act of penetration is more interesting than ever, because you are both floating freely and every movement tends to keep on moving, just as Isaac Newton said it would. In astronautical terms, this becomes a "rendezvous and docking problem." But if astronauts can link multi-ton spacecraft in orbit, a man and a woman should be able to bring themselves together pleasurably. And it's so much fun trying.

Afterward the two of you zip yourselves into the light mesh sleeping bag so that you won't drift around in your sleep and wake yourselves by bumping into a padded wall. You find yourself thinking that living in space all the time might be the kind of lifestyle you would really like. No need for bras or chiropractors up here, and the weightless conditions should be wonderful for the elderly and the infirm—as well as lovers.

Orbital vacations will soon enough replace Niagara Falls, Miami Beach, and even Paris in the springtime. But Apollo 11 astronaut Mike Collins had an even grander vision as he circled the Moon alone while Neil Armstrong and Buzz Aldrin were putting the first footprints on the Moon. Collins imagined:

". . . a spacecraft of the future, with a crew of a thousand ladies, off for Alpha Centauri, with two thousand breasts bobbing beautifully and quivering delightfully in response to their every weightless movement . . . and I am the commander of the craft, and it is Saturday morning and time for inspection . . ."

On to Alpha Centauri!

A Small Kindness ━━━━━━━━━━

To this day, I'm not quite certain of how this story originated. I've been to Athens, and found it a big, noisy, dirty city fouled with terrible automobile pollution—and centered on the awe-inspiring Acropolis. The world's most beautiful building, the Parthenon, is truly a symbol of what is best and what is worst in us. Of its beauty, its grace, its simple grandeur I can add nothing to the paeans that have been sung by so many others. But over the millennia, the dark forces of human nature have almost destroyed the Parthenon. It has been blasted by cannon fire, defaced by conquerors and tourists, and now is being eaten away by the acidic outpourings of automobile exhausts.

A Luddite would say, with justice, that this is a case where human technology is obviously working against the human spirit. A Promethean would say that since we recognize the problem, we ought to take steps to solve it. In a way, that's what *A Small Kindness* is about—I think.

━━━━━━━━━━━

Jeremy Keating hated the rain. Athens was a dismal enough assignment, but in the windswept rainy night it was cold and black and dangerous.

Everyone pictures Athens in the sunshine, he thought. The Acropolis, the gleaming ancient temples. They don't see the filthy modern city with its endless streams of automobiles spewing out so much pollution that the marble statues are being eaten away and the ancient monuments are in danger of crumbling.

Huddled inside his trench coat, Keating stood in the shadows of a deep doorway across the street from the taverna where his target was eating a relaxed and leisurely dinner—his last, if things went the way Keating planned.

He stood as far back in the doorway as he could, pressed against the cold stones of the building, both to remain unseen in the shadows and to keep the cold rain off himself. Rain or no, the automobile traffic still clogged Filellinon Boulevard, cars inching by bumper to bumper, honking their horns, squealing on the slickened paving. The worst traffic in the world, night and day. A million and a half Greeks, all in cars, all the time. They drove the way they lived—argumentatively.

The man dining across the boulevard in the warm, brightly-lit taverna was Kabete Rungawa, of the Tanzanian delegation to the World Government conference. "The Black Saint of the Third World," he was called. The most revered man since Gandhi. Keating smiled grimly to himself. According to his acquaintances in the Vatican, a man had to be dead before he could be proclaimed a saint.

Keating was a tall man, an inch over six feet. He had the lean, graceful body of a trained athlete, and it had taken him years of constant painful work to acquire it. The earlier part of his adult life he had spent behind a desk or at embassy parties, like so many other Foreign Service career officers. But that had been a lifetime ago, when he was a minor cog in the Department of State's global machine. When he was a husband and father.

His wife had been killed in the rioting in Tunis, part of the carefully-orchestrated Third World upheaval that had forced the new World Government down the throats of the white, industrialized nations. His son had died of typhus in the besieged embassy, when they were unable to get medical supplies because the U.S. government could not decide whether it should negotiate with the radicals or send in the Marines.

In the end, they negotiated. But by then it was too late. So now Keating served as a roving attaché to U.S. embassies or consulates, serving where his special talents were needed. He had found those talents in the depths of his agony, his despair, his hatred.

Outwardly he was still a minor diplomatic functionary, an interesting dinner companion, a quietly handsome man with brooding eyes who seemed both unattached and unavailable. That made him a magnetic lure for a certain type of woman, a challenge they could not resist. A few of them had gotten close enough to him to trace the hairline scar across his abdomen, all that remained of the surgery he had needed after his first assignment, in Indonesia. After that particular horror, he had never been surprised or injured again.

With an adamant shake of his head, Keating forced himself to concentrate on the job at hand. The damp cold was seeping into him. His feet were already soaked. The cars still crawled along the rainy boulevard, honking impatiently. The noise was making him irritable, jumpy.

"Terminate with extreme prejudice," his boss had told him, that sunny afternoon in Virginia. "Do you understand what that means?"

Sitting in the deep leather chair in front of the section chief's broad walnut desk, Keating nodded. "I may be new to this part of the department, but I've been around. It means to do to Rungawa what the Indonesians tried to do to me."

No one ever used the words *kill* or *assassinate* in these cheerfully lit offices. The men behind the desks, in their pinstripe suits, dealt with computer printouts and satellite photographs and euphemisms. Messy, frightening things like blood were never mentioned here.

The section chief steepled his fingers and gave Keating a long, thoughtful stare. He was a distinguished-looking man with silver hair and smoothly tanned skin. He might be the board chairman you meet at the country club, or the type of well-bred gentry who spends the summer racing yachts.

"Any questions, Jeremy?"

Keating shifted slightly in his chair. "Why Rungawa?"

The section chief made a little smile. "Do you like having the World Government order us around, demand that we disband our armed forces, tax us until we're as poor as the Third World?"

Keating felt emotions burst into flame inside his guts. All the pain of his wife's death, of his son's lingering agony, of his hatred for the gloating ignorant sadistic petty tyrants who had killed them—all erupted in a volcanic tide of lava within him. But he clamped down on his bodily responses, used every ounce of training and willpower at his command to force his voice to remain calm. One thing he had learned about this organization, and about this section chief in particular: never let anyone know where you are vulnerable.

"I've got no great admiration for the World Government," he said.

The section chief's basilisk smile vanished. There was no need to appear friendly to this man. He was an employee, a tool. Despite his attempt to hide his emotions, it was obvious that all Keating lived for was to avenge his wife and child. It would get him killed, eventually, but for now his thirst for vengeance was a valuable handle for manipulating the man.

"Rungawa is the key to everything," the section chief said, leaning back in his tall swivel chair and rocking slightly.

Keating knew that the World Government, still less than five years old, was meeting in Athens to plan a global economic program. Rungawa would head the Tanzanian delegation.

"The World Government is taking special pains to destroy the United States," the section chief said, as calmly as he might announce a tennis score. "Washington was forced to accept the World Government, and the people went along with the idea because they thought it would put an end to the threat of nuclear war. Well, it's done that—at the cost of taxing our economy for every unemployed black, brown, and yellow man, woman, and child in the entire world."

"And Rungawa?" Keating repeated.

The section chief leaned forward, pressed his palms on his desktop and lowered his voice. "We can't back out of the World Government, for any number of reasons. But we can—with the aid of certain other Western nations—we can take control of it, if we're able to break up the solid voting bloc of the Third World nations."

"Would the Soviets—"

"We can make an accommodation with the Soviets," the

section chief said impatiently, waving one hand in the air.
"Nobody wants to go back to the old cold-war confronta-
tions. It's the Third World that's got to be brought to terms."

"By eliminating Rungawa."

"Exactly! He's the glue that holds their bloc together. 'The
Black Saint.' They practically worship him. Eliminate him
and they'll fall back into their old tangle of bickering selfish
politicians, just as OPEC broke up once the oil glut started."

It had all seemed so simple back there in that comfortable
sunny office. Terminate Rungawa and then set about taking
the leadership of the World Government. Fix up the damage
done by the Third World's jealous greed. Get the world's
economy back on the right track again.

But here in the rainy black night of Athens, Keating knew
it was not that simple at all. His left hand gripped the dart
gun in his trench coat pocket. There was enough poison in
each dart to kill a man instantly and leave no trace for a
coroner to find. The darts themselves dissolved on contact
with the air within three minutes. The perfect murder weapon.

Squinting through the rain, Keating saw through the taverna's
big plate-glass window that Rungawa was getting up from his
table, preparing to leave the restaurant.

Terminate Rungawa. That was his mission. Kill him and
make it look as if he'd had a heart attack. It should be easy
enough. One old man, walking alone down the boulevard to
his hotel. "The Black Saint" never used bodyguards. He was
old enough for a heart attack to be beyond suspicion.

But it was not going to be that easy, Keating saw. Rungawa
came out of the taverna accompanied by three younger men.
And he did not turn toward his hotel. Instead, he started
walking down the boulevard in the opposite direction, toward
the narrow tangled streets of the most ancient part of the city,
walking toward the Acropolis. In the rain. Walking.

Frowning with puzzled aggravation, Keating stepped out of
the doorway and into the pelting rain. It was icy cold. He
pulled up his collar and tugged his hat down lower. He hated
the rain. Maybe the old bastard will catch pneumonia and die
naturally, he thought angrily.

As he started across the boulevard a car splashed by, horn

bleating, soaking his trousers. Keating jumped back just in time to avoid being hit. The driver's furious face, framed by the rain-streaked car window, glared at him as the auto swept past. Swearing methodically under his breath, Keating found another break in the traffic and sprinted across the boulevard, trying to avoid the puddles even though his feet were already wet through.

He stayed well behind Rungawa and his three companions, glad that they were walking instead of driving, miserable to be out in the chilling rain. As far as he could tell, all three of Rungawa's companions were black, young enough and big enough to be bodyguards. That complicated matters. Had someone warned Rungawa? Was there a leak in the department's operation?

With Keating trailing behind, the old man threaded the ancient winding streets that huddled around the jutting rock of the Acropolis. The four blacks walked around the ancient citadel, striding purposefully, as if they had to be at an exact place at a precise time. Keating had to stay well behind them because the traffic along Theonas Avenue was much thinner, and pedestrians, in this rain, were nowhere in sight except for his quarry. It was quieter here, along the shoulder of the great cliff. The usual nightly *son et lumière* show had been cancelled because of the rain; even the floodlights around the Parthenon and the other temples had been turned off.

For a few minutes Keating wondered if Rungawa was going to the Agora instead, but no, the old man and his friends turned in at the gate to the Acropolis, the Sacred Way of the ancient Athenians.

It was difficult to see through the rain, especially at this distance. Crouching low behind shrubbery, Keating fumbled in his trench coat pocket until he found the miniature "camera" he had brought with him. Among other things, it was an infrared snooperscope. Even in the darkness and rain, he could see the four men as they stopped at the main gate. Their figures looked ghostly gray and eerie against a flickering dark background.

They stopped for a few moments while one of them opened the gate that was usually locked and guarded. Keating was more impressed than surprised. They had access to everything they wanted. But why do they want to go up to the Parthenon on a rainy wintry night? And how can I make Rungawa's death look natural if I have to fight my way past three bodyguards?

The second question resolved itself almost as soon as Keating asked it. Rungawa left his companions at the gate and started up the steep, rain-slickened marble stairs by himself.

"A man that age, in this weather, could have a heart attack just from climbing those stairs," Keating whispered to himself. But he knew that he could not rely on chance.

He had never liked climbing. Although he felt completely safe and comfortable in a jet plane and had even made parachute jumps calmly, climbing up the slippery rock face of the cliff was something that Keating dreaded. But he did it, nevertheless. It was not as difficult as he had feared. Others had scaled the Acropolis, over the thirty-some centuries since the Greeks had first arrived at it. Keating clambered and scrambled over the rocks, crawling at first on all fours while the cold rain spattered in his face. Then he found a narrow trail. It was steep and slippery, but his soft-soled shoes, required for stealth, gripped the rock well enough.

He reached the top of the flat-surfaced cliff in a broad open area. To his right was the Propylaea and the little temple of Athene Nike. To his left, the Erechtheum, with its Caryatids patiently holding up the roof as they had for twenty-five hundred years. The marble maidens stared blindly at Keating. He glanced at them, then looked across the width of the clifftop to the half-ruined Parthenon, the most beautiful building on Earth, a monument both to man's creative genius and his destructive folly.

The rain had slackened, but the night was still as dark as the deepest pit of hell. Keating brought the snooperscope up to his eyes again and scanned from left to right.

And there stood Rungawa! Directly in front of the Parthenon, standing there with his arms upraised, as if praying.

Too far away for the dart gun, Keating knew. For some reason, his hands started to shake. Slowly, struggling for absolute self-control, Keating put the "camera" back into his trench coat and took out the pistol. He rose to his feet and began walking toward Rungawa with swift but unhurried, measured strides.

The old man's back was to him. All you have to do, Keating told himself, is to get within a few feet, pop the dart into his neck, and then wait a couple of minutes to make certain the dart dissolves. Then go down the way you came and back to the *pensione* for a hot bath and a bracer of cognac.

As he came to within ten feet of Rungawa he raised the dart gun. It worked on air pressure, practically noiseless. No need to cock it. Five feet. He could see the nails on Rungawa's upraised hands, the pinkish palms contrasting with the black skin of the fingers and the backs of his hands. Three feet. Rungawa's suit was perfectly fitted to him, the sleeves creased carefully. Dry. He was wearing only a business suit, and it was untouched by the rain, as well-creased and unwrinkled as if it had just come out of the store.

"Not yet, Mr. Keating," said the old man, without turning to look at Jeremy. "We have a few things to talk about before you kill me."

Keating froze. He could not move his arm. It stood ramrod straight from his left shoulder, the tiny dart gun in his fist a mere two feet from Rungawa's bare neck. But he could not pull the trigger. His fingers would not obey the commands of his mind.

Rungawa turned toward him, smiling, and stroked his chin thoughtfully for a moment.

"You may put the gun down now, Mr. Keating."

Jeremy's arm dropped to his side. His mouth sagged open; his heart thundered in his ears. He wanted to run away, but his legs were like the marble of the statues that watched them.

"Forgive me," said Rungawa. "I should not leave you out in the rain like that."

The rain stopped pelting Jeremy. He felt a gentle warmth enveloping him, as if he were standing next to a welcoming fireplace. The two men stood under a cone of invisible protection. Jeremy could see the raindrops spattering on the stony ground not more than a foot away.

"A small trick. Please don't be alarmed." Rungawa's

voice was a deep rumbling bass, like the voice a lion would have if it could speak in human tongue.

Jeremy stared into the black man's eyes and saw no danger in them, no hatred or violence; only a patient amusement at his own consternation. No, more: a tolerance of human failings, a hope for human achievement, an *understanding* born of centuries of toil and pain and striving.

"Who are you?" Jeremy asked in a frightened whisper.

Rungawa smiled, and it was like sunlight breaking through the storm clouds. "Ah, Mr. Keating, you are as intelligent as we had hoped. You cut straight to the heart of the matter."

"You knew I was following you. You set up this . . . meeting."

"Yes. Yes, quite true. Melodramatic of me, I admit. But would you have joined me at dinner if I had sent one of my aides across the street to invite you? I think not."

It's all crazy, Jeremy thought. I must be dreaming this.

"No, Mr. Keating. It is not a dream."

An electric jolt flamed through Jeremy. Jesus Chirst, he can read my mind!

"Of course I can," Rungawa said gently, smiling, the way a doctor tells a child that the needle will hurt only for an instant. "How else would I know that you were stalking me?"

Jeremy's mouth went utterly dry. His voice cracked and failed him. If he had been able to move his legs he would have fled like a chimpanzee confronted by a leopard.

"Please do not be afraid, Mr. Keating. Fear is an impediment to understanding. If we had wanted to kill you, it would have been most convenient to let you slip while you were climbing up here."

"What . . ." Jeremy had to swallow and lick his lips before he could say, "Just who are you?"

"I am a messenger, Mr. Keating. Like you, I am merely a tool of my superiors. When I was assigned to this task, I thought it appropriate to make my home base in Tanzania." The old man's smile returned, and a hint of self-satisfaction glowed in his eyes. "After all, Tanzania is where the earliest human tribes once lived. What more appropriate place for me to—um, shall we say, *associate* myself with the human race?"

"Associate . . . with the human race." Jeremy felt breathless, weak. His voice was hollow.

"I am not a human being, Mr. Keating. I come from a far-distant world, a world that is nothing like this one."

"No . . . that can't . . ."

Rungawa's smile slowly faded. "Some of your people call me a saint. Actually, compared to your species, I am a god."

Jeremy stared at him, stared into his deep black eyes, and saw eternity in them, whirlpools of galaxies spinning majestically in infinite depths of space, stars exploding and evolving, worlds created out of dust.

He heard his voice, weak and childlike, say, "But you look human."

"Of course! Completely human. Even to your x-ray machines."

An alien. Jeremy's mind reeled. An extraterrestrial. With a sense of humor.

"Why not? Is not humor part of the human psyche? The intelligences who created me made me much more than human, but I have every human attribute—except one. I have no need for vengeance, Mr. Keating."

"Vengeance," Jeremy echoed.

"Yes. A destructive trait. It clouds the perceptions. It is an obstacle in the path of survival."

Jeremy took a deep breath, tried to pull himself together. "You expect me to believe all this?"

"I can see that you do, Mr. Keating. I can see that you now realize that not *all* the UFO stories have been hoaxes. We have never harmed any of your people, but we did require specimens for careful analysis."

"Why?"

"To help you find the correct path to survival. Your species is on the edge of a precipice. It is our duty to help you avoid extinction, if we can."

"Your duty?"

"Of course. Do not your best people feel an obligation to save other species from extinction? Have not these human beings risked their fortunes and their very lives to protect creatures such as the whale and the seal from slaughter?"

Jeremy almost laughed. "You mean you're from some interstellar Greenpeace project?"

"It is much more complex than that," Rungawa said. "We are not merely trying to protect you from a predator, or from an ecological danger. You human beings are your own worst enemy. We must protect you from yourselves—without your knowing it."

Before Jeremy could reply, Rungawa went on, "It would be easy for us to create a million creatures like myself and to land on your planet in great, shining ships and give you all the answers you need for survival. Fusion energy? A toy. World peace? Easily accomplished. Quadruple your global food production? Double your intelligence? Make you immune to every disease? All this we can do."

"Then why . . ." Jeremy hesitated, thinking. "If you did all that for us, it would ruin us, wouldn't it?"

Rungawa beamed at him. "Ah, you truly understand the problem! Yes, it would destroy your species, just as your Europeans destroyed the cultures of the Americas and Polynesia. Your anthropologists are wrong. There are superior cultures and inferior ones. A superior culture always crushes an inferior, even if it has no intention of doing so."

In the back of his mind, Jeremy realized that he had control of his legs again. He flexed the fingers of his left hand slightly, even the index finger that still curled around the trigger of the dart gun. He could move them at will once more.

"What you're saying," he made conversation, "is that if you landed here and gave us everything we want, our culture would be destroyed."

"Yes," Rungawa agreed. "Just as surely as you whites destroyed the black and brown cultures of the world. We have no desire to do that to you."

"So you're trying to lead us to the point where we can solve our own problems."

"Precisely so, Mr. Keating."

"That's why you've started this World Government," Keating said, his hand tightening on the gun.

"You started the World Government yourselves," Rungawa corrected. "We merely encouraged you, here and there."

"Like the riots in Tunis and a hundred other places."

"We did not encourage that."

"But you didn't prevent them, either, did you?"

"No. We did not."

Shifting his weight slightly to the balls of his feet, Keating said, "Without you the World Government will collapse."

The old man shook his head. "No, that is not true. Despite what your superiors believe, the World Government will endure even the death of 'the Black Saint.' "

"Are you sure?" Keating raised the gun to the black man's eye level. "Are you absolutely certain?"

Rungawa did not blink. His voice became sad as he answered, "Would I have relaxed my control of your limbs if I were not certain?"

Keating hesitated, but held the gun rock-steady.

"You are the test, Mr. Keating. You are the key to your species' future. We know how your wife and son died. Even though we were not directly responsible, we regret their deaths. And the deaths of all the others. They were unavoidable losses."

"Statistics," Keating spat. "Numbers on a list."

"Never! Each of them was an individual whom *we* knew much better than you could, and we regretted each loss of life as much as you do yourself. Perhaps more, because we understand what each of those individuals could have accomplished, had they lived."

"But you let them die."

"It was unavoidable, I say. Now the question is, Can you rise above your own personal tragedy for the good of your fellow humans? Or will you take vengeance upon me and see your species destroy itself?"

"You just said the World Government will survive your death."

"And it will. But it will change. It will become a world dictatorship, in time. It will smother your progress. Your species will die out in an agony of overpopulation, starvation, disease and terrorism. You do not need nuclear bombs to kill yourselves. You can manage it quite well enough merely by producing too many babies."

"Our alternative is to let your people direct us, to become sheep without even knowing it, to jump to your tune."

"No!" Rungawa's deep voice boomed. "The alternative is to become adults. You are adolescents now. We offer you the chance to grow up and stand on your own feet."

"How can I believe that?" Keating demanded.

The old man's smile showed weariness. "The adolescent always distrusts the parent. That is the painful truth, is it not?"

"You have an answer for everything, don't you?"

"Everything, perhaps, except you. You are the key to your species' future, Mr. Keating. If you can accept what I have told you, and allow us to work with you despite all your inner thirst for vengeance, then the human species will have a chance to survive."

Keating moved his hand a bare centimeter to the left and squeezed the gun's trigger. The dart shot out with a hardly audible puff of compressed air and whizzed past Rungawa's ear. The old man did not flinch.

"You can kill me if you want to," he said to Keating. "That is your decision to make."

"I don't believe you," Jeremy said. "I can't believe you! It's too much, it's too incredible. You can't expect a man to accept everything you've just told me—not all at once!"

"We do expect it," Rungawa said softly. "We expect that and more. We want you working with us, not against us."

Jeremy felt as if his guts were being torn apart. "Work with you?" he screamed. "With the people who murdered my wife and son?"

"There are other children in the world. Do not deny them their birthright. Do not foreclose their future."

"You bastard!" Jeremy seethed. "You don't miss a trick, do you?"

"It all depends on you, Mr. Keating. You are our test case. What you do now will decide the future of the human species."

A thousand emotions raged through Jeremy. He saw Joanna being torn apart by the mob and Jerry in his cot screaming with fever, flames and death everywhere, the filth and poverty of Jakarta and the vicious smile of the interrogator as he sharpened his razor.

He's lying, Jeremy's mind shouted at him. He's got to be lying. All this is some clever set of tricks. It can't be true. It can't be!

In a sudden paroxysm of rage and terror and frustration Jeremy hurled the gun high into the rain-filled night, turned abruptly and walked away from Rungawa. He did not look back, but he knew the old man was smiling at him.

It's a trick, he kept telling himself. A goddamned trick. He knew damned well I couldn't kill him in cold blood, with him standing there looking at me with those damned sad eyes of his. Shoot an old man in the face. I just couldn't do it. All he had to do was keep me talking long enough to lose my nerve. Goddamned clever black man. Must be how he lived to get so old.

Keating stamped down the marble steps of the Sacred Way, pushed past the three raincoated guards who had accompanied Rungawa, and walked alone and miserable back to the *pensione*.

How the hell am I going to explain this back at headquarters? I'll have to resign, tell them that I'm not cut out to be an assassin. They'll never believe that. Maybe I could get a transfer, get back into the political section, join the Peace Corps, anything!

He was still furious with himself when he reached the *pensione*. Still shaking his head, angry that he had let the old man talk him out of his assigned mission. Some form of hypnosis, Keating thought. He must have been a medicine man or a voodoo priest when he was younger.

He pushed through the glassed front door of the *pensione*, muttering to himself. "You let him trick you. You let that old black man hoodwink you."

The room clerk roused himself from his slumber and got up to reach Jeremy's room key from the rack behind the desk. He was a short, sturdily-built Greek, the kind who would have faced the Persians at Marathon.

"You must have run very fast," he said to Keating in heavily accented English.

"Huh? What? Why do you say that?"

The clerk grinned, revealing tobacco-stained teeth. "You did not get wet."

Keating looked at the sleeve of his trench coat. It was perfectly dry. The whole coat was as clean and dry as if it had just come from a pressing. His feet were dry; his shoes and trousers and hat were dry.

He turned and looked out the front window. The rain was coming down harder than ever, a torrent of water.

"You run so fast you go between raindrops, eh?" The clerk laughed at his own joke.

Jeremy's knees nearly buckled. He leaned against the desk. "Yeah. Something like that."

The clerk, still grinning, handed him his room key. Jeremy gathered his strength and headed for the stairs, his head spinning.

As he went up the first flight, he heard a voice, even though he was quite alone on the carpeted stairs.

"A small kindness, Mr. Keating," said Rungawa, inside his mind. "I thought it would have been a shame to make you get wet all over again. A small kindness. There will be more to come."

Keating could hear Rungawa chuckling as he walked alone up the stairs. By the time he reached his room, he was grinning himself.

Galactic Geopolitics

Do the kindly, concerned aliens hinted at in *A Small Kindness* actually exist, somewhere out in the depths of interstellar space? Despite the utter lack of evidence, I firmly believe that intelligent life does exist elsewhere in the universe. But I wonder if the old science fiction dream of intelligent civilizations that are far older, wiser and technologically superior to humankind might not just be dead wrong. In *Galactic Geopolitics* I tried to look at what we know of the laws of physics and chemistry, and the shape of the observable universe, to come to some conclusions about where and when we might find intelligent alien civilizations.

Interestingly, these speculations, originally written more than a dozen years ago, have become an "in" subject among astronomers and cosmologists. Symposia have been held to discuss the problem of where They might be and why They have not visited Earth.

Even here, the participants seems to break down into Luddites and Prometheans, pessimists and optimists. And the argument will continue unless and until we do find Them—or (worse luck) They find us.

Let's assume that contact with another intelligent race is inevitable. Sooner or later they will come to visit us, or we'll stumble into them once we get our starships cruising across the Milky Way.

It seems almost certain that we won't find another intelligent species among the planets of our own solar system. Mars and Venus have been blasted from our hopes by the pitiless advance of knowledge, thanks to space probes. Mercury, Pluto and our own Moon were never really counted on as habitats for intelligent races. And the Jovian planets—Jupiter, Saturn, Uranus and Neptune—are *too* alien for us. More on them later.

If we find another intelligent race, it will be out among the stars. Assuming that brainy aliens are out there, what are the chances of having any meaningful, fruitful contacts with them? Not just radio chats, not just an occasional awe-inspiring visit. Real, long-term, continuous interaction, the way the United States interacts with the other nations of Earth—trade, cultural interpenetration, tourism, politics, war.

This all depends, of course, on attaining starflight. More than that, it has to be fast, cheap interstellar transportation. Otherwise there can be no large-scale interactions, no politics or trade, between us and them.

Look at a parallel from Earth's history.

Since at least Roman times, Western Europe knew that China and the Orient existed. In the Middle Ages, Marco Polo got there and back, spreading wondrous tales that grew each year. But Europe didn't interact with China in any significant way. True, Europe engaged in trade with the Arab Middle East and obtained goods from China through Arab middlemen. The Middle East was close enough for Europeans to reach on foot if they had no other way to get there. Europe traded with the Middle East, exchanged scholarly works— which is why most of the stars in the sky have Arabic names—and engaged in the pious slaughters called the Crusades.

But there was no direct trade, and no conflict, with China. Once deep-ocean sailing vessels were perfected, though, Europe did indeed contact China directly and treated the Orient to Western technology, trade, disease and war. Today, of course, with intercontinental rockets and instant communications, everybody on the globe can interact politically with everybody else.

The same rules will apply to interstellar politics. There

may be glorious civilizations in the Orion complex, or even as close as Alpha Centauri. But we know less about them than Hannibal knew about China. No action.

Yet even today it is possible to visualize starships based on technology that is tantalizingly close to our grasp. If and when we can make trips to the nearest stars within a human lifetime, we'll have reached the Marco Polo stage of interstellar contact—adventure, strange tales and stranger artifacts. But no lasting political relations, for better or worse, with the neighbors.

There would be little tourism, except of a scientific variety, when a person could visit the exotic land only once in a lifetime, and the trip would consume a fair portion of his life-span. It is also hard to picture commerce and trade relations based on one ship per human generation. That's more like a cultural exchange. And even the sternest, most fearless and ruthless general might feel a bit foolish about mounting an attack when he knew he could never see the outcome in his own lifetime.

But the real importance of Marco Polo's adventure was the spur it gave to Prince Henry the Navigator and others, including Christopher Columbus. And the importance of the first interstellar contact will be the stimulus it gives to us on Earth.

Now, if you corner a theoretical physicist, the chances are that you can start him mumbling about tachyons and things that go faster than light. Einstein's light barrier is starting to look—well, not leaky, perhaps, but at least a little translucent. Perhaps one day ships will be able to zip among the stars at speeds far greater than light.

Since we're dealing with improbabilities, let's consider this one. With faster-than-light ships, we can get just as close and chummy with our stellar neighbors as we are today with the Chinese.

But we must realize that there will be many races out among the stars that we simply *cannot* interact with in any useful way, even though we may be able to reach them physically.

We may, for example, find races much younger than our own, with a correspondingly simple technology and social development. Aside from letting them worship us as gods, there's probably little that we could do for them—or they could do for us.

Certainly we would want to study them and learn more about how intelligence and societies evolve. That would be best done from orbit, where we could remain "invisible" and not disturb them in any way. What could they offer us, except for their own artifacts or bodies? The artifacts might be interesting as examples of alien art. And no matter how lopsided or gruesome they appear, there will arise at least one art critic who will explain the hidden aesthetic values that everybody else had missed and sell the stuff at a huge markup.

And their bodies?

We wouldn't use them for meat, for a number of reasons. If their bodies contained some precious chemical substances that couldn't be found elsewhere—the key to immortality or something equally exotic—we would be in a lovely ethical bind. But the chances for that sort of situation are vanishingly small. We certainly would not need muscular slaves in our technological society—electricity is cheaper. And we have laws about such things, anyway.

And what could we offer our younger neighbors? Only the things that would destroy their culture as surely as Western Europe destroyed the American Indians. We hope that by the time we reach such a race, we'll have learned not to interfere with them.

If we should try to meddle with a race that's only slightly younger or technologically weaker than we are, their reaction could very well be the same as the Indians'—they would resist us as strongly as they could, probably with guerrilla warfare. We found out in Vietnam exactly what Custer learned nearly a century ago—that "unsophisticated" and "simple" people can use our own technology very effectively against us. But the Indians were either killed or absorbed into our culture, and the Vietnamese are going through the same process. That part of the world will never again be a simple, unspoiled, isolated Asian backwater. The same thing would probably happen to a younger race that fights against us: the very act of resistance will destroy their native culture.

What happens when we contact a race much more advanced than we are? The same situation, only in reverse. We would have precious little to offer them, except possibly curiosity value. And they would be wise enough not to tamper with us. We hope. Playing Cowboys and Indians is no fun when you're on the foredoomed side.

A really far advanced race would most likely go its own way aloof and serene, even if we tried our hardest to make friends. The picture that comes to mind is a puppydog chasing a monorail train.

That leaves us with races that are more or less at our own stage of development, intellectually, morally and technologically. *That's* where the fun—and the danger—will be.

How much of a range is covered by "more or less" is rather hard to say. For a thumbnail definition, let's put it this way: We will interact strongly with races that have something to gain from us, and vice versa. Cavemen and angels have so little in common with us that they won't affect us very much, nor will we affect them. But other humans, even if they're purple and have sixteen legs, will provide the interstellar action.

Further, the races we interact with will probably come from planets enough like our own to make this Earth attractive to them. And their home worlds will similarly be attractive —or at least bearable—to us. This is why, even if intelligent Jovians exist under Jupiter's clouds—or Saturn's or Neptune's or Uranus's—we probably will interact with them about as much as we do with the denizens of the Marianas Trench. There's just no common meeting ground. We don't have political relations with dolphins, even if they are as intelligent as we are. We have nothing to trade or fight over.

So it boils down to this: Although we may meet many strange and marvelous races among the stars, if they are physically or intellectually far removed from us we will have little but the most cursory of contacts with them—except for scientific expeditions.

Yet the races that can stand on our planet in their shirtsleeves, or at least a minimum of protective equipment, and have a technology of a roughly similar level to our own, will be the races that we will talk with, laugh with, trade with and fight with. It may be that intelligent life is too thinly scattered through the Milky Way's stars for us to expect to find such a race close enough to us—close enough in distance *and* maturity—to make interstellar politics likely.

Just what are the chances of meeting another intelligent race that is at our own stage of development, give or take 10,000 years? Below that level are cavemen. Much above that level and we're in the realm of highly advanced civilizations that would regard *us* as cavemen.

The chances for meeting neighbors with whom we can truly interact seem mighty slim. But let's look around anyway and see what the real universe holds for us.

There are 37 stars within 5 parsecs of the Sun. Of these 37 stars, 27 are single, 8 are binary, or double, stars and 2 are triples. Four of these stars are known to have "dark companions"—bodies of planetary mass that are too faint and small to be seen. In fact, two of the nearest five stars have planets. Since planets are extremely difficult to detect, we might suspect that there are plenty of them orbiting the farther stars, but we just cannot perceive them from here.

If the population density of stars is about the same as we go farther away from the Sun, then there should be something like 300,000 stars within 100 parsecs of us, and some 300 million stars within 1,000 parsecs. As we have seen, the Milky Way galaxy as a whole contains more than 100 billion stars. Our galaxy is roughly 30,000 parsecs in diameter, and our solar system is some 10,000 parsecs out from the center.

We have no way of knowing how rare intelligence is. But in every cosmological test that has been applied to the Earth and solar system so far, we find absolutely no evidence for our own uniqueness. Quite the opposite. The Sun is a rather average star. It appears that planets form around stars naturally. Planets at our temperature range from their star should turn out to look roughly like Earth, with plenty of liquid water. Life on those planets should be based on carbon, oxygen and water, making use of some of the most abundant materials and most energetic chemical reactions available. Given enough time, the natural forces that led to the evolution of life on Earth would lead to similar results on similar worlds.

The real question is, What are the ages of the stars around

us? If they are about the same age as the Sun, we might expect to find interesting neighbors.

The Sun's age has been pegged at roughly 5 billion years. This is based chiefly on estimates of the amount of the Sun's original hydrogen that has been converted into helium through the hydrogen fusion processes that make the Sun shine. In turn, these estimates are based largely on theory, since no one can look inside the Sun and actually measure the ratio of hydrogen to helium there. In fact, no one knows how much helium, if any, the Sun had when it first began to shine. But 5 billion years is a reasonable guesstimate, and it tallies well with the ages of the oldest rocks of the Earth, the Moon and the meteorites.

Many of the stars around the Sun are clearly much younger. Table 1 shows the classes of typical stars according to their spectra, together with estimates of their stable life-spans. By "stable life-span" we mean the length of time that the star is on the Main Sequence.

To explain: Stars go through an evolutionary path, a life-span, much as do living creatures. In the vastness of the Milky Way, stars are constantly being born and dying. The evolutionary path for an ordinary star, such as the Sun, goes like this:

1. A "protostar" condenses out of interstellar gas and dust. The protostar, a dark clump of mostly hydrogen, is about a light-year wide. It contracts rapidly, falling inward on itself under the gravitational force of its own mass. As it contracts, it naturally gets denser and hotter. Its interior temperature rises sharply.

2. When the density and temperature at the core of the protostar reach a critical value, hydrogen fusion reactions are triggered. The gravitational collapse stops, because now heat and light produced by fusion are making outward-pushing pressures that balance the inward-pulling gravity. The star shines with fusion energy; it becomes a stable member of the great family of stars that astronomers call the Main Sequence. Its size and surface temperature will remain stable as long as hydrogen fusion provides the star's energy source.

3. The bigger and more massive the star is to start with, the hotter it is, and the faster it runs through its hydrogen fuel

TABLE 1. *Spectral Classes and Life-spans of Stars*

SPEC-TRAL CLASS	SURFACE TEM-PERATURE (°'s KELVIN)	COLOR	STABLE LIFE-SPAN	EXAMPLE
B	11,000–25,000	blue	8 to 400 million yrs.	Rigel, Spica
A	7,500–11,000	blue-white	400 million to 4 billion yrs.	Sirius, Vega
F	6,000–7,500	white	4 to 10 billion yrs.	Canopus, Procyon
G	5,000–6,000	yellow	10 to 30 billion yrs.	Sun, Capella, Alpha Centauri A
K	3,500–5,000	orange	30 to 70 billion yrs.	Arcturus, Aldebaran, Alpha Centauri B
M*	below 3,500	red	more than 70 billion yrs.	Alpha Centauri C, Barnard's star

*Red supergiant stars such as Betelgeuse and Antares are not Main Sequence stars, therefore their stable life-spans in no way correspond with those of the red M-class dwarfs shown on this table.

supply. When the hydrogen runs low, the star begins burning the helium "ash" that is left in its core. Helium fusion, producing oxygen, neon and carbon, runs hotter than hydrogen fusion. The star's central temperature soars, and the outer layers of the star are forced to expand. The star is no longer a Main Sequence member—astronomers call it a red giant. Soon, in astronomical time scales, the helium runs low, and the star begins burning the heavier elements in its core. The star continues to create, and then burn, constantly heavier elements. All the while, the core is getting hotter and the star's outer envelope is swelling enormously. When the Sun goes into its red giant phase, it may get so large that it swallows its inner planets—including Earth.

4. Eventually the star reaches a critical point. It explodes. There are several different types of stellar explosions, and several courses that the evolutionary track might take from

there. For now, we need only realize that the eventual outcome of this stellar violence is a white dwarf star (a fading dim star about the diameter of the Earth or smaller) or an even tinier, denser neutron star. Neutron stars are probably no more than ten kilometers across, yet they contain as much material as the Sun! They are fantastically dense. The pulsars, whose uncannily precise pulses of radio energy led briefly to the "LGM (Little Green Men) theory," are probably fast-spinning neutron stars.

As we can see, a star remains stable for only a certain finite period of time, depending on its mass and temperature. After that, things get pretty dramatic for any planet-dwelling life nearby.

Hot blue giants such as Rigel and Spica won't be stable for more than a few hundred million years. While this is a long time in terms of human life-spans, it is an eyeblink in terms of evolution. This means that such stars cannot be more than a few hundred million years old. In all probability, the dinosaurs never saw Rigel. It wasn't there yet.

We know that it took about 5 billion years for intelligent life to develop on Earth. As a rule of thumb, lacking any better evidence, we can say that we shouldn't expect to find intelligent life on planets circling stars that are less than 5 billion years old. So Rigel and the other young blue giants can probably be ruled out as possible abodes for intelligent life.

The stars that are smaller and cooler than the Sun, such as the K and M dwarfs, have much longer life expectancies. But are they older than the Sun? There's no easy way to tell.

We might be able to get some clues to their ages by looking farther afield. Consider the "geography" of the Milky Way.

The Milky Way is, of course, a spiral galaxy very much like the beautiful nebula in Andromeda. The core of our galaxy is presumably thick with stars, but we never see the core because it is hidden behind thick clouds of interstellar dust. Radio and infrared observations have been able to penetrate the clouds to some extent, and observations of the central regions of other galaxies show that they are so rich with stars that these stars are probably no more than a single light-year from each other, at most.

Stars in the core of a galaxy are also presumably much older than the Sun—red giant stars are common there, and astrophysical theory shows that stars become red giants only after they have used up most of their hydrogen fuel and have ended their stable Main Sequence phases. Also, in the cores of galaxies there are no young, hot, blue giants such as Rigel and Spica. These are found only in the spiral arms of galaxies.

Because the core regions of spiral galaxies seem to have different types of stars, predominantly, than the spiral arms, astronomers refer to the two different stellar constituencies as Population I and Population II. And thereby they sometimes cause confusion.

Population I stars are the kind our Sun lives among. These are the youngish stars of the spiral arms. Their brightest members are the blue giants. Population I stars contain a relatively high proportion of elements heavier than hydrogen and helium. Although the proportion of heavy elements hardly ever amounts to more than one percent, the Population I stars are said to be "metal-rich."

Population II stars are those found in the core regions of a galaxy. They are old, their brightest members are red giants, and they are mostly "metal-poor."

The heavy-element content of a star is an important clue to its history. Why are the stars in a galaxy's core metal-poor and the stars in the spiral arms metal-rich? Because the elements heavier than hydrogen have been created inside the stars. It works this way:

Consider the Milky Way before there were any stars. Cosmologists have estimated that the Milky Way is between 10 and 20 billion years old, that is, some two to four times older than the Sun. Presumably, the whole universe is the same age as the Milky Way. But when you are dealing with tens of billions of years, the numbers tend to get imprecise and hazy.

Regardless of the exact age of our galaxy, it began as an immense dark cloud of gas at least 30,000 parsecs across. The gas might have been entirely hydrogen, or it might have been a hydrogen-helium mixture. Where this gas originally came from is a mystery that cosmologists argue about, but no one has been able to prove which side of their argument is right—if either.

The first stars to form had no elements heavier than helium in them. Perhaps nothing more than hydrogen. All the heavier elements, from lithium to iron, were "cooked" inside these stars as they went from hydrogen-burning to helium-burning to heavier-element-burning. Some of these stars exploded, in the last stages of their lives, with the titanic fury of the supernova. In those star-shattering explosions, still heavier elements were created, beyond iron, all the way up to uranium and even beyond that. There's some evidence that the so-called "man-made" element, Californium 254, was present in the supernova of A.D. 1054, which we know today as the Crab nebula.

So the first generation of stars in the Milky Way began with only hydrogen—perhaps laced with a smattering of helium—and eventually produced all the heavier elements. And the stars threw these heavier elements back into space, where they served as the building material for the next generation of stars. The explosions that marked the death throes of the first-generation stars enriched the interstellar clouds with heavy elements. It is from these clouds that new stars are born.

Judging by the heavy-element content in the stars, most astrophysicists estimate that the Sun must be a third-generation star, a grandson of the original stars of the Milky Way. The elements inside the Sun today were once inside other stars. The atoms that make up the solar system were created inside other stars. The atoms of your own body were made in stars. We are truly star children.

Beware of a clash of jargon when we talk about generations of stars and Population I or II. Population I stars are the younger, late-generation stars. Population II stars are the older, early-generation stars. II came before I, historically.

What has all this to do with meeting the neighbors?

Just this: The first-generation stars *could not produce life*. At least, nothing that we would recognize as life. There was no carbon, no oxygen, no nitrogen . . . nothing but hydrogen and perhaps some helium. If those first stars had planets, they would all be frozen ice balls of hydrogen, somewhat like

Jupiter but not so colorful, because there would be no ammonia or methane or any other chemical compounds to cause gaudy streaks of colored clouds such as we see on Jupiter and Saturn. There wouldn't even be any water. Not yet.

Second-generation stars? It's possible that they would have most of the heavier elements, including the carbon, oxygen, nitrogen, potassium, iron and such that we need to develop life. Planets of such stars might be able to support life, even our own kind of life, if these heavier elements were present in sufficient quantities. And if life has appeared on such planets, there's no reason to suppose it wouldn't eventually attain intelligence. Certainly the long-lived red dwarf stars provide plenty of time for intelligence to develop—5 billion years plus.

Let's grant that an intelligent race could arise on the planetary system of a second-generation star. Could such a race develop a high civilization and technology? It all depends on the abundance of natural resources. Fossil fuels such as coal and oil should be plentiful, since they are the result of the biodegrading of plant and animal remains. But what about metals? Our technology here on Earth is built around metals. Even our history rings with the sounds of the Bronze Age, the Iron Age, the Steel Age, the Uranium Age.

Astronomical evidence is indistinct here. Theory shows that second-generation stars should have a lesser abundance of metals than we third-generation types have. But certainly there should be some metals on second-generation planets.

How much metal is enough? There's no way for us to tell. Planets of second-generation stars might have iron mountains and gold nuggets lying on the open ground. Or they might have very little available metal. Our own Jupiter might easily have more iron in it than Earth does. But if it's there, the iron is mixed with 317.4 Earth-masses of hydrogen, helium, methane, ammonia and whatnot. Try to find it! And get at it!

If there are planets of second-generation stars where heavy metals—iron, copper, silver, tin, gold—are abundant and available, those planets could be sites for highly advanced civilizations. But suppose intelligent races arise on planets where heavy metals are not available? What then?

First, we should clearly realize that intelligence per se does not depend on heavy metals. *Life*, though, does, to some extent. There's an atom of iron at the core of every hemoglobin molecule in your body. And hemoglobin is what makes your red blood cells work. So without iron, and certain other heavy metals, we wouldn't be here!

Mankind rose to intelligence before he discovered heavy metals. He used wood, clay, rock and animal bones for his first technology. In a way, man went through a Ceramics Age, working mostly with clay, before he found metals. In fact, it was wood and ceramics that allowed man to handle fire safely and usefully. Only after fire had been tamed could men start to use metals on a large scale.

The history of man shows that once metals became available, we took a giant leap forward. Metals allowed men to build effective plows. And swords. And chariots. Even today our skyscrapers and computers and engines and spacecraft and weapons and household appliances are made mainly from metals. Metals are strong, tough and cheap. They are rather easily found and easily worked, even with low-grade fire.

Could a race build skyscrapers and spacecraft without metals? Well, today there are many "space age" materials such as plastics and boron-fiber composites. But the machinery that produces them is made of stainless steel, copper, brass, etc. Modern technology is showing that there are nonmetallic materials that can outperform metals in strength, weight and many other performance parameters. But these materials couldn't have been developed before an extensive Metal Age technology. Cavemen, or even the ancient Greeks, could not have produced boron-fiber composites or modern plastics. They didn't have the metals to produce them with!

Would a metal-poor second-generation intelligent race be stymied in its attempts at technology? Who can say? All we know for sure is that *our* technology certainly depends on metals, and until metals were available, our ancestors had no civilization or technology higher than Neolithic.

Another vital point. While we have nothing but the history of our own race to go on, it looks very much as if the whole world of electromagnetic forces would never have been discovered without metals such as iron and copper. Man's discovery of magnetism depended on the abundance of iron on this planet. And from the very beginnings of our experiments with electricity, we used lead, zinc, copper, brass, etc. It's hard to see how the entire chain of study and use of electromagnetic forces—from Volta and Faraday and Hertz through to radio telescopes and television and superconducting magnets—could have happened on a metal-poor planet. And where would our technology be without electricity? Back in the early nineteenth century, at best.

So what about the metal-poor second-generation races? It just might be possible to build a complex technology completely out of nonmetals. But tribes on Earth that never had easy access to heavy metals have never developed a high technology. Coincidence? Maybe.

Could a strong technology be built around the lighter metals, such as lithium, beryllium or boron? Ironically (pardon the pun) those metals are much less abundant in the universe than the heavier metals (iron and up). And for good reason. The light metals make excellent "fuel" for the nuclear fusion reactions inside stars. They are used up inside a star before it explodes and spews out its material for later generations. So the chances of having a sophisticated civilization based on light metals seem slim indeed.

If our own history is any guide, it is the heavy metals that lead to high technology. And they also form a natural gateway into the world of electromagnetic forces and the whole concept of "invisible" forces that act over a distance: magnetism, electricity, gravity, nuclear forces. We can trace a direct line from man's use of heavy metals to electromagnetics, nuclear power, and, we hope, beyond.

For second-generation stars the situation is much cloudier. Either they have enough heavy metals to develop a high technology or they don't. If they do, their races are much older and presumably wiser than we are. Which means they probably won't interact with us at all. We would probably bore them to tears, or whatever they have in place of tears.

Second-generation races that don't have metals are no doubt gamboling innocently through some local version of Eden, and we should leave them strictly alone.

There goes the long-standing science-fiction vision of an immense galactic empire, run by the older and wiser races of the Milky Way's ancient core regions. Like the "steaming jungles" of Venus and desert "cities" of Mars, the empire at the center of the galaxy simply doesn't exist. The first-generation stars produced no life. If there are second-generation intelligences around, chances are they're either *so* far advanced beyond us that empires are meaningless trivialities to them, or they're so metal-starved that they never got past the "Me Tarzan" stage of development.

It's a shame. It would have been pleasant to talk to them—those incredibly ancient, benign and understanding superbeings from the galaxy's core. It's sort of shattering to realize that, if anyone like them does exist, they wouldn't want to be bothered with our chatterings any more than a crotchety grandfather wants to put up with a squalling baby.

On the other hand, science fiction stories abound in which a race only slightly advanced over us—say, a few centuries—does a very ruthless job of conquering Earth. So maybe we should be glad if there's no one older who is interested in us.

Of course, an older race might be benign. If so, it would probably not reveal its presence to us, for fear of damaging irreparably our culture and our spirit. They would prefer to wait until we could meet them on a more equal footing. The "equality" point might be when we've achieved successful starflight for ourselves.

If an older race is not benign, but aggressive, then it might want to gobble us up before we had reached the stage of starflight. That way, we would be alone and defenseless against them.

So if we should be visited by aliens from another solar system *before* we achieve starflight, my hunch is that their intentions will be far from pleasant—no matter what they say.

But the chances of meeting another race that is even within a few centuries of our present stage of development seem rather remote. And remember, the Sun is one of the oldest third-generation stars around this part of the galaxy. There might not be any older races within thousands of parsecs of us.

Could it be that *we* are the oldest, wisest, farthest-advanced race in this neck of the stellar woods?

Now, that's a truly sobering thought!

Priorities

A well-known writer once pontificated that there are only three plots for fiction: (1) Boy meets girl; (2) If this goes on . . . ; and (3) The man who learns better. Well, here's a short-short story about a couple of frustrated Prometheans that might be summarized as a fourth kind of plot: Put the shoe on the other foot.

Dr. Ira Lefko sat rigidly nervous on the edge of the plastic-cushioned chair. He was a slight man, thin, bald, almost timid-looking. Even his voice was gentle and reedy, like the fine thin tone of an English horn.

And just as the English horn is a sadly misnamed woodwind, Dr. Ira Lefko was actually neither timid nor particularly gentle. At this precise moment he was close to mayhem.

"Ten years of work," he was saying, with a barely controlled tremor in his voice. "You're going to wipe out ten years of work with a shake of your head."

The man shaking his head was sitting behind the metal desk that Lefko sat in front of. His name was Harrison Bower. His title and name were prominently displayed on a handsome plate atop the desk. Harrison Bower kept a very neat desktop. All the papers were primly stacked and both the IN and OUT baskets were empty.

"Can't be helped," said Harrison Bower, with a tight smile that was supposed to be sympathetic and understanding. "Everyone's got to tighten the belt. Reordering priorities, you know. There are many research programs going by the boards— New times, new problems, new priorities. You're not the only one to be affected."

With his somber face and dark suit Bower looked like a funeral director—which he was. In the vast apparatus of government, his job was to bury research projects that had run out of money. It was just about the only thing on Earth that made him smile.

The third man in the poorly ventilated little Washington office was Major Robert Shawn, from the Air Force Cambridge Research Laboratories. In uniform, Major Shawn looked an awful lot like Hollywood's idea of a jet pilot. In the casual slacks and sportcoat he was wearing now, he somehow gave the vague impression of being an engineer, or perhaps even a far-eyed scientist.

He was something of all three.

Dr. Lefko was getting red in the face. "But you *can't* cancel the program now! We've tentatively identified six stars within twenty parsecs of us that have—"

"Yes. I know, it's all in the reports," Bower interrupted, "and you've told me about it several times this afternoon. It's interesting, but it's hardly practical, now is it?"

"Practical? Finding evidence of high technology on other planets, not practical?"

Bower raised his eyes toward the cracked ceiling, as if in supplication to the Chief Bureaucrat. "Really, Dr. Lefko. I've admitted that it's interesting. But it's not within our restructured priority rating. You're not going to help ease pollution or solve population problems, now are you?"

Lefko's only answer was a half-strangled growl.

Bower turned to Major Shawn. "Really, Major, I would have thought that you could make Dr. Lefko understand the realities of the funding situation."

Shaking his head, the major answered, "I agree with Dr. Lefko completely. I think his work is the most important piece of research going on in the world today."

"Honestly!" Bower seemed shocked. "Major, you know that the Department of Defense can't fund research that's not directly related to a military mission."

"But the Air Force owns all the big microwave equipment!" Lefko shouted. "You can't get time on the university facilities, and they're too small anyway!"

Bower waggled a finger at him. "Dr. Lefko, you can't have DOD funds. Even if there were funds for your research available, it's not pertinent work. You must apply for research support from another branch of the government."

"I've tried that every year! None of the other agencies have any money for new programs. Dammit, you've signed the letters rejecting my applications!"

"Regrettable," Bower said stiffly. "Perhaps in a few years, when the foreign situation settles down and the pollution problems are solved."

Lefko was clenching his fists when Major Shawn put a hand on his frail-looking shoulder. "It's no use, Ira. We've lost. Come on, I'll buy you a drink."

Out in the shabby corridor that led to the underground garage, Lefko started to tremble in earnest.

"A chance to find other intelligent races in the heavens. Gone. Wiped out . . . The richest nation in the world . . . Oh my God . . ."

The major took him by the arm and towed him to their rented car. In fifteen minutes they were inside the cool shadows of the airport bar.

"They've reordered the priorities," the major said as he stared into his glass. "For five hundred years and more, Western civilization has made the pursuit of knowledge a respectable goal in its own right. Now it's got to be practical."

Dr. Lefko was already halfway through his second rye and soda. "Nobody asked Galileo to be practical," he muttered. "Or Newton. Or Einstein."

"Yeah, people did. They've always wanted immediate results and practical benefits. But the system was spongy enough to let guys like Newton and Plank and even little fish we never hear about—let 'em tinker around on their own, follow their noses, see what they could find."

" 'Madam, of what use is a newborn baby?' " Lefko quoted thickly.

"What?"

"Faraday."

"Oh."

"Six of them," Lefko whispered. "Six point-sources of intense microwave radiation. Close enough to separate from their parent stars. Six little planets, orbiting around their stars, with higher technology microwave equipment on them."

"Maybe the Astronomical Union will help you get more funding."

Lefko shook his head. "You saw the reception my paper got. They think we're crazy. Not enough evidence. And worse still, I'm associated with the evil Air Force. I'm a pariah . . . and I don't have enough evidence to convince them. It takes more evidence when you're a pariah."

"I'm convinced," Major Shawn said.

"Thank you, my boy. But you are an Air Force officer, a mindless napalmer of Asian babies, by definition—your degrees in astronomy and electronics notwithstanding."

Shawn sighed heavily. "Yeah."

Looking up from the bar, past the clacking color TV, toward the heavily draped windows across the darkened room, Lefko said, "I know they're there. Civilizations like ours. With radios and televisions and radars, turning their planets into microwave beacons. Just as we must be an anomalously bright microwave object to them. Maybe . . . maybe they'll find us! Maybe they'll contact us!"

The major started to smile.

"If only it happens in our lifetime, Bob. If only they find us! Find us . . . and blow us to Hell! We deserve it for being so stupid!"

Tor Kranta stood in the clear night chill, staring at the stars. From inside the sleeping chamber his wife called, "Tor . . . stop tormenting yourself."

"The fools," he muttered. "To stop the work because of the priests' objections. To prevent us from trying to contact another intelligent race, circling another star. Idiocy. Sheer idiocy."

"Accept what must be accepted, Tor. Come to bed."

He shook his blue-maned head. "I only hope that the other intelligent races of the universe aren't as blind as we are."

SETI

Why do men and women engage in scientific research? In particular, why do scientists persist in the search for extraterrestrial life? Not one shred of evidence has been found to confirm the belief that life exists elsewhere than on Earth. In fact, the more we explore the solar system with planetary probing spacecraft, the more doubtful the existence of life on those planets appears to be. The more sophisticated our searches of deep space with radio telescopes, the louder seems the absence of intelligent radio signals. *Psychology Today* was curious about the psychological reasons behind our persistent, but so far fruitless, search for other intelligences. Here is the result. As you might expect, I find myself much more in tune with Prometheans Galileo, Sagan and Morrison than Luddite Proxmire.

Sometimes life does imitate art. Several years ago I wrote a novel titled *Voyagers*, in which a radio telescope operated by Harvard University astronomers picked up unmistakable signals from intelligent extraterrestrial creatures. Today, that very radio telescope has become the first instrument to be devoted specifically to the Search for Extraterrestrial Intelligence—SETI.

In my novel, the realization that there are other intelligences in the universe triggered plots and counterplots by the Pentagon, the Kremlin, the Vatican and even certain fundamentalist evangelists. Some people eagerly sought to make meaningful contact with the aliens. Others were terrified of the idea, and actively tried to prevent such contact.

What would happen today, if Harvard's 85-foot radio telescope actually detected a signal from an alien civilization? How would we react to the success of SETI?

When I asked that question of Bruno Bettelheim, the distinguished psychologist, psychiatrist, educator and author, he replied, "There is absolutely no evidence for life in space."

Then why, I asked, are scientists willing to spend their entire careers seeking intelligent life from other worlds? Why is the government spending millions of dollars to fund SETI? Why do tens of millions of people rush to see motion pictures such as *E.T.* and *Close Encounters of the Third Kind*?

Bettelheim chuckled. "People used to believe in gods and demigods. Now they have invented intelligent extraterrestrial life so that they don't have to feel so lonely."

Physicist Philip Morrison, of the Massachusetts Institute of Technology, sees it differently. He believes that every human being carries around in his or her head a "grand internal model" of the universe, a sort of inner map that tells us who and what and where we are in relation to the world around us.

"For me," Morrison said, "exploration is filling in the blank margins of that inner model." He explained that we are constantly trying to fill in the holes in our interior maps, and extending its outermost edges. "This is the essential feature of human exploration, its root cause deep in our minds and in our cultures."

If exploration is a deep-seated drive among human beings, the quest for intelligent creatures beyond the Earth has been an important part of that drive. The search for other creatures equal to us—or even superior to us—has roots that extend far back into prehistory, and deep into the human psyche.

Every human culture has its myths about godlike creatures from realms beyond our own world. When human beings first began studying the skies they quickly saw that there were thousands of stars that remained fixed in their positions against the black bowl of night. But there were others that moved across the heavens. These wandering stars (*planetos* is the Greek word for them) seemed obviously more powerful than the rest. Every culture named the planets after their gods; today we know them by their Romanized names: Mercury, Venus, Mars, Jupiter and Saturn. (Uranus, Neptune and Pluto were so far away that the ancients never knew they existed.)

Spacecraft have visited each of the planets known to the ancients. The Russians have landed spacecraft on the hellish surface of Venus, where the ground is hot enough to melt lead and the air is a choking, thick soup of carbon dioxide laced with clouds of sulfuric acid. American spacecraft have landed on the surface of Mars and found a frozen desert where the air is thinner than Earth's stratosphere and the temperature plummets lower than a hundred degrees below zero every night, even in midsummer.

No trace of life has been found on the Moon or any of the planets. Not a bacterium. Yet the search for life goes on. Astronomers now believe that the giant planet Jupiter, which could swallow a thousand Earths, may be the best place in the solar system to find living organisms. Carl Sagan, the leading scientific figure in the search for extraterrestrial life, believes that Saturn's cloud-covered moon, Titan, may be covered with organic chemicals that are similar to the chemical "soup" in which life arose in Earth's primeval seas.

But not all scientists are equally sanguine about finding life on other worlds. When Harvard biologist George Gaylord Simpson first learned that the study of extraterrestrial life was being undertaken seriously, and had been titled *exobiology*, he commented, ". . . a curious development in view of the fact that this 'science' has yet to demonstrate that its subject matter exists!"

Many biologists agree with Simpson's point of view; they believe that life itself is so complex, and intelligent life so much more so, that we may very well be the only intelligent creatures in the universe.

Tulane University physicist Frank J. Tipler makes an even stronger point. He claims that if intelligent extraterrestrials existed they would already have visited the Earth. Since there is no evidence that they have (UFO reports aside), then there is a strong inference that there are no intelligent aliens to be found.

Yet, since Galileo first turned a telescope toward the heavens and saw that the Earth is not the only world in space, people have been fascinated by the possibility that life and intelligence may exist elsewhere in the universe.

Although early cultures peopled the sky with gods and the underworld with demons, before the rise of modern science no one expected to find mortal creatures like ourselves anywhere except here on Earth. Then Copernicus showed that the Earth is not the center of creation, and Galileo and later astronomers uncovered a universe so staggeringly vast that it humbled human imagination. Our world shrank to the status of a minor dustmote in a whirlpool galaxy of a hundred billion stars or more, part of an expanding universe of billions upon billions of galaxies.

While the astronomers were downgrading the place of Earth in the cosmos, Charles Darwin and the biologists showed that humankind is not separate and distinct from the rest of the animal kingdom. We were toppled from the pinnacle of self-esteem by the theory of evolution. Later, Sigmund Freud delivered another hammer-blow to the human ego by revealing the hidden workings of our minds.

By the end of the nineteenth century, humankind had been reduced to a rather bright species of primate ape living on a small planet circling a mediocre star and harboring an oedipal complex. Yet the human spirit, with its enormous capacity for adaptation, still reached out to seek companionship against the cosmic loneliness. In fact, some thinkers began to use the evidence of the universe's vastness and our own littleness to support the idea that there must be other creatures somewhat like ourselves out there in the starry cosmos.

The universe is *so* large, this argument ran, that it is inconceivable that Earth should be the only place that harbors intelligent life. After all, we are not unique in any other way. Why should the Earth be the only abode for intelligence?

Astronomer Kenneth Franklin, of New York City's Hayden Planetarium, put it this way: "We know that intelligence is 'built into' the universe, because we are intelligent and we're just as much a part of the universe as a tree or a star. So if intelligence is an integral part of the universe, I can't believe that it's arisen only in one place."

While space scientists have spent the past two decades

actively probing the planets of our solar system, radio astronomers have used their giant antennas to listen for possible signals from the depths of interstellar space.

This effort began in 1959 when Morrison and Giuseppi Cocconi, who is also a physicist, suggested that the radio telescopes which astronomers use to study the natural radiowave emissions from stars and interstellar gas clouds might also be able to pick up intelligent signals, if any exist. Admitting that the task would be difficult, and had only a minuscule chance of success, they nevertheless concluded, ". . . but if we never search the chance of success is zero."

Greenbank, West Virginia, became the first place on Earth to host a deliberate search for intelligent extraterrestrial life. Frank Drake, of Cornell University, who then headed the National Radio Astronomy Observatory at Greenbank, used the 85-foot-wide "dish" there to seek radio signals from two relatively nearby stars. Whimsically, Drake called the part-time effort Project Ozma, after the queen of L. Frank Baum's mythical land of Oz. At the cost of a thousand dollars worth of electronic equipment and some two hundred hours of the telescope's heavily-booked time, Drake and his colleagues made the first stab at SETI.

They expected no positive result, and got none. But they were learning how to build the electronic equipment that can sift an intelligent signal out of the constant background of natural radio "noise" emitted by the stars and gas clouds in deep space. Drake and others later used the world's largest radio telescope, the 1000-foot Arecibo dish, which is carved into a hillside in Puerto Rico, to listen and even to send a brief message starward. But these efforts were always on a part-time, very temporary basis. Although a few false alarms temporarily made hearts beat faster, no definite signals were detected.

The biggest alarm came in the summer of 1967, when a group of British astronomers actually thought they might have hit the jackpot. Jocelyn Bell was an undergraduate student at Cambridge University, working on a radio astronomy project that did not involve SETI. She discovered a strange, pulsing signal unlike anything that had ever been picked up before. The signal came in millisecond pulses, bursts that were only

10 to 20 thousandths of a second long, and spaced precisely 1.33730113 seconds apart. It was the precise timing of the pulses, as accurate as any atomic clock, that startled Bell and her colleagues.

For weeks the Cambridge astronomers tried to find a cause for the signals. One of the theories they considered seriously was dubbed LGM—for Little Green Men.

It turned out that the radio pulses were being emitted by entirely natural, though fantastically unusual, astronomical objects. Today they are called pulsars. They are stars like the Sun, but have collapsed down to a size of only a few miles across. A teaspoonful of a pulsar's material would weigh more than the Pacific Ocean.

Musing about those frantic weeks, many years afterward, Bell said, "It is an interesting problem—if one thinks one may have detected life elsewhere in the universe, how does one announce the results responsibly?"

In my novel, when American and Russian astronomers independently detect intelligent radio signals from deep space, both the Pentagon and the Kremlin insist on keeping the information secret. Neither Washington nor Moscow wants the other side to know about the highly advanced technology that might be offered by the aliens. When the Vatican learns of the signals, secrecy is also preferred, because the Church worries how the discovery of intelligent alien creatures would affect the faith of its followers.

The discovery of extraterrestrial life, and intelligence, raises powerful psychological, social and political questions. To begin with, most scientists assume that if we actually do detect intelligent signals from the stars, they will have been sent by a civilization far in advance of our own. After all, we are merely beginning to search for life in the universe. A civilization that is actively transmitting signals over interstellar distances would most likely have been doing so for generations or centuries; its technology would be superior to ours.

What would happen to the human psyche if we suddenly made contact with creatures far advanced over us? Carl Jung once wrote:

"In a direct confrontation with superior creatures from another world, the reins would be torn from our hands and we would, as a tearful old medicine man said to me, find ourselves 'without dreams,' that is, we would find our intellectual and spiritual aspirations so outmoded as to leave us completely paralyzed.''

Dr. Warren H. Jones, associate professor of psychology at the University of Tulsa, sees a more active, and more aggressive, human reaction to the discovery of alien-intelligence creatures.

"The basic human reaction to something that shocking and dramatic," he says, "would be fear, anger . . ." If the classic science fiction scenario of aliens landing their flying saucer on the White House lawn ever really happened, Dr. Jones believes, "We would kill them, if we could."

There is a strong and deep xenophobia lurking within the psyche of the average human being, Dr. Jones explains. "There is good evidence that a fundamental principle of human nature is that we don't really like surprises . . . perhaps we enjoy pleasant surprises occasionally, but we really want the world to be predictable and understandable."

Dr. Jones adds that this desire for a predictable, understandable universe, conversely, is one of the reasons why many scientists believe there *must* be intelligent extraterrestrials elsewhere in the cosmos. "It provides understanding and meaning where there doesn't seem to be any."

Certainly there is plenty of evidence of culture shock in human history. Would our discovery of (or rather, *by*) intelligent aliens start the same kind of tragedy as that suffered by the native American and Polynesian cultures, once they were discovered by the Europeans?

Scientists such as Sagan, who is director of Cornell University's Laboratory for Planetary Studies, have no such fears. Instead, they look forward to interstellar communications with creatures who are more highly developed intellectually than we are. How would such a communication be established, though? What language would the people of Earth have in common with alien intelligences from a distant star?

Sagan wrote, "If it is possible to communicate, we think we know what the first communications will be about: They will be about the one thing the two civilizations are guaranteed to share in common . . . science."

If the astronomers are guilty of projecting their own point of view onto the hypothesized extraterrestrials, there is another attitude that sees alien creatures as potential threats to humankind. In science fiction tales, the aliens are often hostile, heartless and gruesome. No less a writer than the redoubtable H. G. Wells described the Martians in his classic *The War of the Worlds* thus:

". . . minds that are to our minds as ours are to those of the beasts that perish, intellects vast and cool and unsympathetic, regarded this earth with envious eyes, and slowly and surely drew their plans against us."

The astronomers may expect to meet angels, or at least college professors, but the fantasists warn that the dark side of intelligence exists side by side with the bright.

People who have reported seeing Unidentified Flying Objects and their crews, however, almost invariably describe the UFO aliens as humanlike in appearance, and utterly benign.

Dr. Janet Jeppson, training and supervising analyst at the William Alanson White Institute of Psychoanalysis in Manhattan, believes that the similarities among all the thousands of UFO "contactee" stories points to the conclusion that these are reports of unconscious wish-fulfillment, rather than descriptions of reality.

"The aliens are always so saintly," Dr. Jeppson remarks. "They always are motivated only by the best interests of the human race." Dr. Jeppson, who is the wife of science fiction writer Isaac Asimov and a writer herself, is in the unique position of seeing the UFO phenomenon from several different points of view.

Tulsa's Dr. Jones agrees that UFO sightings and reports of contacts with alien astronauts are a form of "substitute religion . . . a modernistic, mechanistic modern religion [which] combines the best of science fiction and religion. On the one hand, [the UFO aliens represent] a race of people who are technologically superior, who can solve age-old human frailties and shortcomings: they can stops wars, cure all disease, allow us to live forever . . . and that is fused with the much more ancient notion of a superhuman being out there somewhere in the sky who watches over us, and protects us, and has our best interests at heart."

But to date, no one has found any evidence acceptable to the vast majority of humankind that we have been visited by aliens. Nor has any evidence been found to show that life exists beyond the Earth. Although most scientists are convinced that life should arise wherever the natural conditions for it exist, none of our space probes have found so much as an organic molecule or a fossilized spore, and none of our radio telescopes have yet picked up an intelligible signal.

For years, the federal government supported NASA's planetary exploration programs in the hopes of finding life elsewhere in the solar system. But when the Viking landers showed that Mars was so barren it would make Death Valley look like the Garden of Eden, much of Capitol Hill's enthusiasm for planetary exploration evaporated. NASA's funds for planetary sciences were severely cut, and new probes of the planets were slashed almost entirely out of the space agency's budget.

Meanwhile, the radio astronomy approach to SETI was also under attack in Washington, particularly by Senator William Proxmire (Democrat, Wisconsin). In 1978 Proxmire was chairman of the Senate Committee that controlled NASA's funding. He had won a place for himself in the Washington limelight by giving out each month a Golden Fleece award for "the most ironic or most ridiculous example of wasteful [government] spending."

In February 1978 Proxmire gave his Golden Fleece award to NASA for "riding the wave of popular enthusiasm for *Star Wars* and *Close Encounters of the Third Kind*, [by] proposing to spend $14 to $15 million over the next seven years to try to find intelligent life in outer space. . . . At a time when the country is faced with a $61-billion budget deficit, the attempt to detect radio waves from solar systems should be postponed until right after the federal budget is balanced and income and social security taxes are reduced to zero."

Proxmire succeeded in getting all funding for SETI cut from the NASA budget. Later, when he learned that the space agency was still spending roughly a million dollars a year on research that could be applied to SETI, he got the Congress to prohibit NASA specifically from doing any work connected with the search for extraterrestrial intelligence.

There may have been more afoot than merely an attempt to save the taxpayers' dollars. After all, Proxmire himself always voted in favor of the two-billion-dollar milk subsidy every year. Those who resist the relatively inexpensive research involved in SETI might have psychological motivations for their political stance. They may not want to see the human race displaced even further from the center of the universe's stage. Forced by scientific evidence to accept the fact that the Earth is not unique, and that humans evolved from "lower" animals, many people still unconsciously cling to the faith that life itself—and certainly intelligent life—is singular to our world.

When media pundits, politicians and religious leaders learned that the spacecraft we have sent to Mars detected no traces of life, Sagan observed, "They were unmistakably *relieved*."

The shock of contact with intelligent extraterrestrials will be very different from its depiction in films such as *E.T.* If and when we meet alien creatures, they will undoubtedly look nothing like human beings; biologists have warned us repeatedly that it would be foolish to expect evolution to follow exactly the same course on a distant different world. This is why the typical UFO "contact" story is regarded so skeptically by most scientists: such reports almost always depict the UFO aliens as humanlike in appearance. Biologists are more inclined to believe in science fiction's "bug-eyed monsters" than in aliens from a distant star looking more-or-less human.

Thinking about the likelihood that very advanced intelligent aliens will undoubtedly look most un-human, author Arthur C. Clarke pointed out, "The rash assertion that 'God created man in His own image' is ticking like a time bomb at the foundations of many faiths."

Despite these fears and forebodings, the main body of scientists and space enthusiasts chafed unhappily over the cutbacks in planetary exploration and the Proxmire-mandated death of SETI. Once again it was Sagan who spearheaded the counterattack. He wrote a petition calling for a systematic search for extraterrestrial intelligence, which was subsequently signed by 73 scientists from 14 nations, including seven Nobel Prize winners. He and other scientists began meeting with the politicians in Washington, including Proxmire, to "educate" them about the intellectual and practical benefits of SETI. On the practical side, for example, the development of computer technology necessary for SETI will have many other applications in science, business and national defense.

Sagan is also president of the Planetary Society, a grass-roots space activist organization of some 100,000 members. Since 1982, the Planetary Society has been funding an effort at Harvard, directed by physicist Paul Horowitz, to scan 128,000 radio channels simultaneously, using the 85-foot radio telescope at Harvard's Oak Ridge Station. The actual observation work began in March 1983, when Horowitz's compact electronic gear—nicknamed "suitcase SETI" because of its portability—was linked to the radio telescope.

This multi-year program is the first "dedicated" search for intelligent signals. The electronic receiving equipment that Horowitz and his colleagues have devised will enable the radio telescope to make observations within minutes that would have taken Drake and his Project Ozma team thousands of years to perform.

The "moral suasion" by the scientists on Capitol Hill also met with some degree of success, and Proxmire relented in his opposition to SETI enough to allow NASA to spend a total of $12.5 million over the next several years to develop advanced technology to listen for messages from the stars. Proxmire now describes his attitude as "skeptical neutrality," as opposed to his earlier active hostility.

And although NASA's planetary exploration program is still under severe financial constraints, the agency was permitted to develop the Galileo spacecraft to explore Jupiter. The orbiter will fire a probe vehicle down into the giant planet's swirling sea of clouds on a one-way mission to sample the gases there and see if they contain the chemicals of life.

Perhaps Bettelheim is correct, and we are inventing imaginary creatures to protect ourselves against cosmic loneliness. Tipler, who argues forcefully against the existence of extra-terrestrials, also points out that there is no certain way to *prove* that they do not exist; no matter how many negative returns we get, the "pro-life" scientists can always hope that ET is waiting to be discovered just beyond the reach of our latest probe.

Typically, Sagan makes a virtue even out of such negativism. If we find no evidence for life or intelligence, he says, it will simply help us to appreciate how rare and precious we ourselves are in the universe.

No matter which argument ultimately turns out to be correct, SETI is now going ahead, at a total cost of a few pennies per taxpayer per year. The benefits of new knowledge that we gain, even if no trace of life is found, will make the effort a fiscal bargain.

Nearly four centuries ago, Galileo wrote, "Astronomers . . . seek to investigate the true constitution of the universe—the most important and most admirable problem that there is." This quest for knowledge, for understanding, this drive to explore, is a fundamental part of the human psyche. We reach out to seek others like ourselves, regardless of the consequences, and in doing so we learn more about the universe—and about ourselves, as well.

Perhaps Lee DuBridge put it best, back when he was President Eisenhower's science advisor. He said, "Either we are alone in the universe or we are not; either way is mind-boggling."

The Great Supersonic Zeppelin Race ▬▬▬

Although I count myself among the Prometheans, I do recognize that sometimes Prometheanism can run amok. When the Luddites among us succeeded in stopping the American effort to develop a supersonic transport plane, I found myself writing this story. If nothing else, it shows that a true Promethean is never stopped for long.

The part about the Busemann biplane, incidentally, is true. At least, that's what I heard from these two aerodynamicists one day at lunch in the laboratory cafeteria in Everett.

————————

"You can make a supersonic aircraft that doesn't produce a sonic boom," said Bob Wisdom.

For an instant the whole cafeteria seemed to go quiet. Bob was sitting at a table by the big picture window that overlooked Everett Aircraft Co.'s parking lot. It was drizzling out there, as it usually did in the spring. Through the haze, Mt. Olympia's snow-topped peak could barely be seen.

Bob smiled quizzically at his lunch pals. He was tall and lanky, round-faced in a handsome sort of way, with dark, thinning hair and dark eyes that were never somber, even in the midst of Everett Aircraft's worst layoffs and cutbacks.

"A supersonic aircraft," mumbled Ray Kurtz from inside his beard.

"With no sonic boom," added Tommy Rohr.

Bob Wisdom smiled and nodded.

"What's the catch?" asked Richard Grand in a slightly Anglified accent.

The cafeteria resumed its clattering, chattering noises. The drizzle outside continued to soak the few scraggly trees and pitiful shrubs planted around the half-empty parking lot.

"Catch?" Bob echoed, trying to look hurt. "Why should there be a catch?"

"Because if someone could build a supersonic aircraft that doesn't shatter people's eardrums, obviously someone would be doing it," Grand answered.

"We could do it," Bob agreed pleasantly, "but we're not."

"Why not?" Kurtz asked.

Bob shrugged elaborately.

Rohr waggled a finger at Bob. "There's something going on in that aerodynamicist's head of yours. This is a gag, isn't it?"

"No gag," Bob replied innocently. "I'm surprised that nobody's thought of the idea before."

"What's the go of it?" Grand asked. He had just read a biography of James Clerk Maxwell and was trying to sound English, despite the fact that Maxwell was a Scot.

"Well," Bob said, with a bigger grin than before, "there's a type of wing that the German aerodynamicist Adolph Busemann invented. Instead of making the wings flat, though, you build your supersonic aircraft with a ringwing. . . ."

"Ringwing?"

"Sure." Leaning forward and propping one elbow on the cafeteria table, Bob pulled a felt-tip pen from his shirt pocket and sketched on the paper placemat.

"See? Here's the fuselage of a supersonic plane." He drew a narrow cigar shape. "Now we wrap the wing around it, like a sleeve. It's actually two wings, one inside the other, and all the shock waves that cause the sonic boom get trapped inside the wings and get canceled out. No sonic boom."

Grand stared at the sketch, then looked up at Bob, then stared at the sketch some more. Rohr looked expectant, waiting for the punch line. Kurtz frowned, looking like a cross between Abe Lincoln and Karl Marx.

"I don't know much about aerodynamics," Rohr said slowly,

"but that is a sort of Busemann biplane you're talking about, isn't it?"

Bob nodded.

"A hah . . . and isn't it true that the wings of a Busemann biplane produce no lift?"

"Right," Bob admitted.

"No lift?" Kurtz snapped. "Then how the hell do you get it off the ground?"

Trying to look completely serious, Bob answered, "You can't get it off the ground if it's an ordinary airplane. It's got to be lighter than air. You fill the central body with helium."

"A zeppelin?" Kurtz squeaked.

Rohr started laughing. "You sonofabitch. You had us all going there for a minute."

Grand said, "Interesting."

John Driver sat behind a cloud of blue smoke that he puffed from a reeking pipe. His office always smelled like an opium den gone sour. His secretary, a luscious and sweet-tempered girl of Greek-Italian ancestry, had worn out eight strings of rosary beads in the vain hope that he might give up smoking.

"A supersonic zeppelin?" Driver snapped angrily. "Ridiculous!"

Squinting into the haze in an effort to find his boss, Grand answered, "Don't be too hasty to dismiss the concept. It might have some merit. At the very least, I believe we could talk NASA or the Transportation people into giving us money to investigate the idea."

At the sound of the word "money," Driver took the pipe out of his teeth and waved some of the smoke away. He peered at Grand through reddened eyes. Driver was lean-faced, with hard features and a gaze that he liked to think was piercing. His jaw was slightly overdeveloped from biting through so many pipe stems.

"You have to spend money to make money in this business," Driver said in his most penetrating *Fortune* magazine acumen.

"I realize that," Grand answered stiffly. "But I'm quite

willing to put my own time into this. I really believe we may be onto something that can save our jobs."

Driver drummed his slide-rule-calloused fingertips on his desktop. "All right," he said at last. "Do it on your own time. When you've got something worth showing, come to me with it. Not anyone else, you understand. Me."

"Right, Chief." Whenever Grand wanted to flatter Driver, he called him Chief.

After Grand left his office, Driver sat at his desk for a long, silent while. The company's business had been going to hell over the past few years. There was practically no market for high-technology work any more. The military was more interested in sandbags than supersonic planes. NASA was wrapping tourniquets everywhere in an effort to keep from bleeding to death. The newly reorganized Department of Transportation and Urban Renewal hardly understood what a Bunsen burner was.

"A supersonic zeppelin," Driver muttered to himself. It sounded ridiculous. But then, so had air-cushion vehicles and Wankel engines. Yet companies were making millions on those ideas.

"A supersonic zeppelin," he repeated. "SSZ."

Then he noticed that his pipe had gone out. He reached into his left-top desk drawer for a huge blue-tipped kitchen match and started puffing the pipe alight again. Great clouds of smoke billowed upward as he said: "SSZ . . . no sonic boom . . . might not even cause air pollution."

Driver climbed out of the cab, clamped his pipe in his teeth, and gazed up at the magnificent glass and stainless steel facade of the new office building that housed the Transportation and Urban Renewal Department.

"So this is TURD headquarters," he muttered.

"This is it," replied Tracy Keene, who had just paid off the cabbie and come up to stand beside Driver. Keene was Everett Aircraft's crackerjack Washington representative, a large, round man who always conveyed the impression that he knew things nobody else knew. Keene's job was to find new customers for Everett, placate old customers when Everett inevitably alienated them, and pay off taxicabs. The job involved grotesque amounts of wining and dining, and Keene—who had once been as wiry and agile as a weak-hitting shortstop—seemed to grow larger and rounder every time Driver came to Washington. But what he was gaining in girth, he was losing in hair, Driver noticed.

"Let's go," Keene said. "We don't want to be late." He lumbered up the steps to the magnificent glass doors of the magnificent new building.

The building was in Virginia, not the District of Columbia. Like all new government agencies, it was headquartered outside the city proper. The fact that one of this agency's major responsibilities was to find ways to revitalize the major cities and stop urban sprawl somehow had never entered into consideration when the site for its location was chosen.

Two hours later, Keene was half-dozing in a straight-backed metal chair, and Driver was taking the last of an eight-inch-thick pile of viewgraph slides off the projector. The projector fan droned hypnotically in the darkened room. They were in the office of Roger K. Memo, Assistant Under Director for Transportation Research of TURD.

Memo and his chief scientific advisor, Dr. Alonzo Pencilbeam, were sitting on one side of the small table, Keene was resting peacefully on the other side. Driver stood up at the head of the table, frowning beside the viewgraph projector. The only light in the room came from the projector, which now threw a blank glare onto the wan, yellow wall that served in place of a screen. Smoke from Driver's pipe sifted through the cone of light.

Driver snapped the projector off. The light and the fan's whirring noise abruptly stopped. Keene jerked fully awake and, without a word, reached up and flicked the wall switch that turned on the overhead lights.

Although the magnificent building was sparkling new, Memo's office somehow looked instant-seedy. There wasn't enough furniture in it for its size: only an ordinary steel desk and swivel chair, a half-empty bookcase, and this little conference table with four chairs that didn't match. The walls and floor were bare, and there was a distinct echo when anyone spoke or even walked across the room. The only window had vertical slats instead of a curtain, and it looked out on an automobile graveyard. The only decoration on the walls was a diploma: Memo's doctorate degree, bought from an obscure Mohawk Valley college for $200 without the need to attend classes.

Driver stood by the projector, frowning through his own smoke.

"Well what do you think?" he asked subtly.

Memo pursed his lips. He was jowly fat, completely bald, wore glasses and rumpled gray suits.

"I don't know," he said firmly. "It sounds . . . unusual . . ."

Dr. Pencilbeam was sitting back in his chair and smiling beautifully. His Ph.D. had been earned during the 1930s, when he had had to work nights and weekends to stay alive and in school. He was still very thin, fragile looking, with the long skinny limbs of a praying mantis.

Pencilbeam dug in his jacket pockets and pulled out a pouch of tobacco and cigarette paper. "It certainly looks interesting," he said in a soft voice. "I think it's technically feasible . . . and lots of fun."

Memo snorted. "We're not here to enjoy ourselves."

Keene leaned across the table and fixed Memo with his best here's-something-from-behind-the-scenes look:

"Do you realize how the Administration would react to a sensible program for a supersonic aircraft? With the Concorde going broke and the Russian SST grounded . . . you could put this country out in front again."

"H'mm," said Memo. "But . . ."

"Balance of payments," Keene intoned knowingly. "Gold outflow . . . aerospace employment . . . national prestige . . . the President would be awfully impressed."

"H'mm," Memo repeated. "I see . . ."

The cocktail party was in full swing. It was nearly impossible to hear your own voice in the swirling babble of chatter and clinking glassware. In the middle of the sumptuous living room, the Vice President was demonstrating his golf swing. Out in the foyer, three senators were comparing fact-finding tours they were arranging for the Riviera, Rio de Janeiro, and American Samoa, respectively. The Cabinet wives held sway in the glittering dining room.

Roger K. Memo never drank anything stronger than ginger ale. He stood in the doorway between the living room and foyer, lip-reading the senators' conversation about travel plans. When the trip broke up and Senator Goodyear (R., Ohio) headed back toward the bar, Memo intercepted him.

"Hello, Senator!" Memo shouted heartily. It was the only way to be heard over the party noise.

"Ah . . . hello." Senator Goodyear obviously knew that he knew Memo, but just as obviously couldn't recall his name, rank or influence rating.

Goodyear was nearly six feet tall, and towered over Memo's paunchy figure. Together they shouldered their way through the crowd around the bar. Goodyear ordered bourbon on the rocks, and therefore so did Memo. But he merely held onto his glass, while the senator immediately began to gulp at his drink.

A statuesque blonde in a spectacular gown sauntered past them. The senator's eyes tracked her like a range finder following a target.

"I hear you're going to Samoa," Memo shouted as they edged away from the bar, following the girl.

"Eh . . . yes," Goodyear answered cautiously, in a tone he usually employed with newspaper reporters.

"Beautiful part of the world," Memo yelled.

The blonde slipped an arm around the waist of a young, long-haired man and they disappeared into another room together. Goodyear turned his attention back to his drink.

"I said," Memo repeated, standing on tiptoes, "that Samoa is a beautiful part of the world."

Nodding, Goodyear said, "I'm going to investigate the ecological conditions there . . . my committee is considering legislation on ecology."

"Of course, of course. You've got to see things firsthand if you're going to enact meaningful laws."

Slightly less guardedly, Goodyear said, "Exactly."

"It's such a long way off, though," Memo said. "It must take considerable thought to decide to make such a long trip."

"Well . . . you know we can't think of our own comforts when we're in public service."

"Yes, of course . . . Will you be taking the SST? I understand Qantas flies it out of San Francisco . . ."

Suddenly alert again, Goodyear snapped, "Never! I always fly American planes on American airlines."

"Very patriotic," Memo applauded. "And sensible, too. Those Aussies don't know how to run an airline. And any plane made by the British *and* the French . . . well, I don't know. I understand it's financially in trouble."

Goodyear nodded again. "That's what I hear."

"Still—it's a shame that the United States doesn't have a supersonic aircraft. It would cut your travel time in half. Give you twice as much time to stay in Samoa . . . investigating."

The hearing room in the Capitol was jammed with reporters and cameramen. Senator Goodyear sat in the center of the long front table, as befitted the committee chairman.

All through the hot summer morning the committee had listened to witnesses: John Driver, Roger K. Memo, Alonzo Pencilbeam and many others. The concept of the supersonic zeppelin unfolded before the newsmen and started to take on definite solidity right there in the rococo-trimmed hearing room.

Senator Goodyear sat there solemnly all morning, listening to the carefully rehearsed testimony, watching the greenery outside the big sunny window. Whenever he thought about the TV cameras, he sat up straighter and tried to look lean and tough, like Gary Cooper. Goodyear had a drawer full of Gary Cooper movies on video cassettes in his Ohio home.

Now it was his turn to summarize what the witnesses had said. He looked straight at the nearest camera, trying to come across strong and sympathetic, like the sheriff in *High Noon*.

"Gentlemen," he began, immediately antagonizing the eighteen women in the audience, "I believe that what we have heard here today can mark the beginning of a new program that will revitalize the aerospace industry and put America back in the forefront of international commerce . . ."

One of the younger senators at the far end of the table interrupted:

"Excuse me, Mr. Chairman, but my earlier question about pollution was never answered. Won't the SSZ use the same kinds of jet engines that the SST was going to use? And won't they cause just as much pollution?"

Goodyear glowered at the junior member's impudence, but controlled his temper well enough to say only, "Em . . . Dr. Pencilbeam, would you care to answer that question?"

Pencilbeam, seated at one of the witness tables, looked startled for a moment. Then he hunched his bony frame around the microphone in front of him and said:

"The pollution arguments about the SST were never substantiated. There were wild claims that if you operated jet engines up in the high stratosphere, you would eventually cause a permanent cloud layer over the whole Earth or destroy the ozone up there and thus let in enough solar ultraviolet radiation to cause millions of cancer deaths. But these claims were never proved."

"But it was never disproved, either, was it?" the junior senator said.

Before Pencilbeam could respond, Senator Goodyear grabbed his own microphone and nearly shouted, "Rest assured that we are all well aware of the possible pollution problems. At the moment, though, there is no problem because there is no SSZ. Our aerospace industry is suffering, employment is way down and the whole economy is in a bad way. The SSZ project will provide jobs and boost the economy. As part of the project, we will consult with the English and French and see what their pollution problems are—if any. And our own American engineers will, I assure you, find ways to eliminate any and all pollution coming from the SSZ engines."

Looking rather disturbed, Pencilbeam started to add something to Goodyear's statement. But Memo put a hand over the scientist's microphone and shook his head in a strong negative.

Mark Sequoia was hiking along a woodland trail in Fairmont Park, Philadelphia, when the news reached him.

Once a flaming crusader for ecological salvation and against pollution, Sequoia had made the mistake of letting the Commonwealth of Pennsylvania hire him as the state ecology director. He had spent the past five years earnestly and honestly trying to clean up Pennsylvania, a job that had driven four generations of the original Penn family into early graves. The deeper that Sequoia buried himself in the solid wastes and politics of Pittsburgh, Philadelphia, Chester, Erie and other hopeless cities, the fewer followers and national headlines he attracted.

Now he led a scraggly handful of sullen high school students through the soot-ravaged woodlands of Fairmont Park on a steaming July afternoon, picking up empty beer cans and loaded prophylactics—and keeping a wary eye out for muggers. Even full daylight was no protection against assault. And the school kids with him wouldn't help. Half of them would jump in and join the fun.

Sequoia was broad-shouldered, almost burly. His face had been seamed by weather and press conferences. He looked strong and fit, but lately his back had been giving him trouble, and his old trick knee . . .

He heard someone pounding up the trail behind him.

"Mark! Mark!"

Sequoia turned to see Larry Helper, his last and therefore most trusted aide, running along the gravel path toward him, waving a copy of the *Evening Bulletin* over his head. Newspaper pages were slipping from his sweaty grasp and fluttering off across the grass.

"Littering," Sequoia mumbled in the tone sometimes used by bishops when faced with a case of heresy.

"Some of you men," Sequoia said in his best Lone Ranger voice, "pick up those newspaper pages."

A couple of kids lackadaisically ambled after the fluttering sheets.

"Mark, look here!" Helper skidded to a stop and breathlessly waved the front page of the newspaper. "Look!"

Sequoia grabbed his aide's wrist and took the newspaper from him. He frowned at Helper, who cringed and stepped back.

"I . . . I thought you'd want to see . . ."

Satisfied that he was in control of things, Sequoia turned his attention to the front page headline.

"Supersonic *zeppelin!*"

By nightfall, Sequoia was meeting with a half-dozen men and women in the basement of a prosperous downtown church that specialized in worthy causes capable of filling the pews upstairs.

Sequoia was pacing across the little room in which they were meeting. There was no table, just a few folding chairs scattered around, and a locked bookcase stuffed with books on sex and marriage.

"No, we've got to do something dramatic!" Sequoia pounded a fist into his open palm. "We can't just drive down to Washington and call a press conference . . ."

"Automobiles pollute," said one of the women, a comely redhead, whose eyes never left Sequoia's broad, sturdy-looking figure.

"We could take the train; it's electrical."

"Power stations pollute."

"Airplanes pollute, too."

"What about riding down on horseback? Like Paul Revere!"

"Horses pollute."

"They do?"

"Ever been around a stable?"

"Oh."

Sequoia pounded his fist again. "I've got it!" His hand stung; he had hit it too hard.

"What?"

"A balloon! We'll ride down to Washington in a non-polluting, helium-filled balloon. That's the dramatic way to emphasize our point!"

"Fantastic!"

"Marvelous!"

The redhead was panting with excitement. "Oh, Mark, you're so clever. So dedicated." There were tears in her eyes.

Helper said softly, "Uh . . . does anybody know where we can get a balloon? And how much they cost?"

Sequoia glared at him.

When the meeting finally broke up, Helper had the task of finding a suitable balloon, preferably for free. Sequoia would spearhead the effort to raise money for a knockdown fight against the SSZ. The redhead volunteered to assist him. They left arm in arm.

*   *   *

The auditorium in Foggy Bottom was crammed with newsmen. TV lights were glaring at the empty podium. The reporters and cameramen shuffled, coughed, talked to each other. Then:

"Ladies and gentlemen, the President of the United States."

They all stood up and applauded politely as the President strode across the stage toward the podium in his usual bunched-together, shoulder-first football style. His dark face was somber under its beetling brows.

The President gripped the lectern and nodded, with a perfunctory smile, to a few of his favorites. The newsmen sat down. The cameras started rolling.

"I have a statement to make about the tragic misfortune that has overtaken one of our finest public figures—Mark Sequoia. According to the latest report I have received from the Coast Guard—no more than ten minutes ago—there is still no trace of him or his party. Apparently the balloon they were riding in was blown out to sea two days ago, and nothing has been heard from them since.

"Now let me make this perfectly clear. Mr. Sequoia was frequently on the other side of the political fence from me, your President. He was often a critic of my policies and actions, the policies and actions of your President. He was on his way to Washington to protest our new SSZ project, when this unfortunate accident occurred—to protest the SSZ project despite the fact that it will employ thousands of aerospace engineers who are otherwise unemployable and untrainable. Despite the fact that it will save the American dollar on the international market and salvage American prestige in the technological battleground of the world.

"Now, in spite of the fact that some of us—such as our Vice President, as is well known—feel that Mr. Sequoia carried the constitutional guarantee of free speech a bit too far, despite all this, mind you, I—as your President and Commander-in-Chief—have dispatched every available military, Coast Guard, and Boy Scout plane, ship, and foot patrol to search the entire coastline and coastal waters between Philadelphia and Washington. We will find Mark Sequoia and his brave party of misguided ecology nuts . . . or their remains.

"Are there any questions?"

The Associated Press reporter, a hickory-tough old man with huge, thick glasses and a white goatee, stood up and asked in stentorian tones: "Is it true that Sequoia's balloon was blown off course by a flight of Air Force fighter planes that buzzed it?"

The President made a smile that looked somewhat like a grimace and said: "I'm glad you asked that question . . ."

Ronald Eames Trafalgar was Her Majesty's Ambassador Plenipotentiary to the Government of the Union of Soviet Socialist Republics.

He sat rather uneasily in the rear seat of the Bentley, watching the white-boled birch trees flash past the car windows. The first snow of autumn was already on the ground, the trees were almost entirely bare, the sky was a pewter gray. Trafalgar shivered with the iron cold of the steppes, even inside his heavy woolen coat.

Next to him sat Sergei Mihailovitch Traktor, Minister of Technology. The two men were old friends, despite their vast differences in outlook, upbringing and appearance. Trafalgar could have posed for Horatio Hornblower illustrations: he was tall, slim, poised, just a touch of gray at his well-brushed temples. Traktor looked like an automobile mechanic (which he once was): stubby, heavy-faced, shifty eyes.

"I can assure you that this car is absolutely clean," Trafalgar said calmly, still watching the melancholy birch forest sliding by. The afternoon sun was an indistinct bright blur behind the trees, trying to burn its way through the gray overcast.

"And let me assure you," Traktor said in flawless English, a startling octave higher than the Englishman's voice, "that *all* your cars are bugged."

Trafalgar laughed lightly. "Dear man. We constantly find your bugs and plant them next to tape recordings of the Beatles."

"You only find the bugs we want you to find."

"Nonsense."

"Truth." Traktor didn't mention the eleven kilos of electronic gear that had been strapped to various parts of his fleshy anatomy before he had been allowed to visit the British embassy.

"Ah, well, no matter . . ." Trafalgar gave up the argument with an airy wave of his hand. "The basic question is quite simple: What are you going to do about this ridiculous supersonic zeppelin idea of the Americans?"

Traktor pursed his lips and studied his friend's face for a moment, like a garage mechanic trying to figure out how much a customer will hold still for.

"Why do you call it ridiculous?" he asked.

"You don't think it's ridiculous?" Trafalgar asked.

They sparred for more than an hour before they both finally admitted that (a) their own supersonic transport planes were financially ruinous, and (b) they were both secretly working on plans to build supersonic zeppelins.

After establishing that confidence, both men were silent for a long, long time. The car drove out to the limit allowed by diplomatic protocol for a British embassy vehicle, then headed back for Moscow. The driver could clearly see the onion-shaped spires of churches before Trafalgar finally broke down and asked quietly:

"Em . . . Sergei, old man, . . . do you suppose that we could work together on this zeppelin thing? It might save us both a good deal of money and time. And it would help us to catch up with the Americans."

"Impossible," said Traktor.

"I'm sure the thought has crossed your mind before this," Trafalgar said.

"Working with a capitalist nation . . ."

"Two capitalist nations," Trafalgar corrected. "The French are in with us."

Traktor said nothing.

"After all, you've worked with the French before. It's difficult, I know. But it can be done. And my own government is now in the hands of the Socialist Party."

"Improbable," said Traktor.

"And you *do* want to overtake the Americans, don't you?"

The President's desk was cleared of papers. Nothing cluttered the broad expanse of redwood except three phones (red, white and black), a memento from an early Latin America tour (a fist-sized rock), and a Ping-Pong paddle.

The President sat back in the elevated chair behind the desk and fired instructions at his personal staff.

"I want to make it absolutely clear," he was saying to his press secretary, "that we are not in a race with the Russians or anybody else. We're building our SSZ for very sound economic and social reasons, not for competition with the Russians."

"Right, Chief," said the press secretary.

He turned to his top congressional liaison man. "And you'd better make darned certain that the Senate Appropriations Committee votes the extra funds for the SSZ. Tell them that if we don't get the extra funding, we'll fall behind the Reds."

"And I want you," he said to the Director of TURD, "to spend every nickel of your existing SSZ money as fast as you can. Otherwise we won't be able to get Congress to put in more money."

"Yes sir."

"But, Chief," the head of Budget Management started to object.

"I know what you're going to say," the President said to the top BUM. "I'm perfectly aware that money doesn't grow on trees. But we've got to make the SSZ a success . . . and before next November. Take money from education, from poverty, from the space program—anything. I want that SSZ flying by next spring, when I'm scheduled to visit Paris, Moscow and Peking."

The whole staff gasped in sudden realization of the President's master plan.

"That's entirely correct," he said, smiling slyly at them. "I want to be the first Chief of State to cross the Atlantic, Europe and Asia in a supersonic aircraft."

The VA hospital in Hagerstown had never seen so many reporters. There were reporters in the lobby, reporters lounging in the halls, reporters bribing nurses, reporters sneaking into elevators and surgical theaters (where they inevitably fainted). The parking lot was a jumble of cars bearing press stickers.

Only two reporters were allowed to see Mark Sequoia on any given day, and they had to share their story with all the other newsmen. Today the two—picked by lot—were a crusty old veteran from UPI and a rather pretty blonde from *Women's Wear Daily*.

"But I've told your colleagues what happened at least a dozen times," Sequoia mumbled from behind a swathing of bandages.

He was hanging by both arms and legs from four traction braces, his backside barely touching the bed. Bandages covered eighty percent of his body.

The two reporters stood by his bed. UPI looked flinty as he scribbled some notes on a rumpled sheet of paper. The blonde had a tiny tape recorder in her hand.

She looked misty-eyed. "Are . . . are you in much pain?"

"Not really," Sequoia answered bravely, with a slight tremor in his voice.

"Why the damned traction?" UPI asked in a tone reminiscent of a cement mixer riding over a gravel road. "The docs said there weren't any broken bones."

"Splinters," Sequoia said weakly.

"Bone splinters? Oh, how awful!" gasped the blonde.

"No—" Sequoia corrected. "Splinters. When the balloon came down, it landed in a clump of trees just outside of Hagerstown. We all suffered from thousands of splinters. It took the surgical staff here three days to pick all the splinters out of us. The chief of surgery said he was going to save the wood and build a scale model of the *Titanic* with it. . . ."

"Oh, how painful!" The blonde insisted on gasping. She gasped very well, Sequoia noted, watching her blouse.

"And what about your hair?" asked UPI gruffly.

Sequoia felt himself blush. "I . . . I must have been very frightened. After all, we were aloft in an open balloon for six days, without food, without anything to drink except a six-pack of beer that one of my aides brought along. We went through a dozen different thunderstorms . . ."

"With lightning?" the blonde asked.

Nodding painfully, Sequoia added, "We all thought we were going to die."

UPI frowned. "So your hair turned white from fright. There was some talk that cosmic rays might have done it."

"Cosmic rays? We weren't that high. . . . Cosmic rays don't have any effect until you get to very high altitudes . . . isn't that right?"

"How high did you go?"

"I don't know," Sequoia answered. "We didn't have an altimeter with us. Those thunderstorms pushed us pretty high, the air got kind of thin . . ."

"But not high enough for cosmic-ray damage."

"I doubt it."

"Too bad," said UPI. "Would've made a better story than just being scared. Hair turned white by cosmic rays. Maybe even sterilized."

"Sterilized?"

"Cosmic rays do that, too," UPI said. "I checked."

"Well, we weren't that high."

"You're sure?"

"Yeah . . . well, I don't think we were that high."

"But you could have been."

Shrugging was sheer torture, Sequoia found out.

"Okay, but those thunderstorms could've lifted you pretty damned high . . ."

The door opened and a horse-faced nurse said firmly, "That's all, please. Mr. Sequoia must rest now."

"Okay, I think I got something to hang a story onto," UPI said with a happy grin on his seamed face.

The blonde looked shocked and terribly upset. "You . . . you don't think you were really sterilized, do you?"

Sequoia tried to make himself sound worried and brave at the same time. "I don't know. I just . . . don't know."

Late that night the blonde snuck back into his room. If she knew the difference between sterilization and impotence, she didn't tell Sequoia about it. On his part, he forgot about his still-tender skin and his traction braces. The day nurse found him the next morning, unconscious, one shoulder dislocated, his skin terribly inflamed, most of his bandages rubbed off and a silly grin on his face.

*   *   *

"Will you look at this!"

Senator Goodyear tossed the morning *Post* across the break-fast table to his wife. She was a handsome woman: nearly as tall as her husband, athletically lean, shoulder-length dark hair with just a wisp of silver. She always dressed for break-fast just as carefully as for dinner. This morning she was going riding, so she wore slacks and a turtleneck sweater that outlined her figure.

But the senator was more interested in the *Post* article. "That Sequoia! He'll stop at nothing to destroy me! Just because the Ohio River melted his houseboat once, years ago . . . he's been out to crucify me ever since."

Mrs. Goodyear looked up from the newspaper. "Sterilized? You mean that people who fly in the SSZ could be sterilized by cosmic rays?"

"Utter nonsense!" Goodyear snapped.

"Of course," his wife murmured soothingly.

But after the senator drove off in his chauffeured limousine, Mrs. Goodyear made three phone calls. One was to the Smithsonian Institution. The second was to a friend in the Zero Population Growth movement. The third was to the underground Washington headquarters of the Women's International Terrorist Conspiracy from Hell. Unbeknownst to her husband or any of her friends or associates, Mrs. Goodyear was an undercover agent for WITCH.

The first snow of Virginia's winter was sifting gently past Roger K. Memo's office window. He was pacing across the plastic-tiled floor, his footsteps faintly echoing in the too-large room. Copies of the *Washington Post*, *New York Times* and *Aviation Week* were spread across his desk.

Dr. Pencilbeam sat at one of the unmatched conference chairs, all bony limbs and elbows and knees.

"Relax, Roger," he said calmly. "Congress isn't going to stop the SSZ. It means too many jobs, too much international prestige. And besides, the President has staked his credibility on it."

"That's what worries me," Memo mumbled.

"What?"

But Memo's eye was caught by movement outside his window. He waddled past his desk and looked out at the street below.

"Oh, my God."

"What's going on?" Pencilbeam unfolded like a pocket ruler into a six-foot-long human and hurried to the window.

Outside, in the thin mushy snow, a line of somber men was filing down the street past the TURD building. Silently they bore screaming signs:

> STOP THE SSZ
> DON'T STERILIZE THE HUMAN RACE
> SSZ MURDERS UNBORN CHILDREN
> ZEPPELINS, GO HOME

"Isn't that one with the sign about unborn children a priest?" Pencilbeam asked.

Memo shrugged. "Your eyes are better than mine."

"Ah-hah! And look at this!"

Pencilbeam pointed further down the street. A swarm of women was advancing on the building. They also carried signs:

> SSZ FOR ZPG
> ZEPPELINS SI! BABIES NO
> ZEPPELINS FOR POPULATION CONTROL
> UP THE SSZ

Memo visibly sagged at the window. "This . . . this is awful . . ."

The women marched through the thin snowfall and straight into the line of picketing men. Instantly the silence was shattered by shouts and taunts. Shrill female voices battled against rumbling baritones and basses. Signs wavered. Bodies pushed. Someone screamed. One sign struck a skull and then bloody war broke out.

Memo and Pencilbeam watched aghast until the helmeted TAC squad police doused the whole scene with riot gas, impartially clubbed men and women and dragged everyone off.

*   *   *

The huge factory assembly bay was filled with the skeleton of a giant dirigible. Great aluminum ribs stretched from titanium nosecap back toward the more intricate cagework of the tail fins. Tiny men with flashing laser welders crawled along the ribbing like maggots cleaning the bones of a noble whale.

Even the jet engines sitting on their loading pallets dwarfed human scale. Some of the welders held clandestine poker games inside them. John Driver and Richard Grand stood beside one of them, craning their necks to watch the welding work going on far overhead. The assembly bay rang to the shouts of working men, the hum of electrical machinery and the occasional clatter of metal against metal.

"It's going to be some Christmas party if Congress cancels the project," Driver said gloomily from behind his inevitable pipe.

"Oh, they wouldn't dare cancel it, now that Women's Liberation is behind it," said Grand with a sardonic little smile.

Driver glared at him. "With those bitches for allies, you don't need any enemies. Half those idiots in Congress will vote against us just to prove that they're not scared of Women's Lib."

"Do you really think so?" Grand asked.

He always acts as if he knows more than I do, Driver thought. It had taken him several years to realize that Grand actually knew rather less than most people—but had a way of hiding this behind protective language.

"Yes, I really think so!" Driver snapped. Then he pulled his pipe out of his mouth and jabbed it in the general direction of Grand's eyeballs. "And listen to me, kiddo. I've been working on that secretary of mine since the last goddamned Christmas party. If this project falls through and the party's a bust, that palpitating hunk of female flesh is going to run home and cry. And so will I!"

Grand blinked several times, then murmured, "Pity."

The banner saying HAPPY HOLIDAYS drooped sadly across one wall of the cafeteria. Outside in the darkness, lights glimmered, cars were moving, and a bright moon lit the snowy peak of Mt. Olympia.

But inside Everett Aircraft's cafeteria there was nothing but gloom. The Christmas party had been a dismal flop, especially so since half the company's employees had received their layoff notices the day before.

The tables had been pushed to one side of the cafeteria to make room for a dance floor. Syrupy music was oozing out of the loudspeakers in the acoustic-tile ceiling. But no one was dancing.

Bob Wisdom sat at one of the tables, propping his aching head on his hands. Ray Kurtz and Tommy Rohr sat with him, equally dejected.

"Why the hell did they have to cancel the project two days before Christmas?" Rohr asked rhetorically.

"Makes for more pathos," Kurtz muttered from inside his beard.

"It's pathetic, all right," Wisdom said. "I've never seen so many secretaries crying at once."

"Even Driver was crying," Rohr said.

"Well," Kurtz said, staring at his half-finished drink on the table before him, "Sequoia did it. He's a big national hero again."

"And we're on the bread line," Rohr said.

"You get laid off?"

"Not yet—but it's coming. This place will be closing its doors before another year is out."

"It's not that bad," said Wisdom. "There's still the Air Force work."

Rohr frowned. "You know what gets me? The way the whole project was scrapped, without giving us a chance to build one of the damned zeps and see how they work. Without a goddam chance!"

Kurtz said, "Congressmen are scared of being sterilized."

"Or castrated by Women's Lib."

"Next time you dream up a project, Bob, make it underground. Something in a lead mine. Then the congressmen won't have to worry about cosmic rays."

Wisdom started to laugh, then held off. "You know," he said slowly, "you just might have something there."

"What?"

"Where?"

"A supersonic transport—in a tunnel."

"Oh, for Chri—"

Wisdom sat up straight in his chair. "No, listen. You could make an air-cushion vehicle go supersonic. If you put it in a tunnel, you get away from the sonic boom and the pollution . . ."

"Hey, the safety aspects would be a lot better, too."

Kurtz shook his head. "You guys are crazy! Who the hell's going to dig tunnels all over the United States?"

But Wisdom waved him down. "Somebody will. Now, the way I see the design of this . . . SSST, I guess we call it."

"SSST?"

"Sure," he answered, grinning. "Supersonic subway train."

Blessed Be the Peacemakers ▬▬▬▬▬

While the Supersonic Zeppelin is obviously a spoof, the possibility of building defenses in orbit that can protect us against nuclear missile attack is very real. The automatic Luddite reaction to President Reagan's speech of 23 March 1983 was a loud, "No!" But this is a case that involves life and death for the entire human race, and it must be examined very carefully, honestly and *openly* by Luddites and Prometheans alike. We may have a chance to remove the terrible threat of nuclear devastation. But like a man defusing a live bomb, we must approach this task with great care and caution.

It is a hopeful sign that, at their summit meeting in Geneva in 1985, President Reagan and General Secretary Gorbachev took the first step toward the cooperative program I have advocated.

———————

President Reagan's call for a defense against nuclear attack, using the most scientifically advanced means possible, marks the beginning of a new era in international politics.

In a small way, it is an era I helped to create. I worked at the laboratory where the first breakthrough into truly high-power lasers was made. In February 1966 I helped to arrange the first top secret meeting in the Pentagon to reveal to the Defense Department what our laboratory had accomplished. A group of scientists from our lab, the Avco Everett Research Laboratory, spent more than an hour explaining that lasers of truly enormous power output could now be made. When the last slide was shown, the slide projector turned off and the overhead lights came on, there was a long moment of awed silence—from the best scientists the Pentagon could bring together.

Within months, we were not only developing the technology of high-power lasers, we were also studying how they might be used. Some of the potential uses of such lasers were peaceful: drilling tunnels in hard rock, welding and cutting metal at high speeds, communicating over interplanetary distances.

The most significant weapons application for high-power lasers, however, appeared to be in space—where there is no air to absorb or distort the laser's beam of energy, where the distances between laser and target could be thousands of miles, and where the targets themselves would be moving at thousands of miles per hour.

To give you an idea of the kinds of power outputs these lasers can produce, in 1970 Avco Everett sold a relatively low-power laser to Caterpillar Tractor Company's research laboratory in Muncie, Indiana. This laser produced a mere 10,000 watts output, too low to be of interest to the military. That 10-kilowatt beam cut through three-quarter-inch steel at rates of 50 to 100 inches per minute. Today, Avco sells 100-kilowatt lasers on the commercial marketplace. Military classification begins at higher power levels.

Since the mid-sixties I have been thinking and writing about the technical, political and human implications of using high-power lasers in orbit as a defense against nuclear missile attack. In novels such as *Millennium* and nonfiction books such as *The High Road* I have examined various scenarios dealing with the inevitable time when such weaponry is put in space. It could bring about the end of the threat of nuclear holocaust. But it might also, instead, trigger the very nuclear Armageddon we all fear.

Today all Americans are hostage to the nuclear missiles of the Soviet Union. By deliberate government policy, every American man, woman and child is defenseless against a Soviet missile attack. We have agreed, by the terms of the SALT I accord, not even to attempt to defend our cities and our population. And the Russians have agreed to the same terms.

Since Hiroshima, strategic policy has been based entirely on the idea that there is no visible defense against a determined nuclear attack. Our official policy is literally MAD: Mutual Assured Destruction. We strive to maintain a nuclear attack force that is so strong that even if the Soviets launch a first strike at us, our counterstrike will annihilate the Soviet Union. And the Russians do the same.

This MAD policy has produced the continuing nuclear arms race that has terrified so many people around the world. The nuclear freeze movement is an attempt by people in Europe and America to stop the constant escalation of nuclear weapons. It is a well-intended movement, but it is doomed to failure—unless someone, somewhere, finds a way to assure the leaders in Washington and Moscow that they can actually protect their nations from nuclear annihilation.

Now technology offers the possibility of creating a workable defense against nuclear missiles. Critics of the idea claim that it is impossible, or at least undesirable. Crazy as it may seem, there are some allegedly thoughtful people in America whose instant reaction to the President's suggestion was that it is preferable to live under a nuclear Sword of Damocles than to build a credible defense against nuclear war. This is akin to Neville Chamberlain's hope, when he was Prime Minister of Great Britain in the 1930s, that he could appease Hitler and avert war.

I, for one, do not choose to spend the rest of my life, and the lives of my children, and *their* children, under the constant threat of nuclear holocaust. If there is a way to defend us, it is deadly nonsense to ignore it.

But—and this is the point on which our entire future will turn—we must be prepared not only to open our minds to bold new technological concepts; we must be prepared to consider fairly and openly equally bold new *political* ideas. For just as the technology of gunpowder eventually blew away the political system based on kings and emperors, just as the technology of aircraft ended Britain's snug, smug feeling of safety on their tight little isle, the new technology of space weaponry is going to change international politics forever.

The first political reality we must face is that we no longer live in a bipolarized world of two superpowers, their various allies and satellites, and a scattering of small, poor nations that don't count when it comes to political power. True, our major military concerns all center on the Soviet Union. But the People's Republic of China has nuclear-tipped missiles. So do France and Great Britain. India is launching satellites with its own rockets, and has tested its own nuclear bomb. Pakistan, the most likely target of India's missiles, is undoubtedly trying to produce its own nuclear arsenal so that it, too, can engage in a MAD policy.

What will the world be like in the 1990s, when nations such as Argentina and Libya may have nuclear weapons and missiles to deliver them? Will Iraq finally produce its own nuclear bombs, and if it does, will it use them first against Iran or Israel?

It may be that none of the smaller nations would ever dream of aiming a nuclear-tipped missile at an American city. But would you bet your life on that?

A second fact we must face is that we are not the only nation in the world that might build orbital defenses. Most American pundits who have come out against what they call "the Star Wars defense" have tacitly assumed that if the United States does not place defensive weapons in orbit, nobody will. That is arrant foolishness. We can decide if *we* will build orbital defense weapons; we cannot decide if the Soviets or other nations will.

Make no mistake: the Soviet Union has been developing this technology for almost as long as we have, and in several key areas of development they are far ahead of us.

In the 1960s, as we at Avco Everett were working on the earliest high-power lasers, we watched the Russian scientific literature carefully. At that time, the Soviets did not classify theoretical work. We saw them developing the same ideas that we ourselves had developed only a year or two earlier. And when those ideas converged on the realization that lasers of virtually unlimited power could be built, all that work disappeared from the open, unclassified scientific journals.

Through the 1970s, as the American space program became moribund after Washington killed the Apollo program, the Soviets sent scores of cosmonauts into orbit aboard a succession of space stations they call Salyuts. Salyut 7 is in orbit today. It is larger than any previous Soviet space station, and may well be the permanent platform from which the Russians will test their own orbital energy weapons.

Soviet scientists have worked hard not only on lasers, but also on particle-beam devices, which fire a stream of subatomic particles such as protons. As a weapon, particle-beam devices may prove to be more effective than lasers. The Soviets have also pushed development of the kinds of electrical power systems that are needed to "drive" high-power lasers and particle-beam weapons.

For nearly twenty years the Soviets have flown military weaponry in space. While both the United States and the USSR have placed into orbit satellites for military surveillance, communications, early warning, weather observation and mapping, only the Soviets have put actual weapons into space. They have an operational antisatellite weapon system, and unconfirmed leaks from intelligence sources claim that they have blinded American surveillance satellites by firing lasers at them from the ground.

As much as we may want to keep space free of weaponry, the fact is that the military got into space before anyone else did, and that space is already a theater of military operations. The best thing we can do, the wisest thing we can do, is to try to use space in a way that will shield us against nuclear attack.

Is it possible? Technologically, yes. There is no reason why we cannot develop orbital weapons that will find, track and destroy ballistic missiles bearing nuclear warheads. Satellites armed with lasers, particle-beam weapons, or even pellet guns or small missiles could destroy ballistic missiles while their rocket engines are still boosting them, when they are still over their own territory and very vulnerable to attack.

Earlier proposals for defense against ballistic missiles were based on the idea of firing antimissile missiles from the ground at incoming nuclear warheads. Tests proved that you could shoot down a single warhead that way, but that such an antimissile system would be easily overwhelmed by a full-scale attack of hundreds of warheads, decoys and radar-jamming techniques.

The idea of defending against missile attack with ground-based antimissile missiles was something like trying to play football by giving your opponent the ball on your own five-yard line, and allowing him five hundred downs in which to score—and in a situation that is truly "sudden death." So the United States agreed to the SALT I treaty provision that limits us—and the USSR—to building only one antimissile system. We soon gave up even on that, convinced that a ground-based system would not work. The Soviets have built their system to protect Moscow, whether it works or not.

Orbital defenses, in which weapons aboard satellites fire at the attacking missiles as soon as they are launched, is more like playing football in midfield, or even on your opponent's five-yard line.

Critics of the idea claim that building an orbital defense system would violate the 1972 ABM treaty. However, the treaty specifically allows *research and development* efforts on missile defense to be carried out. That is what we should be doing. It is undoubtedly what the Soviet Union is already doing. When we are convinced that R&D efforts will lead to an effective defense, it is time to return to the bargaining table.

The loudest argument that critics of orbital defenses make, however, is their claim that such a system will not work. Their forefathers made similar claims against repeating rifles, submarines, airplanes, ballistic missiles and almost every other new idea they ever heard of.

The critics point out that no defense system is perfect, and that some attacking missiles will get through to deliver their nuclear warheads on target. That is quite true. But remember that the goal we pursue is *deterrence*. No one wants to dare the Soviet Union to attack us. We wish to prevent them from deciding that they can or should attack.

If the USSR knows that a substantial portion of its missile force will be destroyed long before the missiles reach their targets, and that a powerful American force will survive a Soviet first strike and be capable of a devastating counterstrike, the decision-makers in the Kremlin will no doubt stay their hand, even though they could inflict considerable damage on the United States. As Admiral Yamamoto reflected after the Japanese attack on Pearl Harbor, it does not pay to enrage a giant.

How would the Soviets respond to such an American buildup of orbital defenses? Perhaps they would respond by producing more ballistic missiles, so that they could overwhelm our defenses and deliver enough warheads on target to demolish our counterstrike missiles, bombers and submarines.

Or, more likely, they would launch a strike when it became clear to them that we are building defenses that will ultimately make their attack forces obsolete and useless. Already the Kremlin has branded Star Wars as a threat against the USSR. In their view, a system that protects the United States against Soviet nuclear attack would lead the U.S. to think that it could attack Russia with impunity. Therefore, Moscow would feel justified in launching a preemptive strike before the U.S. could complete its defensive shield.

All of this reasoning works both ways, of course. What the Soviets are doing in space to defend themselves against our missiles could be seen as a direct threat to America.

It seems clear that orbital defensive systems can be built; if not this year, then certainly in the foreseeable future. Thus the question of whether or not they *should* be built becomes of primary importance now, today.

It will cost tens or even hundreds of billions of dollars to build such an orbiting defensive shield. But what price tag do you place on survival? How much are you willing to pay to prevent nuclear war from happening?

If we match the technological wizardry of high-power lasers and satellite defense systems with equally high-powered political initiatives, we do have a chance—a good chance—of making nuclear war almost impossible.

The key to this is simple in concept, but terribly difficult in practice. It is this: invite the Soviets, the Chinese, the Europeans—everyone in the world—to join us in the effort to build and deploy such defensive satellites.

If we have the moral courage to make this program completely open, and invite the rest of the world to participate in it, sharing our knowledge with theirs, and placing the orbiting satellites under international control, then we may have found the way to prevent *any* nation from launching a nuclear attack on any other nation.

What we need is a form of Swiss Guard in orbit, an international organization that has the power to destroy any rocket launched from anywhere in the world, if that rocket has not been inspected and found to be carrying only a peaceful payload.

Such an organization would discourage nations from developing nuclear arsenals, or from enlarging the arsenals they already have. And an international program could spread the costs of the system among all the participating nations.

Would the United States voluntarily give up its right to attack its enemies? Would we willingly place our own defense in the hands of some international organization? That *must* be the basis for a full and thorough political dialogue within our own society.

Would the Soviet Union, with its historic fear of invasion and almost-paranoiac insistence on secrecy, be willing to allow such an international organization to control its defenses? I believe the Kremlin would join such an effort, for two reasons:

First, most of the rest of the world would quickly agree to such a global defense system, and the Soviets would find themselves facing not only the U.S. and Western Europe, but almost the whole world. It would be more advantageous to the Soviet Union to join the peace-keeping force than to isolate itself.

Second, by neutralizing the world's nuclear arsenals, the Soviets—with their heavy preponderance of conventional military arms—would feel more secure than they do today. By removing the threat of nuclear war, their advantages in numbers of tanks, guns and planes becomes more important to them. And to us.

Clearly, orbital defenses against nuclear-armed missiles are not the answer to every problem that faces the world. But they can be the answer to nuclear Armageddon, and that is a major step forward for the human race's prospects of survival.

If it is impossible to freeze nuclear weapons, we should at least try to melt them.

The Weathermakers ▬▬▬▬▬

The dream of controlling the weather all around the world is one of the ultimate Promethean fantasies. The Luddite in us warns that we should not even attempt to do it. The practical problems of weather *forecasting*, without even thinking of modifying the weather, are enormous. But when you stop to think that we are just as helpless in the face of the weather as any Stone Age hunter was, you begin to wonder if it wouldn't be a better world where the weather was under firm human control; where, in the words of lyricist Alan Jay Lerner, "The rain may never fall 'til after sundown/By nine p.m. the moonlight must appear . . ."

▬▬▬▬▬

Ted Marrett gathered us around the mammoth viewscreen-map that loomed over his desk in the THUNDER control center. The map showed a full-fledged hurricane—Nora—howling up the mid-Atlantic. Four more tropical disturbances, marked by red danger symbols, were strung out along the fifteenth parallel from the Antilles Islands to the Cape Verdes.

"There's the story," Ted told us, prowling impatiently along the foot of the viewscreen. He moved his tall, powerful body with the feline grace of a professional athlete. His stubborn red hair and rough-hewn face made him look more like a football gladiator than "the whiz-kid boss of Project THUNDER," as the news magazines had called him.

Gesturing toward the map, Ted said, "Nora's no problem;

she'll stay out at sea. Won't even bother Bermuda much. But these four lows'll bug us."

Tuli Noyon, Ted's closest buddy and chief of the Air Chemistry Section, said in his calm Oriental way, "This is the day we have all been dreading. There are more disturbances than we can handle. One of them, possibly two, will get past us and form hurricanes."

Ted looked sharply at him, then turned to me. "How about it, Jerry? What's the logistics picture?"

"Tuli's right," I admitted. "The planes and crews have been working around the clock for the past few weeks and we just don't have enough . . ."

"Skip the flute music. How many of these Lows can we hit?"

I shrugged. "Two, I'd say. Maybe three if we really push it."

Barney—Priscilla Barneveldt—said, "The computer just finished an updated statistical analysis on the four disturbances. Their storm tracks all threaten the East Coast. The two closest ones have point-eight probabilities of reaching hurricane strength. The farther pair are only point-five."

"Fifty-fifty," Ted muttered, "for the last two. But they've got the longest time to develop. Chances'll be better for 'em by tomorrow."

Barney was slim and blond as a Dutch jonquil, and had a true Hollander's stubborn spirit. "It's those two closest disturbances that are the most dangerous," she insisted. "They each have an eighty percent chance of turning into hurricanes that will hit the East Coast."

"We can't stop them all," Tuli said. "What will we do, Ted?"

Project THUNDER: Threatening Hurricane Neutralization, Destruction and Recording. Maybe we were young and daring and slightly fanatical, as the newsmen had said of us. But it took more than knowledge and skill. THUNDER was Ted Marrett's creation, the result of nearly four years of his single-minded determination. None of us would have dared it, even if there were a hundred more of us, without Ted to lead the way. He had brought the Project into being, practically with his own strong hands.

Yet it wasn't enough, not for Ted Marrett. He wasn't satisfied with an experimental program to modify potential hurricanes. Ted wanted to control the weather, fully. Nothing less. To him THUNDER was only a small shadow of what could be done toward controlling the weather. He had said as much to the press, and now the world expected us to prevent all hurricanes from striking the islands of the Caribbean and the North American mainland.

It was an impossible task.

"Where's the analysis?" Ted asked Barney. "I want to go over the numbers."

She looked around absently. "I must have left it on my desk. I'll go get it."

Ted's phone buzzed. He leaned across the desk and flicked the switch. "Dr. Weis calling from Washington," the operator said.

He made a sour face. "Okay, put him on." Sliding into his desk chair, Ted waved us away as Dr. Weis's tanned, well-creased face came on the phone viewscreen.

"I've just seen this morning's weather map," the President's science advisor said with no preliminaries. "It looks to me as though you're in trouble."

"Got our hands full," Ted said.

I started back for my own cubicle. I could hear Dr. Weis's nasal voice, a little edgier than usual, saying, "The opposition has turned Project THUNDER into a political issue, with only six weeks to the election. If you hadn't made the newsmen think that you could stop every hurricane . . ."

The rest was lost in the chatter and bustle of the control room. THUNDER's nerve center filled the entire second floor of our Miami bayfront building. It was a frenetic conglomeration of people, desks, calculating machines, plotting boards, map printers, cabinets, teletypes, phones, viewscreens and endless piles of paper. Over it all hung Ted's giant electronic plotting screen, showing our battlefield—all of North America and the North Atlantic Ocean. I made my way across the cluttered windowless room and stepped into my glass-walled cubicle.

It was quiet inside, with the door closed. Phone screens lined the walls, and half my desk was covered with a private switchboard that put me in direct contact with a network of THUNDER support stations ranging from New Orleans to ships off the coast of Africa to the Atlantic Satellite Station, in synchronous orbit 23,000 miles above the mouth of the Amazon River.

I looked across the control center again, and saw Ted still talking earnestly into the phone. Dr. Weis called every day. THUNDER was important to him, and to the President. If we failed . . . I didn't like to think of the consequences.

There was work to be done. I began alerting the Navy and Air Force bases that were supporting THUNDER, trying to get ready to hit those hurricane threats as hard and fast as we could.

While I worked, I watched Barney and Ted plowing through the thick sheaf of computer printout sheets that contained the detailed analysis of the storm threats. They made a good-looking couple, and everyone assumed that she was Ted's girl. Including Ted himself. But he never bothered to ask Barney about it. Or me.

As soon as I could, I went down and joined them.

"Okay," he was saying, "if we leave those two farther-out Lows alone, they'll develop into hurricanes overnight. We can knock 'em out now without much sweat, but by tomorrow they'll be too much for us."

"The same applies to the second disturbance," Barney said, "only more so. It's already better developed than the two farther lows."

"We'll have to skip the second one. The first one—off the Leewards—is too close to ignore. So we'll hit Number One, skip the second, and hit Three and Four."

Barney took her glasses off. "That won't work, Ted," she said firmly. "If we don't stop the second one today it certainly will develop into—"

"A walloping big hurricane. I know." He shrugged. "But if we throw enough planes at Number Two to smother it, we'll have to leave Three and Four alone. Then they'll both develop and we'll have *two* brutes on our hands.''

"But this one . . ."

"There's a chance that if we knock out the closest Low, Number Two'll change its track and head out to sea."

"That's a terribly slim chance. The numbers show—"

"Okay, it's a slim chance. But it's all we've got to work with. Got any better ideas?"

"Isn't there anything we can do?" she asked. "If a hurricane strikes the coast . . ."

"Weis is already looking through his mail for my resignation," Ted said. "Okay, we're in trouble. Best we can do is hit Number One, skip Two, and wipe out Three and Four before they get strong enough to make waves."

Barney stared at the numbers on the computer sheets. "That means we're going to have a full-grown hurricane heading for Florida within twenty-four hours."

"Look," Ted snapped, "we can sit around here debating till they *all* turn into hurricanes. Let's scramble. Jerry, you heard the word. Get the planes up."

I headed back to my cubicle and sent out the orders. A few minutes later, Barney came by. Standing dejectedly in the doorway, she asked herself out loud:

"Why did he agree to take on this Project? He knows it's not the best way to handle hurricanes. It's too chancy, too expensive, we're working ourselves to death . . ."

"So are the aircrews," I answered. "And the season's just starting to hit its peak."

"Then why did he have to make the newsmen think we could run up a perfect score the first year?"

"Because he's Ted Marrett. He not only thinks he can control the weather, he thinks he *owns* it."

"There's no room in him for failure," she said. "If this storm does hit, if the Project is canceled . . . what will it do to him?"

"What will it do to you?" I asked her.

She shook her head. "I don't know, Jerry. But I'm afraid we're going to find out in another day or two."

*   *   *

Tropical storms are built on seemingly slight differences of air temperature. A half-dozen degrees of difference over an area a hundred miles in diameter can power the giant heat engine of a hurricane. Ted's method of smothering tropical disturbances before they reached hurricane strength was to smooth out the temperature difference between the core of the disturbance and its outer fringes.

The nearest disturbance was developing quickly. It had already passed over the Leeward Islands and entered the Caribbean by the time our first planes reached it. The core of the disturbance was a column of warm, rising air, shooting upward from the sea's surface to the tropopause, some ten miles high. Swirling around this warm column was cooler air sliding down from the north into the low-pressure trough created by the warm column.

If the disturbance were left to itself, it would soak up moisture from the warm sea and condense it into raindrops. The heat released by the condensation would power winds of ever-mounting intensity. A cycle would be established: winds bring in moisture, the water vapor condenses into rain, the heat released builds the winds' power. Finally the core would switch over into a cold, clear column of downward-rushing air—the eye of a full-grown hurricane. A thousand megatons of energy would be loose, unstoppable, even by Project THUNDER.

Our job was to prevent that cycle from establishing itself. We had to warm up the air flowing into the disturbance and chill down its core until air temperatures throughout the disturbance were practically the same. A heat engine that has all its parts at the same temperature—or close to it—simply won't work.

We had been doing that job successfully since July. But now, in mid-September, with the hurricane season nearing its peak, there were more disturbances than we could handle simultaneously.

As I started giving out the orders for three missions at once, Tuli stuck his head into my cubicle.

"I'm off to see the dragon firsthand." He was grinning excitedly.

"Which one?"

"Number One dragon; it's in the Caribbean now."

"I know. Good luck. Kill it dead."

He nodded, a round-faced, brown-skinned St. George working against the most destructive menace man had ever faced.

As I parceled out orders over my phones, a battery of gigajoule lasers aboard the Atlantic Station began pumping their energy into the northern peripheries of the storms. The lasers were part of our project. Similar to the military type mounted in the missle-defense satellites, they had been put aboard the Atlantic Station at Ted's request, and with the personal backing of Dr. Weis and the White House. Only carefully selected Air Force personnel were allowed near them. The entire section of the satellite Station where they were installed was under armed guard, much to the discomfort of the civilians aboard.

Planes from a dozen airfields were circling the northern edges of the disturbances, sowing the air with rain-producing crystals.

"Got to seed for hours at a time," Ted had once told me. "That's a mistake the early experimenters made—never stayed on the job long enough to force an effect on the weather."

And thanks to chemical wizards like Tuli, we had a wide assortment of seeding materials that could squeeze rain from almost any type of air mass. Producing the tonnage of crystals we needed had been a problem, but the Army's Edgewood Arsenal had stepped in with their mass-production facilities to help us.

I was watching the disturbance in the Caribbean. That was the closest threat, and the best-developed of all the four disturbances. Radar plots, mapped on Ted's giant viewscreen, showed rain clouds expanding and showering precipitation over an ever-widening area. As the water vapor in the seeded air condensed into raindrops, the air temperature rose slightly. The satellite-borne lasers were also helping to heat the air feeding into the disturbance.

It looked as though we were just making the disturbance bigger. But Ted and the other technical staff people had figured out the energy balances in the storm. They knew what they were doing . . . but I still found myself frowning worriedly.

Tuli was in an Air Force bomber, part of two squadrons of planes flying at staggered altitudes. From nearly sea level to fifty thousand feet, they roared into the central column of warm air in precise formation and began dumping tons of liquid nitrogen into the rising tropical air.

The effect was spectacular. The TV screen alongside the big plotting screen showed what the planes saw: tremendous plumes of white sprang out behind each plane as the cryogenic liquid flash-froze the water vapor in the warm column. It looked as though some cosmic wind had suddenly spewed its frigid breath through the air. The nitrogen quickly evaporated, soaking up enormous amounts of heat. Most of the frozen vapor simply evaporated again, although radar plots showed that some condensation and actual rainfall occurred.

I made my way to Ted's desk to see the results of the core freezing.

"Looks good," he was saying into a phone.

I checked the teletype chugging nearby. It was printing a report from the observation planes that followed the bombers.

Ted stepped over to me. "Broke up the core okay. Now if she doesn't re-form, we can scratch Number One off the map."

It was early evening before we could tell for sure. The disturbance's source of energy, the differing temperatures of the air masses it contained, had been taken away from it. The plotting screen showed a large swatch of concentric, irregular isobars, like a lopsided bull's-eye, with a sullen red "L" marking its center, just north of Jamaica. The numbers of the screen showed a central pressure of 991 millibars, nowhere near a typical hurricane's. Wind speeds had peaked at fifty-two knots and were dying off now. Kingston and Guantanamo were reporting moderate-to-heavy rain, but at Santo Domingo, six hundred miles to the east, it was already clearing.

The disturbance was just another small tropical storm, and a rapidly weakening one at that. The two farther disturbances, halfway out across the ocean, had been completely wiped out. The planes were on their way home. The laser crews aboard the Atlantic Station were recharging their energy storage coils.

"Shall I see if the planes can reload and fly another mission tonight?" I asked Ted. "Maybe we can still hit the second disturbance."

He shook his head. "Won't do any good. Look at her," he said pointing toward the plotting map. "By the time the planes get to her, she'll be a full-grown hurricane. There's nothing we can do about it now."

So we didn't sleep that night. We stayed at the control center and watched the storm develop on the TV picture being beamed from the Atlantic Station. At night they had to use infrared cameras, of course, but we could still see—in the ghostly IR images—a broad spiral of clouds stretching across four hundred miles of open ocean.

Practically no one had left the control center, but the big room was deathly quiet. Even the chattering, calculating machines and teletypes seemed to have stopped. The numbers on the spotting screen steadily worsened. Barometric pressure sank to 980, 965, 950 millibars. Wind velocity mounted to 50 knots, 60, 80. She was a full-grown hurricane by midnight.

Ted leaned across his desk and tapped out a name for the storm on the viewscreen's keyboard: *Omega*.

"One way or the other, she's the end of THUNDER," he murmured.

The letters glowed out at the top of the plotting screen. Across the vast room, one of the girls broke into sobs.

Through the early hours of the morning, Hurricane Omega grew steadily in size and strength. An immense band of clouds towered from the sea to some sixty thousand feet, pouring two inches of rain per hour over an area of nearly 300,000 square miles. The pressure at her core had plummeted to 942 millibars and central wind speeds were gusting at better than 100 knots, and still rising.

"It's almost as though she's alive," Tuli whispered as we watched the viewscreen intently. "She grows, she feeds, she moves."

By 2:00 a.m. Miami time, dawn was breaking over Hurricane Omega. Six trillion tons of air packing the energy of a hundred hydrogen bombs, a mammoth, mindless heat engine turned loose, aiming for civilization, for us.

Waves lashed by Omega's fury were spreading all across the Atlantic and would show up as dangerous surf on the beaches of four continents. Seabirds were sucked into the storm against their every exertion, to be drenched and battered to exhaustion; their only hope was to make it to the eye, where the air was calm and clear. A tramp steamer on the New York-to-Capetown run, five hundred miles from Omega's center, was calling frantically for help as mountainous waves overpowered the ship's puny pumps.

Omega churned onward, releasing every fifteen minutes as much energy as a ten-megaton bomb.

We watched, we listened, fascinated. The face of our enemy, and it made all of us—even Ted—feel completely helpless. At first Omega's eye, as seen from the satellite cameras, was vague and shifting, covered over by cirrus clouds. But finally it steadied and opened up, a strong column of downward-flowing air, the mighty central pillar of the hurricane, the pivotal anchor around which her furious winds wailed their primeval song of violence and terror.

Barney, Tuli and I sat around Ted's desk, watching his face sink deeper into a scowl as the storm worsened.

We didn't realize it was daylight once more until Dr. Weis phoned again. He looked haggard on the tiny desktop viewscreen.

"I've been watching the storm all night," he said. "The President called me a few minutes ago and asked me what you were going to do about it."

Ted rubbed his eyes. "Can't knock her out, if that's what you mean. Too big now; be like trying to stop a forest fire with a blanket."

"Well, you've got to do something!" Weis snapped. "All our reputations hang on that storm. Do you understand? Yours, mine, even the President's! To say nothing of the future for weather-control work in this country, if that means anything to you."

He might just as easily have asked Beethoven if he cared about music.

"Told you back in Washington when we started this game,"

Ted countered, "that THUNDER was definitely the wrong way to tackle hurricanes . . ."

"Yes, and then you announced to the press that no hurricanes would strike the United States! So now, instead of being an act of nature, hurricanes are a political issue."

Ted shook his head. "We've done all we can do."

"No, you haven't. You can try to steer the hurricane . . . change its path so that it won't strike the coast."

"Won't work."

"You haven't tried it!"

"We could throw everything we've got into it and maybe budge it a few degrees. It'll still wind up hitting the coast somewhere. All we'll be doing is fouling up its track so we won't know for sure where it'll hit."

"Well, we've got to do something. We can't just sit here and let it happen to us. Ted, I haven't tried to tell you how to run THUNDER, but now I'm giving an order. You've got to make an attempt to steer the storm away from the coast. If we fail, at least we'll go down fighting. Maybe we can salvage something from this mess."

"Waste of time," Ted muttered.

Dr. Weis's shoulders moved as though he were wringing his hands, off camera. "Try it anyway. It might work. We might just be lucky . . ."

"Okay," Ted said, shrugging. "You're the boss."

The screen went dark. Ted looked up at us. "You heard the man. We're going to play Pied Piper."

"But we can't do it," Tuli said. "It can't be done."

"Doesn't matter. Weis is trying to save face. You ought to understand that, buddy."

Barney looked up at the plotting screen. Omega was northeast of Puerto Rico and boring in toward Florida. Toward us.

"Why didn't you tell him the truth?" she asked Ted. "Why didn't you tell him that the only way to stop the storm is to control the weather across the whole East Coast."

"Been all through this half a million times," Ted grumbled, slouching back in his chair wearily. "Weis won't buy weather control. Hurricane-killing is what he wants."

"But we can't kill Omega. THUNDER has failed, Ted. You shouldn't have—"

"Shouldn't have what?" he snapped. "Shouldn't have taken THUNDER when Weis offered to let us try it? Think I didn't argue with him? Think I didn't fight it out, right in the White House? I know THUNDER's a shaky way to fight hurricanes. But it's all I could get. I had to take what they were willing to give us."

Barney shook her head. "And what has it got you? A disaster."

"Listen," he said, sitting up erect now and pressing his big hands on the desk. "I spelled it out to the President and to Weis. I told 'em both that chasing tropical disturbances and trying to smother hurricanes before they develop is doing things the hard way. Showed 'em how we could control the weather over the whole country. They wouldn't take the chance. Too risky. Think the President wants to get blamed for every cloudy day in Arizona, or every rainfall in California, or every chill in Chicago?"

He stood up and began pacing. "They wanted something spectacular but safe. So they settled on killing hurricanes—very spectacular. But only by making weather mods out at sea, where nobody would complain about 'em—that's safe, see? I told 'em it was the hard way to do the job. But that's what they wanted. And that's what I took. Because I'd rather do *something*, even if it's not the best something. I wanted to show 'em that we can kill hurricanes. If we had gone through this year okay, maybe they would've tried real weather control next year."

"Then why," she asked, very softly, "did you tell the newsmen that we would stop every hurricane threat? You knew we couldn't do it."

"Why? How should I know? Maybe because Weis was sitting there in front of the cameras looking so blasted sure of himself. Safe and serene. Maybe I was crazy enough to think we could really sneak through a whole hurricane season okay. Maybe I'm just crazy, period. I don't know."

"But what do we do now?" I asked.

He cocked an eye at the plotting-screen. "Try to steer Omega. Try saving Weis's precious face." Pointing to a symbol on the map several hundred miles north of the storm, he said, "This's a Navy sonar picket, isn't it? I'm going to buzz out there, see if I can get a firsthand look at this monster.''

"That could be dangerous," Barney countered.

He shrugged.

"Ted, you haven't thought this out," I said. "You can't run the operation from the middle of the ocean."

"Picket's in a good spot to see the storm . . . at least, the edge of it. Maybe I can wangle a plane ride through it. Been fighting hurricanes all season without seeing one. Besides, the ship's part of the Navy's antisubmarine-warning net; loaded with communications gear. Be in touch with you every minute, don't worry."

"But if the storm comes that way . . ."

"Let it come," he snapped. "It's going to finish us anyway." He turned and strode off, leaving us to watch him.

Barney turned to me. "Jerry, he thinks we blame him for everything. We've got to stop him."

"No one can stop him. You know that. Once he gets his mind set on something . . ."

"Then I'll go with him." She got up from her chair. I took her arm.

"No, Jerry," she said. "I can't let him go alone."

"Is it the danger you're afraid of, or the fact that he's leaving?"

"Jerry, in the mood he's in now . . . he's reckless . . ."

"All right," I said, trying to calm her. "All right. I'll go with him. I'll make sure he keeps his feet dry."

"I don't want either one of you in danger!"

"I know. I'll take care of him."

She looked at me with those misty gray-green eyes. "Jerry . . . you won't let him do anything foolish, will you?"

"You know me," I said. "I'm no hero."

"Yes, you are," she said. And I felt my insides do a handspring.

I left her there with Tuli and hurried out to the parking lot. The bright sunshine outdoors was a painful surprise. It was hot and muggy, even though the day was only an hour or so old.

Ted was getting into one of the Project staff cars when I caught up with him.

"A landlubber like you shouldn't be loose on the ocean by himself," I said.

He grinned. "Hop aboard, salt."

The day was sultry. The usual tempering sea breezes had died off. As we drove along the Miami bayfront, the air was oppressive, ominous. The sky was brazen, the water calm. The old-timers along the fishing docks were squinting out at the horizon to the south and nodding to each other. It was coming.

The color of the sea, the shape of the clouds, the sighting of a shark near the coast, the way the sea birds were perching— all these became omens.

It was coming.

We slept for most of the flight out to the sonar picket. The Navy jet landed smoothly in the calm sea and a helicopter from the picket brought us aboard. The ship was similar in style to the deep-sea mining dredges my father operated out in the Pacific. For antisubmarine work, though, the dredging equipment was replaced by a fantastic array of radar and communications antennae.

"Below decks are out of bounds to visitors, I'm afraid," the chunky lieutenant who welcomed us to his ship told us as we walked from the helicopter landing pad toward the bridge. "This bucket's a floating sonar station. Everything below decks is classified except the galley, and the cook won't let even me in there."

He laughed at his own joke. He was a pleasant-faced type, about our own age, square-jawed, solidly built, the kind that stayed in the Navy for life.

We clambered up a ladder to the bridge.

"We're anchored here," the lieutenant said, "with special bottom gear and arresting cables. So the bridge isn't used for navigation as much as a communications center."

Looking around, we could see what he meant. The bridge's aft bulkhead was literally covered with viewscreens, maps, autoplotters and electronics controls.

"I think you'll be able to keep track of your hurricane without much trouble." The lieutenant nodded proudly toward the communications setup.

"If we can't," Ted said, "it won't be your fault."

The lieutenant introduced us to the chief communications technician, a scrappy little sailor who had just received his engineering degree and was putting in two Navy years. Within minutes, we were talking to Tuli back in THUNDER headquarters.

"Omega seems to have slowed down quite a bit," he told us, his face impassive. "She's almost stopped dead in her tracks, about halfway between your position and Puerto Rico."

"Gathering strength," Ted muttered.

They fed the information from Ted's big plotting screen in Miami to the picket's autoplotter, and soon we had a miniature version of the giant map to work with.

Ted studied the map, mumbling to himself. "If we could feed her some warm water . . . give her a shortcut to the outbound leg of the Gulf Stream . . . then maybe she'd stay off the coast."

The lieutenant watched us from a jumpseat that folded out of the port bulkhead.

"Just wishful thinking," Ted muttered on. "Fastest way to move her is to set up a low-pressure cell to the north . . . make her swing more northerly, maybe bypass the coast."

He talked it over with Tuli for the better part of an hour, perching on a swivel chair set into the deck next to the chart table. Their conversation was punctuated with equations and aerodynamics jargon that no one else on the bridge could understand.

"Are they talking about weather?" the ship's executive officer asked the lieutenant. "I know as much about meteorology as most of us do, and I can't make out what they're saying."

I walked over to them. "Standard meteorology is only part of Ted's game. They're looking at the hurricane as an aerodynamics problem—turbulent-boundary-layer theory, I think they call it."

"Oh." The expression on their faces showed that they heard it, but didn't understand it, or even necessarily believe me.

The cook popped through the bridge's starboard hatch with a tray of sandwiches and coffee. Ted absently took a sandwich and mug, still locked in talk with Tuli Noyon.

Finally he said to the viewscreen, "Okay, then we deepen this trough off Long Island and try to make a real storm cell out of it."

Tuli nodded, but he was clearly unhappy.

"Get Barney to run it through the computer as fast as she can, but you'd better get the planes out right now. Don't wait for the computer run. Got to hit while she's still sitting around. Otherwise . . ." His voice trailed off.

"All right," Tuli said. "But we're striking blindly."

"I know. Got any better ideas?"

Tuli shrugged.

"Then let's scramble the planes." He turned to me. "Jerry, we've got a battle plan figured out. Tuli'll give you the details."

Now it was my turn. I spent the better part of the afternoon getting the right planes with the right payloads off to the exact places where their work had to be done. Through it all, I was calling myself an idiot for tracking out to this mid-ocean exile. It took twice as long to process the orders as it would have back at headquarters.

"Don't bother saying it," Ted said when I finished. "So it was kinky coming out here. Okay. Just had to get away from that place before I went over the hill."

"But what good are you going to do here?" I asked.

He gripped the bridge's rail and looked out past the ship's prow to the softly billowing sea and clear horizon.

"We can run the show from here just as well . . . maybe a little tougher than back in Miami, but we can do it. If everything goes okay, we'll get brushed by the storm's edge. I'd like to see that . . . want to feel her, see what she can do. Better than sitting in that windowless cocoon back there."

"And if things don't go well?" I asked. "If the storm doesn't move the way you want it to?"

He turned away. "Probably she won't."

"Then we might miss the whole show."

"Maybe. Or she might march right down here and blow down our throats."

"Omega might . . . we might be caught in the middle of it?"

"Could be," he said easily. "Better get some sleep while you can. Going to be busy later on."

The exec showed us to a tiny stateroom with two bunks in it. Part of the picket's crew was on shore leave, and they had a spare compartment for us. I tried to sleep, but spent most of the late afternoon hours squirming nervously. Around dusk, Ted got up and went to the bridge. I followed him.

"See those clouds, off the southern horizon?" he was saying to the lieutenant. "That's her. Just her outer fringes."

I checked back with THUNDER headquarters. The planes had seeded the low-pressure trough off Long Island without incident. Weather stations along the coast, and automated observation equipment on satellites and planes, were reporting a small storm cell developing.

Barney's face appeared on the viewscreen. She looked very worried. "Is Ted there?"

"Right here," he said, stepping into view.

"The computer run's just finished," she said, pushing a strand of hair from her face. "Omega's going to turn northward, but only temporarily. She'll head inland again late tomorrow. In about forty-eight hours she'll strike the coast somewhere between Cape Hatteras and Washington."

Ted let out a low whistle.

"But that's not all," she continued. "The storm track crosses right over the ship you're on. You're going to be in the center of it!"

"We'll have to get off here right away," I said.

"No rush," Ted said. "We can spend the night here. I want to see her develop firsthand."

Barney said, "Ted, don't be foolish. It's going to be dangerous."

He grinned at her. "Jealous? Don't worry, I just want to get a look at her, then I'll come flying back to you."

"You stubborn—" The blond curl popped back over her eyes again and she pushed it away angrily. "Ted, it's time you stopped acting like a little boy. You bet I'm jealous. I'm tired of competing against the whole twirling atmosphere! You've got responsibilities, and if you don't want to live up to them . . . well, you'd better, that's all!"

"Okay, okay. We'll be back tomorrow morning. Be safer traveling in daylight anyway. Omega's still moving slowly; we'll have plenty of time."

"Not if she starts moving faster. This computer run was just a first-order look at the problem. The storm could move faster than we think."

"We'll get to Miami okay, don't worry."

"No, why should I worry? You're only six hundred miles out at sea with a hurricane bearing down on you."

"Just an hour away. Get some sleep. We'll fly over in the morning."

The wind was picking up as I went back to my bunk, and the ship was starting to rock in the deepening sea. I had sail-boated through storms and slept in worse weather than this. It wasn't the conditions of the moment that bothered me. It was the knowledge of what was coming.

Ted stayed out on the bridge, watching the southern skies darken with the deathly fascination of a general observing the approach of a much stronger army. I dropped off to sleep, telling myself that I'd get Ted off this ship as soon as a plane could pick us up, even if I had to have the sailors wrap him in anchor chains.

By morning, it was raining hard and the ship was bucking severely in the heavy waves. It was an effort to push through the narrow passageway to the bridge, with the deck bobbing beneath my feet and the ship tossing hard enough to slam me into the bulkheads.

Up on the bridge they were wearing slickers and life vests. The wind was already howling evilly. One of the sailors handed me a slicker and vest. As I turned to tug them on, I saw that the helicopter pad out on the stern was empty.

"Chopper took most of the crew out about an hour ago," the sailor hollered into my ear. "Went to meet the seaplane out west of here, where it ain't so rough. When it comes back we're all pulling out."

I nodded and thanked him.

"She's a beauty, isn't she?" Ted shouted at me. "Moving up a lot faster than we thought."

I grabbed a handhold between him and the lieutenant. To the south of us was a solid wall of black. Waves were breaking over the bows and the rain was a battering force against our faces.

"Will the helicopter be able to get back to us?" I asked the lieutenant.

"Certainly," he yelled back. "We've had worse blows than this . . . but I wouldn't want to hang around for another hour or so!"

The communications tech staggered across the bridge to us. "Chopper's on the way, sir. Ought to be here in ten–fifteen minutes."

The lieutenant nodded.

"I'll have to go aft and see that the helicopter's dogged down properly when she lands. You be ready to hop on when the word goes out."

"We'll be ready," I said.

As the lieutenant left the bridge, I asked Ted, "Well, is this doing you any good? Frankly, I would've been just as happy in Miami . . ."

"She's a real brute," he shouted. "This is a lot different from watching a map."

"But why . . ."

"This is the enemy, Jerry. This is what we're trying to kill. Think how much better you're going to feel after we've learned how to stop hurricanes."

"If we live long enough to learn how!"

The helicopter struggled into view, leaning heavily into the raging wind. I watched, equally fascinated and terrified, as it worked its way to the landing pad, tried to come down, got blown backward by a terrific gust, fought toward the pad again, and finally touched down on the heaving deck. A team of sailors scrambled across the wet square to attach heavy lines to the landing gear, even before the rotor-blades started to slow down. A wave smashed across the ship's stern and one of the sailors went sprawling. Only then did I notice that each man had a stout lifeline around his middle. They finally got the 'copter secured.

I turned back to Ted. "Let's go before it's too late."

We started down the slippery ladder to the main deck. As we inched back toward the stern, a tremendous wave caught the picket amidships and slued her around broadside. The little ship shuddered violently and the deck seemed to drop out from under us. I sagged to my knees.

Ted pulled me up. "Come on, buddy, Omega's breathing down our necks."

Another wave smashed across us. I grabbed for a handhold, and as my eyes cleared, saw the helicopter pitching crazily over to one side, the moorings on her landing gear flapping loosely in the wind.

"It's broken away!"

The deck heaved again and the 'copter careened over on its side, its rotors smashing against the pad. Another wave caught us. The ship bucked terribly. The helicopter slid backward along its side and then, lifted by a solid wall of foaming green, smashed through the gunwale and into the sea.

Groping senselessly on my hands and knees, soaking wet, battered like an overmatched prizefighter, I watched our only link to safety disappear into the raging sea.

From somewhere behind me I heard Ted shouting, "Four years! Four years of killing ourselves and it has to end like this!"

I clambered to my feet on the slippery deck of the Navy picket. The ship shuddered again and slued around. A wave hit the other side and washed across, putting us knee-deep in foaming water until the deck lurched upward again and cleared the waves temporarily.

"Omega's won," Ted roared in my ear, over the screaming wind. "The 'copter's washed overboard. We're trapped."

We stood there, hanging onto the handholds. The sea was impossible to describe—a furious tangle of waves, with no sense or pattern to them, their tops ripped off by the wind, spray mixing with the blinding rain.

The lieutenant groped by, edging along hand over hand on the lifeline that ran along the superstructure bulkhead.

"Are you two all right?"

"No broken bones, if that's what you mean."

"You'd better come back up to the bridge," he shouted. We were face to face, close enough to nearly touch noses, yet we could hardly hear him. "I've given orders to cast off the anchors and get up steam. We've got to try to ride out this blow under power. If we just sit here, we'll be swamped."

"Is there anything we can do?" I asked.

"Sure. Next time you tinker with a hurricane, make it when I'm on shore leave!"

We followed the lieutenant up to the bridge. I nearly fell off the rain-slicked ladder, but Ted grabbed me with one of his powerful paws.

The bridge was sloshing from the monstrous waves and spray that were drenching the decks. The communications panels seemed to be intact, though. We could see the map that Ted had set up on the autoplotter screen; it was still alight. Omega spread across the screen like an engulfing demon. The tiny pinpoint of light marking the ship's location was well inside the hurricane's swirl.

The lieutenant fought his way to the ship's intercom while Ted and I grabbed for handholds.

"All the horses you've got, Chief," I heard the lieutenant bellow into the intercom mike. "I'll get every available man on the pumps. Keep those engines going. If we lose power we're sunk!"

I realized he meant it literally.

The lieutenant crossed over toward us and hung on to the chart table.

"Is that map accurate?" he yelled at Ted.

The big redhead nodded. "Up to the minute. Why?"

"I'm trying to figure a course that'll take us out of this blow. We can't stand much more of this battering. She's taking on more water than the pumps can handle. Engine room's getting swamped."

"Head southwest then," Ted said at the top of his lungs. "Get out of her quickest that way."

"We can't! I've got to keep the sea on our bows or else we'll capsize!"

"What?"

"He's got to point her into the wind," I yelled. "Just about straight into the waves."

"Right!" The lieutenant agreed.

"But you'll be riding along with the storm. Never get out that way. She'll just carry us along all day!"

"How do you know which way the storm's going to go? She might change course."

"Not a chance." Ted pointed to the plotting screen. "She's heading northwesterly now and she'll stay on that course the rest of the day. Best bet is heading for the eye."

"Toward the center? We'd never make it!"

Ted shook his head. "Never get out of it if you keep heading straight into the wind. But if you can make five knots or so, we can spiral into the eye. Be calm there."

The lieutenant stared at the screen. "Are you sure? Do you know exactly where the storm's moving and how fast she's going to go?"

"We can check it out."

So we called THUNDER headquarters, transmitting up to the Atlantic Station satellite for relay to Miami. Barney was nearly frantic, but we got her off the line quickly. Tuli answered our questions and gave us the exact predictions for Omega's direction and speed.

Ted went inside with a soggy handful of notes to put the information into the ship's course computer. Barney pushed her way on to the viewscreen.

"Jerry . . . are you all right?"

"I've been better, but we'll get through it okay. The ship's in no real trouble," I lied.

"You're sure."

"Certainly. Ted's working out a course with the skipper. We'll be back in Miami in a few hours."

"It looks . . . it looks awful out there."

Another mammoth wave broke across the bow and drenched the bridge with spray.

"It's not picnic weather," I admitted. "But we're not worried, so don't you go getting upset." *No, we're not worried*, I added silently. *We're scared white.*

Reluctantly, the lieutenant agreed to head for the storm's eye. It was either that or face a battering that would split the ship within a few hours. We told Tuli to send a plane to the eye, to try to pick us up.

Time lost all meaning. We just hung on, drenched to the skin, plunging through a wild, watery inferno, the wind shrieking evilly at us, the seas absolutely chaotic. No one remained on the bridge except the lieutenant, Ted and me. The rest of the ship's skeleton crew were below decks, working every pump on board as hard as they could be run. The ship's autopilot and computer-run guidance system kept us heading on the course Ted and Tuli had figured.

Passing into the hurricane's eye was like stepping through a door from bedlam to a peaceful garden. One minute we were being pounded by mountainous waves and merciless winds, the rain and spray making it hard to see even as far as the bow. Then the sun broke through and the wind abruptly died. We limped out into the open, with nothing but a deep swell to mar a tranquil sea.

Towering clouds rose all about us, but this patch of ocean was safe. A vertijet was circling high overhead, sent out by Tuli. The plane made a tight pass over us, then descended onto the helicopter landing pad on the ship's fantail. Her landing gear barely touched the deck and her tail stuck out over the smashed railing where the helicopter had broken through.

We had to duck under the plane's nose and enter from a hatch in her belly because the outer wing jets were still blazing, but the plane took us all aboard. As we huddled in the crammed passenger compartment, the plane hoisted straight up. The jetpods swiveled back for horizontal flight and the wings slid to supersonic sweep. We climbed steeply and headed up for the sky.

As I looked down at the fast-shrinking little picket, I realized the lieutenant was also craning his neck at the port for a last look.

"I'm sorry you had to lose your ship."

"So am I," he said. "But headquarters gave permission to abandon her. We couldn't have stayed in the eye indefinitely, and another hour or so in those seas would have finished us."

"You did a darned good job to get us through," Ted said.

The lieutenant smiled wearily. "We couldn't have done it without your information on the storm. Good thing your numbers were right."

Barney was waiting for us at the Navy airport with dry clothes, the latest charts and forecasts on Omega, and a large

share of feminine emotion. I'll never forget the sight of her
running toward us as we stepped down from the vertijet's
main hatch. She threw her arms around Ted's neck, then
around mine, and then around Ted again.

"You had me so worried, the two of you!"

Ted laughed. "We were kind of ruffled ourselves."

It took more than an hour to get out of the Navy's grasp.
Debriefing officers, brass hats, press corps men, photo-
graphers—they all wanted to hear how Ted and the lieutenant
described the situation. We finally got to change our clothes
in an officer's wardroom and then battled our way out to the
car Barney had come in, leaving the lieutenant and his crew
to tell their story in detail.

"Dr. Weis has been on the phone all day," Barney said as
the driver pulled out for the main highway leading to the
Miami bayfront and THUNDER headquarters.

Ted frowned and spread the reports on Omega across his
lap.

Sitting between the two of us, she pointed to the latest
chart. "Here's the storm track . . . ninety percent reliability,
plus-or-minus two percent."

Ted whistled. "Right smack into Washington and then up
the coast. She's going to damage more than reputations."

"I told Dr. Weis you'd phone him as soon as you could."

"Okay," he said reluctantly. "Let's get it over with."

I punched out the Science Advisor's private number on the
phone set into the car's forward seat. After a brief word with
a secretary, Dr. Weis appeared on the viewscreen.

"You're safe," Dr. Weis said flatly. He looked wearier
than we felt.

"Disappointed?" Ted quipped.

"The way this hurricane is coming at us, we could use a
martyr or two."

"Steering didn't work. Only thing left to try is what we
should've done in the first place . . ."

"Weather control? Absolutely not! Being hit with a hurricane is bad enough, but if you try tinkering with the weather
all across the country, we'll have every farmer, every vaca-
tionist, every mayor and governor and traffic cop on our
necks!"

Ted fumed. "What else are you going to do? Sit there and take it? Weather control's the only way to stop this beast . . ."

"Marrett, I'm almost ready to believe that you set up this storm purposely to force us into letting you try your pet idea!"

"If I could do that, I wouldn't be sitting here arguing with you."

"Possibly not. But you listen to me. Weather control is out. If we have to take a hurricane, that's what we'll do. We'll have to admit that THUNDER was too ambitious a project for the first time around. We'll have to back off a little. We'll try something like THUNDER again next year, but without all the publicity. You may have to lead a very quiet life for a year or two, but we'll at least be able to keep going . . ."

"Why back down when you can go ahead and stop this hurricane?" Ted insisted hotly. "We can push Omega out to sea—I know we can!"

"The way you steered her? That certainly boomeranged on you."

"We tried moving six trillion tons of air with a feather duster! I'm talking about total control of the weather patterns across the whole continent. It'll work!"

"You can't guarantee that it will, and even if you did I wouldn't believe you. Marrett, I want you to go back to THUNDER headquarters and sit there quietly. You can operate on any new disturbances that show up. But you are to leave Omega strictly alone. Is that clear? If you try to touch that storm in any way, I'll see to it that you're finished. For good."

Dr. Weis snapped off the connection. The viewscreen went dark, almost as dark as the scowl on Ted's face. For the rest of the ride back to Project headquarters he said nothing. He simply sat there, slouched over, pulled in on himself, his eyes blazing.

When the car stopped he looked up at me.

"What would you do if I give the word to push Omega off the coast?"

"But Dr. Weis said—"

"I don't care what he said, or what he does afterward. We can stop Omega."

Barney turned and looked at me.

"Ted . . . I can always go back to Hawaii and help my father make his twelfth million. But what about you? Weis can finish your career permanently. And what about Barney and the rest of the Project personnel?"

"It's my responsibility. Weis won't care about the rest of 'em. And I don't care what he does to me . . . I can't sit here like a dumb ape and let that hurricane have its own way. I've got a score to settle with that storm."

"Regardless of what it's going to cost you?"

He nodded gravely. "Regardless of everything. Are you with me?"

"I guess I'm as crazy as you are," I heard myself say. "Let's go do it."

We piled out of the car and strode up to the control center. As people started to cluster around us, Ted raised his arms for silence. Then he said loudly:

"Listen: Project THUNDER is over. We've got a job of weather-making to do. We're going to push that hurricane out to sea."

Then he started rattling off orders as though he had been rehearsing for this moment all his life.

As I started for my glass-walled office, Barney touched my sleeve. "Jerry, whatever happens later, thanks for helping him."

"We're accomplices," I said. "Before, after and during the fact."

"Do you think you could ever look at a cloud in the sky again if you hadn't agreed to help him try this?"

Before I could think of an answer she turned and started toward the computer section.

We had roughly thirty-six hours before Omega would strike the Virginia coast and then head up Chesapeake Bay for Washington. Thirty-six hours to manipulate the existing weather pattern over the entire North American continent.

Within three hours Ted had us around his desk, a thick pack of notes clenched in his right hand. "Not as bad as it could've been," he told us, waving the notes toward the plotting screen. ''This big high sitting near the Great Lakes—good cold, dry air that can make a shield over the East Coast if we can swing it into position. Tuli, that's your job.''

Tuli nodded, bright-eyed with excitement.

''Barney, we'll need pinpoint forecasts for every part of the country, even if it takes every computer in the Weather Bureau to wring 'em out.''

''Right, Ted.''

''Jerry, communications're the key. Got to keep in touch with the whole blinking country. And we're going to need planes, rockets, even slingshots maybe. Get the ball rolling before Weis finds out what we're up to.''

''What about the Canadians? You'll be affecting their weather, too.''

''Get that liaison guy from the State Department and tell him to have the Canadian Weather Bureau check with us. Don't spill the beans to him, though.''

''It's only a matter of time until Washington catches on,'' I said.

''Most of what we've got to do has to be done tonight. By the time they wake up tomorrow, we'll be on our way.''

Omega's central wind speeds had climbed to 120 knots by evening, and were still increasing. As she trundled along toward the coast, her howling fury was nearly matched by the uproar of action at our control center. We didn't eat, we didn't sleep. We worked!

A half-dozen military satellites armed with anti-ICBM lasers started pumping streams of energy into areas pinpointed by Ted's orders. Their crews had been alerted weeks earlier to cooperate with requests from Project THUNDER, and Ted and others from our technical staff had briefed them before the hurricane season began. They didn't question our messages. Squadrons of planes flew out to dump chemicals and seeding materials just off Long Island, where we had created a weak storm cell in the vain atttempt to steer Omega. Ted wanted that low deepened, intensified—a low-pressure trough into which that high on the Great Lakes could slide.

''Intensifying the low will let Omega come in faster, too,'' Tuli pointed out.

"Know it," Ted answered. "But the numbers're on our side, I think. Besides, the faster Omega moves, the less chance she gets to build up higher wind velocities."

By ten o'clock we had asked for and received a special analysis from the National Meteorological Center in Suitland, Maryland. It showed that we would have to deflect the jet stream slightly, since it controlled the upper-air flow patterns across the country. But how do you divert a river of air that's three hundred miles wide, four miles thick, and racing at better than three hundred miles per hour?

"It would take a hundred-megaton bomb," Barney said, "exploded about fifteen miles up, just over Salt Lake City."

"Forget it!" Ted snapped. "The UN would need a month just to get it on the agenda. Not to mention the sovereign citizens of Utah and points east."

"Then how do we do it?"

Ted grabbed the coffeepot standing on his desk and poured a mug of steaming, black liquid. "Jet stream's a shear layer between the polar and mid-latitude tropopauses," he muttered, more to himself than any of us. "If you reinforce a polar air mass, it can nudge the stream southward . . ."

He took a cautious sip of the hot coffee. "Tuli, we're already moving a high southward from the Great Lakes. Take a couple of your best people—and Barney, give him top priority on the computers. See if we can drag down a bigger polar air mass from Canada and push the jet stream enough to help us."

"We don't have enough time or equipment to operate in Canada," I said. "And we'd need permission from Ottawa."

"What about reversing the procedure?" Tuli asked. "We could expand the desert high over Arizona and New Mexico until it pushes the jet stream from the south."

Ted raised his eyebrows. "Think you can do it?"

"I'll have to make some calculations."

"Okay, scramble."

In Boston, people who had gone to bed with a weather forecast of "warm, partly cloudy," awoke to a chilly, driving northeast rain. The low we had intensified during the night had surprised the local forecasters. The Boston Weather Bureau office issued corrected predictions through the morning as the little rainstorm moved out, the Great Lakes high slid in and caused a flurry of frontal squalls, and finally the sun broke through. The cool, dry air of the high dropped local temperatures more than ten degrees within an hour. To the unknowing New Englanders it was just another day, slightly more bewildering than most.

Dr. Weis was on the phone at seven-thirty that morning.

"Marrett, have you lost your mind? What do you think you're doing? I told you . . ."

"Can't talk now, we're busy," Ted shot back.

"I'll have your hide for this!"

"Tomorrow you can have my hide. I'll bring it up myself. But first I'm going to find out if I'm right or wrong about this."

The President's Science Advisor turned purple. "I'm going to send out an order to all government installations to stop . . ."

"Better not. Then we'll never find out if it worked. Besides, most of the mods've already been made. Damage's done. Let's see what good it does."

Barney rushed up with a ream of computer printout sheets as Ted cut the phone connection.

"There's going to be a freeze on the central plains and northern Rockies," she said, pushing back her tousled hair. "There'll be some snow. We haven't fixed the exact amount yet."

A harvest-time freeze. Crops ruined, cities paralyzed by unexpected snow, weekend holidays ruined, and, in the mountains, deaths from exertion and exposure.

"Get the forecast out on the main Weather Bureau network," Ted ordered. "Warn 'em fast."

The plotting screen showed the battle clearly. Omega, with central windspeeds of 175 knots now, was still pushing toward Virginia. But her forward progress was slowing, ever so slightly, as the Great Lakes high moved southeastward past Pittsburgh.

By noontime, Ted was staring at the screen and muttering, "Won't be enough. Not unless the jet stream comes around a couple degrees."

It was raining in Washington now, and snow was beginning to fall in Winnipeg. I was trying to handle three phone calls at once when I heard an ear-splitting whoop from Ted. I looked at the plotting screen. There was a slight bend in the jet stream west of the Mississippi that hadn't been there before.

As soon as I could, I collared Tuli for an explanation.

"We used the lasers from the Atlantic Station and every plane and ounce of exothermic catalyst I could find. The effect isn't very spectacular, no noticeable weather change. But the desert high has expanded slightly and pushed the jet stream a little northward, temporarily."

"Will it be enough?" I asked.

He shrugged.

Through the afternoon we watched that little curl travel along the length of the jet stream's course, like a wave snaking down the length of a long, taut rope. Meanwhile, the former Great Lakes high was covering all of Maryland and pushing into Virginia. Its northern extension shielded the coast well into New England.

"But she'll blast right through it," Ted grumbled, watching Omega's glowering system of closely-packed isobars, "unless the jet stream helps to push 'er off."

I asked Barney. "How does the timing look? Which will arrive first, the jet stream change, or the storm?"

She shook her head. "The machines have taken it down to four decimal places and there's still no sure answer."

Norfolk was being drenched with a torrential downpour; gale-force winds were snapping power lines and knocking down trees. Washington was a darkened, windswept city. Most of the federal offices had closed early, and traffic was inching along the rain-slicked streets.

Boatmen from Hatteras to the fishhook angle of Cape Cod—weekend sailors and professionals alike—were making fast extra lines, setting out double anchors, or pulling their craft out of the water altogether. Commercial airlines were juggling their schedules around the storm and whole squadrons of military planes were winging westward, away from the danger, like great flocks of migrating birds. Storm tides were piling up all along the coast, and flood warnings were flashing from Civil Defense centers in a dozen states. The highways were filling up with people moving inland before the approaching fury.

And Omega was still a hundred miles out to sea.

Then she faltered.

You could feel the electricity crackle through our control center. The mammoth hurricane hovered off the coast as the jet stream deflection finally arrived. We all held our breaths. Omega stood off the coast uncertainly for an hour, then turned to the northeast. She began to head out to sea.

We shouted our foolish heads off.

When the furor died down, Ted hopped up on his desk. "Hold on, heroes. Job's not finished yet. We've got a freeze in the midwest to modify. And I want to throw everything we've got into Omega, weaken her as much as possible. Now *scramble!*"

It was nearly midnight before Ted let us call it quits. Our Project people—real weathermakers now—had weakened Hurricane Omega to the point where she was only a tropical storm, fast losing her punch over the cold waters off the North Atlantic. A light snow was sprinkling much of the upper midwest, but our warning forecasts had been in time, and the weathermakers were able to take most of the snap out of the cold front. The local weather stations were reporting only minor problems from the unexpected freeze, and Barney's final computer run showed that the snow would be less than an inch.

Most of the Project people had left for sleep. There was only a skeleton crew left in the control center. Barney, Tuli and I gravitated to Ted's desk. He had commandeered a typewriter, and was pecking on the keys.

"How do you spell 'resignation'?" he asked me.

Before I could answer, the phone buzzed. It was Dr. Weis.

"You didn't have to call," Ted said. "Game's over. I know it."

Dr. Weis looked utterly exhausted, as though he had personally been battling the storm. "I had a long talk with the President tonight, Marrett. You've put him in a difficult position, and me in an impossible one. To the general public you're a hero. But I wouldn't trust you as far as I could throw a cyclotron."

"Guess I don't blame you," Ted answered calmly. "Don't worry, you won't have to fire me. I'm resigning. You'll be off the hook."

"You can't quit," Dr. Weis said. "You're a national resource, as far as the President's concerned. He spent the night comparing you to nuclear energy: you've got to be tamed and harnessed."

"Harnessed? For weather control?"

Weis nodded wordlessly.

"The President wants to really work on weather control?" Ted broke into a huge grin. "That's a harness I've been trying to get into for four years."

"You're lucky, Marrett. Very lucky. If the weather patterns had been slightly different, if things hadn't worked out so well . . ."

Ted's grin vanished. "Wasn't luck. It was work, a lot of people's work, and brains, and guts. That's where weather control—*real* weather control—wins for you. It doesn't matter what the weather patterns are if you're going to change all of them to suit your needs. You don't need luck, just time and sweat. You can *make* the weather you want. That's what we did. That's why it's got to work, if you just do it on a big enough scale."

"All right, you've won," Dr. Weis said. "Luck or skill or guts, it doesn't matter. Not now. The President wants to see you."

"How about tomorrow . . . I mean later this morning?"

"Fine," Dr. Weis said, although his face was still sullen.

"We've won," Tuli said as Ted shut off the phone. "We've actually won."

Barney sank into the nearest chair. "It's too much happening all at once. I don't think I can believe it all."

"It's real," Ted answered quietly. "Weather control is a fact now. Nobody can say it doesn't work, or that it can't have any important effect on the country."

"So you're seeing the President tomorrow," I said.

"Later today," he corrected, "and I want you three guys with me."

"Guys," Barney echoed.

"Hey, that's right. You're a girl. Come on, Girl, I'll take you home. Looks like you won't have to be playing second fiddle to hurricanes anymore." He took her arm and started for the door. "Think you can stand being the center of my attention?"

Barney looked back at me. I got up and took her other arm. "If you don't mind, she's going to be the center of my attention, too."

Tuli shook his head as he joined us. "You barbarians. No wonder you're nervous wrecks. You never know who's going to marry whom. I've got my future wife all picked out; our families agreed on the match when we were both four."

"That's why you're here in the States," Ted joked.

Barney said, "Tuli, don't do anything to make them change their minds. I haven't had this much attention since *I* was four."

Down the main stairway we went, and out into the street. The sidewalks were puddled from rain, a side effect of Omega, but overhead the stars were shining through tattered, scudding clouds.

"Today the world's going to wake up and discover that man can control the weather," Ted said.

"Not really," Tuli cautioned. "We've only made a beginning. We still have years of learning ahead. Decades. Maybe centuries."

Ted nodded, a contented smile on his face. "Maybe. But we've started, that's the important thing."

"And the political problems this is going to cause?" I asked. "The social and economic changes that weather control will bring? What about them?"

He laughed. "That's for administrators like you and the President to worry about. I've got enough to keep me busy: six quadrillion tons of air . . . and one mathematician."

It was more than a year later, in October, when the United Nations convened an extraordinary session in Washington to hear an address by the President.

The delegates met at a special outdoor pavilion, built along the banks of the Potomac for their meeting. Ted, Barney,

Tuli—most of the key people from the Weather Bureau and Congress and government were in the audience. Beyond the seats set on the grass for the UN delegates and invited guests, a huge thronging crowd looked on, and listened to the President.

". . . For mankind's technology," he was saying, "is both a constant danger and a constant opportunity. Through technology, man has attained the power to destroy himself, or the power to unite this planet in peace and freedom—freedom from war, from hunger, from ignorance.

"Today we meet to mark a new step in the peaceful use of man's growing technical knowledge: the establishment of the United Nations Commission for Planetary Weather Control . . ."

Like Ted's victory over Hurricane Omega, this was only a first step. Total control of the weather, and total solution of the human problems involved, was still a long way off. But we were started along the right road.

As we sat listening to the President, a gentle breeze wafted by, tossing the flame-colored trees, and tempering the warmth of the sun. It was a crisp, golden October day; bright blue sky, beaming sun, occasional puffs of cottonball cumulus clouds. A perfect day for an outdoor ceremony.

Of course.

Man Changes the Weather ━━━━━

The following excerpts from *Man Changes the Weather* were written more than ten years ago. Sadly (or happily, if you're a Luddite) not very much has happened in the past decade to improve our ability to manipulate the weather deliberately. The biggest improvements have come in the field of electronic computers, where new "fifth-generation" computers of unprecedented capacity and speed just might be able to handle all the data and do all the "number crunching" that is necessary for truly accurate long-range weather forecasts. And perhaps another breakthrough of sorts is on the horizon, as well. If the United States or other nations place gigantic lasers in orbit as defenses against ballistic missile attack, those lasers might be used eventually to pump energy into carefully-selected pinpoint target areas among brewing weather systems. If antimissile lasers can some-day help to modify the weather, the Prometheans will smile and quote Biblical prophecies about swords and plowshares.

━━━━━━

I. A Handful of Dry Ice

Year 1946—It was cold and windy on the hill.

Dr. Irving Langmuir stood out there with a pair of binoculars in his hands. At the age of 65, when most men are ready to retire, he was just starting a new career: changing the weather.

It was November 13, 1946. Langmuir was out on the parking lot of the General Electric Company's Research Laboratory, not far from Schenectady, N. Y. With the binoculars he watched a small plane flying over Mt. Greylock, Massachusetts, about 30 miles away.

A long, gray cloud hung over the mountain. The plane circled over it. Suddenly snow began to fall from the cloud.

"This is history!" Langmuir shouted.

For the first time, man had deliberately and predictably made a change in the weather. Six pounds of "dry ice" pellets had caused a man-made snowfall over the mountain.

Born in 1881, Langmuir was a world-known figure in science. He had received a Nobel Prize in 1932.

The man in the plane was Vincent Schaefer, who was then 40 years old. It was he who had discovered that dry ice could cause snow or rain.

Coaxing the Clouds

Deliberately changing the weather is an old, old dream. Ever since our remote ancestors cowered under trees during a rainstorm, they've wanted to be able to control the weather.

They've fired arrows into the sky in an effort to bring rain down from the clouds. In later centuries they switched to cannons. Men have tried dancing, praying, shouting, beating on drums, and all manner of weird gadgets that produced noise and sometimes steam—but seldom produced rain.

Most of man's attempts at changing the weather have been aimed at bringing rainfall. Ever since mankind invented farming—some 10,000 years ago—rainfall has been a crucial factor. Without the right amount of rain, the crops won't grow. But if there's too much rain at the wrong time of the year, that's almost as bad. In most cases, though, the problem is not enough rain. So most of man's efforts to influence the weather have been in the area of rainmaking.

As we'll soon see, there's a modern industry of rainmaking that does millions of dollars' worth of business each year in the United States alone. It's based on the techniques invented by Schaefer, Langmuir, and Bernard Vonnegut when they worked together at the GE Research Laboratory in the late 1940s.

The trick in rainmaking is to coax the clouds into dropping more moisture than they would do naturally. No one knows how to bring rain out of a clear, dry sky. But modern rainmakers can squeeze rainfall from clouds that might not have produced rain unless men tinkered with them.

The key to modern rainmaking is knowing how a cloud produces rain naturally.

A raincloud consists of millions upon millions of tiny water droplets. These droplets are so small and light they actually float on air: air pressure and currents keep them buoyed up. They're too light to fall! In fact, the water droplets are so small that a cubic yard of the darkest, most threatening cloud contains only about a tenth of an ounce of water.

Rainfall only happens when these droplets get big enough and heavy enough to fall out of the cloud. To begin with, the droplets are usually only about one hundredth of a millimeter in diameter (0.01 mm). Under the right conditions in a cloud, they'll start to combine into bigger drops. The usual raindrop that splatters on the ground is about one millimeter in diameter: 1 mm is about the width of the lead in a mechanical pencil.

The drops in a fine drizzle can be as small as 0.1 mm in diameter, while the drops in a heavy summer shower are sometimes as big as 6 mm.

How do the tiny droplets become raindrops? There are two possible ways. First, they can grow fat and heavy by *coalescing*, simply bumping together inside the cloud and merging. Coalescing is something like a tiny droplet inching down a windowpane, merging with other drops on the glass and getting bigger and heavier.

In many clouds there are ice crystals present, as well as droplets, because the air inside the cloud is below the freezing temperature. The water droplets can remain liquid even at temperatures below freezing: this is known as a *supercooled cloud*. The smaller the droplet, the lower the temperature at which it can remain liquid. Large drops can remain liquid down to about 5°F; all droplets, no matter how small, freeze at –40°F.

In a supercooled cloud, the ice crystals tend to grow and get bigger, while the droplets get smaller. The water in the cloud goes mainly into the ice crystals as time moves on, and eventually the crystals become heavy enough to fall out of the cloud. If the air temperature below the cloud is warm enough, the crystals will melt and reach the ground as raindrops.

This ice-crystal system is called the *Bergeron process* of droplet growth, after Tor Bergeron, a Swedish meteorologist.

Whether the raindrops form by coalescence or the Bergeron process, it's important to realize that each tiny droplet needs a speck of dust or sand or salt to form around. If there were no dust in our atmosphere, or no sand or salt from the oceans, there could be no rain or snow. Most of the water in the air exists as water vapor, a gas, which comes from the oceans, lakes and rivers, evaporated by the sun. The vapor cannot condense into even the tiniest of droplets unless there's a particle of some sort for it to condense onto. The particles are called *condensation nuclei*, since each particle forms the nucleus of a droplet.

The Deep-Freeze Laboratory

In 1946, Schaefer was trying to find some way to trigger ice crystal formation in clouds. His "laboratory" was a deep-freeze chest, the kind of freezer that housewives store food in. The freezer holds cold, moist air, under conditions that are very similar to the conditions inside a cloud. The particular freezer that Schaefer was working with was a top loader (a GE model, of course); its lid was on the top.

Schaefer wanted to trigger the Bergeron process in his deep-freeze laboratory. His idea was to throw different materials into the cold, moist air inside the freezer, to see if they would produce ice crystals. He felt that if he could make enough ice crystals form inside the freezer's air, much of the moisture in that air would condense onto the crystals and form a miniature snowfall.

He started by simply blowing his own breath into the freezer. Then he tried hundreds of different substances, from talcum powder to sand. Nothing worked.

On July 12, 1946, he came back from lunch and saw that the freezer had been left open and had warmed up slightly (only slightly, because the cold air in the freezer was denser than the room-temperature air outside, and therefore mixed very little with the room air). To quickly get the freezer's air temperature back down to where he wanted it, Schaefer tossed a handful of dry ice into the freezer.

A tiny snowstorm sprang up!

Dry ice is frozen carbon dioxide (CO_2). Carbon dioxide is one of the gases in our air; we breathe it out as a waste gas, but plants breathe it in—it's as important to them as oxygen is to us. It's called dry ice because frozen carbon dioxide doesn't melt into a liquid, as water ice does. It goes straight from a solid frozen state into a gas, with no liquid phase in between, under ordinary conditions.

Solid carbon dioxide is much colder than water ice. It freezes at $-109.3°F$. At this very chilly temperature, it's an excellent material for quickly cooling down a freezer, which is why Schaefer threw it into his freezer chest.

The air in the freezer chest was well below the $32°F$ temperature at which water freezes. (After all, that's what a freezer is for!) But that doesn't mean that all the water vapor in the air inside the freezer had turned to ice crystals. Just as in a supercooled cloud, the moist air in the freezer had some water droplets in it, as well as ice crystals. It was supercooled.

But at the dry-ice temperature of lower than $-100°F$ even the tiniest droplet freezes instantly. So when Schaefer tossed the dry ice into his freezer, he turned all the microscopic water droplets into ice crystals. Water-ice crystals. Snowflakes.

It took some time for Schaefer and Langmuir to be certain that this was what had happened. They repeated the experiment many times, until they were convinced that they knew what was going on, and why.

Then they decided to try a "real-life" experiment. They needed a supercooled cloud, some dry ice and an airplane. Four months and one day after his semi-accidental discovery, Schaefer tossed six pounds of dry ice into the supercooled cloud over Mt. Greylock while Langmuir, watching from the parking lot of the laboratory, saw the first man-made snowfall in history.

While all this was going on, another GE scientist was methodically working on another way to cause clouds to give up their moisture.

Bernard Vonnegut was trying to find a microscopic crystal that had the same size and shape as an ordinary ice crystal. He reasoned that if water droplets sometimes condense onto ice crystals to form snowflakes or raindrops, then perhaps they could be "fooled" into forming around another type of crystal that has the same size and shape as an ice crystal.

Working systematically to find a crystal that closely resembles natural ice crystals, Vonnegut hit upon silver iodide. A mixture of silver iodide and other chemicals can be put into a special type of burner; the resulting smoke contains crystals of silver iodide, which work just as well as dry ice to cause supercooled clouds to release precipitation.

Moreover, the silver iodide burners—which are also called generators—can stay on the ground. You don't need to carry them aloft in a plane; their smoke wafts upward, bringing the crystals to the clouds.

This technique of putting dry ice or silver iodide crystals into a cloud to cause precipitation is called *cloud seeding*. The "seed" material triggers the cloud's natural mechanisms for making rain or snow. Once started by man's hand, the precipitation continues just as it naturally would. Thus a tiny amount of seeding material can cause billions of gallons of water to drop out of a cloud.

Project Cirrus

By 1947, Langmuir, Schaefer and Vonnegut had proved that it was possible to alter the weather deliberately, to wring rain or snow from a supercooled cloud—sometimes.

This was a startling new idea, and many professional meteorologists refused to believe it. But Langmuir was enthusiastic and insistent. He claimed that *weather modification* was too important an idea to ignore. With his international reputation as a scientist, he was able to convince some people to take weather modification seriously.

Some of the people he convinced were in the Department of Defense. Military men have battled against the weather just as often as they've fought opposing armies and navies.

The men in the Pentagon knew that even small weather "mods"—such as clearing fog from an airport—could save many lives. Moreover, in 1947, with World War II still a very fresh memory and the cold war threatening to plunge the world into destruction once again, the Pentagon had plenty of money for research. After all, research had produced the radars and rockets and nuclear bombs of World War II. Could research now offer a way of taming the weather?

Langmuir was set up in New Mexico, and his work was code-named *Project Cirrus*.

On one of the first Project Cirrus flights, an Air Force plane dropped 15 pounds of dry ice along a path 20 miles long through a heavy layer of cloud. Within minutes, a 20-mile-long clearing had been carved out of the cloud bank. The plane's pilot said, "Its sides were as sharp and steep as though someone had taken a spade and shoveled a path through a snowdrift."

By October 1948, both silver iodide and dry ice were being used. On October 14, four different cloud-seeding flights were made near Albuquerque. Half an inch of rain fell over an area of 4000 square miles.

By July 1949, Langmuir was running silver iodide generators on the ground for hours at a time. On July 21, he ran them for more than ten hours straight. Although the Weather Bureau predicted no rain for that day, an afternoon cloudburst dropped nearly an inch and a half of rain on Langmuir's equipment. Heavy rain also hit other parts of New Mexico. Creeks that were normally dry overflowed with sudden rainwater. Langmuir calculated that Project Cirrus had caused nearly 500 billion gallons of water to fall in New Mexico in just two days.

But how can you tell "man-made" rain from "natural" rain?

In other words, how could Langmuir be certain that it was Project Cirrus causing the rainfalls? Perhaps it would have rained anyway, without the silver iodide or dry ice. Many people, including scientists and meteorologists, began to dispute Langmuir's claims.

His only defense was in statistics, using numbers to show that the laws of chance were on his side. Langmuir showed that unusually heavy rainfalls almost always happened only when he seeded the clouds. He claimed it happened too often to be just a coincidence.

But statistics are tricky, and they're not as powerful as other forms of evidence—especially when people decide not to believe the numbers that the statistics produce.

The more his claims were doubted, the stronger Langmuir made his claims. He showed—with statistics—that his cloud-seeding operations had changed rainfall patterns clear across the eastern two-thirds of the United States. When he seeded clouds in New Mexico, sudden and unusual rainstorms came a few days later and as far away as Florida. Langmuir insisted that this happened because the prevailing westerly winds across the U.S. carried his cloud-seeding crystals from New Mexico eastward.

The doubters still doubted him. But now other people began to blame Project Cirrus for storms and floods. Some of them went to court to sue Langmuir and the U.S. Government for damaging their property. Others blamed *droughts* on the cloud seedings!

To make matters worse, cloud seeding became a popular activity. Other agencies of the government began cloud-seeding experiments. Universities, newspapers, amateur scientists and self-styled "rainmakers" started seeding clouds all over the country. A host of private companies sprang up and began selling rainmaking services to farmers, especially in the drier midwestern and southwestern regions of the nation.

Many of these private companies were run by reputable, professional meteorologists who had closely followed the work of Langmuir and his associates. But many others were run by people who only knew that you dumped some chemicals out of an airplane and took in cash.

The result was chaos. Langmuir had wanted to do orderly experiments and lay the scientific foundation for weather modification. But his work was being drowned out in arguments, claims and counterclaims. Instead of a controlled scientific experiment, he had a three-ring circus on his hands.

Worst of all, since there were so many wild claims being made on all sides, the word began to spread that *all* rainmakers were charlatans. Langmuir's evidence came to be regarded as rather weak. "After all," said the nonbelievers, "it's only statistics." The implication was that you could rig statistics any way you wanted to.

The Committee on Weather Control

But all this fuss about rainmaking had attracted the interest of some of the nation's most important people: the farmers.

Most farmers didn't know very much about Langmuir's statistics. But they knew that an extra ten or fifteen percent of rainfall often spelled the difference between a good year and a failure. So congressmen and senators from farm states became interested in weather mods and cloud seeding.

In 1953, with Langmuir still claiming great success and predicting a future when men would control the weather almost completely, while skeptical scientists called the whole business little more than a hoax, Congress established an Advisory Committee on Weather Control. The committee was set up to study the whole question of weather modification and to recommend to the Congress whether or not the government should allow, encourage or support weather modification work.

Government committees have a reputation for being leisurely. In most cases, this reputation isn't deserved. But the Advisory Committee on Weather Control took four years before releasing its report, on the last day of 1957. The report was sober, factual—and cautious.

The committee reported that the only evidence for successful rainmaking was statistical evidence, and the numbers showed that cloud seeding had probably increased rainfall in mountainous areas by ten to fifteen percent. In the flatlands, where most of the farms are, the results were so unclear that the committee couldn't say anything about them, one way or the other.

Rightly or wrongly, this report put a sharp pin into the bubble of hope that men could someday alter or even control the weather. Cloud seeding got a rather bad name in government circles, and even in most research laboratories. (Even science fiction writers, who should have known better, turned their backs on weather control.)

Langmuir died in 1957, shortly before the report was released. But he knew what was in it, and he must have died a very disappointed man.

But on the other hand, he probably knew better than anyone else that his battle was an important one in the long road toward man's eventual control of the weather.

II. Taming the Clouds

The history of any new idea generally follows a rather predictable pattern. Whether the new idea is a laser, a superconducting magnet, artificial satellites, artificial hearts, weather modifications or what-have-you, it always seems to go the same way.

At first the new idea generates a tremendous burst of excitement and enthusiasm. The enthusiasm builds very quickly to a high peak as predictions are made about the new idea. It will solve everybody's problems faster, better, cheaper than ever before.

Soon, though, it becomes clear that the new idea won't solve *everyone's* problems. In fact, there are problems raised by the new idea itself, and bugs in it that need to be worked out. Disenchantment sets in and many of the original followers drop away. Some of the people who thought that the new idea would help them become rather bitter and suspicious of *all* new ideas.

In time, the new idea will either prove itself or disappear into the dusty shelves of reference libraries.

By 1958, cloud seeding and weather modification work had reached the point of disenchantment. Langmuir, Schaefer and Vonnegut had shown that it worked—sometimes. But the original hopes of being able to change the weather at will had given way to statistics, arguments and the 1957 report by the Advisory Committee on Weather Control.

An Industry Is Born

While most people in Washington and elsewhere turned their backs on weather modification, a few determined men quietly pressed on. Langmuir died, but Schaefer and Vonnegut continued their work, and both of them eventually became teachers and researchers at the State University of New York.

And almost without anyone realizing it, a new industry took shape—rainmaking.

Farmers in the Midwest and Southwest live every year on the edge of failure. The success of their crops depends on the amount of rain they get, and even a ten to fifteen percent increase in rainfall can be critically important to them. Ever since settlers moved into these relatively dry western areas from the rain-rich east coast, they've had to battle against a lack of water, a scarcity of rain. For decades they've failed when the rains were too sparse.

By the mid-1950s, though, there were a handful of men who had followed the work of Langmuir, Schaefer and Vonnegut. They knew the scientific basis for producing rain. So they went into the modern rainmaking business.

There were others who were out-and-out fakes, whose only knowledge of cloud seeding was what they read in the newspapers. But the professional rainmakers included meteorologists of the highest caliber.

Modern rainmakers sell rainfall by the inch. That is, the farmer pays only for the rainfall he gets that's over and above what neighboring areas get. Honest rainmakers never claim they can bring rain from a clear sky; they don't even pretend that they can make every cloud drop moisture. What they can do—under the right circumstances—is squeeze extra rainfall from clouds that would sooner or later drop rain anyway. They can modify a natural weather situation to make it more useful to the farmer. Hence the term *weather modification*, or weather ''mods.''

Pulling extra rainfall from the clouds or *redistributing* rainfall that would naturally come, so that it falls on farmlands rather than cities, is a multimillion-dollar business in the United States today.

Science and a New Frontier

Although interest and enthusiasm over weather mods dropped to an all-time low when the report of the Advisory Committee on Weather Control was released, some work went on.

The report itself recommended that the National Science Foundation should conduct basic research into the possibilities of modifying the weather. This approach—quiet, sober, university research—was so much less than the news stories had promised about rainmaking and storm-killing that the public never paid much attention to the recommendation.

But the White House did. In 1958, Congress passed a law that allowed the National Science Foundation to investigate weather modification and weather control. Small-scale studies were started at several universities. The professional rainmakers, meanwhile, continued to sell rainfall by the inch to the American farmers.

And that's where matters stood until 1961, when the Kennedy Administration came to Washington. President John Kennedy's campaign theme had been "New Frontiers"; he wanted to expand America's activities in all areas, to reach for excellence in everything we did.

His science advisor was Jerome Weisner of MIT. Weisner strongly believed that science and technology should be put to work in areas that would encourage international cooperation. Everyone in the world knew that science helped to make weapons; Weisner wanted to show that science could also help to make the world safer, healthier.

Weather modification was one exciting possibility to demonstrate "peaceful" science at its best. Many new technical ideas had been developed in the few years between 1957 and 1961. Weisner and several other scientists believed that practical weather mods might be much closer at hand than most people ever realized.

Among the new ideas were new mathematical techniques that promised more reliable weather forecasts, faster and larger computers that could handle the enormous amounts of data needed to understand weather processes on a large scale, and artificial satellites and other observational tools that could keep the entire world's weather under constant scrutiny.

One of the key people in pushing the "weather frontier" with the Kennedy Administration was Thomas F. Malone, vice president and research director of the Travelers Insurance Company. This company had been a leader in private weather forecasting and research for many years. Malone was also chairman of the Committee on Atmospheric Sciences. In 1963, he appointed a special panel to report to the Academy on the progress in rainmaking and other weather mods. Chairman of this Panel on Weather and Climate Modification was Gordon J. F. MacDonald of the University of California at Santa Barbara.

Although it's not an official arm of the government, the National Academy of Sciences (founded by President Lincoln) represents the nation's foremost scientists and acts as an advisory group to the government on scientific matters.

By October 1964, the MacDonald Panel released a preliminary report. It said that weather mods were possible, given enough time and research money to work out the problems. It also stated that statistical evidence still showed no strong proof that cloud seeding produced rain reliably. In other words, the scientists' conclusions were pretty much the same as they had been seven years earlier, even though the report was phrased in much more optimistic language.

Then a curious thing happened.

The commercial rainmakers, some of whom had been making their living for nearly twenty years from cloud seeding, launched a counterattack.

The National Academy Panel and the earlier Advisory Committee on Weather Control had never seen all the evidence that the commercial rainmakers had amassed. The rainmakers had mainly ignored the Advisory Committee back in the 1950s. But faced with another "official" decision that rainmaking didn't work, the commercial cloud seeders marched on Washington armed with their records—proof of their successes.

This was unexpected. MacDonald had a vacancy to fill on his panel, and wanted to fill it with someone who could tackle the newly-arrived data from the rainmakers. He picked James C. McDonald of the University of Arizona. McDonald (the "Mc" McDonald, not MacDonald, the panel chairman), a highly respected cloud physicist, was at that time openly skeptical about rainmaking. But he was known to be a fair and impartial scientist. In fact, he had been one of the few professional scientists who had publicly called for a careful investigation of Unidentified Flying Objects, to determine just what the "flying saucers" really were. Most scientists avoided making any comments on controversial subjects such as UFOs and cloud seeding. But not McDonald.

Through all of 1965, McDonald studied the rainmakers' private data. Not satisfied with his own efforts, which included the help of several Arizona graduate students, he called for separate checks of the evidence by experts from Rand Corporation, the University of Chicago and the Weather Bureau.

In January 1966, the panel issued a new report. It said that rainfall can be increased by cloud seeding in mountainous areas by ten to fifteen percent, just as the 1957 report had concluded. But it added that commercial rainmaking operations had apparently increased rainfall by as much as twenty percent—sometimes—in non-mountainous areas. Most important of all, the new report concluded that the evidence was clear that cloud seeding could produce rain under proper conditions.

Today, rainmaking is an accepted part of modern science and technology (even though a few states, such as Maryland, have passed laws against cloud seeding). It's not as reliable as turning on an electric light, and there's a staggering amount of knowledge still to be learned. We simply don't know enough about how the weather works to predict natural weather events more than a few days—or sometimes only a few hours—in advance. And if we can't predict natural weather processes, then deliberate weather mods are going to be hit-or-miss affairs for some time to come.

Still, there's a great deal of work being done: determined men are trying to understand and control some of the damaging and destructive forces of the weather—hurricanes, tornadoes, lightning, hail, fog.

And they're succeeding!

Clouds and Rain, Hail and Lightning

Most of the weather modification work that's been done to date has involved seeding clouds, very much as Schaefer and Vonnegut did more than twenty years ago.

In a way, clouds are like storehouses of energy. Within

their water droplets, they've captured the energy that helps to make the weather. It takes energy to evaporate water from the surface of a lake or sea, and when water vapor condenses into a droplet, this energy is released into the air. This give-and-take of energy is the driving force behind our weather. It's still not very well understood by atmospheric scientists, which is why weather forecasts can't be made very far ahead.

For this reason, many research teams are vitally interested in studying clouds, to see how they work. They hope to learn more about the give-and-take of energy from the clouds' mixtures of water vapor, droplets and ice crystals. One way to study these processes in clouds is to deliberately try to alter a cloud by seeding it.

While this kind of research-oriented cloud seeding can help tell scientists quite a lot about the way clouds work, it doesn't really have much of an influence on the weather. A single cloud, or even a small group of clouds, doesn't really affect the weather over much territory. So cloud research doesn't run much risk of causing damaging weather effects such as severe storms or floods.

As we've already seen, many farmers are willing to pay for influencing the weather: they want rain, and they pay professional cloud seeders for it.

For more than twenty years now, professional rainmakers have been making their living from seeding clouds. And for just that long, an argument has raged among meteorologists as to whether the cloud seeding does more harm than good.

The doubters claim that seeding doesn't always produce rain, and in fact may prevent rain that might otherwise have fallen. At best, they feel, all that can be done by cloud seeding is to *redistribute* rainfall that will come down anyway, and make rainfall heavier in one location by causing less rainfall somewhere else. This is "robbing Peter to pay Paul."

But even if cloud seeding does nothing more than redistribute rain and snowfalls, this can still be put to good use. For example, the U.S. Bureau of Reclamation is using cloud seeding techniques to cause extra rain and snow in certain areas of the western United States. The idea is to produce as much precipitation as possible in areas that will help fill water

reservoirs serving the growing and thirsty cities and farmlands of the west. Winter storms are seeded in the hope of
keeping the reservoirs filled during the dry summer.

Further east, cloud seeding operations on the American
side of the Great Lakes are aimed at redistributing the snowfalls that often cripple upper New York State. Under normal
conditions, the moist cold air blowing in over the Lakes
dumps heavy snowfalls along the shore, crippling cities such
as Buffalo and Rochester, while a few miles inland there's no
snow at all. By seeding the clouds over the Lakes, it's been
possible to slightly redistribute the snowfall: the shoreside
cities get less snow, and the inland areas get enough to make
winter sports possible.

Hail Suppression: A strong hailstorm with large hailstones
can ruin a farmer's crop. In the Midwest it's not uncommon
to find hailstones as big as baseballs. Hailstorms cause
some $200 to $300 million of damage to crops each year
in the United States—more than the damage tornadoes
inflict.

One way to ease the sting of hailstorms is to make the
stones small and soft enough so that they won't cause much
damage. This can sometimes be done by overseeding the
clouds where the hailstorms are being formed. By pouring a
huge amount of condensation nuclei into the clouds, many
small hailstones form, rather than a smaller number of big
ones.

Hail-suppression operations have been going on for many
years all over the world. In Russia, France and Italy, men fire
rockets or cannon shells loaded with silver iodide or dry ice
into clouds that look threatening. In the United States, silver
iodide ''smoke'' generators are more frequently used.

Although it's impossible to say that a particular cloud
would have dropped hailstones big enough to cause damage if
it hadn't been seeded, the records of many years show that
cloud seeding operations have resulted in far fewer destructive hailstorms. At a relatively slight cost, farmers in many
nations have saved themselves many millions of dollars in
crop damages.

Lightning Suppression: Lightning bolts strike the Earth about a hundred times every second. That's more than five million strokes each day. More people are killed by lightning strokes than by any other aspect of the weather, including hurricanes and tornadoes. And most of the forest fires that destroy valuable timber are caused not by man, but by lightning.

The U.S. Forest Service started Project Skyfire in an attempt to reduce lightning-caused forest fires. The aim of the cloud seeding here was to change the electrical nature of the clouds and reduce the number of lightning strokes that reached the ground. Skyfire didn't show very dramatic results, although some meteorologists believed that the clouds weren't seeded enough.

Another attempt at reducing lightning strikes is being made by scientists of the Environmental Research Laboratories, which are part of the National Oceanographic and Atmospheric Agency (NOAA). Strips of aluminized foil, called chaff, are either dropped into the clouds from airplanes or fired into the clouds by rockets launched from the ground. The chaff strips are electrically charged, and under the proper circumstances can cause the cloud to dissipate its electrical energy without making lightning bolts that strike the ground. Some indications of reduced lightning activity have been found, but much more work needs to be done in this area.

Fog: Nobody likes fog. And many government agencies and private companies have worked at methods of getting rid of fog.

Cloud seeding techniques have been used on fog: after all, fog is merely a cloud that's sitting on or near the ground. Cloud seeding can dissipate cold fog, just as seeding can cause supercooled clouds to release precipitation. The seeding crystals produce precipitation in the fog; the fog melts away and the ground gets wet.

But seeding works only on cool fogs, and ninety-five percent of the fogs that occur in the United States are too warm for seeding to be effective. Some research teams have tried to come up with seeding agents that will work on warm fogs. To date, they haven't been very successful.

There are simpler ways to get rid of fog, though. Simpler, but more expensive than seeding.

One is called FIDO. It dates back to World War II. FIDO stands for Fog Investigation and Dispersal Operations. The problem was to get rid of fog shrouding airfield runways. The solution was to set up large drums of kerosene along the runway and set the kerosene on fire. The currents of hot air created by the fires caused updrafts that lifted the fog off the ground. Also, the heat from the fires helped to "bake out" some of the fog droplets, turning them back into water vapor.

Orly Airport, which serves Paris, now has a series of gas turbine jet engines placed underground alongside the runways. When fog develops, the turbine engines produce hot air, just as FIDO oil fires did, and the fog is blown away.

Several research teams in the United States have considered using high-powered lasers to break up fog. If a laser beam had enough energy in it—many megawatts of continuous power—it could theoretically bake off the fog droplets. It could produce clearings in a fog bank exactly where you wanted them, and very quickly too. A laser "fog knife" would be a very handy tool, if lasers of sufficient power could be built, and if they would be economical enough to operate.

As for economics, officials of the Air Transport Association of America and of United Airlines have reported that fog seeding is definitely a money-saving operation. Flights that are cancelled because of fog, or are re-routed to another airport because fog has "socked in" the airport that the flight was scheduled to land at, cost the airlines more than $75 million each year. United Airlines has for years been involved in seeding cool fogs at the airports it uses in the Pacific Northwest and Alaska. The airline claims that it's saved five dollars for every dollar spent on fog seeding.

Taming Hurricanes

Going from individual clouds or cloud systems to a hurricane is like stepping from a quiet meadow into downtown Manhattan at rush hour.

A hurricane is an organized storm that's often several

hundred miles in diameter. It releases a megaton of energy every fifteen minutes or so. Hurricanes have dropped more than a foot of rain per hour over thousands of square miles of territory. Wind speeds of two hundred miles per hour are not uncommon in a full-grown hurricane. These winds blow out windows, knock over electric cables and their poles, uproot trees, tear down signs, rip off roofs and pile up tidal waves that sweep over low-lying coastal lands and cause enormous damage.

Over the five-year period of 1965–1969, hurricanes caused more than $2.4 *billion* worth of damage in the United States alone, and killed nearly 500 people. One hurricane that hit Galveston in 1900 killed 6000 people. Today, better prediction and warnings have cut down the death toll greatly, especially since airplanes and satellites have been used to spot hurricanes while they're still far out at sea.

Hurricanes are a class of *tropical cyclones*, in the language of the meteorologists. The word "cyclone" simply means a revolving, roughly circular mass of low-pressure air. Meteorologists use terms such as *cyclonic depression* and *cyclonic storm*.

Most of the property damage and killing done by a hurricane stems from its enormously powerful winds, which can blow down buildings and pile up waves that sweep everything in their path. It's been estimated that if we could somehow reduce the force of a hurricane's winds by as little as fifteen percent, the damage caused by the storm would be cut in half.

In 1961, Project Stormfury was born. Operated jointly by the Department of Commerce and the Department of Defense, Stormfury saw the cooperative efforts of the National Weather Service, Navy, Air Force and Marines pitted against the fury of the hurricane.

For all of its strength and frightening power, a hurricane is actually a rather delicate balance of forces. Some meteorologists have described it as a heat engine. It works this way: Winds and warm air of the storm sweep up water vapor from the warm ocean. The vapor condenses into droplets, a process that releases heat energy. This heat energy provides the driving force that builds up the wind speeds, and allows the storm to sweep up still more water vapor. Once a hurricane runs onto dry land, or over cold northern waters, it's cut off from its basic supply of energy: warm water. Then it dies, although usually it takes several days to break up completely.

This very rough outline leaves many questions to be answered. The details of just how a hurricane does all this are yet to be understood. And even more puzzling is the fact that, although there are hundreds of tropical disturbances over the ocean in a year, only a few of them develop into hurricanes. Why don't they all? What happens to the disturbances that *don't* become hurricanes? Can we use such knowledge to prevent a hurricane from forming?

Such thoughts of preventing hurricanes from forming, or steering full-grown hurricanes so that they don't hit populated land areas, lie in the future. At present, Project Stormfury's aim is to seed the hurricane's clouds and see if this can help to reduce the wind speeds in the storm. Answer: Yes, it can and does.

The aim of Stormfury's seeding is to smooth out the differences in air pressure around the eye of the hurricane. Air pressure in the relatively calm eye is very low. Just next to it, in the bands of clouds that spiral around the eye, the air pressure is much higher. In these wall clouds are located the strongest winds of the storm.

Seeding the wall clouds causes many of their supercooled water droplets to freeze into ice crystals. This process releases heat and makes the seeded area of the clouds warmer, more buoyant, lower in pressure. The difference in air pressure between the eye and the wall clouds becomes less and, theoretically, the wind speed should go down.

Hurricanes were first seeded by Stormfury planes in 1961 and 1963. The results looked interesting, but not really clear. The wind speeds in the hurricanes diminished slightly right after the seeding flights, but picked up again almost immediately.

Between 1963 and 1969 several factors combined to keep the Stormfury planes away from hurricanes: For one thing, the Project people had agreed at the outset of their work that they'd seed only hurricanes that showed little likelihood of reaching land areas. This is because no one could predict what long-term effects seeding would have on a storm. If seeding operations turned out to make a storm stronger, or change its course, then it could cause more harm than good.

Secondly, the work on the first hurricanes showed that the meteorologists needed to know a great deal more about the behavior of tropical clouds. So, much of the time was spent seeding individual clouds and learning how they are affected.

Then, in August 1969, along came Hurricane Debbie. It was in the right place at the right time for Stormfury's handful of airplanes and its little group of determined men and women.

A little armada of planes flew into Hurricane Debbie at carefully selected altitudes and along precise flight paths. The planes seeded the hurricane with silver iodide crystals, and took measurements of the storm. Not just once a day, as had been done in earlier years—Debbie was seeded five times within eight hours on August 18 and again on August 20.

The results were perfectly clear. On August 18, the strongest winds in Debbie dropped from 98 knots to 68 knots within a few hours after seeding: a decrease of 31 percent. On August 19 there were no seeding flights and the storm re-intensified. On August 20, maximum wind speeds were 99 knots before seeding and 84 knots afterward, a decrease of 15 percent.

Man can change a hurricane. What's been done to date is only a tiny start on a huge task. But at least we know that we needn't sit helplessly in the face of nature's most furious storms. Someday we may understand how to prevent the storm from causing any damage at all.

Taming Tornadoes

While the prospects of dealing with hurricanes are beginning to look encouraging, tornadoes are still very much an enigma to meteorologists.

Compared to a hurricane, a tornado is a tiny storm. It packs only a ten-thousandth the energy of a hurricane. A tornado funnel forms suddenly under a threatening, thunderstorm filled sky. The funnel streaks across a few miles of landscape and then breaks up as suddenly as it formed. But in its wake, the tornado funnel leaves nothing but pure destruction.

Tornado winds have never been measured accurately. Usually there's nothing left to measure with when a tornado hits. It's been estimated that wind speeds in the "twister's" funnel may reach 400 miles per hour or more. And the air pressure inside the funnel is so low that the funnels have been seen to suck up ponds of water and even pull snow off the ground, like some wild vacuum cleaner. Trucks, roofs, trees—twisters have lifted them all and hurled them around like matchsticks.

This extremely-low-presure air is one of the tornado's most terrifying weapons. When a tornado hits a building, the air pressure inside the funnel is so low that the normal air pressure inside the building blows the windows and sometimes even the walls outward. Whole buildings have exploded themselves this way, when a tornado strikes.

Although meteorologists can generally forecast the weather conditions that will spawn tornadoes, it's still impossible to predict exactly where and when an individual funnel will form. So attempts at controlling tornadoes are aimed at changing the general weather pattern that might produce tornadoes, rather than trying to stop an individual funnel once it's formed. It all happens so fast, and so violently, that there's not much chance for altering the intensity or direction of an individual twister.

Usually "tornado weather" is caused by the movement of a cold air front into a mass of warm, very moist air. Tornadoes are always associated with the severe thunderstorms that mark the advance of such a cold front.

In general, the types of seeding operations that have been aimed at reducing lightning might help to prevent tornadoes from forming. The basic hope is to seed the areas where severe thunderstorms and tornadoes might break out, but to date there's been little success in taming killing "twisters."

Where Do We Stand?

Although men have been seeding clouds for decades, we can see that the work on taming storms has really just begun.

Weather-changing men can coax extra rainfall from clouds with some success. Their attempts at reducing the damage from hailstorms have been successful; attempts at reducing lightning, less so. Hurricanes have been modified, tornadoes have not. Fog can be cleared under some conditions, and work goes on toward clearing it under all conditions.

In 1958, the magazine *Science Newsletter* ran a survey of professional meteorologists, to find out what they thought about weather modification. Among the questions asked was: Do you believe that men will learn to *control* the large-scale features of the weather? The question was not concerned with merely modifying individual clouds or storms, but controlling weather.

Thirty percent of the meteorologists answered that they did believe weather control would be possible by the end of this century.

The work on weather modification that's been done since 1958 gives some evidence that weather control might indeed be possible some day. The real question now is, Should we try to control the weather?

III. Should We Control the Weather?

It's a long, long way from the weather mods of today to intentional control of the weather.

But the work that's been done so far—and the *unintentional* changes we make in the weather every day—are making weather control more than a possibility. The day might come when we'll *have to* deliberately control the weather.

John von Neumann (1903–1957) was one of the principal geniuses behind the development of modern electronic computers. In addition to many other interests, he was fascinated by the idea of using computers to help predict the weather. One enormous problem in weather forecasting is that there's so much information to be taken into account that it's difficult to make a forecast that's accurate for more than a few hours ahead. Von Neumann once said that he thought it might be easier to control the weather than to predict it. That is, if we take control of all the forces in our atmosphere that make the weather happen, then we'll know exactly what's going on, and forecasting will become simple.

What do we need to know, and what must we do to achieve weather control? Thomas Malone, chairman of the National Academy of Sciences' Committee on Atmospheric Sciences, pointed out in 1966 that four key developments were needed:

One: We need a much better understanding of the basic physical nature of the atmosphere and its behavior.

At present, weather forecasting is done partly by understanding how the atmosphere behaves, but mostly by matching today's weather patterns against old patterns. That is, weather forecasters know that certain patterns produce certain changes in the weather. When they see a major storm coming from the west, for example, they know that it will follow roughly the same track that most storms follow, so they make their forecasts accordingly.

No meteorologist on Earth can predict how much rain a certain storm will produce, or exactly where the storm will hit, or when. No one knows precisely how storm systems are created.

If we could know these things, precisely and in detail, weather forecasts could be made accurate for many days, weeks, perhaps even months, ahead. The amount of information that would be needed to make such forecasts is staggering, of course. But modern computers offer the hope of storing and digesting such mountains of data.

Two: The second need that Malone pointed out was improved computers, which can handle all the data necessary for understanding the weather patterns all around the world. Such computers are being developed.

Three: Malone showed that we need a huge worldwide network of observational instruments to monitor and measure weather conditions around the world continuously, every minute of the day.

Before the first artificial satellites went into orbit, only about five percent of the world's surface was monitored for weather conditions. In the industrial and populated regions of North America and Europe, there were plenty of weather observation stations. But in the other parts of the world, and across the broad oceans and polar ice caps (where the weather is made) there were no observation stations.

Satellites such as TIROS and NIMBUS and the Russian METEOR have changed all that. Orbiting the planet every few hours, or hanging in stationary orbit where they can watch half the world continuously, satellites have given meteorologists their first chance to see the planet's weather on a truly global scale.

And there are other observational systems going into action, too. Huge buoys are being placed in the oceans, with a complex of measuring instruments powered by small nuclear electric generators. These buoys monitor weather and sea conditions around the world, and give valuable information about how the oceans and the air affect each other. Long-range balloons that carry meteorological sensors are "orbiting" the world in the upper atmosphere, measuring weather conditions and automatically radioing the data to ground stations, under a program called Project GHOST (which stands for Global Horizontal Sounding Technique).

Four: New mathematical techniques must be worked out, techniques that will allow long-range forecasts of the weather and show *before the fact* what the effects of possible weather modifications will be.

It would be terribly foolish to try to change the weather in any major way without knowing in detail how this change will affect the world's weather. For example, suppose we learn how to smother a hurricane so completely that the storm dies away altogether before it ever reaches full strength. What effect will this have on the rainfall in the regions that the hurricane would have hit? Would killing the storm cause problems with the weather in other parts of the world?

If and when computers become large and fast enough to handle the job, men will make their weather changes on paper (or magnetic tape) first, and then let the computer tell them what the long-range effects of such changes will be. Only then can we make major weather changes in the real world safely.

There's a fifth item that Malone didn't include in his list, but it's necessary before large-scale weather alterations can be made: *energy sources*.

So far, the only halfway reliable method we've found to change the weather is cloud seeding. In effect, seeding triggers energy changes in the cloud, makes the cloud release the energy it's stored up in its water droplets and/or ice crystals.

If we're going to make any major changes in the weather, we must find better energy sources—more reliable triggers. Think of the energy involved in the weather: a quarter-inch rainfall over a 100-mile-square area (about the size of the District of Columbia) releases some 20 million kilowatts.

Certainly man isn't going to match the energy of the weather on a head-to-head basis. But neither did man match the strength of the mammoths, head-to-head, back in the Ice Age. Still, Ice Age men slaughtered the mammoths. Not by using brute strength, but by using cunning.

Will we be clever enough to control the weather someday? The answer is most likely yes. But this brings us back to the question that started this discussion: Should we try to control the weather?

As we've seen earlier, man is constantly changing the weather around him without even thinking about it. Unless we begin to control the ways we pour heat and pollution into the atmosphere, we may cause disasters much worse than the killing smogs of Donora and London.

When it comes to pollution and the unconscious effects man has on the weather, it seems that we *must* exert some controls. We can control these aspects of the weather mainly by controlling ourselves.

It can be done.

The great city of London has been famous for some of the most impenetrable fogs (and smogs) on record. Up until a few years ago, everyone knew that these fogs were at least partially man-made, but no one did anything about it. Most of the homes in London are heated by coal-burning furnaces, and the coal used most often was rich in sulfur. Coal smoke pouring out of millions of chimneys and factory smokestacks produced countless particles of sulfur-bearing soot, which in turn produced droplets of water and sulfur dioxide.

In the terrible smog of December 1952, about 4000 residents died, most of them from lung ailments brought on by the action of the sulfur dioxide. Trains couldn't run. Birds couldn't see to fly. An opera was cancelled because the singers couldn't see the orchestra conductor. Movies shut down because people couldn't see the screen. Prize cattle, brought into the city for a livestock show, lay down and died on the spot.

Londoners finally decided that they'd had enough. Parliament tackled the problem, and after much argument and investigation, passed the British Clean Air Act of 1956. It was a very mild law. Basically, all it did was to make it illegal to burn smoke-producing fuels in certain parts of the vast city.

But the law was *enforced*. The local London government paid up to seventy percent of the cost to any homeowner who had to change his heating furnace so that he could burn smokeless fuel. The suppliers where people bought their fuel stopped selling the smoke-producing kind. Police patrolmen simply noted whose chimneys were smoking and asked them to comply with the law. For the most part people cooperated and worked together to save their city—and their own lives.

The result: sunshine!

The amount of sunshine in London during the winter months has increased fifty percent since 1956. The number of dense fogs has gone down by eighty percent. Bird species that hadn't been seen in London's parks for decades have started to reappear. And some of the city's finest stone buildings—from Buckingham Palace to St. Paul's Cathedral—have been cleaned up and had the soot of two centuries scraped off them, revealing lovely warm colors of stone beneath their pollution-gray coats.

What happened in London can be done in other cities. The pollution problems of New York and Los Angeles seem much tougher, but London's success offers hope that even these cities can be saved.

This form of weather control—controlling man's unconscious effects on the weather—can be made to work. What about more deliberate alterations of the natural weather?

For example, Eugene Bollay, one of the nation's leading commercial rainmakers, has proposed a bold scheme for adding a million or more acre-feet of water to the Colorado River. The Colorado and its tributaries provide the water for Southern California, Arizona and part of Mexico. A million acre-feet of additional water each year would help to solve the growing water shortages caused by explosive growth of the area's population and industry.

Bollay's scheme is to set up a "picket fence" of ground-based seeding generators near the snowpack atop the Rockies, where the Colorado River-system begins. The snow on these mountains feeds the river system. During the winter months, approaching storms would be seeded so that they would yield ten to fifteen percent more snowfall than they would normally. Bollay calculated that this would add a million acre-feet of water to the rivers when the snow melted in the spring.

This kind of weather control can be done now. In the future, it might be possible to control most of the large-scale features of the weather around the world. Man may learn to regulate the amount of rainfall that a given section of land receives; control when, where and how much rain and snow falls. Destructive storms might be weakened or steered away from populated areas. Weather might be made perfect for farmers, so that they can grow all the food that's needed to feed the hungry billions of the world.

But—who will control the weather? Who will make the decision? Will weather control be used for good or evil?

During the summer of 1967, riots erupted in many American cities. Detroit and Washington burned. People died in the streets. Two particular riots were very interesting because they did *not* happen.

During one week of that violent summer, in Milwaukee and then a few days later in Washington, riots that were just getting started suddenly broke up when heavy rain showers drenched the streets and made everybody run home. In both cases, the showers were caused by completely natural weather patterns.

But what if a government could control the weather well enough to drown out a street demonstration? What if a government could actually control the weather for its farmers and businessmen and vacationers? Would it be a step toward a police state, where you did what you were told or you didn't get good weather?

Suppose government decided to use weather control as a weapon against other nations. By causing droughts, or floods, or violent storms, weather control could ruin a nation just as effectively as an invading army. And the nation might not even know it was being attacked!

The United States isn't the only nation working on weather modification and control. Suppose the ability to control weather was mastered by some of the nations that now have nuclear weapons: the U.S., Russia, England, France and China. In such a world, every rainstorm might signal an enemy action.

If half a dozen countries tried to tinker with each other's weather, the resulting chaos might cause a disaster for us all. Because of this, the chances are that weather control might become a subject for international cooperation, instead of conflict.

Some people worry that cloud seeding and rainmaking are merely taking rainfall away from where it would naturally fall and giving it to the area that's been seeded. Perhaps, on the small scale that's been attempted up to now, the cloud seeders really are "robbing Peter to pay Paul."

But, as Secretary of the Interior Stewart Udall pointed out in 1967, there are some 47.5 *billion* acre-feet of water flowing across the United States in "rivers in the sky." If we could learn to squeeze just an extra two percent out of this treasure, it would benefit everyone in the nation without hurting anyone, since most of this moisture would fall into the oceans, anyway.

Our atmosphere is a precious resource, much more vital to us than gold or oil. We're just starting to understand this, and are beginning to learn how to use this resource wisely, rather than use it as a dumping ground. If the nations of the world act together, weather control can help to erase some of the ancient causes for war—hunger and poverty.

Should we try to control the weather? That's for you to

decide. It seems clear that before we can ever hope to really control the weather, we must learn to control ourselves.

If we do, then someday we might have the kind of world where it will never rain until everyone's safely under shelter, where snow will come on schedule and never be allowed in cities (where it's not really appreciated), where there will always be fair winds for sailors and sunshine for us all.

It might be a pleasant world to live in.

The Man Who ... ▆▆▆▆▆▆▆

Of all the new capabilities that science has offered human-kind, none are so powerful as genetic engineering. When we take the very material of life itself into our hands and begin to tinker with it, we put ourselves on Nietzsche's tightrope between immortality and oblivion. *The Man Who ...* looks into one possible use of "the new biology" in a field that has been quick to adapt for its own purposes such new technologies as television and computers: the field of politics.

▆▆▆▆▆▆▆

"He doesn't have cancer!"

Les Trotter was a grubby little man. He combed his hair forward to hide his baldness, but now as I drove breakneck through the early Minnesota morning, the wind had blown his thinning hair every which way, leaving him looking bald and moon-faced and aging.

And upset as hell.

"Marie, I'm telling you, he doesn't have cancer." He tried to make it sound sincere. His voice was somewhere between the nasality of an upper-register clarinet and its Moog synthesis.

"Sure," I said sweetly. "That's why he's rushed off to a secret laboratory in the dead of night."

Les' voice went up still another notch. "It's not a secret lab! It's the Wellington Memorial Laboratory. It's world-famous. And . . . goddammit, Marie, you're *enjoying* this!"

"I'm a reporter, Les." Great line. Very impressive. It

hadn't kept him from making a grab for my ass, when we had first met. "It's my job."

He said nothing.

"And if your candidate has cancer . . ."

"He doesn't."

"It's news."

We whipped past the dead bare trees with the windows open to keep me from dozing. It had been a long night, waiting for Halliday at the Twin Cities Airport. A dark horse candidate, sure, but the boss wanted *all* the presidential candidates covered. So we drew lots and I lost. I got James J. Halliday, the obscure. When his private jet finally arrived, he whisked right out to this laboratory in the upstate woods.

I love to drive fast. And the hours around dawn are the best time of the day. The world's clean. And all yours . . . a new day coming. This day was starting with a murky gray as the sun tried to break through a heavy, late-winter overcast.

"There's ice on the road, you know," Les sulked.

I ignored him. Up ahead I could see lighted buildings.

The laboratory was surrounded by a riot-wire fence. The guard at the gate refused to open up and let us through. It took fifteen minutes of arguing and a phone call from the guard shack by Les before the word came back to allow us in.

"What'd you tell them?" I asked Les as I drove down the crunchy gravel driveway to the main laboratory building.

He was still shivering from the cold. "That it was either see you or see some nasty scare headlines."

The lab building was old and drab, in the dawning light. There were a few other buildings farther down the driveway. I pulled up behind a trio of parked limousines, right in front of the main entrance.

We hurried through the chilly morning into the lobby. It was paneled with light mahogany, thickly carpeted, and *warm*. They had paintings spotted here and there—abstracts that might have been amateurish or priceless. I could never figure them out.

A smart-looking girl in a green pantsuit came through the only other door in the lobby. She gave me a quick, thorough inspection. I had to smile at how well she kept her face straight. My jeans and jacket were for warmth, not looks.

"Governor Halliday would like to know what this is all about," she said tightly. Pure efficiency: all nerves and smooth makeup. Probably screwed to a metronome beat. "He is here on a personal matter; there's no news material in this visit."

"That depends on his x-rays, doesn't it?" I said.

Her eyes widened. "Oh." That's all she said. Nothing more. She turned and made a quick exit.

"Bright," I said to Les. "She picks up right away."

"His whole staff's bright."

"Including his advance publicity man?" *With the overactive paws,* I added silently.

"Yes, including my advance publicity man."

I turned back toward the door. Walking toward me was James J. Halliday, Governor of Montana, would-be President of these United States: tall, cowboy-lean, tanned, good-looking. He was smiling at me, as if he knew my suspicions and was secretly amused by them. The smile was dazzling. He was a magnetic man.

"Hello, Les," Halliday said as he strode across the lobby toward us. "Sorry to cause you so much lost sleep." His voice was strong, rich.

And Les, who had always come on like a lizard, was blooming in the sunshine of that smile. He straightened up and *his* voice deepened. "Perfectly okay, Governor. I'll sleep after your inauguration."

Halliday laughed outright.

He reached out for my hand as Les introduced, "This is Marie Kludjian of—"

"I know," Halliday said. His grip was firm. "Is *Now*'s circulation falling off so badly that you have to invent a cancer case for me?" But he still smiled as he said it.

"Our circulation's fine," I said, trying to sound unimpressed. "How's yours?"

He stayed warm and friendly. "You're afraid I'm here for a secret examination or treatment, is that it?"

I wasn't accustomed to frankness from politicians. And he was just radiating warmth. Like the sun. Like a flame.

"You . . . well . . ." I stammered. "You come straight to the point, at least."

"It saves a lot of time," he said. "But I'm afraid you're

wasting yours. I'm here to visit Dr. Corio, the new director
of the lab. We went to school together back East. And Les
has such a busy schedule arranged for me over the next week
that this was the only chance I had to see him.''

I nodded, feeling as dumb as a high school groupie.

"Besides," he went on, "I'm interested in science. I think
it's one of our most important national resources. Too bad the
current administration can't seem to recognize a chromosome
from a clavicle."

"Uh-huh." My mind seemed to be stuck in neutral. *Come
on!* I scolded myself. *Nobody can have that powerful an
effect on you! This isn't a gothic novel.*

He waited a polite moment for me to say something else,
then cracked, "The preceding was an unpaid political
announcement."

We laughed, all three of us together.

Halliday ushered Les and me inside the lab, and we stayed
with him every minute he was there. He introduced me to Dr.
Corio—a compactly built intense man of Halliday's age, with
a short, dark beard and worried gray eyes. I spent a yawn-
provoking two hours with them, going through a grand tour
of the lab's facilities. There were only five of us: Halliday,
Corio, the girl in the green suit, Les and me. All the lab's
offices and workrooms were dark and unoccupied. Corio
spent half the time feeling along the walls for light switches.

Through it all something buzzed in my head. Something
was out of place. Then it hit me. *No staff. No flunkies. Just
the appointments secretary and Les . . . and I dragged Les
here.*

It was a small thing. But it was different. *A politician
without pomp?* I wondered.

By seven in the morning, while Corio lectured to us about
the search for carcinoma antitoxins or some such, I decided I
had been dead wrong about James J. Halliday.

By seven-thirty I was practically in love with him. He was
intelligent. And concerned. He had a way of looking right at
you and turning on that dazzling smile. Not phony. Knee-
watering. *And unattached,* I remembered. *The most available
bachelor in the Presidential sweepstakes.*

By eight-thirty I began to realize that he was also as tough as a grizzled mountain man. I was out on my feet, but he was still alert and interested in everything Corio was showing me.

He caught me in mid-yawn, on our way back to the lobby. "Perhaps you'd better ride with us, Marie," he said. "I'll have one of Corio's guards drive your car back to the airport."

I protested, but feebly. I *was* tired. And, after all, it's not every day that a girl gets a lift from a potential President.

Halliday stayed in the lobby for a couple of minutes while Les, the appointment girl and I piled into one of the limousines. Then he came out, jogged to the limo and slid in beside me.

"All set. They'll get your car back to the airport."

I nodded. I was too damned sleepy to wonder what had happened to the people who had filled the other two limousines. And all the way back to Minneapolis, Halliday didn't smile at me once.

Sheila Songard, the managing editor at *Now*, was given to making flat statements, such as: "You'll be back in the office in two weeks, Marie. He won't get past the New Hampshire primary."

You don't argue with the boss. I don't, anyway. Especially not on the phone. But after Halliday grabbed off an impressive 43% of the fractured New Hampshire vote, I sent her a get-well card.

All through those dark, cold days of winter and early spring I stayed with Jim Halliday, got to know him and his staff, watched him grow. The news and media people started to flock in after New Hampshire.

The vitality of the man! Not only did he have sheer animal magnetism in generous globs, he had more energy than a half-dozen flamenco dancers. He was up and active with the sunrise every day and still going strong long after midnight. It wore out most of the older newsmen trying to keep up with him.

When he scored a clear victory in Wisconsin, the Halliday staff had to bring out extra buses and even arrange a separate plane for the media people to travel in, along with The Man's private 707 jet.

I was privileged to see the inside of his private jetliner. I was the only news reporter allowed aboard during the whole campaign, in fact. He never let news or media people fly with him. Superstition, I thought. Or just a desire to have a place that can be really private—even if he had to go 35,000 feet above the ground to get the privacy. Then I'd start daydreaming about what it would be like to be up that high with him. . . .

The day I saw the plane, it was having an engine overhauled at JFK in New York. It was still cold out, early April, and the hangar was even colder inside than the weakly sunlit out-of-doors.

The plane was a flying command post. The Air Force didn't have more elaborate electronics gear. Bunks for fifteen people. *There goes the romantic dream*, I thought. No fancy upholstery or decorations. Strictly utilitarian. But row after row of communication stuff: even picturephones, a whole dozen of them.

I had known that Jim was in constant communication with his people all over the country. But picturephones—it was typical of him. He wanted to be *there*, as close to the action as possible. Ordinary telephones or radios just weren't good enough for him.

"Are you covering an election campaign or writing love letters?" Sheila's voice, over the phone, had that bitchy edge to it.

"What's wrong with the copy I'm sending in?" I yelled back at her.

"It's too damned laudatory, and you know it," she shrilled. "You make it sound as if he's going through West Virginia converting the sinners and curing the lepers."

"He's doing better than that," I said. "And I'm not the only one praising him."

"I've watched his press conferences on TV," Sheila said. "He's a cutie, all right. Never at a loss for an answer."

"And he never contradicts himself. He's saying the same things here that he did in New York . . . and Denver . . . and Los Angeles."

"That doesn't make him a saint."

"Sheila, believe it. He's *good*. I've been with him nearly four months now. He's got it. He's our next President."

She was unimpressed. "You sound more like you're on his payroll than *Now*'s."

Les Trotter had hinted a few days earlier that Jim wanted me to join his staff for the California primary campaign. I held my tongue.

"Marie, listen to Momma," Sheila said, softer, calmer. "No politician is as good as you're painting him. Don't let your hormones get in the way of your judgment."

"That's ridiculous!" I snapped.

"Sure . . . sure. But I've seen enough of Halliday's halo. I want you to find his clay feet. He's got them, honey. They all do. It might hurt when you discover them, but I want to see what The Man's standing on. That's your job."

She meant it. And I know she was right. But if Jim had clay feet, nobody had been able to discover it yet. Not even the nastiest bastards Hearst had sent out.

And I knew that I didn't want to be the one who did it.

So I joined Jim's staff for the California campaign. Sheila was just as glad to let me go. Officially I took a leave of absence from *Now*. I told her I'd get a better look inside The Man's organization this way. She sent out a lank-haired slouchy kid who couldn't even work a dial telephone, she was that young.

But instead of finding clay feet on The Man, as we went through the California campaign, I kept coming up with gold.

He was beautiful. He was honest. Everyone of the staff loved him and the voters were turning his rallies into victory celebrations.

And he was driving me insane. Some days he'd be warm and friendly and . . . well, it was just difficult to be near him without getting giddy. But then there were times—sometimes the same day, even—when he'd just turn off. He'd be as cold and out of reach as an Antarctic iceberg. I couldn't understand it. The smile was there, his voice and manners and style were unchanged, but the vibrations would be gone. Turned off.

There were a couple of nights when we found ourselves sitting with only one or two other people in a hotel room, planning the next days' moves over unending vats of black coffee. We made contact then. The vibes were good. He wanted me, I know he did, and I certainly wanted him. Yet somehow we never touched each other. The mood would suddenly change. He'd go to the phone and come back . . . different. His mind was on a thousand other things.

He's running for President, I raged at myself. *There's more on his mind than shacking up with an oversexed ex-reporter.*

But while all this was going on, while I was helping to make it happen, I was also quietly digging into the Wellington Memorial Laboratory, back in Minnesota. And its director, Dr. Corio. If Jim did have feet of clay, the evidence was there. And I had to know.

I got a friend of a friend to send me a copy of Corio's doctoral thesis from the Harvard library, and while I waited for it to arrive in the mail, I wanted more than anything to be proved wrong.

Jim was beautiful. He was so much more than the usual politician. His speech in Denver on uniting the rich and poor into a coalition that would solve the problems of the nation brought him as much attention for its style as its content. His position papers on R&D, the economy, tax reform, foreign trade, were all called "brilliant" and "pace-setting." A crusty old economist from Yale, no less, told the press, "That man has the mind of an economist." A compliment, from him. A half-dozen of Nader's Raiders joined the Halliday staff because they felt, "He's the only candidate who gives a damn about the average guy."

A political campaign is really a means for the candidate to show himself to the people. And *vice versa*. He must get to know the people, all the people, their fears, their prides, their voices and touch and smell. If he can't feel for them, can't reach their pulse and match it with his own heartbeat, all the fancy legwork and lovely ghostwriting in the universe can't help him.

Jim had it. He grew stronger every minute. He kept a backbreaking pace with such ease and charm that we would have wondered how he could do it, if we had had time enough to catch our own breaths. He was everywhere, smiling, confident, energetic, *concerned*. He identified with people and they identified with him. It was uncanny. He could be completely at ease with a Missouri farmer and a New York corporation chairman. And it wasn't phony; he could *feel* for people.

And they felt for him.

And I fell for him; thoroughly, completely, hopelessly. He realized it. I was sure he did. There were times when the electric current flowed between us so strongly that I could barely stand it. He'd catch my eye and grin at me, and even though there were ninety other people in the room, for that instant everything else went blank.

But then an hour later, or the next day, he'd be completely cold. As if I didn't exist . . . or worse yet, as if I was just another cog in his machine. He'd still smile, he'd say the same things and look exactly the same. But the spark between us just wouldn't be there.

It was driving me crazy. I put it down to the pressures of the campaign. He couldn't have any kind of private life in this uproar. I scolded myself, *Stop acting like a dumb broad!*

Corio's thesis arrived three days before the California primary. I didn't even get a chance to unwrap it.

Jim took California by such a huge margin that the TV commentators were worriedly looking for something significant to say by ten that evening. It was no contest at all.

As we packed up for the last eastern swing before the national convention, I hefted Corio's bulky thesis. Still unopened. I was going to need a translator, I realized; his doctoral prose would be too technical for me to understand. We were heading for Washington, and there was a science reporter there that I knew would help me.

Besides, I needed to get away from Jim Halliday for a while, a day or so at least. I was on an emotional roller coaster, and I needed some time to straighten out my nerves.

The phone was ringing as the bellman put my bags down in my room at the Park Sheraton. It was Sheila.

"How are you?" she asked.

She never calls for social chatter. "What do you want,

Sheila?'' I asked wearily. It had been a long, tiring flight from the coast, and I knew my time zones were going to be mixed up thoroughly.

"Have you found anything . . . clay feet, I mean?"

The bellman stood waiting expectantly beside me. I started fumbling with my purse while I wedged the phone against my shoulder.

"Listen, Marie," Sheila was saying. "He's too good to be true. *Nobody* can be a masterful politician *and* a brilliant economist *and* a hero to both the ghetto and the suburbs. It's physically impossible."

I popped a handful of change from my wallet and gave it over to the bellman. He glanced at the coins without smiling and left.

"He's doing it," I said into the phone. "He's putting it all together."

"Marie," she said with great patience, as I flopped on the bed, "he's a puppet. A robot that gets wound up every morning and goes out spouting whatever they tell him to say. Find out who's running him, who's making all those brilliant plans, who's making his decisions for him."

"He makes his own decisions," I said, starting to feel a little desperate. If someone as intelligent as Sheila couldn't *believe* in him, if politics had sunk so low in the minds of the people that they couldn't recognize a knight in brilliant armor when he paraded across their view . . . then what would happen to this nation?

"Marie," she said again, with her Momma-knows-best tone, "listen to me. Find out who's running him. Break the story in *Now*, and you'll come back on the staff as a full editor. With a raise. Promise."

I hung up on her.

She was right in a way. Jim was superman. More than human. *If only he weren't running for President! If only we could*—I shut off that line of thought. Fantasizing wasn't going to help either one of us. Lying there on the hotel bed, I felt a shiver go through me. It wasn't from the air-conditioning.

Even with translation into language I could understand, Corio's thesis didn't shed any light on anything. It was all about genetics and molecular manipulation. I didn't get a chance to talk with the guy who had digested it for me. We met at National Airport, he sprinting for one plane and me for another.

My flight took me to San Francisco, where the national convention was due to open in less than a week.

The few days before a national convention opens are crazy in a way nothing else on Earth can match. It's like knowing you're going to have a nervous breakdown and doing everything you can to make sure it comes off on schedule. You go into a sort of masochistic training, staying up all night, collaring people for meetings and caucuses, yelling into phones, generally behaving like the world is going to come to an end within the week—and you've got to help make it happen.

Jim's staff was scattered in a half-dozen hotels around San Francisco. I got placed in the St. Francis, my favorite. But there wasn't any time for enjoying the view.

Jim had a picturephone network set up for the staff. For two solid days before the convention officially convened, I stayed in my hotel room and yet was in immediate face-to-face contact with everyone I had to work with. It was fantastic, and it sure beat trying to drive through those jammed, hilly streets.

Late on the eve of the convention's opening gavel—it was morning, actually, about two-thirty—I was restless and wide awake. The idea wouldn't have struck me, I suppose, if Sheila hadn't needled me in Washington. But it *did* hit me, and I was foolish enough to act on the impulse.

None of Jim's brain-trusters are here, I told myself. *They're all safe in their homes, far from this madhouse. But what happens if we need to pick at one of their mighty intellects at some godawful hour? Can we reach them?*

If I hadn't been alone and nervous and feeling sorry for myself, sitting in that hotel room with nothing but the picturephone to talk to, I wouldn't have done it. I knew I was kidding myself as I punched out the number for Professor Marvin Carlton, down in La Jolla. I could hear Sheila's *listen to Momma* inside my head.

To my surprise, Carlton's image shaped up on the phone's picture-screen.

"Yes?" he asked pleasantly. He was sitting in what looked like a den or study—lots of books and wood. There was a drink in his hand and a book in his lap.

"Professor . . ." I felt distinctly foolish. "I'm with Governor Halliday's staff . . ."

"Obviously. No one else has the number for this TV phone he gave me."

"Oh."

"What can I do for you . . . or the governor? I was just about to retire for the night."

Thinking with the speed of a dinosaur, I mumbled, "Oh well, we were just . . . um, checking the phone connection . . . to make certain we can reach you when we have to. . . ."

He pursed his lips. "I'm a bit surprised. The governor had no trouble reaching me this afternoon."

"This afternoon?"

"Yes. We went over the details of my urban restructuring program."

"Oh—of course." I tried to cover up my confusion. I had been with Jim most of the afternoon, while he charmed incoming delegates at various caucuses. We had driven together all across town, sitting side by side in the limousine. He had been warm and outgoing and . . . and then he had changed, as abruptly as putting on a new necktie. *Was it something I said? Am I being too obvious with him?*

"Well?" the professor asked, getting a bit testy. "Are you satisfied that I'm at my post and ready for instant service?

"Oh, yes . . . yes sir. Sorry to have disturbed you."

"Very well."

"Um—Professor? One question? How long did you and the governor talk this afternoon? For our accounting records, you know. The phone bill, things like that."

His expression stayed sour. "Lord, it must have been at least two hours. He dragged every last detail out of me. The man must have an eidetic memory."

"Yes," I said. "Thank you."

"Good night."

I reached out and clicked the phone's off switch. If Jim had spent two hours talking with Professor Carlton, it couldn't have been that afternoon. He hadn't been out of my sight for more than fifteen minutes between lunch and dinner.

I found myself biting my tongue and punching another number. This time it was Rollie O'Malley, the guy who ran our polling services. He was still in New York.

And sore as hell. "Goin' on five o'clock in the motherin' morning and you wanna ask me what?"

"When's the last time you talked with The Man?"

Rollie's face was puffy from sleep, red-eyed. His skin started turning red, too. "You dizzy broad . . . why in the hell—"

"It's important!" I snapped. "I wouldn't call if it wasn't."

He stopped in mid-flight. "Whassamatter? What's wrong?"

"Nothing major . . . I hope. But I need to know when you talked to him last. And for how long."

"Christ." He was puzzled, but more concerned than angry now. "Lessee . . . I was just about to sit down to dinner here at the apartment . . . musta been eight, eight-thirty. 'Round then."

"New York time?" That would put it around five or so our time. *Right when Jim was greeting the Texas delegation.*

"No! Bangkok time! What the hell is this all about, Marie?"

"Tell you later," and I cut him off.

I got a lot of people riled. I called the heads of every one of Jim's think-tank teams: science, economics, social welfare, foreign policy, taxation, even some of his Montana staff back in Helena. By dawn I had a crazy story: eleven different people had each talked *personally* with The Man that afternoon for an average of an hour and a half apiece, they claimed. Several of them were delighted that Jim would spend so much time with them just before the convention opened.

That was more than sixteen hours of face-to-face conversation on the picturephones. All between noon and 7 p.m., Pacific Daylight Time.

And for most of that impossible time, Jim had been in my presence, close enough to touch me. And never on the phone once.

I watched the sun come up over the city's mushrooming

skyline. My hands were shaking. I was sticky damp with a cold sweat.

Phony. I wanted to feel anger, but all I felt was sorrow. And the beginnings of self-pity. *He's a phony. He's using his fancy electronics equipment to con a lot of people into thinking he's giving them his personal attention. And all the while he's just another damned public relations robot.*

And his smiles, his magnetism, the good vibes that he could turn on or off whenever it suited him. *I hate him!*

And then I asked myself the jackpot question: *Who's pulling his strings?* I had to find out.

But I couldn't.

I tried to tell myself that it wasn't just my emotions. I told myself that, puppet or not, he was the best candidate running. And God knows we needed a good President, a man who could handle the job and get the nation back on the right tracks again. But, at that bottom line, was the inescapable fact that I loved him. As wildly as any schoolgirl loved a movie star. But this was real. I wanted Jim Halliday . . . I wanted to be *his* First Lady.

I fussed around for two days, while the convention got started and those thousands of delegates from all over this sprawling nation settled preliminary matters like credentials and platform and voting procedures. There were almost as many TV cameras and news people as there were delegates. The convention hall, the hotels and the streets were all crawling with people asking each other questions.

It was a steamroller. That became clear right at the outset when all the credentials questions got ironed out so easily. Halliday's people were seated with hardly a murmur in every case where an argument came up.

Seeing Jim privately, where I could ask him about the phony picturephone conversations, was impossible. He was surrounded in his hotel suite by everybody from former party chieftains to movie stars.

So I boiled in my own juices for two days, watching helplessly while the convention worked its way toward the inevitable moment when The Man would be nominated. There was betting down on the streets that there wouldn't even be a first ballot: he'd be nominated by acclamation.

I couldn't take it. I bugged out. I packed my bag and headed for the airport.

I arrived at Twin Cities Airport at 10 p.m., local time. I rented a car and started out the road toward the Wellington Lab.

It was summer now, and the trees that had been bare that icy morning, geologic ages ago, were now full-leafed and rustling softly in a warm breeze. The moon was high and full, bathing everything in cool beauty.

I had the car radio on as I pushed the rental Dart up Route 10 toward the laboratory. Pouring from the speaker came a live interview with James J. Halliday, from his hotel suite in San Francisco.

". . . and we're hoping for a first-ballot victory," he was saying smoothly, with that hint of earnestness and boyish enthusiasm in his voice. *I will not let myself get carried away,* I told myself. *Definitely not.*

"On the question of unemployment . . ." the interviewer began.

"I'd rather think of it as a mismatch between—"

I snapped it off. I had written part of that material for him. But dammit, he had dictated most of it, and he never said it the same way twice. He always added something or shaded it a little differently to make it easier to understand. If he was a robot, he was a damnably clever one.

The laboratory gate was coming up, and the guard was already eyeing my car as I slowed down under the big floodlights that lined the outer fence.

I fished in my purse for my Halliday staff ID card. The guard puzzled over it for a second or two, then nodded.

"Right, Ms. Kludjian. Right straight ahead to the reception lobby."

No fuss. No questions. As if they were expecting me.

The parking area was deserted as I pulled up. The lobby was lit up, and there was a girl receptionist sitting at the desk, reading a magazine.

She put the magazine down on the kidney-shaped desk as I

pushed the glass door open. I showed her my ID and asked if Dr. Corio was in.

"Yes he is," she said, touching a button on her phone console. Nothing more. Just the touch of a button.

I asked, "Does he always work this late at night?"

She smiled very professionally. "Sometimes."

"And you too?"

"Sometimes."

The speaker on her phone console came to life. "Nora, would you please show Ms. Kludjian to Room A-14?"

She touched the button again, then gestured toward the door that led into the main part of the building. "Straight down the corridor," she said sweetly, "the last door on your right."

I nodded and followed instructions. She went back to her magazine.

Jim Halliday was waiting for me inside Room A-14.

My knees actually went weak. He was sitting on the corner of the desk that was the only furniture in the little, tile-paneled room. There was a mini-TV on the desk. The convention was roaring and huffing through the tiny speaker.

"Hello, Marie." He reached out and took my hand.

I pulled it away, angrily. "So that 'live' interview from your hotel was a fake, too. Like all your taped phone conversations with your think-tank leaders."

He smiled at me. Gravely. "No, Marie. I haven't faked a thing. Not even the way I feel about you."

"Don't try that . . ." But my voice was as shaky as my body.

"That was James J. Halliday being interviewed in San Francisco, live, just a few minutes ago. I watched it on the set here. It went pretty well, I think."

"Then . . . who the hell are you?"

"James J. Halliday," he answered. And the back of my neck started to tingle.

"But—"

He held up a silencing hand. From the TV set, a florid speaker was bellowing, "This party *must* nominate the man who has swept all the primary elections across this great land. The man who can bring together all the elements of our people back into a great, harmonious whole. The man who will lead us to *victory* in November. . . .''—The roar of applause swelled to fill the tiny bare room we were in—''. . . The man who will be our next President!'' The cheers and applause were a tide of human emotion. The speaker's apple-round face filled the little screen: ''James J. Halliday, of Montana!''

I watched as the TV camera swept across the thronged convention hall. Everybody was on their feet, waving Halliday signs, jumping up and down. Balloons by the thousands fell from the ceiling. The sound was overpowering. Suddenly the picture cut to a view of James J. Halliday sitting in his hotel room in San Francisco, watching *his* TV set and smiling.

James J. Halliday clicked off the TV in the laboratory room and we faced each other in sudden silence.

''Marie,'' he said softly, kindly, ''I'm sorry. If we had met another time, under another star . . .''

I was feeling dizzy. ''How can you be there . . . and here . . .''

''If you had understood Corio's work, you'd have realized that it laid the basis for a practical system of cloning human beings.''

''Cloning . . .''

''Making exact replications of a person from a few body cells. I don't know how Corio does it—but it works. He took a few patches of skin from me, years ago, when we were in school together. Now there are seven of us, all together.''

''Seven?'' My voice sounded like a choked squeak.

He nodded gravely. ''I'm the one that fell in love with you. The others . . . well, we're not *exactly* alike, emotionally.''

I was glancing around for a chair. There weren't any. He put his arms around me.

''It's too much for one man to handle,'' he said, urgently, demandingly. ''Running a Presidential campaign takes an inhuman effort. You've got to be able to do everything—either that or be a complete fraud and run on slogans and gimmicks. I didn't want that. I want to be the best President this nation can elect.''

''So . . . you . . .''

''Corio helped replicate six more of me. Seven exactly similar James J. Hallidays. Each an expert in one aspect of the Presidency such as no Presidential candidate could ever hope to be, by himself.''

''Then that's how you could talk on the picturephones to everybody at the same time.''

''And that's how I could know so much about so many different fields. Each of us could concentrate on a few separate problem areas. It's been tricky shuffling us back and forth—especially with all the newspeople around. That's why we keep the 707 strictly off-limits. Wouldn't want to let the public see seven of us in conference together. Not yet, anyway.''

My stomach started crawling up toward my throat.

''And me . . . us . . . ?''

His arms dropped away from me. ''I hadn't planned on something like this happening. I really hadn't. It's been tough keeping you at arm's length.''

''What can we do?'' I felt like a little child—helpless, scared.

He wouldn't look at me. Not straight-on. ''We'll have to keep you here for a while, Marie. Not for long. Just 'til after the Inauguration. 'Til I . . . we . . . are safely in office. Corio and his people will make you comfortable here.''

I stood there, stunned. Without another word Jim suddenly got up and strode out of the room, leaving me there alone.

He kept his promises. Corio and his staff made life very comfortable for me here. Maybe they're putting things in my food or something, who can tell? Most likely it's for my own good. I do get bored. And so lonely. And frightened.

I watched his Inauguration on television. They let me see TV. I watch him every chance I get. I try to spot the tiny difference that I might catch among the seven of them. So far, I haven't been able to find any flaw at all.

He said they'd let me go to him after the Inauguration. I hope they remember. His second Inauguration is coming up soon, I know.

Or is it his third?

The Seeds of Tomorrow ━━━━

This final piece is excerpted from the only book of mine to be cited as a reference in the *Encyclopaedia Britannica*. It shows how the Promethean ideal affects our society. After all, scientific research and new technological developments do not occur in a vacuum. The way we shape our society determines how well we use—or misuse—the products of research and development. While comparatively few men and women in any society become research scientists, it is critically important that *every* citizen in a democracy understand what science can and cannot do. The only real "enemy of the people" is ignorance. Those who do not understand science and technology inevitably become Luddites, through and through. And the terrible consequence of the Luddite philosophy is that we lose the golden opportunities that science and technology offer us, because we are afraid of the unknown, unsure of our own abilities, unwilling to trust ourselves.

We build our own future, each one of us, day by day. We build it by the things we do and the things we fail to do. Each time we turn away from knowledge, from learning, we take a step backward toward the darkness. Each time we use our brains and our skills to build some new capability, we take a step toward the stars, toward the abode of the gods, toward the citadel where Prometheus waits to welcome us.

━━━━━

I. The Revolutionaries:
Science and Technology

Technology has brought us changes, most of which we should welcome, rather than reject. Wealth is the least important of these changes. Of greater importance is change itself. Those young humanists who think themselves revolutionaries are nothing compared to technology.

—Lewis M. Branscomb

America celebrated its Bicentennial in 1976, commemorating two hundred years of independence, two centuries since the start of the American Revolution. To celebrate our Bicentennial year, we landed a pair of Viking spacecraft on the surface of Mars, and automated laboratories aboard the Viking landers began to search the Martian soil for evidence of life.

Sending spacecraft to another world is a particularly fitting tribute to the revolutionary spirit of America, for science and technology were important ingredients in the American Revolution of 1776.

The seeds of our revolution were actually planted in Europe during the fifteenth and sixteenth centuries. In 1454, in the German city of Mainz, Johann Gutenberg published the first book printed from movable metal type. The printing press was a revolutionary invention. For the first time in history, knowledge could be spread to everyone, instead of being restricted to the elite upper classes of society. Books could be made cheaply enough and in large enough numbers so that even the poorest people could afford them. Knowledge became available to all and was no longer a rare and guarded secret.

In 1492, of course, Columbus discovered the New World, although he didn't realize at the time that he had not reached the East Indies (modern Indonesia), which was his target. The fact that mariners could voyage across the open ocean, instead of hugging the shoreline, was the result of several technological breakthroughs, such as the development of deep-water sailing ships and crude but serviceable navigation instruments.

As small and fragile as Columbus's ships were, they can still be compared to today's spacecraft—technological wonders that could travel into realms where earlier generations of vessels had dared not go.

In 1543, Nicolaus Copernicus, the Polish astronomer, published the most revolutionary book of all time. It was entitled *De Revolutionibus*, and its "inflammatory" contents dealt with the idea that perhaps the Earth was not the center of the universe, but instead was a planet that revolved around the Sun.

Copernicus was so timid about his idea that he didn't allow his book to be published until he was on his deathbed. As a civil employee of the Roman Catholic Church, he could foresee quite clearly the furor that his book would cause.

Copernicus's idea flew in the face of the Church's teachings. It was bad enough that Columbus had given a practical demonstration of the fact that the Earth was not flat. But to believe that it was not the fixed and immovable center of the universe? Heresy!

In the sixteenth century the Church was a powerful political force as well as a spiritual one. The Church was rich in land holdings and gold, and it could command armies when the need arose. But the Church was threatened by the Protestant Reformation, which had thrown all of Europe into turmoil. For the first time since the Roman Empire had adopted Catholicism as its official state religion, Europeans were turning away from the Church, to the new teachings of Martin Luther and other Protestants. The Church responded with force, and even war, in many parts of Europe, to the challenge of its dogma.

Many in the Church, as well as other European intellectuals (including Luther!), wanted Copernicus's book suppressed.

A century earlier that would have been a simple matter. The few painfully reproduced copies of the book could have been quietly taken off the rare library shelves in the universities and either locked up or burned. But by 1543 large numbers of books were being printed and distributed throughout Europe. There was no way for the authorities to prevent people from reading Copernicus's revolutionary ideas.

Not only did Copernicus's ideas fly in the face of the acknowledged authorities of that era, they also ran contrary to the common belief that the Sun and Moon and stars revolved around the Earth.

Men of learning argued about Copernicus's concept for more than half a century. For despite all that the authorities of the day could do to suppress the idea—including burning people at the stake—the Copernican revolution would not die.

In the early summer of 1609, the great Italian physicist and astronomer, Galileo Galilei, made the first astronomical observations using a telescope. The startling things he discovered confirmed Copernicus's concept that the Earth revolves around the Sun. Although the Church forced Galileo to recant his statements about these discoveries, under threat of torture and imprisonment, the world knew by then that the Earth does move and it is not the center of the universe.

Copernicus had won. But what has this to do with the American Revolution? Just this: The Copernican revolution showed the world that new ideas can be developed, tested and confirmed no matter what the authorities of the day say or do. Men began investigating the world around them for themselves, rather than letting the authorities tell them what they should think. The scientific way of thinking, based on evidence and logic, was developed by Roger Bacon and others. During the seventeenth century this scientific attitude led to the Age of Enlightenment, during which thinking men across all of Europe prided themselves on their acceptance and understanding of the scientific method of thought.

England's Isaac Newton uncovered some of the basic principles that govern our universe, such as gravitation and the laws of motion. But equally important, in the eighteenth century, philosophers and social thinkers such as the Frenchmen Voltaire and Rousseau began to apply the scientific method of thought to social problems. Instead of accepting society as they found it, they began to question the rules laid down by the authorities: Why should people be governed by a king and hereditary nobles? Where does the rightful power of government lie? And what rights do the common people have?

Meanwhile, on a completely different level, a technological revolution was taking place. In the early Renaissance years of the fifteenth century, gunpowder and cannons made it possible for kings to overpower their barons and gather all the political power and authority of the land into their own hands. Throughout the Middle Ages, feudal barons had ruled small principalities, and the acknowledged king of each land was merely one of the barons with a grander title—but little more wealth or power—than the rest.

The technology of gunpowder changed all that. As the Middle Ages gave way to the Renaissance, gunpowder was as strange and new as intercontinental missiles are today. Only the richest, most farsighted and powerful could gather and train enough men to create an army proficient in the use of cannons and muskets. The men who were able to bring such armies into existence became kings. They battered down the other barons' castle walls with cannons and shot their armored knights with muskets.

By the time the fledgling American colonies were beginning to grumble about taxation and other grievances against Mother England, the technology of gunpowder had trickled down from the rich into the hands of the common people.

By 1776 even the ragged, embattled farmers who stood against the Redcoats at Lexington and Concord had guns in their hands—guns made by their neighbors, and gunpowder and shot that they had made for themselves. The richest kings of Europe no longer had a technological advantage over the common people. Revolution could succeed. And did.

Scientific thinking, which examines the world around us in a questioning, critical light, allowed people to begin examining their own way of life and to search for better ways of living. Timid Copernicus was the intellectual grandfather of Thomas Jefferson. And you can see the reasoned, scientific mode of thought in every line of the Declaration of Independence.

Technological development, which eventually made the yeoman farmer equal to the professional soldier in firepower, provided the military basis on which the Revolutionary War was won. By 1814, Andrew Jackson's ragtag collection of defenders was able to riddle a strong, professional British Army at New Orleans and send it reeling in flight because the Americans had accurate long-range rifles in their hands, while the British still used old-fashioned muskets.

In the 1960s, the "unsophisticated" guerillas of Southeast Asia often battled the U.S. Army to a standstill, using modern technological devices such as transistorized radios, cheap mortars and mass-produced submachine guns.

Today many Americans complain about the government's use of electronic surveillance techniques and phone taps to pry into the lives of private citizens. Modern electronics technology is in the same stage of development as gunpowder was during the Renaissance: It is new enough, strange enough and expensive enough so that only the very rich and powerful elements of our society can use it. Electronics technology has not yet filtered down to the common people, as gunpowder technology had by 1776. But it will.

The point of all this history is to show that political and social revolutions have never occurred without being accompanied—or preceded—by scientific or technological revolutions. Science and technology have always been revolutionary forces. Most other forces in our society—religion, politics, tradition, law—are essentially conservative. They look backward, not forward. They seek to maintain the status quo, to keep everything exactly the way it was yesterday.

Science and technology, by their very nature, are forward-looking. Every new idea, every new invention or development, upsets the status quo, changes people and society.

Certainly science and technology are not the only revolutionary forces in human history. Nor are they the only revolutionary forces at work in our world today. The urge to be free, the desire of poor people to gain a fairer share of their national wealth, and new religious and political ideas are all revolutionary forces. But science and technology are crucially important to all of us, now more than at any time in our past.

We live today in a world that has been shaped by science and technology. This world faces enormous problems. Overpopulation threatens to reduce every nation to poverty and starvation. Already there are food shortages in Africa and

Asia. In the wealthy nations of Europe and North America (and in Japan and Australia, too) pollution of the air and water makes it actually dangerous to breathe and eat.

We face energy crises and shortages of such critical raw materials as copper and potassium. Looming behind all these problems is the ever-present threat of nuclear devastation. Each year more nations acquire the means to build and deliver nuclear bombs. Each year the moment when one madman can destroy the world comes closer.

Some people feel that science and technology are to blame for these problems. They would like to somehow stop our modern world, end our reliance on science and technology, and turn back the clock to an earlier, simpler time when these shattering problems did not exist.

But that is no answer. Imagine the situation for yourself. Picture what would happen if today, right *now*, we shut down all the research laboratories in the world, all the science and engineering colleges, all the factories, engineering offices, and electrical power plants, and all the automobiles, trucks, trains, planes and ships that use engines of any sort. Picture a world without electricity, without radio or television, without tractors or chemical fertilizers, computers, telephones, plastics, antibiotics, air-conditioning or central heating.

If all these products of modern science and technology were eliminated today, almost everyone in the world would die within a month. Billions of human beings would starve. Food from the world's farms could not reach most of the people without modern transport vehicles and the electronically assisted intelligence to send the food to the places where it is needed. Four and a half billion human beings cannot all feed themselves on their own little plots of self-sufficient farms. Organic, family-style farms cannot produce enough food to feed everyone in the world. There isn't enough arable land on Earth to feed four billion people that way.

It would not be a case of people going hungry for a while, until they learned how to grow their own food. Most people would starve to death—within a month. And those who did not starve would be attacked by disease within a short time.

A world without science and technology is not the Garden of Eden; it is Death Valley. A human being without science and technology would not be a yeoman farmer or a noble savage; he'd be a dead naked ape.

We are caught on the horns of a painful dilemma. We cannot live without science and technology. That statement is true in the most literal sense: We cannot live, eat, breathe, love, exist, without science and technology. On the other hand, byproducts of science and technology have made our world overcrowded, overpolluted and overly dangerous. Nuclear war is an ever-present threat. Pollution silently kills millions every year and threatens to poison our air and seas to the point where they can no longer sustain life. Our antibiotic medicines and insecticides have led to the rise of bacteria and insects that are stronger and more menacing to our health than the weaker strains we have eliminated.

How can this be? Are science and technology good, or are they evil? The answer is . . . neither, and both. Science is a way of thinking. Technology is a tool. Each can be put to evil uses or good uses. It is *people* who do good and evil. A hammer has no moral sense. Neither does an atom.

It is quite true that science and technology have played an enormous part in shaping the world we live in today, both the good and the bad. And we do face staggering problems. Science and technology can be used to help solve our problems and lead us toward a future that is bright with hope and promise. They are the seeds of tomorrow that we can plant today, seeds that can yield a beautiful harvest of knowledge and wealth for all the world's people.

II. Citizens of the World

New sources of energy; information systems that can bring new knowledge and wealth to all the world's people; expansion into the solar system's vast domain of new resources; the challenges, dangers, and breathless opportunities of the new biological sciences—these are the seeds of the future that can bring a golden era of peace and plenty to the entire human race. But it is necessary for us to begin planting those seeds now, today, if this bright future is to blossom into reality.

Because, as we know, the seeds of our own destruction have already been planted by earlier generations of shortsighted, selfish people.

The harvest that these bad seeds will yield has been outlined in the Club of Rome's study, *The Limits to Growth*: choking pollution, soaring death rate, crumbling cities, exhausted farmlands, chaos, war, the end of civilization and quite possibly the end of humanity. Yet we possess the scientific knowledge and the technological tools not merely to avert the predicted disaster, but to make life better and richer than it has ever been for every member of the human race.

But a basic problem exists. How do we use this knowledge and these wonderful tools? How can we employ our science and technology to solve the problems of overpopulation, starvation, ignorance, and greed? How can you and I, for example, turn the experimental studies of fusion reactors into practical controlled thermonuclear reactors that will supply all the world's energy needs cheaply and efficiently? And how do we get to where we want to be from where we are today?

These questions are largely political and social rather than scientific. But since the days of Copernicus, every advance in scientific thinking and technological capability has involved crucial political and social questions. Galileo faced torture and imprisonment; Einstein's work in nuclear energy resulted in Hiroshima; today's molecular biologists are more worried about social consequences than the ultimate success of their work.

The problems we face today are global ones. The disaster that awaits us will hit everyone. The solutions to global problems must also be global in scope. It will do little good for the United States, alone, to maintain a high standard of living while the rest of the world starves. Our economy is too dependent on the economies of other nations. And we would soon find ourselves attacked by hungry, jealous and frightened nations. And most important, it would be *wrong*—by any reasonable standard of morality.

We must find ways of using our scientific and technological skills on a global scale, to attack and defeat the problems that threaten us. How can this be done?

Ask yourself: Where are the citizens of the world? If you

live in Maine, or California, or Montana, or Alabama, you still consider yourself to be an American. But how many Americans—or Englishmen, Chinese, Czechs, New Zealanders or Nigerians—consider themselves to be citizens of the world?

With the exception of a few idealists who have renounced their national citizenship, every human being on Earth gives his highest political allegiance to a nation-state: the United States of America, the Union of Soviet Socialist Republics, India, Libya, Uruguay.

True, there are still a handful of primitive societies in which the individual members give their highest allegiance to their own tribe or clan. In some rural areas of Southeast Asia the true allegiance of most of the people is to their village; the only connection they have with a national government is when a tax collector comes to the village or when soldiers turn their rice paddies into battlefields.

For most of the Earth's four billion people, the strongest political loyalty professed is to a nation. We consider ourselves to be Americans, or Germans, Canadians, Turks, Israelis, Australians, etc. No more than a tiny fraction of the world's population thinks of itself as citizens of the world.

We may *say* that we think of ourselves as human beings first and as national citizens second, but we *act* as if the citizens of nations other than our own are something less than truly human. Foreigners are *them*, not *us*. Our policies of trade and commerce, finance, politics, even our behavior at the Olympic Games, show the force of nationalism. We're Number One! Buy American! See America First! Don't Sell America Short! America, love it or leave it!

Make no mistake about it: the United States of America is, to me, the finest nation in the world. You have only to travel overseas a little to realize that the rights and freedoms we take for granted here in the United States are very rare and extremely precious. Nor is nationalistic zeal restricted to America. It is not even restricted to the industrialized nations of the West. The newly emerging nations of the Third World burn with fierce nationalistic ambition. In Latin America nations have gone to war over soccer games, so intense is their national rivalry.

If nationalism were entirely stupid, evil or harmful, it

would have disappeared centuries ago. Human beings may be shortsighted and greedy, but they seldom cling to something very long, once they realize that it is harming them.

The roots of nationalism go back to the Middle Ages, when royal houses such as the Tudors in England and the Bourbons of France were struggling to increase their power over the power of rival noble families. In time, such European struggles transformed the patchworks of medieval baronies and duchies into modern nations with centralized leadership and government.

Today, in many of the new nations of the Third World, small, educated groups of leaders are struggling to bring their villagers and tribesmen into the twentieth century. To accomplish this, they must get their peoples' thinking habits to leapfrog from tribalism to the concept of nationalism. This is why so many of the new members of the United Nations display so much pomp and pride of nationalism. It is only this new and exciting idea of a nation that is holding their people together.

So nationalism has its uses. But it also has very real limitations. And, as we said earlier, the global disaster that lurks in our future cannot be solved piecemeal, by individual nations. It requires an international, global response.

How do we go from nationalism to a global community? How can a world divided into nations learn to work together, in a unified way, to meet global problems? How can the United States or Soviet Russia or Zaire surrender any of its national power and authority to an international organization?

Alexander Hamilton, one of the founders of the United States, saw the situation quite clearly almost two hundred years ago: "Do not expect nations to take the initiative in imposing restrictions upon themselves," he said.

In other words, no national government is going to willingly give up any of its power to an international organization. For years people have complained that the United Nations is little more than a debating society, that it has no real power in the arena of international politics. This is very true. But it is true because the nations that created the United Nations built powerlessness into its very foundations. How well would the U.S. government work if one single state in the Union could nullify any piece of federal legislation simply by casting a veto?

Americans fought the bloody Civil War to affirm the supremacy of the federal government over the powers of the individual states. We still have legal wrangles over states' rights. The United Nations is effectively powerless because any member nation of the Security Council can veto almost any action. It was the most powerful nations of the world, including the United States, that wrote the veto into the UN charter.

The few idealistic persons who have proclaimed themselves citizens of the world have not brought about a step forward in international cooperation. In fact, by renouncing their citizenship in any particular nation, they have become legally stateless persons. They have no citizenship anywhere on Earth. They have no legal residence, no voting privileges, no passports, no civil rights. They are literally exiles from every nation on this planet. Without citizenship in a nation, an individual human being has no legal protection from any government. He is as helpless as an Ice Age hunter who belonged to no tribe: a single, frail human being all alone in a cold and dangerous world.

Perhaps, in our increasingly complex and dangerous world, it would be desirable to have a single, unified world government. Perhaps not. Leaving that question aside for the moment, let us see if there are any trends on the world scene today that are moving the separate nations toward more international cooperation.

Clearly, the influence of modern technology is to unite the world socially and culturally, if not politically. Electronic communications has turned the world into a "global village," in the words of Marshall McLuhan. Diplomats can fly from one capital to another at the speed of sound, shuttling back and forth over more miles in a single day than Talleyrand, the nineteenth-century French statesman and diplomat, covered in a lifetime. Rock singers are known instantly all over the world. Western clothing styles, business methods and social attitudes can be found from Tokyo to Timbuktu.

Spearheaded by our science-based technology, Western culture is homogenizing most of the world. All the industrialized nations and most of the emerging ones have adopted a Western form of society. As *The Limits to Growth* has shown, it is this very industrialization and its resulting population explosion that is causing most of the world's problems today. Can the same high-technology industrialization become part of the solution to these problems?

Western culture may be literally conquering the world socially and economically, but what is happening politically? There has been some movement toward supra-national (*supra*, meaning "beyond, over, more than") groupings of nations. These alliances among nations have been spurred mainly by the military confrontation between the West and the Soviet Bloc. NATO, in the West, and the East's Warsaw Pact are supra-national organizations that are mainly military alliances.

Most of the nations of Western Europe have banded together to form the European Economic Community, the so-called Common Market. But this has done rather little to bring these nations together *politically*.

Economically, socially, culturally and technologically, we are moving toward a unified world, whether we like it or not. But politically we are still divided into separate, suspicious, hostile nations. Many writers and researchers who deal in forecasts have said that it is modern technology that will lead the way toward uniting the world's peoples and nations. "First come the scientists," they say, "then the engineers, the financiers, the businessmen and finally—way behind— come the politicians."

How far behind are the politicians? A few years? A decade? A generation? How far behind can we allow them to be when they have their fingers on the H-bomb buttons? In a world simmering with little wars, with vast nuclear armaments, with growing gaps between the rich and the poor, and with steadily rising population and steadily dwindling resources, how much longer can we remain divided into nation-states and expect to survive?

Look at history. Most historians agree that the most brilliant civilization on Earth prior to our modern age was that of ancient Greece. Many feel that the Greeks, particularly the Athenians, produced the highest civilization humankind has yet achieved.

Yet that beautiful civilization was swept away by people who were barbarians, compared to the Athenians. The Macedonians, and later the Romans, conquered all of Greece and ended the glory of Athens and the other Greek city-states. Greek culture permeated the conquerors, true enough. But the wisdom of the Greeks never advanced an inch further after the Macedonians conquered Greece.

The brilliant and beautiful Greek culture stagnated under Macedonian and Roman rule. Would it have advanced further if it had remained free? Would there had been a scientific revolution fifteen hundred years before Copernicus's time? If Greece had remained free, perhaps we would not have had to wait fifteen centuries between Aristotle and Galileo. Perhaps today, in the twentieth century, our knowledge and abilities would be *fifteen hundred years* ahead of where we are now. Perhaps.

But this much we do know for certain. No citizen of Athens thought of himself as a Greek. He was an Athenian. There were no Greeks. There were Spartans and Thebans and Corinthians. No citizen of the Greek city-states had a political allegiance higher than that to his city. The Greeks could band together temporarily to fight off invaders. But even when a handful of Athenians, Spartans, *et al.* threw back the full might of the Persian Empire, the victors marched home to the separate cities and resumed squabbling among themselves. They never realized that, united, they were the most powerful force in the world. They destroyed themselves with intercity wars. The Macedonians conquered an exhausted Athens.

To paraphrase the philosopher George Santayana, those who ignore the lessons of history are doomed to repeat the mistakes. The civilization of ancient Greece fell because the Greek people never developed a political loyalty to any entity higher than their city-states. Today we live in a world where our highest political allegiance is given to the nation-state. Yet it seems clear that the global problems that threaten us cannot be solved by individual nations, each working by itself. The problems of nationalism now outweigh the advantages.

Nationalism has served us well in the past. It has provided the framework for the development of nation-states the size of

whole continents, and for empires of globe-spanning propor-
tions. But today, nationalism is not part of the solution; it is
part of the problem.

In his book *The Story of Man*, anthropologist Carleton S.
Coon warns:

> Because it now takes less time to fly around the world
> than it took President Washington to travel from his
> home in Virginia to Independence Hall in Philadelphia . . .
> what prevents the peoples of the world from pooling their
> efforts . . . is not distance, time, or technology.
>
> It is the retention by twentieth-century, Atom Age
> men of the Neolithic point of view that says: *You stay
> in your village, and I will stay in mine. If your sheep eat
> our grass we will kill you, or we may kill you anyhow
> to get all the grass for our own sheep. Anyone who tries
> to make us change our ways is a witch and we will kill
> him. Keep out of our village.*

This "Neolithic point of view" has been with us since the
end of the Ice Age. It must change, if we are to survive.

We are biological creatures, and to some extent so are our
societies. Biological forces are extremely conservative. The
basic motivating principle among biological creatures seems
to be, "Do it today exactly as you did it yesterday." Human
societies are very complex biological entities, but they follow
the same basic conservative rule. They change slowly, and
very reluctantly.

Yet biological organisms do change. If they did not, this
planet would be inhabited by nothing more than viruses.
People do change. And so do societies. Sooner or later there
will be an effective international organization of some sort,
and the limitations of today's nationalism will be over-
come. The seeds for this tomorrow exist today in our technology, in our growing interdependence with all the peoples
of this planet, in our minds and our hopes for a better
future.

But we are definitely in a race against time. For if we do
not take the necessary steps to solve the problems that threaten
us, we will be overwhelmed by them and go down to destruc-

tion under a bloody tide of population, pollution, starvation and war.

In 1974 the Club of Rome published a second report, entitled *Mankind at the Turning Point*. The club's first report, *The Limits of Growth*, was devoted to showing the disaster awaiting us within a few decades, in the strongest possible manner. That first report had to catch the attention of the whole world, had to make people realize that we must face tomorrow's problems today. It succeeded in doing that.

In *Mankind at the Turning Point*, the investigators showed that there are ways to avoid the impending disaster, scientific and technological approaches that we can take to solve key problems such as energy, food, information and natural resources. The Club of Rome's second report also stresses the fact that international cooperation will be absolutely indispensable, if we are to succeed in solving these problems.

The final paragraph of *Mankind at the Turning Point* states:

> Mankind cannot afford to wait for change to occur spontaneously and fortuitously. Rather, man must initiate on his own changes of necessary but tolerable magnitude in time to avert intolerably massive [and destructive] change. A strategy for such change can be evolved only in the spirit of truly global cooperation, shaped in free partnership by the world's diverse regional communities and guided by a rational master plan for long-term organic growth. All our computer simulations have shown quite clearly that this is the only sensible and feasible approach to avoid major regional and ultimately global catastrophe, and that the time that can be wasted before developing such a global world system is running out. *Clearly the only alternatives are division and conflict, hate and destruction.*

The problem is clear and real, global in its scope and frightening in its complexity and seriousness. But the human race has struggled through Ice Ages, plagues, wars, famines—and, yes, even the collapse of whole civilizations.

We have the knowledge and the tools to meet the problems of the coming decades. We have the skill and the courage to make the twenty-first century a Golden Age for all the human race, rather than a Dark Age of misery and death.

But we do have the heart and the willpower to change our own ways of living, our own views of the world? Are we willing to act *now*, to plant the seeds of tomorrow that will bring forth a good future?

Science and technology hold the key to our future. We must all learn as much as we can about what science and technology can do for us, and what they cannot do—where the shortcomings and pitfalls are. Then we must use our knowledge in the political arena, and see to it that our governments use these powerful tools wisely, for the benefit of all the people.

We live in a world brim-full of new energy sources, new information-handling techniques, new scientific capabilities all around us. We can lift the scourge of hunger and fear from all people, everywhere. We can expand outward to new worlds in space, and improve our own minds and bodies to the point where we can challenge immortality itself.

But we must start now. Each one of us. This golden future will never come to be if we do not plant the good seeds of tomorrow in today's waiting ground. The old saying holds for each one of us: "If you're not part of the solution, you're part of the problem."